BADGER'S MOON

By Peter Tremayne and featuring Sister Fidelma

*forthcoming

BADGER'S MOON

Peter Tremayne

 St. Martin's Minotaur ⋈ New York

www.minotaurbooks.com

Library of Congress Cataloging-in-Publication Data

Tremayne, Peter.
    Badger's moon / Peter Tremayne.—1st St. Martin's Minotaur ed.
        p. cm.
    ISBN 0-312-32341-7
    EAN 978-0312-32341-7
    1. Fidelma, Sister (fictitious character)—Fiction. 2. Ireland—History—To 1172—Fiction. 3. Women detectives—Ireland—Fiction. 4. Girls—Crimes against—Fiction. 5. Celtic Church—Fiction. 6. Catholics—Fiction. 7. Nuns—Fiction. I. Title

PR6070.R366B33 2005
823'.914—dc22   2004061441

First published in Great Britain by Headline Book Publishing

First St. Martin's Minotaur Edition: March 2005

10 9 8 7 6 5 4 3 2 1

For Denis, The O'Long of Garranelongy,
descendant of the Eoghanacht Prince Longadh,
eponymous ancestor of the O'Longs who was a
contemporary of Sister Fidelma, and for Lester,
Madam O'Long, with gratitude for their friendship
and hospitality.

May no demons, no ill, no calamity or terrifying dreams
Disturb our rest, our willing, prompt repose.

An Evening Prayer
ascribed to St Patrick, 5th century

Historical Note

The Sister Fidelma mysteries are set mainly in Ireland during the mid-seventh century AD.

Sister Fidelma is not simply a religieuse, a former member of the community of St Brigid of Kildare. She is also a qualified *dálaigh*, or advocate of the ancient law courts of Ireland. As this background will not be familiar to many readers encountering the Sister Fidelma stories for the first time, this Historical Note is designed to provide a few essential points of reference to make the stories more appreciated.

The Ireland of Fidelma's day consisted of five main provincial kingdoms; indeed, the modern Irish word for a province is still *cúige*, literally 'a fifth'. Four provincial kings – of Ulaidh (Ulster), of Connacht, of Muman (Munster) and of Laigin (Leinster) – gave their qualified allegiance to the *Ard Rí* or High King, who ruled from Tara, in the 'royal' fifth province of Midhe (Meath), which means the 'middle province'. Even among the provincial kingdoms, there was a decentralisation of power to petty kingdoms and clan territories.

The law of primogeniture, the inheritance by the eldest son or daughter, was an alien concept in Ireland. Kingship, from the lowliest clan chieftain to the High King, was only partially hereditary and mainly electoral. Each ruler had to prove him or herself worthy of office and was elected by the *derbfhine* of their family – a minimum of three generations from a common ancestor gathered in conclave. If a ruler did not pursue the commonwealth of the people, he was impeached and removed from office. Therefore the monarchical system of ancient Ireland had more in common with a modern day republic than with the feudal monarchies which had developed in medieval Europe.

Ireland, in the seventh century AD, was governed by a system of sophisticated laws called the Laws of the Fénechus, or land-tillers, which became more popularly known as the Brehon Laws, deriving from the word *breaitheamh* – a judge. Tradition has it that these laws were first gathered in 714 BC by order of the High King, Ollamh Fódhla. Over a thousand years later, in AD 438, the High King, Laoghaire, appointed a commission of nine learned people to study, revise and commit the laws to the new writing in Latin characters. One of those serving on the commission was Patrick, eventually to become

ix

patron saint of Ireland. After three years, the commission produced a written text of the laws, which is their first known codification.

The first complete surviving texts of the ancient laws of Ireland are preserved in an eleventh-century manuscript book in the Royal Irish Academy, Dublin. It was not until the seventeenth century that the English colonial administration in Ireland finally suppressed the use of the Brehon law system. To even possess a copy of the Irish law books was punishable often by death or transportation.

The law system was not static and every three years, at the Féis Temhach (Festival of Tara), the lawyers and administrators gathered to consider and revise the laws in the light of changing society and its needs.

Under these laws, women occupied a unique place. The Irish laws gave more rights and protection to women than any other western law code at that time or until recent times. Women could, and did, aspire to all offices and professions as co-equal with men. They could be political leaders, command their people in battle as warriors, be physicians, poets, artisans, local magistrates, lawyers and judges. We know the names of many female judges of Fidelma's period – Bríg Briugaid, Áine Ingine Iugaire and Darí among others. Darí, for example, was not only a judge but also the author of a noted law text written in the sixth century AD.

Women were protected by law against sexual harassment, against discrimination and against rape. They had the right of divorce on equal terms from their husbands, with equitable separation laws, and could demand part of their husband's property as a divorce settlement; they had the right of inheritance of personal property and the right of sickness benefits when ill or hospitalised. Ancient Ireland had Europe's oldest recorded system of hospitals. Seen from today's perspective, the Brehon Laws might appear to enshrine an almost ideal society.

Fidelma went to study law at the bardic school of the Brehon Morann of Tara and, after eight years of study, she obtained the degree of *anruth*, only one degree below the highest offered in either bardic or ecclesiastical universities in ancient Ireland. The highest degree was *ollamh*, which is still the modern Irish word for a professor. Fidelma's studies were in both the criminal code of the *Senchus Mór* and the civil code of the *Leabhar Acaill*. Thereby she became a *dálaigh* or advocate of the law courts.

Her main role could be compared to a modern Scottish sheriff-substitute whose job is to gather and assess the evidence, independent of the police, to see if there is a case to be answered. The modern French *juge d'instruction* holds a similar role. However, sometimes

Fidelma is faced with the task of prosecuting in the courts, of defending or even rendering judgements in minor cases when a Brehon was not available.

In those days most of the professional or intellectual classes were members of the new Christian religious houses, just as, in previous centuries, all intellectuals and members of the professions had been Druids. Fidelma became a member of the religious community of Kildare, established in the late fifth century by St Brigid. But by the time the action of this story takes place, Fidelma has left Kildare in disillusionment. The reason why may be found in the title story of the short story collection *Hemlock At Vespers*.

While the seventh century is considered part of the European Dark Ages, for Ireland it was the period of Golden Enlightenment. Students from every corner of Europe flocked to the Irish secular and ecclesiastic colleges to receive their education, including the sons of many of the Anglo-Saxon kings. At the great ecclesiastical university of Durrow at this time, it is recorded that no fewer than eighteen different nations were represented among the students. At the same time, Irish male and female missionaries were setting out to return Europe to Christianity, as it had fallen to the pagan invasions. They established churches, monasteries, and centres of learning as far east as Kiev, in the Ukraine, as far north as the Faroes, and as far south as Taranto in southern Italy. Ireland was a byword for literacy and learning.

However, what we now call the Celtic Church was in constant dispute with Rome on matters of liturgy and ritual. Rome had begun to reform itself in the fourth century, changing its dating of Easter and aspects of its liturgy. The Celtic Church and the Eastern Orthodox Church maintained their independence from Rome in such matters. The Celtic Church of Ireland, during Fidelma's time, was much concerned with this conflict so that it is impossible to write on church matters without referring to the philosophical warfare between them.

One thing that was shared by both the Celtic Church and Rome in the seventh century was that the concept of celibacy was not universal. In spite of previous explanations on this matter, however, a few readers were surprised when in *The Haunted Abbot* it was revealed that Sister Fidelma and her companion Brother Eadulf had undertaken one of the nine legal forms of marriage under Irish law.

While there were always ascetics in the churches who sublimated physical love in dedication to the deity, it was not until the Council of Nice in AD 325 that clerical marriages were condemned (but not banned) by the hierarchy of the Western Church. Celibacy was not a popular concept. It arose in Rome mainly from the customs practised by the pagan priestesses of Vesta and the priests of Diana, which became an inheritance of Roman culture.

By the fifth century, Rome had forbidden its clerics from the rank of abbot and bishop to sleep with their wives – implying they were still marrying – and, shortly after, even to marry at all. The main reason appears to be property concerns, for Pope Pelagius I (AD 536–61) decreed that sons of priests should not be allowed to inherit church property. The general clergy were discouraged from marrying by Rome but not expressly forbidden to do so.

The celibacy lobby in Rome became strong and it was Peter Damian (AD 1000–1072), a leading theologian whose writings reveal him to be a misogynist, who became a major influence and persuaded Pope Leo IX (AD 1049–54) to enforce celibacy on all clergy. Leo IX ordered the wives of priests to be sent as slaves to Rome for the Pope to 'dispose of'. In AD 1139, Innocent II tried a softer approach by requesting all priests to divorce their wives. But Pope Urban II, in AD 1189, decreed that wives of priests could be seized and sold as slaves by any of the European feudal lords. The priests fought back. It took Rome a long time to enforce universal celibacy. The Celtic Church took centuries to give up its anti-celibacy and fall in line with Rome, while in the Eastern Orthodox Church priests below the rank of abbot and bishop have retained their right to marry until this day.

An awareness of these facts concerning the liberal attitudes towards sexual relations in the Celtic Church is essential towards understanding the background to the Fidelma stories.

The condemnation of the 'sin of the flesh' remained alien to the Celtic Church for a long time after Rome's attitude became a dogma. In Fidelma's world, both sexes inhabited abbeys and monastic foundations, which were known as *conhospitae*, or double houses, where men and women lived raising their children in Christ's service.

Fidelma's own house of St Brigid of Kildare was one such community of both sexes during her time. When Brigid established her community of Kildare (*Cill Dara* – church of the oaks) she invited a bishop named Conláed to join her. Her first surviving biography, completed fifty years after her death in AD 650, during Fidelma's lifetime, was written by a monk of Kildare named Cogitosis, who makes it clear that it continued to be a mixed community after her death.

It should also be pointed out, demonstrating their co-equal role with men, that women were priests of the Celtic Church in this period. Brigid herself was ordained a bishop by Patrick's nephew, Mel, and her case was not unique. In the sixth century, Rome actually wrote a protest at the Celtic practice of allowing women to celebrate the divine sacrifice of Mass.

Unlike the Roman Church, the Irish Church did not have a system of 'confessors' where 'sins' had to be confessed to clerics who then had the authority to absolve the penitent of those sins in Christ's name. Instead, people chose a 'soul friend' (*anam chara*), clerical or lay, with whom they discussed matters of emotional and spiritual well-being.

To help readers more readily identify personal names, a list of the principal characters is given.

In response to the numerous readers who have asked for help in pronouncing the Irish names and words, I have included a pronunciation guide.

Thus armed, we may now enter Fidelma's world. The events of this story take place in AD 667 in the days following the night known as *Gelach a' bhruic*, the Badger's Moon, which is the full moon of October in whose light the ancient Irish believed that the badger dried grass to build its nest.

Pronunciation Guide

As the Fidelma series has become increasingly popular, many English-speaking fans have written wanting assurance about the way to pronounce the Irish names and words.

Irish belongs to the Celtic branch of the Indo-European family of languages. It is closely related to Manx and Scottish Gaelic and a cousin of Welsh, Cornish and Breton. It is a very old European literary language. Professor Calvert Watkins of Harvard maintained it contains Europe's oldest *vernacular* literature, Greek and Latin being a *lingua franca*. Surviving texts date from the seventh century AD.

The Irish of Fidelma's period is classed as Old Irish; after AD 950 the language entered a period known as Middle Irish. Therefore, in the Fidelma books, Old Irish forms are generally adhered to, whenever possible, in both names and words. This is like using Chaucer's English compared to modern English. For example, a word such as *aidche* ('night') in Old Irish is now rendered *oiche* in modern Irish.

There are only eighteen letters in the Irish alphabet. From earliest times there has been a literary standard but today four distinct spoken dialects are recognised. For our purposes, we will keep to Fidelma's dialect of Munster.

It is a general rule that stress is placed on the first syllable but, as in all languages, there are exceptions. In Munster the exceptions to the rule of initial stress are a) if the second syllable is long then it bears the stress; b) if the first two syllables are short and the third is long then the third syllable is stressed – such as in the word for fool, *amadán*, pronounced amad-awn; and c) where the second syllable contains ach and there is no long syllable, the second syllable bears the stress.

There are five short vowels – a, e, i, o, u – and five long vowels – á, é, í, ó, ú. On the long vowels note the accent, like the French acute, which is called a *fada* (literally, 'long'), and this is the only accent in Irish. It occurs on capitals as well as lower case.

The accent is important for, depending on where it is placed, it changes the entire word. *Seán* (Shawn) = John. But *sean* (shan) = old and *séan* (she-an) = an omen. By leaving out the accent on his name, the actor Sean Connery has become 'Old' Connery!

These short and long vowels are either 'broad' or 'slender'. The six broad vowels are:

a pronounced 'o' as in cot   á pronounced 'aw' as in law
o pronounced 'u' as in cut   ó pronounced 'o' as in low
u pronounced 'u' as in run   ú pronounced 'u' as in rule

The four slender vowels are:

i pronounced 'i' as in hit   í pronounced 'ee' as in see
e pronounced 'e' as in let   é pronounced 'ay' as in say

There are double vowels, some of which are fairly easy because they compare to English pronunciation – such as 'ae' as s*ay* or 'ui' as in q*ui*t. However, some double and even triple vowels in Irish need to be learnt.

ái pronounced like 'aw' in law (*dálaigh* = daw-lee)
ia pronounced like 'ea' in near
io pronounced like 'o' in come
éa pronounced like 'ea' in bear
ei pronounced like 'e' in let
aoi pronounced like the 'ea' in mean
uai pronounced like the 'ue' in blue
eoi pronounced like the 'eo' in yeoman
iai pronounced like the 'ee' in see

Hidden vowels

Most people will have noticed that many Irish people pronounce the word film as fil-um. This is actually a transference of Irish pronunciation rules. When **l**, **n** or **r** is followed by **b**, **bh**, **ch**, **g** (not after **n**), **m** or **mh**, and is preceded by a short stressed vowel, an additional vowel is heard between them. So *bolg* (stomach) is pronounced bol-ag; *garbh* (rough) is gar-ev; *dorcha* (dark) is dor-ach-a; *gorm* (blue) is gor-um and *ainm* (name) is an-im.

The consonants

b, **d**, **f**, **h**, **l**, **m**, **n**, **p**, **r** and **t** are said more or less as in English

g is always hard like the 'g' in gate
c is always hard like the 'c' in cat
s is pronounced like the 's' in said except before a slender vowel
when it is pronounced 'sh' as in shin

In Irish the letters **j**, **k**, **q**, **w**, **x**, **y** or **z** do not exist and **v** is formed
by the combination of **bh**.

Consonants can change their sound by aspiration or eclipse. Aspiration is caused by using the letter **h** after them.

bh is like the 'v' in voice
ch is a soft breath as in loch (not pronounced as lock!) or as
in Ba*ch*
dh before a broad vowel is like the 'g' in gap
dh before a slender vowel is like the 'y' in year
fh is totally silent
gh before a slender vowel can sound like 'y' as in yet
mh is pronounced like the 'w' in wall
ph is like the 'f' in fall
th is like the 'h' in ham
sh is also like the 'h' in ham

Consonants can also change their sound by being eclipsed, or
silenced, by another consonant placed before it. For example *na
mBan* (of women) is pronounced nah *m*'on; *i bpaipéar* (in the paper)
i *b*'ap'er and *i gcathair* (in the city) i *g*'a'har.

p can be eclipsed by **b**, **t**
t can be eclipsed by **d**
c can be eclipsed by **g**
f can be eclipsed by **bh**
b can be eclipsed by **m**
d and **g** can be eclipsed by **n**

For those interested in learning more about the language, it is worth
remembering that, after centuries of suppression during the colonial
period, Irish became the first official language of the Irish state on
independence in 1922. The last published census of 1991 showed
one third of the population returning themselves as Irish-speaking.
In Northern Ireland, where the language continued to be openly
discouraged after Partition in 1922, only 10.5 per cent of the population

were able to speak the language in 1991, the first time an enumeration of speakers was allowed since Partition.

Language courses are now available on video and audio-cassette from a range of producers from Linguaphone to RTÉ and BBC. There are some sixty summer schools and special intensive courses available. Teilifís na Gaeilge is a television station broadcasting entirely in Irish and there are several Irish language radio stations and newspapers. Information can be obtained from Comhdháil Náisiúnta na Gaeilge, 46 Sráid Chill Dara, Baile Atha Cliath 2, Éire.

Readers might also like to know that *Valley of the Shadow*, in the Fidelma series, was produced on audio-cassette, read by Marie McCarthy, from Magna Story Sound (SS391 – ISBN 1-85903-313-X).

Principal Characters

Sister Fidelma of Cashel, a *dálaigh* or advocate of the law courts of seventh-century Ireland
Brother Eadulf of Seaxmund's Ham in the land of the South Folk, her companion

At Cashel

Colgú, King of Muman, Fidelma's brother
Ségdae, bishop of Imleach, *comarb* of Ailbe
Sárait, the nursemaid

At Rath Raithlen

Becc, chieftain of the Cinél na Áeda
Adag, the steward to Becc
Accobrán, tanist, or heir apparent, to Becc
Lesren the tanner, father of Beccnat
Bébháil, mother of Beccnat
Seachlann the miller, father of Escrach
Brocc, brother of Seachlann
Sirin, cook at Rath Raithlen, uncle of Ballgel
Berrach, aunt of Ballgel, sister to Sirin
Goll the woodcutter
Fínmed, his wife
Gabrán, son of Goll
Liag the apothecary
Gobnuid, a smith
Tómma, Lesren's assistant
Creoda, a tanner's assistant
Síoda, a boy
Menma, a hunter
Suanach, his wife

At the abbey of the Blessed Finnbarr

Abbot Brogán
Brother Solam
Brother Dangila
Brother Nakfa
Brother Gambela

Brother Túan, steward of the house of Molaga

Conrí, war chief of the Uí Fidgente

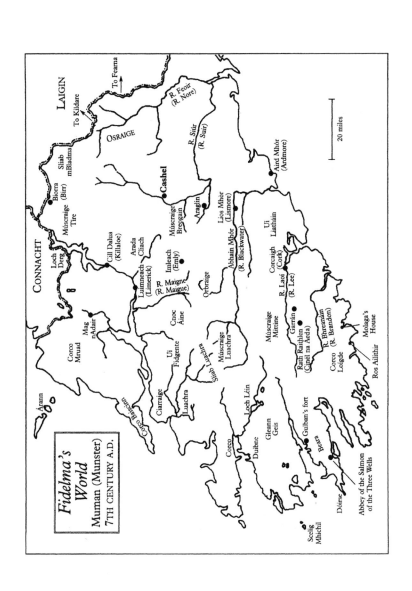

Fidelma's
World
Muman (Munster)
7TH CENTURY A.D.

CONNACHT

LAIGIN

To Fearna

To Kildare

OSRAIGE

Sliab mBladma (Birr)

R. Feoir (R. Nore)

R. Siúr (R. Suir)

Cashel

Aird Mhór (Ardmore)

Biorra (Birr)

Múscraige Tíre

Loch Derg

Cill Dalua (Killaloe)

Arada Cliach

Luimneach (Limerick)

Imleach (Emly)

Múscraige Breogain

Anaglin

Líos Mhór (Lismore)

Abhain Mhór (R. Blackwater)

Uí Liatháin

Corcaigh (Cork)

R. Maigne (R. Maigue)

Orbraige

Múscraige Mittine

R. Laoi (R. Lee)

Garrán

Rath Raithlen (Cinél na Aeda)

R. Bhreanáin (R. Brandon)

Corco Loigde

Molaga's House

Ros Ailithir

Arann

Corco Mruad

Mag nAdair

Uí Fidgente

Luachra

Ciarraige

Cnoc Áine

Sliab Luachra

Múscraige Luachra

Corco Baiscinn

Loch Léin

Corco Dubne

Gleann Geis

Gulban's fort

Beara

Dóirse

Abbey of the Salmon of the Three Wells

Sceitg Mhichil

20 miles

Chapter One

It seemed as if the great white disc of the moon dominated the sky. Low hanging, remorselessly bright and cold, it filled the heavens with such luminosity that all darkness seemed to vanish. He felt visible and naked before it, standing shivering in its unmerciful icy illumination. Some distant thought registered that it was curious, in spite of a feeling of body coldness, that his head appeared to be on fire, the palms of his hands were sweating, and his breathing was swift and shallow. He felt almost sexually aroused. His heartbeat was throbbing in excitement. His nostrils were filled with the fragrance of the mixed nocturnal scents. He raised his arms towards the giant smudged white disc, stretching forth his fingertips as if he would pluck the moon from the sky, straining forward a little, the muscles rippling in his back and shoulders as he stretched.

His lips drew back from his teeth, snarling a little in his grin of exultation. He felt a thrill of knowledge, an intoxication of superiority over his fellows. He, alone of all people, would dare to speak the forbidden sacred name of the moon because he shared her enlightenment, her secret wisdom. He, alone, dared speak her name while his fellows would call her by myriad euphemisms and epithets because they were too frightened to stand before the unforgiving goddess of the night and utter her true, hallowed identity. They would uneasily refer to her as 'the brightness', 'the radiance', or 'the place where knowledge is gathered', and when sailors went on board a ship they thought they would bring misfortune on themselves unless they simply called her 'Queen of the Night'. But he knew her true name and only he would dare to utter it.

Only he had the privilege of pronouncing her name, and it was a token of his power, a show of his authority and skill in defining the named. The God of the New Faith would not reveal his own name even to his beloved Moses. Didn't the priests of the New Faith say that when Moses asked for the name of the deity who was about to use him, the God replied: 'I am who I am.' Was it not true that all the gods wanted to declare their divine freedom from any manipulation or control by concealing the knowledge and use of their names? Names and naming imparted power. He held that power. He felt that power now.

1

He stretched forth his hands again and spread his fingertips as if to caress the stern, smutty face of the moon.

He could feel that stirring, the strange pulsating of the *sreang na imleacáin*, the umbilical cord, which bound him to her white orb and demanded his unquestioning service and obedience, in return for which he held dominion beneath her rays.

He knew that the time had come once again when he could no longer resist her demands. The compulsion was now irresistible.

He turned from the clearing and moved into the woods with a curious loping gait. He knew where he was going although he had not consciously worked it out. He carried himself with an animal-like ease, moving swiftly along the darkened forest path. He negotiated its impediments without difficulty, his breath soft and not taxed at all by his efforts. The main track was near. The trees were thinning and he could see the dark outlines of the old rath of the chieftain on the hill to his right. He paused at the sight. He observed the flicker of the lanterns that marked the gates of the fortress. He knew that in the shadows behind the lamps there would be at least two warriors on watch. That did not matter. He did not intend to go any closer to the fortress than he was now. That was not his purpose.

The moonlight revealed that the track, which lay alongside the woods, winding its way up to the fortress, was deserted. He glanced up at the orb above him and his lips compressed momentarily into a thin determined line.

Was it too late? Could he have missed the moment? Surely not. The impulse which guided him assured him that all would be right. He had the knowledge. He was omniscient.

There was a movement at the gates of the rath. The squeal of metal hinges disturbed the silence of the night. He could hear voices and someone called in a masculine drawl: 'Safe home, Ballgel!' A soft female voice answered cheerfully. Then he heard the rasping sound of the gates shutting.

A shadowy figure began to swing down the hill.

He let out a breath of thanks. He had arrived in time. The slight female figure, apparently carrying a basket on one arm, became visible in the moonlight once away from the dark shadows of the fortress walls. The figure walked with a confident youthful step.

He smiled to himself and drew back a little into the cover of the trees. He could feel the throb of his pulse begin to increase its pressure again, the sweat on the palms of his hands began to itch. Unconsciously he rubbed them up and down on his thighs to dry them and ease the itching sensation.

The figure drew nearer, walking swiftly, unconcerned. The girl drew abreast of him and he moved slightly, causing the undergrowth to rustle gently.

She halted at once and swung in his direction.

'Who is there?' she demanded, peering into the darkness, her voice showing no fear.

He hesitated only a moment, peering swiftly around in the shadows to make sure that they were alone, and then stepped forward into the moonlight. She recognised him and visibly relaxed.

'Oh, so it's you! What are you doing here?'

He cleared his dry throat and forced a smile. His voice was pitched to that of warm friendliness. 'I was on my way home, Ballgel. I thought I saw you coming down the track from the rath. Isn't it late to be going home?'

The girl dismissed the hour with laugh. 'Becc had many guests this evening. I had to stay to help my uncle in the kitchen. There was a great tidying to do. Isn't it always the same at the rath every night our chieftain entertains? I am often forced to stay until about this time. I thought you knew that.'

He nodded absently. He did know it. He was counting on it. 'I'll walk along the way with you.'

'Suit yourself,' she replied. 'It's straight home for me. It's been an exhausting day.'

She turned and recommenced her interrupted walk. She knew that his house lay in the general direction of her own and was not surprised at his offer to accompany her. He fell in step at her side.

He was smiling now. It was a fox-like smile but, in the gloom, she did not see the cunning mould of his features.

'If you want to get home quickly, then the quicker path lies along the woodland shortcut over the shoulder of the hill. It takes fifteen minutes off the journey by this track where you have to go all round the base of the hill.'

'Across the Thicket of Pigs at this time of night?' She laughed again. 'With wolves and who knows what wild animals along the way? And aren't you forgetting what has happened in those woods up on the hill?'

He paused and spread his arms as if he would sweep the dangers aside.

'I am here to protect you, aren't I?' he demanded. 'Neither beast nor man would dare attack two grown adults. Come on. I am in a hurry to get home too and have further to go than you. That path is a full fifteen minutes in the saving of our journey. Surely that's a good prospect?'

The girl hesitated, reluctantly seeing the logic of his argument.

'It's dark along the woodland path,' she protested, but in a half-hearted fashion.

'What? Dark? With the moon at its full, there's light enough for us to see the passing of a badger below the bushes at twenty paces. Come on! There is nothing to be fearful of since you are with me.'

She hesitated only a fraction of a moment more and then slowly nodded agreement. 'Very well. But I mean to hurry along the path.'

She went before him and for a second he raised his face to the great hanging white orb of the moon, eyes closed exultantly, letting the death-white flesh of his face bathe in the chilly white light.

'Come on, then,' he heard her call impatiently. 'What are you waiting for?'

'I am coming,' he replied hastily. His heart was beating so loud that it seemed to drown out all other sounds. He felt the sweat trickling down his forehead and around his eye sockets. He raised a hand to wipe his face. Then he set off with slow sure steps after her shadowy form, as it seemed to momentarily vanish along the pathway into the moonlit woods.

'My lord Becc, come quickly!'

Becc, chieftain of the Cinél na Áeda, glanced up in annoyance as Adag, his steward, burst into his bedchamber without even the courtesy of knocking. It was an unforgivable lapse of social etiquette and he opened his mouth to deliver a reprimand, but the servant was continuing.

'Brother Solam from the abbey has just arrived at the gates. The abbey is under attack,' gasped the rotund and balding man. 'Abbot Brogán asks that you go to his assistance immediately.'

Becc had been up late, feasting and drinking with his guests. His head ached and his mouth was dry. He groaned a little and reached for a flagon that stood on a table near his bed. He raised it and took a mouthful or two directly from it. His face screwed into a look of distaste as the stale liquor washed down. His steward looked on with disapproval.

'Wine is sweet in the drinking but bitter in the paying,' observed Becc in self-defence, wiping his mouth with the back of his hand.

Adag focused beyond the chieftain's shoulder and piously intoned: 'He who drinks only water will not be drunk.'

Becc gazed at him sourly, opened his mouth and then closed it again. Another aphorism came unbidden into his mind. Let you be drunk or sober, keep your thoughts to yourself.

He rose and began to move rapidly, dressing quickly and ignoring his disapproving steward until he had buckled on his sword.

A dishevelled Brother of the Faith was waiting in agitation in the anteroom beyond. He was young, with fair hair.

'Brother Solam,' Becc greeted him. 'What is this news that you bring me?'

'The abbey is under attack, my lord Becc. My abbot bids you—'

Becc made a cutting motion with his hand, silencing the man.

'The abbey is under attack? Who is attacking it?' he demanded sharply.

'The villagers, my lord. Yet another body, the body of the young girl named Ballgel, was found in the woods this morning . . .'

The chieftain's eyes widened with shock. 'Ballgel? But she works in my kitchen. She was here last night until late because we had guests . . .' He turned quickly to his steward, who had followed him. 'Adag, at what time did Ballgel leave the rath last night?'

'Just after midnight, lord. I was at the gate when she left. She went alone.'

Becc turned to Brother Solam. 'It is certain that it was Ballgel who was killed?'

'It is certain. The villagers are in an ugly mood. This is the third young girl of the village who has been killed in as many months. A crowd has marched on the abbey and called upon the abbot to hand over the three visiting religious. The abbot refuses and now they are in fury, rage and clamour. They say they will attack the brethren and set fire to the abbey unless the strangers are handed over.'

'Why the strangers? Do the villagers have evidence that they killed Ballgel?'

Brother Solam shook his head quickly. 'The villagers are full of fear and suspicion, lord. But that does not make them any the less dangerous.'

'I have already alerted the guard, my lord Becc,' Adag intervened. 'The horses should be saddled by now.'

'Then let us ride for the abbey!' Becc ordered decisively, turning to lead the way to the courtyard. 'Brother Solam can ride behind one of our warriors.'

The abbey of the Blessed Finnbarr was only a short ride away, a cluster of wooden buildings gathered by the banks of the River Tuath. The buildings were encompassed by a wooden stockade which served to keep out wolves and other nocturnal scavengers. Before the wooden gates, which were hardly strong enough to exclude one determined man, a group of forty or fifty men and women had gathered. Facing them stood a slightly built, elderly religieux with silver hair. His clothing proclaimed him as a senior member of the community. At either side of him stood two young, nervous-looking brethren.

The old man was holding up his hands as if calling for quiet. However, the shouting and outrage of the crowd drowned out his words.

'Hand over the strangers! We will deal with them!'

At the forefront of the crowd was a thickset villager with a dark black beard and an angry expression. He carried a thick cudgel in one of his large hands. Those around him roared their approval of his belligerent leadership.

'This is a house of God!' The thin, reedy tone of the old man made itself heard in a momentary lull of the angry murmurs. 'No one dare enter the house of the Lord with violent intent. Go back to your homes.'

At this the people howled their disapproval. Someone threw a small stone from the back of the crowd. It passed over the people's heads and struck harmlessly at the walls. But the implication was dangerous.

'In the name of God, Brocc, take these people away from this place before harm is done.' The old man appealed directly to the burly leader. They were almost face to face, so that no one else could probably hear the words of appeal.

'Harm has already been done, Abbot Brogán,' replied the man as loudly as he could so that those around would know what was being said. 'More harm shall be done if you refuse to give up the strangers to justice.'

'Give them up to vengeance is what you mean. Our visitors walk in the shadow of God. They are protected not only under the ancient laws of hospitality but under the sacred rule of sanctuary.'

'You would protect the murderers of our children?'

'Where is your proof against them?'

'The proof is the mutilated bodies of our daughters!' cried Brocc, raising his voice so that all the people could hear him.

A loud acclamation greeted his words.

'You have no proof,' countered one of the younger Brothers of the Faith at the abbot's side. Unlike the abbot's, his voice was young and strong and carried. 'You have come here only because these religious are strangers in our land and for no other reason. You fear them simply because they are strangers.'

Another missile was aimed from the back of the crowd. This time it caught the young Brother a glancing blow on the forehead, causing a red gash of blood, and the impact made him stagger back a step or two. The crowd growled menacingly, like an animal, in their approval of the bloodshed.

'Unless you wish to suffer the same fate as the strangers, Abbot Brogán,' threatened Brocc, 'you will hand them over.'

'You dare to threaten the abbot?' cried the second Brother, his expression aghast. 'You have already raised your hands against the brethren of this community, for which God's punishment will surely pursue you. But you dare to threaten—'

'Enough of words!' Brocc yelled and raised his cudgel menacingly.

It was then that the chieftain Becc, with Adag his steward and four of his warriors, came riding up, pushing their horses through the crowd. The people fell back with sullen expressions at the sight of their chieftain and his armed horsemen.

Brother Solam, who had been riding behind one of the warriors, slipped off the horse and hurried to the abbot before turning to the crowd, standing in front of the abbot in an attitude of protection. The people had suddenly fallen into an uneasy quiet. However, Brocc did not wish to lose the momentum he had gained.

'Well, lord Becc,' he called in a sneering tone, 'have you come to sanction the punishment of the murderers or do you support those that would protect them?' He flung out a hand and pointed accusingly at the abbot. 'The abbot refuses to hand the murderers over to justice.'

'I have come here to tell you that this is not the law,' cried Becc sharply. 'Disperse back to your homes.'

Brocc placed his feet apart and one hand remained on his hip while the other held his cudgel in easy fashion. He had his reputation as a strong man to maintain and his stance had more than a trace of a swagger to it.

'So you seek to protect the murderers too, lord Becc?' He raised his voice almost triumphantly.

'It is enough that I am your chieftain for you to obey me,' Becc snapped at him in irritation. 'I say, go back to your homes lest you incur my displeasure.'

The crowd began to mutter uneasily and several of them turned away with pale, sullen faces.

'Hold fast!' Brocc yelled. He remained in his defiant position. His sharp voice halted those who were half-hearted among the mob. He turned insolently back to the chieftain. 'Do not try to intimidate us, lord Becc. We will have justice.'

Becc's face had become red with anger.

'You do not seek justice, Brocc,' he retorted. 'What you seek is bloodshed and with no just cause but your prejudice against the strangers.' He raised his voice again to the others. 'I call on you once more to disperse to your homes. You currently stand in contravention of the *Cáin Chiréib* – the law of riot. The consequences of continuing your actions are dire. Do you understand?'

Once again the faint-hearted would have turned away, accepting the inevitable, but Brocc held up a hand to stay them yet again.

'I am a *céile*, a free clansman. I work my land, pay my taxes for the upkeep of this community and am the first to join the chieftain's troops in time of war and danger. I have a voice in the clan assembly and while I may not be of the *derbfhine* of your family, that band of relatives who elected you as chieftain, my voice should and shall be heard.'

Becc, sitting easily on horseback, continued to appear relaxed, only his eyes now narrowed slightly.

'Your voice is being heard, Brocc,' the chieftain pointed out softly. Only those who knew him well could appreciate the dangerous tone in his voice.

But Brocc did not know him so well. He turned to the crowd and appealed to those who had held their ground.

'There have been deaths in this community. Violent, terrible deaths of young girls. Last night Ballgel, a cousin of mine who worked in the kitchens of our own chieftain's fortress, was slaughtered on her way home. She is now the third young girl to be slaughtered at the time of the full moon. Did not Escrach, my brother's only child, suffer this same terrible death last month? And when did these slaughters begin? They began at the time when Abbot Brogán first gave hospitality to the three dark strangers. Black is their colour and black are their deeds. We shall have justice. Bring them out to face punishment.'

There was a murmur of approval, slightly more muted than previously in view of the armed warriors. But it was clear that Brocc had strong support among the local people.

Becc leant forward a little in his saddle. 'Where is your evidence, Brocc?' His tone was reasonable, almost conversational.

'Evidence was given to your Brehon Aolú,' replied the man.

'Which he found not to be any evidence at all.'

'And now the old fool is dead. Bring forth a new Brehon and I will give my evidence again.'

'Aolú told you that you had no evidence. What evidence do you now present against the strangers to charge them before a Brehon? Evidence is what is required under the law of this land.'

Brocc laughed harshly. 'Their very appearance is the evidence against them!'

In spite of the growing mutters of approval, the chieftain sat back and smiled grimly.

'So, you have no evidence save your own prejudice?' he sneered. 'It is as I have said. You do not want justice; you simply want a sacrifice to your own prejudice. I say again to you, Brocc, and to everyone who now remains before these gates, you stand under the shadow of the *Cáin Chiréib*. This is the second time that I have uttered this warning to you. I do not want to utter it a third time.'

Brocc would not be put off. He stood immovable, shaking his head.

'We will not be frightened away from our intention. We aim to enter the abbey and take the strangers and no one will stop us, neither clergy nor you, Becc, and your warriors, if you stand in the way.'

He lifted his stout cudgel into a menacing position across his chest. He turned to the crowd and raised his voice. 'Follow me and I will give you justice!'

No one moved. They were looking beyond Brocc to where Becc and his warriors were seated on their horses. When Brocc turned back he found that Becc had taken his bow and now an arrow was drawn against its string and aimed at him. Brocc was no coward. He blinked in surprise for a moment and then he smiled in his defiance.

'You cannot shoot me down, Becc. I am a *céile*, a free clansman.'

Becc had lifted the bow slightly in order to bring the arrow flights to the level of his eye. The bow was now fully drawn.

'For the third time, Brocc, I warn you that you stand in the shadow of the *Cáin Chiréib*. I ask for the third and last time that you proceed to your home and no harm shall come to you. Stay and you will meet the consequences of your disobedience to the law.'

'May you fester in your grave! You would not kill your own people, Becc,' sneered Brocc. 'You would not kill us to protect strangers.' He raised his cudgel and called to the crowd. 'Follow me! Let us have just—'

His words ended in a scream of pain.

Becc had released his arrow, and it had embedded itself in Brocc's thigh. For a moment the man stood, his eyes wide, an aghast expression on his features. Then he collapsed and fell writhing to the ground, groaning in agony. No one else moved. No one spoke.

Becc turned with an angry frown. 'You have been warned three times. Now, disperse to your homes!' His voice was harsh.

With a quiet muttering but with alacrity, the mob vanished. Within a moment there was no one left out of the menacing crowd but the crumpled figure of Brocc.

Becc swung down from his horse as Abbot Brogán came hurrying forward.

'Thanks be to God that you came quickly, my lord Becc. I feared that the abbey would be violated.'

Becc turned to his steward, Adag, who was also dismounting. 'Take Brocc to the *forus tuaithe* and have them tend his wound. It is only a flesh wound, painful but not debilitating. Ensure that he is confined there to await a hearing before a Brehon for his violation of the law.'

The *forus tuaithe* was, literally, 'the house of the territory', which served as the clan hospital. Each territory had such hospitals, either secular ones governed under the direct cognisance of the Brehons or monastic charitable institutions under the direction and management of the local abbot.

Adag hauled Brocc to his feet, perhaps a little too roughly. The burly man groaned and clutched at him for support. Blood was spurting from his wound.

'May a great choking come on you,' Brocc groaned, his eyes smouldering with hate at Becc. 'May you die roaring!'

Becc smiled back into the man's malignant features. 'Your curses are not harmful to me, Brocc. And remember, when you pronounce your maledictions, that it is said that under a tree falls its own foliage.'

He glanced at Adag and nodded slightly. The steward began to drag the wounded man away in none too gentle a fashion.

'In case you don't know the old saying, Brocc,' Adag, the steward, whispered in cheerful explanation, 'it means that if you invoke a curse and it does not harm the person against whom you have aimed it, it will fall on your own head. I would seek an act of contrition before the abbot to avoid its consequence.'

Behind them, Becc had turned back to the old abbot.

'This is a bad business, Abbot Brogán,' the chieftain was saying as he unstrung his bow and hooked it onto his saddle.

The old religieux nodded. 'I fear that the people are terror-stricken. If it was not Brocc, then someone else would put their terror to some ill use. Three young girls have been butchered and each one at the full of the moon.' He shivered, crossed himself and mumbled, '*Absit omen!*'

'What do the strangers have to say about their whereabouts last night?'

'They each swear that they did not stir from the abbey and, in this matter, I do not know what to do. Should I tell them to be gone from the sanctuary of the abbey? That I can no longer give them protection and hospitality?'

Becc shook his head quickly. 'If they are not guilty that would be an injustice and we would be guilty of a great crime for violating the law of hospitality. If they are guilty, then, equally, it would be wrong, for we would have dispersed them into the world without trial and, perhaps, to perpetuate their crimes elsewhere.'

'Then what must we do?' queried the abbot. 'I can see no solution.'

Becc stood rubbing his chin as though deep in thought. In fact, he had been considering the problem ever since Brother Solam had brought him the news a short while before, and his plan was already in place. But Becc was not one who wished it to appear that his decisions were arbitrary. Aolú had been Brehon of the Cinél na Áeda for forty years when, three weeks previously, the old man had taken sick and died. Becc had been contemplating how he could replace the old judge. Within the Cinél na Áeda there were several minor judges but none of the rank and authority to replace Aolú as the senior judge of the clan.

'I believe that we should call in the services of a Brehon from outside our territory. The local Brehons, upright and honourable justices though they may be, might not carry the influence and potency to quell the panic that is growing among the villagers.'

The abbot nodded slowly. 'I agree, my lord Becc. We must first calm the fears of the people and then find out who is behind these senseless killings.'

Becc pulled a face.

'No killing is without a kind of sense to the person who commits it,' he rejoined. 'However, we must find a Brehon of authority.'

'Where would you find such a Brehon, my lord Becc?' demanded the abbot dubiously.

'I am going to take one of my men and we shall ride to the king's court at Cashel. King Colgú will advise us, for we can appeal to no higher authority in the land than our king.'

'Cashel?' Abbot Brogán's eyes widened a little. 'But that will mean that you will be away for several days upon your journey. It is a long road between here and Cashel.'

'Have no fear. I will leave Accobrán, my tanist, in command with strict orders for your protection and that of the strangers.' Accobrán had been the tanist, or heir apparent, to the chieftain of the Cinél na Áeda for less than a year. He was a young warrior, who had proved his courage in the recent wars against the rebellious Uí Fidgente. Becc smiled complacently. 'I doubt whether anyone will attempt to attack the abbey again in view of the manner in which I have dealt with Brocc. The people will think twice about rioting having seen the consequences of their disobedience.'

'There is that, of course,' the abbot agreed. 'But I was thinking of the potential harm coming to any more of our young women.'

Becc fingered his beard thoughtfully for a moment. 'I would have thought that observation would discount such a fear, abbot.'

The old man frowned. 'I do not understand.'

'The three young women were all slaughtered on the full of the moon. A ritual and gruesome death. We now lack an entire month until the next full of the moon. Our young women should be safe until then.'

The abbot's face was grave. Becc had articulated the very fear that he had been trying to drive from his mind since the news of the second slaughter had been brought to him and had now been reinforced by the third killing.

'The full of the moon,' he sighed. 'Then you agree, Becc, we are dealing with some madman . . . someone who needs to perform his or her killing ritual by the light of the full moon?'

'That much is self-evident, Abbot Brogán. I will leave for Cashel this afternoon in search of a Brehon of reputation. We have until the next full of the moon before evil strikes at us once again.'

Chapter Two

Eadulf entered the chamber where Fidelma was stretched out in a chair in front of a fire. There was an autumnal chill in the early evening air which permeated the great grey stone halls of the palace of Cashel in spite of the woollen tapestries that covered the walls and the rugs that cushioned the flags of the floors and were supposed to give warmth to the rooms. Eadulf wore a scowl of annoyance on his face and he swung the heavy oak door shut behind him none too gently.

Fidelma glanced up from the book that she was reading with a frown of irritation. Her book was one of the small satchel books, called a *tiag liubhair*, intended to be carried easily on pilgrimages and missions to far-off countries. She liked to read beside the fire and such small books could be held in the hand and were ideal for the purpose.

'Hush! You'll wake Alchú,' she said reprovingly. 'He's only just gone to sleep.'

Eadulf's scowl deepened as he crossed the room to the fire.

'Is something wrong?' enquired Fidlema, suppressing a sudden yawn and laying aside the book. She could recognise the signs when Eadulf was annoyed.

'I have just encountered that old fool, Bishop Petrán,' Eadulf said tersely, dropping into a chair opposite her. 'He started giving me a lecture on the benefits of celibacy.'

Fidelma gave a tired smile. 'He would, wouldn't he? Bishop Petrán is a leading advocate of the idea that all members of the religious should be celibate. He holds that celibacy is the ideal of the Christian victory over the evil of worldly things.'

Eadulf's expression was moody.

'Such an ideal victory would see humankind disappear from the earth within a few generations.'

'But why did you get involved in argument with old Petrán?' demanded Fidelma. 'Everyone knows that he is a woman hater and that is probably the cause of his own celibacy. No woman would look at him anyway,' she added uncharitably.

'He does not approve of our marriage, Fidelma.'

'That is his personal choice. Thanks be to God that there is no law which demands celibacy among the religious . . . not even among those

13

who give their allegiance, like Petrán, to the rules and philosophies now accepted in Rome. There are certain groups in the New Faith who argue that those who serve and give their love to the Christ cannot give their love to a single, fellow human being as well. They are misguided. If there were laws telling us to put our natural emotions in chains, the world would be so much the poorer.'

Eadulf grimaced dourly. 'Bishop Petrán claims that Paul of Tarsus demanded the practice of celibacy among his followers.'

Fidelma sniffed in disapproval. 'Then you should have quoted to him Paul's letter to Timothy – "Some will desert from the Faith and give their minds to subversive doctrines inspired by devils, through the specious falsehoods of men whose own conscience is branded with the devil's sign. They forbid marriage and inculcate abstinence from certain foods, though God created them to be enjoyed with thanksgiving by believers who have inward knowledge of the truth. For everything that God created is good, and nothing is to be rejected when it is taken with thanksgiving, since it is hallowed by God's own word and by prayer." Ask Petrán if he denies that God created man and woman and whether marriage is made an honourable estate by him.'

'I don't think Petrán was disposed to discuss the finer points of the matter with me.'

Fidelma stretched slightly in her chair. 'I suspect that Petrán also disapproves of many things that we of Éireann do since he has spent some years in a Frankish monastery among those advocating and practising celibacy. The only chaste men and women are those who are unable to find love with their fellows and so they wrap themselves in cloaks of chastity and pretend they love the intangible, shying away from people of real flesh and blood. If people are forced to suppress the emotion of love for their fellow human beings then they certainly can't have love for anything else, including God. Anyway, it probably does not matter to us what Petrán thinks as he is shortly to leave on a pilgrimage to the city of Lucca, which is north of Rome, where the Blessed Fridian of Éireann was bishop about a hundred years ago.'

Eadulf was torn a little between admiration for her philosophical arguments and a feeling of inadequacy. He wished he had the retentive knowledge to quote entire sections of the scriptures, as Fidelma was able to do. The scholars of Éireann had, for centuries, practised the art of memorising entire passages of learning. Indeed, Fidelma had told him that in the times before the New Faith had come to the country, it was traditional that no philosophies of the old religious should be written down. Men and women would spend as many as twenty years learning the ancient codes and practices solely by memory.

'I suppose we are twice damned in Bishop Petrán's eyes,' Eadulf said, rising and moving to the corner of the room where a crib stood.

'Don't wake him,' Fidelma instructed sharply.

'I won't,' Eadulf assured her. He gazed down at the baby that lay asleep there. There were fine strands of red hair across its forehead. Eadulf's features lightened in a smile of paternal pride. 'It is still difficult to realise that we have a son,' he said softly, half to himself.

Fidelma rose swiftly to join him, laying a hand on his arm. 'You've had four months to grow used to the fact of little Alchú's arrival in this world.'

'Gentle hound.' Eadulf translated the name softly as he gazed down at the baby. 'I wonder what he will grow up to be?'

Fidelma's mouth turned down almost in disapproval. 'There is a great deal of growing ahead of him before we can begin to ask that question, Eadulf.' She turned back to the fire and sat down again. 'Sárait should be here soon to look after him for we have been asked to attend a feasting in my brother's hall this evening.'

Eadulf rejoined her at the fire. Sárait was Fidelma's servant, who also occupied the position of nursemaid to little Alchú. While living in her brother's palace of Cashel, Fidelma was not treated as a religieuse of the Faith but, according to her right, as an Eóghanacht princess, sister to the king of Muman.

'What is the occasion for this feasting?' Eadulf asked.

'I am told that the chieftain of the Cinél na Áeda arrived this afternoon and is seeking my brother's help. Colgú has asked us to join him at the meal.'

'Help? What sort of help?'

Fidelma shrugged indifferently. 'I do not know, and have been wondering what brings him to Cashel at this time. Doubtless, our curiosity will be assuaged at the feasting.'

'And who are the Cinél na Áeda? I thought I knew most peoples of your kingdom but I cannot recall hearing of them.'

'They dwell in the hills south of the River Bride. That's an easy two-day ride to the south-west of here. The chieftain's fortress is a place called Rath Raithlen. The chieftain is called Becc and he is a distant cousin of mine, for his people are a sept of the Eóghanacht. Becc's grandfather Fedelmid was king of Cashel some four score years ago. I haven't seen Becc or been in his territory since I was a little girl.'

'So, it is not often that he visits Cashel?'

'He visits rarely,' agreed Fidelma. 'Except for important convocations of the assembly of the kingdom, Becc never comes here on social visits.'

In fact, Fidelma was more curious about the reason for her distant cousin's visit than Eadulf. She was still turning the matter over in her mind when she and Eadulf made their way to the private chambers of Colgú, king of Muman. The king's steward had informed them that Colgú wanted to see them in his private chambers before going into the feasting hall. The young king was waiting alone to receive them. There was no doubt as to the relationship of Colgú and Fidelma for both had the same tall build, the same red hair and changeable green eyes. They shared the same facial structure and the same indefinable quality of movement.

Colgú came quickly to meet them with a warm smile and embraced his sister before reaching out a hand to Eadulf.

'The little one is well?' he enquired.

'Alchú is well, indeed. He is in the safe hands of Sárait,' replied Fidelma. She glanced quickly round the room. 'I see that your guest is not here, brother. This means that you have some news that you wish to discuss with us before we greet him.'

Colgú grinned. 'As ever, you have a discerning sense, Fidelma. In fact, I did want a word with you before the feasting. However, the news is something that I want you to hear directly from the mouth of our cousin. I want to bring him in to speak with you before we go into the feasting hall where the atmosphere will not be congenial to anything but the most superficial discussion.'

Eadulf coughed awkwardly. 'Perhaps I should withdraw, if this is a matter concerning your family?'

Colgú threw out a hand towards him in a staying motion. 'You are part of this family now. Husband to my sister and father to her child. Besides, this matter also concerns you, so stay.'

Fidelma seated herself in one of the chairs before the fire and Eadulf waited for Colgú to indicate that he could also be seated before he sank into another. This was protocol, because Fidelma, aside from being sister to the king, was also qualified to the level of *anruth* and thus could sit unbidden in the presence of provincial kings and even speak before they did. She could even seat herself in the presence of the High King, if invited to do so. Eadulf, as a stranger in the kingdom, albeit the husband of Fidelma, had to wait until invited to be seated.

'From your remarks, Colgú, I presume that the matter Becc wishes to discuss is not some superficial family concern?' said Fidelma.

'Far from it,' agreed Colgú. 'He brings talk of evil and death. There is a great fear abroad among the Cinél na Áeda.'

Fidelma raised her eyebrows in surprise.

'Evil and death?' she repeated softly. 'Evil is an emotive word but death is always with us. How do they come together?'

'He talks of superstition and, perhaps, the spectre of unholy rituals among the dwellers in the dark woods that surround his people.'

'You intrigue me, brother. Tell us more.'

'I will bring Becc in to tell his story,' replied Colgú. 'It is best, as I say, that you hear his tale at first hand.' He reached forward to a side table and took up a small silver bell. Scarcely had the sharp peal of the bell died away when the king's steward opened the door and, on receiving a nod from Colgú, stood aside to usher in an elderly man, with a bushy beard, whose face retained the good looks of his youth and whose general appearance showed the well-muscled figure of a warrior which age had not yet diminished.

'Becc, chieftain of the Cinél na Áeda,' announced the steward before withdrawing and closing the door.

Only Eadulf stood up awkwardly as the handsome chieftain, his tall frame belying the meaning of the name he bore – for Becc meant 'small one – came forward. He bowed formally to Colgú before turning to Fidelma with a soft smile and the faintest forward motion of his head.

'Fidelma, I scarcely recognise you as the little girl whom I met many years ago. Now your fame precedes you in all the corners of our kingdom.'

'You are kind, cousin Becc,' replied Fidelma gravely. 'Allow me to present my companion, Brother Eadulf of Seaxmund's Ham, in the land of the South Folk.'

Becc turned to acknowledge Eadulf. The chieftain's quizzical blue-green eyes examined the other humorously.

'I have heard Brother Eadulf's name mentioned in the same breath as that of Fidelma of Cashel. They are names synonymous with law and justice.'

Eadulf was not looking exactly happy. He had a vague suspicion of something prompting these compliments and a hidden purpose behind this meeting.

'Be seated,' invited Colgú and both men obeyed. 'I have asked Fidelma and Eadulf to come here and listen to your story before we go in to the feasting, Becc.'

The chieftain pursed his lips and a dark shadow seemed to cross his features.

17

'It may well be that you can point the way out of the mire into which the Cinél na Áeda have descended,' he said hopefully.

Fidelma gazed at him thoughtfully. 'Tell your story, Becc, and we will see how best we may help you.'

'The first killing was two months ago,' Becc began without preamble. 'The victim was Beccnat, the daughter of Lesren who is our tanner and leather worker. She had just reached her seventeenth summer. A young, innocent girl.'

He fell silent, apparently meditating on the event.

'In what manner was she killed?' prompted Fidelma, after a few moments.

'Brutally,' returned Becc at once. 'Brutally.' His voice was suddenly sharp. 'Her body was found one morning in the woods not far from my fortress. She had been stabbed many times, almost as if the flesh was ripped apart in some unspeakable ritual way.'

'You said that this was the first killing. So I deduce that there have been others?'

'A month ago, another young girl was slain. This time it was Escrach, the daughter of our miller. She was found in a similar manner. She, too, was no more than seventeen or eighteen years of age.'

'Was she found in the same woods?'

Becc nodded. 'And not far from where the first body was found. Then a few nights ago the third girl was found. Her name was Ballgel. She was of the same age as the others. She worked in the kitchens at my fortress. She, too, was slaughtered in an unspeakable manner.'

'Unspeakable?' Fidelma grimaced dourly. 'When things are unspeakable I often find that they are best described in words.'

Becc sighed and gave a shake of his head.

'I do not choose my words lightly,' he said reprovingly. 'Have you ever seen the results when a butcher has slaughtered a hog?'

Eadulf's mouth was tight. 'That bad?'

Becc gazed evenly at him.

'Perhaps worse, Brother Saxon,' he agreed quietly.

There was a silence for a moment or so. Then Fidelma spoke again.

'You say that this was the third girl? And each killing was spaced a month apart?'

'At each full of the moon.'

Fidelma let out a soft breath and glanced quickly towards Eadulf.

'At the full of the moon,' she repeated softly.

Becc nodded to emphasise the significance.

'That is an implication which has not been lost on myself, or on Abbot Brogán,' he said.

18

'Abbot Brogán?'

'Nearby is the abbey where the Blessed Finnbarr was born.' Becc glanced at Eadulf. 'Finnbarr founded a school in the marshlands by the River Laoi and taught many years there.'

'We know well who Finnbarr was,' interposed Colgú roughly, 'for was not our father, Faílbe Fland mac Aedo Duib, king at Cashel during those days?'

Becc inclined his head, not bothering to explain that he was addressing his remarks to Eadulf.

'I had not forgotten. Anyway, Abbot Brogán is a venerable man who was trained at Finnbarr's college by the River Laoi. He took over the stewardship of the abbey near to us two decades ago. The abbey stands just below the wooded hill where these killings took place. We call the woods the Thicket of Pigs and now the hill bears that name.'

Fidelma leant back in her chair. 'So, from what you say, there have been three young girls murdered, each killing made on the full moon? Has your own Chief Brehon investigated this matter? I fail to understand why you bring this tale to Cashel.'

Becc shifted in embarrassment. 'My Chief Brehon was Aolú. A man of wit and wisdom who served the Cinél na Áeda for forty long years in that office. He was old and frail and three weeks ago he died from a fever produced from a chill.'

'Who succeeded him?' demanded Fidelma.

'Alas, I have not been able to appoint a successor. We have several judges of lower rank and ability, none of them of sufficient experience to be appointed as Chief Brehon. Until such an appointment can be made, we are without the wisdom of an experienced judge.'

Fidelma let out a sighing breath. She now realised what lay behind Becc's arrival at Cashel.

'When Aolú was alive was he able to take evidence and investigate the early deaths?'

'He was.'

'Are there any clues as to who would perpetrate such acts?'

Becc raised his shoulders and let them fall in an eloquent symbolism. 'None that Aolú considered worthy of pursuing. My tanist, Accobrán, made some inquiries for Aolú was infirm at the time and could not move from my rath. Alas, he learnt nothing. But as for suspects . . .' His expression became suddenly serious.

Fidelma caught the expression and her eyes narrowed. 'You appear troubled, cousin? There is a suspect?'

Becc hesitated for a moment and then made a gesture with one hand that seemed to express a sense of helplessness. 'It is that which prompted me to come here, Fidelma, and as a matter of urgency. There was a riot at the gates of the abbey of the Blessed Finnbarr. I had to use my warriors to save the religious from being attacked and I had to wound a man as an example to prevent the inevitable injury and destruction of the religious community.'

'The religious? At the abbey?' Fidelma could not conceal her surprise. 'Why there? Are you saying that the religious are suspected of these killings?'

'Not exactly the religious of the abbey. Brocc, who works with his brother at our local mill and is related to two of the victims, persuaded many of our people that some strangers who are staying in the abbey are responsible for the murders.'

'On what evidence?'

'I fear on no more evidence than his own prejudice. The strangers arrived and were given hospitality at the abbey only days before the first killing. As such a thing had never happened before, Brocc argues that it was undoubtedly the work of these visitors. It is unfortunate that something about them generates the fear and prejudice of our people. Brocc tried to lead the people in storming the gates of the abbey with the idea of seizing the strangers. Had he done so, they would undoubtedly have been killed and the brethren would have been harmed for trying to protect them.' Becc smiled grimly and shrugged. 'I thrice told them of the Law of Riots and its consequences. When Brocc still refused to depart to his home, I shot him in the thigh with an arrow. This caused everyone to pause for thought.'

Eadulf pursed his lips in an expression without humour.

'I should imagine it would. Drastic but effective,' he said with clear approval.

'And these strangers are under the protection of the abbey?' Fidelma asked. 'Were the people informed?'

'They are and they were. The strangers reside there under the sacred laws of hospitality as well as the rule of sanctuary that the New Faith has adopted.'

'Is there not a danger of the abbey's being attacked in your absence?' Edulf queried.

'Brocc, the main trouble-maker, will not be active for a while yet.' Becc smiled grimly. 'Also, I have left Accobrán, my tanist, in command. He will protect the abbey and the strangers.'

'Are you and Abbot Brogán totally satisfied of the innocence of these strangers?' Fidelma asked.

'We only know that you cannot punish strangers on no other evidence than suspicion. We lack a fully qualified Brehon to resolve the matter.'

There was a silence while Fidelma leant back in her chair, her eyes almost shut in thought. She gave a long sigh.

'I am only a minor Brehon. I am merely a *dálaigh* or advocate and qualified to the level of *anruth*. You need an *ollamh* of law. I would suspect that you have better qualified Brehons among the Cinél na Áeda than myself.'

'But none with your reputation, cousin,' replied Becc immediately.

'What is it that you expect from me?'

Becc was silent for a moment and then he cleared his throat nervously.

'Expect? Far be it for me to expect anything of you, Fidelma of Cashel. However, I would like to ask something of you. Would you come to Rath Raithlen, with Brother Eadulf of course, and solve this evil mystery which is afflicting our community?'

Eadulf glanced sharply at Fidelma. He had had a growing suspicion where this conversation was leading right from the start. Now, with foreboding, he saw the glint of excitement in her eyes. Fidelma's features were animated. He knew that she could not refuse the stimulant that was being offered to her intellect. Since they had returned from the land of the South Folk, even during the months of her confinement and the birth of little Alchú, Eadulf realised that she had not been completely happy. Fidelma was not a person to whom marriage and maternity was everything. Indeed, he had a sneaking suspicion that he might possess more of the maternal spirit than she did.

For some time now he had realised that she longed to get back to the thing that impassioned her most – the solving of conundrums, and the application of law to the answers. These were the things that brought her alive and invigorated her senses. In short, during these last months he had realised that she was bored. Bored with life at Cashel, with looking after Alchú with nothing else to occupy her highly attuned intellectual faculties. Oh, he had a sense of guilt when he thought about it because it was not that she was a bad or indifferent mother. It was not that she did not love Alchú. He knew her too well to condemn her for being true to her nature. Eadulf was aware that he was losing her almost before he spoke. He cleared his throat quickly.

'There is Alchú to consider,' he said quietly.

Fidelma's lips compressed in irritation.

'Sárait is a good nurse,' intervened Colgú before she could speak. 'You would not be away more than a week, perhaps ten days at most. She could look after him until you return. It is not as if Cashel is a stranger to babies and children.'

'We feel that you are our only hope in clearing up this mystery,' added Becc, a pleading note in his voice. 'We do not ask this of you as a mere whim of the moment.'

Fidelma looked at Eadulf with a faintly sad expression, as if she understood that he realised that the request provided an incentive that he could not displace – not even little Alchú could entice her to surrender this part of her life. It was what she had been born for, trained for, the thing she needed the way people need air to breathe, sleep by night and light during the day.

She turned back to Becc. 'These three strangers whom you mention. When you say "strangers", do you mean that they are strangers to the Cinél na Áeda, strangers to our kingdom of Muman or strangers to the five kingdoms of Éireann?'

'They are strangers from over the seas, from some distant land that I have never heard of.'

'Then, if they are unjustly accused or attacked, it becomes a matter of the honour of the kingdom and not just that of the Cinél na Áeda.'

Eadulf sighed softly in resignation. He had lost her.

Colgú was nodding in approval.

'There is that aspect to be considered,' he agreed. 'It is an important aspect. That is why it is vital that this matter be resolved before there are any more attacks on the abbey of the Blessed Finnbarr.'

'Or, indeed, any other young girls are murdered,' Fidelma added drily. She turned to Eadulf once again. 'Then I must go. There is no choice. Will you come with me, Eadulf? I shall need your help. Sárait will be a good nurse to Alchú.'

Eadulf hesitated only a second and then surrendered completely.

'Of course,' he said gruffly. 'As your brother says, Sárait is a good nurse. She will take care of the baby while we are away.'

Fidelma's features broadened in a smile of satisfaction. 'Then we shall be able to leave for Rath Raithlen at dawn tomorrow.'

Colgú had reached forward and rung the silver handbell once again. 'Before we conclude this discussion, there is one more task I must accomplish.'

This time it was Colgú's religious counsellor who entered. Ségdae was the elderly bishop of Imleach and *comarb*, official successor, of the Blessed Ailbe who first brought the Faith to Muman. The ageing but hawk-faced man, whose dark eyes missed nothing, carried a small, oblong box with him.

Colgú stood up and, as protocol demanded, they all stood. Ségdae's stern features softened a little in brief greeting to them all before he handed the box to Colgú. The king turned to Fidelma.

'In view of the nature of this matter, as you have already pointed out, Fidelma, we must treat it as a matter of concern for the honour of the kingdom. We have given hospitality to these strangers; if they are unjustly accused and harmed, it reflects on our honour. If they have abused our hospitality and committed these criminal acts, then it is we who are responsible for seeing that they answer for that abuse.' He opened the box. 'You have acted as my authority once before, Fidelma, and now you must act as my authority again.'

He took from the box a small wand of white rowan on which was fixed a figurine in gold in the image of an antlered stag. This was the personal symbol of the Eóghanacht princes of Cashel, the symbol of their regal authority. He handed it to Fidelma.

'This is the symbol of my personal authority, sister. You have used it well in the past and will use it again in justice in the future.'

Fidelma took the wand of authority in her hand, inclining her head briefly. Then brother and sister embraced in the official manner of the court.

There was a solemnity between them for a moment and then both stood back and their features broke into grins like children sharing a secret. Colgú turned to them all, still smiling.

'Now let us proceed into the feasting hall or the rest of our guests will be wondering what ails us.'

Chapter Three

The party left Cashel the next morning, but not at dawn as Fidelma had suggested. In fact, the sun was creeping towards its zenith before they left because the feasting had lasted late into the night and there had been music and dancing. Bards, accompanying themselves on small stringed instruments, which they plucked, had sung the praises of the ancestry of Colgú in what Fidelma explained to Eadulf was one of the oldest forms of poetry known to her people – the *forsundud* or 'praise poem'. In all the time that he had been in the five kingdoms of Éireann, Eadulf had never heard this ancient form and found the words of the chants recited the various reigns of the kings of Cashel and their noble deeds. The recitation was accompanied by an exuberant music which, to Eadulf's ears, was both strange and wild. The wine circled well among the company. When the party departed for the territory of the Cinél na Áeda, the palace of Cashel still had an air of sleep about it and Eadulf and Becc seemed strained and silent. Fidelma, knowing the alcoholic cause of their wretchedness, was not sympathetic.

It took three days of easy riding to reach the fortress of the Cinél na Áeda at Rath Raithlen. They rode in just after dark and were greeted in the courtyard by Accobrán, the tanist. He was a tall, muscular young man, with dark hair which he wore in the shoulder-length fashion but clean-shaven. His features were pleasant but there seemed some ruthless quality about his mouth. Something indiscernibly cruel. His eyes were dark and Fidelma distrusted his ability to smile too quickly. She identified the quiet vanity of his manner and the self-satisfaction of the consciously handsome.

'Has all been quiet while I have been in Cashel?' was Becc's first question as he was dismounting.

The young man gestured with diffidence. 'Brocc has recovered from his wound. He demands to be released.'

'He has a hide like a bull,' muttered Becc. 'I thought he might have learnt his lesson and stopped trying to provoke discord.'

Accobrán smiled quickly but there was no humour in the expression. 'There is no need for him to provoke what is already in the people's hearts, Becc. But his incarceration is creating disaffection among the people.'

'Have him released into the care of his brother, Seachlann the millwright,' Becc said. 'Seachlann must stand ready to pay for any misbehaviour until we have dealt properly with this matter.'

The young tanist acknowledged the order before turning to where Eadulf was assisting Fidelma to dismount. There was a frown of disapproval on his face.

'I thought that you were going to return with a Brehon? The last thing we need here is more religious. The people are suspicious and angry enough.'

Becc clucked his tongue in annoyance at the young man's discourtesy to his guests.

'This is Fidelma of Cashel, sister to the king, and our cousin. You should also know that she is a qualified *dálaigh* . . . and this is her companion, Eadulf of Seaxmund's Ham.'

The tanist's eyes widened a fraction and then he recovered from his surprise.

'Forgive me, lady.' Accobrán's expression changed to a disarming smile of welcome. 'I did not know you by sight but I have heard much of your reputation. Your name has been spoken much in this kingdom.' His easy charm was something to which Fidelma felt an immediate aversion. The tanist went on, oblivious of the expression of dislike on the Saxon monk's face. 'You do us much honour in coming here.'

'There is little honour in having to respond to crime, tanist of the Cinél na Áeda,' replied Fidelma softly, gazing keenly at the young man. His face was like some pliable mask. She felt distrust towards someone who could assume emotions and abandon them with lightning facility. 'My companion Eadulf is well versed in law, and he is also my *fer comtha*.'

Accobrán must have been astonished at this statement of her marital relationship to the Saxon but his features remained respectful.

'I shall order your rooms and bathing facilities to be prepared immediately,' he muttered. 'Excuse me.' He turned and made his way into the complex of buildings that constituted the great hall of Becc within the fortress.

The elderly chieftain had observed Fidelma's irritated expression and grimaced defensively.

'My tanist is young, cousin. He was only elected to the office a year ago and therefore is not yet fully polished in the ways of chiefly etiquette. He is my nephew. When the time comes to replace me and he takes over guiding the fortunes of the Cinél na Áeda, his manners will hopefully become more considerate.'

'You do not have to apologise,' muttered Fidelma, slightly embarrassed that her reaction had been so obvious.

The old chieftain smiled quickly.

'I am only offering an explanation, not an apology,' he replied quietly. 'And now, come into my hall and take refreshment while your rooms are being prepared.'

They followed him into a hall of moderate size with a log fire crackling away in the hearth and wine already heated for their comfort. They seated themselves before the blazing wood. Servants had carried their bags in while others went to attend to their horses.

'When will you begin your investigation?' asked Becc after he had given all the necessary orders, mulled wine had been served and they were joined once again by the youthful tanist, Accobrán, who announced that bathing water would be ready heated within the hour.

Fidelma paused a moment to savour the inner warmth of the wine.

'I will begin at once,' she replied, to everyone's surprise.

'But it is dark—' began Becc in protest.

'I mean that I will begin in terms of gathering some background details about the victims,' she responded patiently. 'I would like to know some precise details about each of the girls.'

Becc frowned and glanced at Accobrán before returning his gaze to Fidelma.

'There is little more I could tell you. I could summon Lesren the tanner and Seachlann the miller to the fortress tomorrow.'

'They are the fathers of Beccnat and Escrach, the first and second victims,' interposed Accobrán by way of explanation.

'In the circumstances, I would rather visit them where they live or work,' replied Fidelma. 'However, I thought that perhaps you, tanist, might be able to give me some of the information I need.'

Accobrán looked astonished. 'I am not sure that I . . .'

'Come, Accobrán. You are a young man and would surely know most of the young girls in the territory?'

The tanist frowned for a moment before he shrugged and forced a soft smile to part his lips. 'That depends on what information you need, lady.'

'Well, let us begin with the first victim, Beccnat. This was the daughter of the tanner named Lesren?'

'She was. Lesren works on the far side of the hill, in the valley by the river there.'

'What do you know about her? Was she attractive?'

Accobrán lifted a shoulder slightly and let it fall without expression.

'She was young. She had just celebrated reaching her seventeenth year. She was due to wed the son of Goll the woodcutter.'

'That's right,' Becc intervened. 'Lesren didn't like the boy – the son of Goll, that is – and, at first, it was thought that the boy might have been the murderer. Well, Lesren accused the boy, anyway.'

'What did you say his name was?'

'The name of the son of Goll? His name is Gabrán.'

'And you say that he was suspected? Then what evidence cleared him?'

'I doubt whether Lesren has stopped suspecting him,' Accobrán intervened. 'But the boy had a sound enough alibi. He was away from the territory on a journey to collect some supplies. At the time of the full moon he was twelve miles from here staying at the house of Molaga on the coast.'

'I know the abbey of Molaga,' nodded Fidelma. 'So what were the circumstances of Beccnat's murder?'

'As I mentioned before, lady,' intervened Becc, 'her body was found in the woods less than a quarter of a mile from here. It looked as if it had been torn to pieces by a pack of wolves.'

Fidelma leaned forward, her brows raised in interrogation. 'What, then, made the community suspicious of murder and made Lesren suspicious of Gabrán, the son of Goll? Is it not conceivable that wolves or some other wild animals could have attacked the girl?'

'Conceivable but unlikely,' replied the tanist. 'Wolves do not usually attack humans, and adult humans at that, unless they are driven to it by dire necessity. However, Liag, our apothecary, pointed out that the wounds could only have been inflicted by a knife. It was after he had examined the body that we were alerted to the facts.'

'Did this apothecary, Liag . . . did he examine all three victims?'

'He did,' affirmed Becc.

'Then we shall want to see him,' Fidelma instructed. 'Does he reside at the fortress?'

Accobrán shook his head. 'He dwells in the woods on a hillock by the River Tuath. He is something of a strange person who dislikes the company of others. He is almost a hermit. Yet he is a good apothecary and has cured many of various ailments.'

'Very well. Did he arrive at any conclusions as to any commonality between the victims?'

Becc again shook his head, a little puzzled. 'I am not sure that I understand you.'

'I refer to the manner of their deaths. Were they all killed in the same manner? Was there a similarity in the way in which all the victims died?'

'Oh, Liag certainly felt that they had all died by human hand and not from attacks by beasts. He also told me that he felt it was by the same human hand because of the frenzied manner of the attacks.'

'I think you said that the second victim was about the same age?' Fidelma seemed to change her train of thought.

Becc nodded sadly. 'Escrach, the youngest daughter of Seachlann. She was a lovely young girl.'

'Seachlann has taken his grief badly,' added Accobrán. 'His brother is Brocc, the one who has been stirring up the people against the religious.'

'The one who claims that these visiting religious are the killers?' Fidelma sought clarification.

'That is so.'

'Does Seachlann share his brother's views?'

'He does.'

'Then we must certainly question them both and try to find out their reasons for accusing the religious. What did you say is Seachlann's profession?'

'He is the miller. His mill is on the hill due south of us.'

'And what of the third victim? Can you tell me something of this girl Ballgel?'

'Indeed we can,' Becc said. 'We knew her very well. She worked here in my kitchen with her uncle, Sirin, who is the cook.'

'Did she live here?'

Accobrán answered with a shake of his head. 'She did not. She lived with Berrach, an elderly aunt—'

'Sirin's wife?' interposed Eadulf.

'Sirin is unmarried. No, Berrach is Sirin's sister but was also sister to Ballgel's mother. Both of Ballgel's parents are dead. Berrach looked after her. Berrach has a small *bothán* more than half an hour's walk away. It was doubtless wrong of our steward, Adag, to let the girl walk home alone after midnight in view of the previous two killings.'

Fidelma gazed thoughtfully at Accobrán.

'A logical observation,' she replied, before turning to Becc. 'Why was she allowed to walk home alone? In fact, why was she here so late on that night?'

Becc pursed his lips defensively. 'I was entertaining guests that night. The services of Sirin and Ballgel were essential and they were needed until late. It was not unusual and nothing had ever happened before. I was concerned with my guests and had no knowledge of the time when the girl left . . .' He paused and added, almost with a tone of affronted dignity, 'I *am* the chieftain of the Cinél na Áeda.'

Fidelma smiled softly. 'I was not suggesting that you were personally in charge of the arrangements for those who serve in your fortress, Becc. However, it might help if you send for your steward, who would know the arrangements.' She paused and then added, 'Is Sirin within the fortress at present?'

Accobrán uttered an affirmative.

'Then ask him to come here.'

After Accobrán rose and left to carry out the task, Fidelma turned again to Becc.

'I presume that all your guests spent the night at the fortress and that you were up until late into the night?'

'We were up until dawn's first glimmering. Oh, with the exception of Abbot Brogán who returned to the abbey early and, indeed, was the first to leave the company.'

'What time did he leave? Before or after Ballgel?'

Becc shrugged. 'That I cannot say. You will have to ask my steward. It was only the next morning that Adag told me that Ballgel had left soon after midnight. I did not observe the time when the abbot left. Perhaps Adag could tell you.'

'Apart from the abbot, who were the other guests?'

'Local neighbouring chiefs. There were three. They slept well and were not disturbed, even though Adag my steward had to rouse me early. That was when the people, having found Ballgel's body, were marching on the abbey. As I have told you.'

Fidelma was frowning. 'It occurs to me that Accobrán is younger and stronger than you, Becc. Why didn't he go to deal with this disturbance instead of you?'

'He was not here,' Becc explained.

'Oh? He did not attend this meal?'

'He was not at the fortress that night.'

Accobrán re-entered at that moment and announced that Adag and Sirin would join them shortly.

'I am told that you were not in the fortress on the night of Ballgel's death,' Fidelma said, turning to him.

The tanist nodded as he resumed his seat. 'I had duties that took me to the border of our territory on the River Comar. Some cattle had been stolen and I went to sort the matter out. I returned the following day, some time about mid-morning, just before Becc departed for Cashel.'

'The Comar is a confluence to the west of our territory,' explained Becc. 'It forms our western boundary.'

'These duties – did anyone accompany you?' asked Fidelma.

'I went alone,' replied the tanist.

They were interrupted by a knock at the door and the steward, Adag, entered. 'Did you send for me, lord Becc?'

'And for Sirin the cook,' added Fidelma.

Adag glanced towards her and then turned back to Becc.

'Sirin is waiting outside,' he replied directly to his chief.

'Then bring him in,' instructed Fidelma sharply.

The steward continued to look at Becc who nodded slightly to confirm the order.

Sirin was almost the double of Adag the steward. He was a round-faced, rotund figure with thinning hair. His features were lugubrious. At first Fidelma thought his mournful, joyless countenance reflected his grief for the death of his niece, but she soon learnt that his melancholy was a permanent expression.

The corpulent man shuffled forward to stand before his chief while Adag stood quietly in the background.

'Sirin, this is Fidelma of Cashel. She is a *dálaigh* and has come to inquire into the murders. She has questions to ask of you and you must answer them to the best of your knowledge.'

'I will do so, lord,' replied the man in a sonorous tone that matched his plumpness. He turned with a questioning expression to Fidelma.

'Sirin, let me begin by saying that I am sorry for the tragedy that has befallen your family.'

Sirin inclined his head towards her but said nothing.

'There are some questions that I need to ask you. Tell me something of your niece and her background.'

Sirin spread his hands in a gesture which seemed to give him the appearance of an almost comic, doleful figure.

'She was young, seventeen years old. Her parents died from the Yellow Plague two years ago. That terrible scourge almost wiped out our family. My sister and I and poor Ballgel were the only ones who remained alive. Now . . . now Ballgel is gone.'

'I understand that she lived with her aunt?'

'With my sister, Berrach . . . she did so. She came to work with me here in the kitchens of the fortress two years ago.'

'She was not married, or betrothed? Did she have a young male friend?' queried Fidelma.

Sirin shook his head. 'She used to say that she had never met the right one. It is true that many of the young boys sought her company. But she was not interested.'

'Any young boys in particular?'

Sirin smiled sadly. 'She was an attractive girl. I could name most of the lads of Rath Raithlen. There was no one in particular.' A sudden frown crossed his brow. Fidelma saw it.

'You have had a thought?'

Sirin shrugged. 'It was only an incident. Gobnuid, who is one of the smiths working in the fortress – well, it was nothing.'

Fidelma leaned forward encouragingly. 'Let me be the judge.'

'Well, it was at a feasting a month ago.' He glanced at Becc. 'It was the feast day of the Blessed Finnbarr who founded our little abbey here,' he said, as if feeling a need to explain.

'And what happened?'

'Nothing really. Gobnuid wanted to dance with Ballgel and she refused and Gobnuid seemed mortified. Ballgel was with some of her young friends and, frankly, Gobnuid is old enough to be her father. I am afraid that the young lads mocked him and he turned away with a few angry words. That's all.'

'I see. So, returning to the night she died, I understand that she left the fortress at midnight or soon after on that night?'

'She did.'

'When was her body discovered?'

'Early next morning by one of the villagers gathering mushrooms.'

'And the abbey was immediately attacked. Why was that?'

'I did not attack the abbey.' Sirin's voice was unexpectedly harsh. 'I was in grief and so was my sister Berrach. It was my cousin Brocc who roused the people to that action. Brocc had already lost his own niece to this evil.'

Becc intervened. 'It is true that Sirin was not among those who threatened the abbey. He and Berrach were certainly not there.'

Fidelma nodded but continued to address herself to Sirin.

'Do you believe that the strangers at the abbey could have done this?'

Sirin looked blank. 'I do not know. Many claim that they did. I have yet to see proof of Brocc's assertions.'

'Did your cousin share his suspicions with you?'

'He does not like the strangers because they are strangers.'

'You do not appear to share that view,' she observed.

'I want the guilty punished, but let us first know that they are guilty,' replied the man.

'Do you suspect them or anyone else? Do you have any thoughts as to why Ballgel was killed?'

Sirin screwed up his face in a negative gesture. 'I believe only some beast or madman could have done this terrible thing. I can offer you nothing else. But I tell you this, Sister: once I know who is guilty it is vengeance that I want in return. Do not tell me about justice. I am of the Faith and did not Paul of Tarsus write to the Galatians that whatsoever a man sows, that shall he also reap? Whoever has done this terrible deed has planted a thorn in my heart. He must not expect to pluck a rose from it.'

Fidelma was sympathetic but returned his look with disapproval. 'Blood will not wash out blood, Sirin.'

'Eye for eye, tooth for tooth, hand for hand, foot for foot . . .'

Fidelma sighed. 'Very well, Sirin.'

The man was about to turn away, realising that she had finished her questions, when Eadulf suddenly leant forward.

'You say that Brocc is your cousin, Sirin. Are you also related to Adag?'

Sirin thrust out his lower lip in a sullen expression.

'I am not,' he snapped. 'May I go now?'

'You may return to your kitchen,' Fidelma assured him in some amusement. It was true that the steward and the cook might be taken for brothers, for they did look alike.

When Sirin had gone, Fidelma turned to Becc with a sad smile.

'Heraclitus said that it is difficult to fight against anger, for a man will buy revenge with his soul. It seems that Brocc is not the only one out for vengeance at this place, Becc.'

There was an uncomfortable silence. Then Fidelma turned to the steward who had been waiting patiently by the door.

'I am told that the abbot was the first to leave the feasting on the night of which we are talking. What time did the abbot depart from the fortress?' she asked.

Adag frowned and glanced to his chieftain as if in unspoken question.

Fidelma exhaled in exasperation. 'Adag, mark me well. When I ask you a question, you do not have to seek permission of Becc or anyone else before you answer me. If you do not respect the fact that I am a *dálaigh*, although you should obey the law, then respect the fact that I am sister to your king who sits at Cashel. Even your chieftain, Becc, my cousin, defers to me in this matter.'

Becc looked embarrassed.

'I apologise for my steward, Fidelma. He has a quaint idea of loyalty,' he said, before turning with a glance of wrath at the man. 'You will obey my cousin, Fidelma, with the same alacrity as you obey me, Adag, otherwise I shall be looking for a new steward.'

The steward flushed and gave a nervous grimace.

'What was your question, lady?' he asked in an apologetic tone.

'I asked, at what time did the abbot depart from the fortress on the night Ballgel was killed?'

'A little after midnight, I think,' he answered.

'And was that before or after Ballgel left?'

He stared at her in surprise and hesitated before replying. 'The abbot left afterwards, I think.'

'You think?' Fidelma's voice was sharp. 'Is there anyone else who would know exactly?'

Adag coloured in annoyance. 'I was at the gate and bade good night to Ballgel. She left before the abbot. I am sure of it.'

'So you were the last person to see her alive?' intervened Eadulf, who had been silent for some time.

Adag sniffed contemptuously. 'Her killer would be the last person to do so, Brother Saxon.'

Fidelma decided to let the insult to Eadulf go unchallenged for the moment.

'How long was it between Ballgel's leaving and when the abbot left?' she pressed. 'Moments later or a longer period?'

'It was some time later . . . perhaps half an hour or so.'

'And the path to the abbey lies in the same direction as the woods where she was found?'

'At the bottom of the hill you would have to turn right to the abbey, while the place where Ballgel was found was to the left, away from the abbey. The abbot could not have caught up with her.'

Fidelma regarded him with some amusement.

'Why do you think that extra information is of importance?' she asked softly.

Adag's mouth thinned in annoyance. 'I thought that you were accusing—'

'When I accuse anyone,' interrupted Fidelma, still speaking softly, 'I shall say so directly. At the moment, I am still looking for information. I am asking questions and I expect answers and not opinions or prevarication. Questions must be answered with courtesy and respect. Brother Eadulf of Seaxmund's Ham, who is my *fer comtha*, is also worthy of a respectful response, for he was a lawyer among his own people.'

Adag hung his head in mortification. His cheeks were crimson.

'I only meant that—'

'I know perfectly well what you meant,' Fidelma replied shortly. 'Now, as to that last exchange of words that you had with Ballgel . . .'

Adag looked startled for a moment. 'Last exchange?'

'Your conversation at the gates of the fortress when she went home that night. I presume you did exchange some words?'

'As I said, I merely bade her good night,' acknowledged Adag hurriedly. 'She responded. She left and that was the last I saw of her.'

Fidelma paused in reflection for a moment.

'The moon was full that night. It was bright. Was Ballgel nervous of going home alone? She was aware that two other young girls had been killed in those woods, wasn't she?'

Adag sighed and nodded. 'Ballgel was a very stubborn and self-willed girl. Nothing seemed to make her nervous. But I suppose that it was not until after her death that most of us generally realised the significance of the full moon.'

'Significance?' Eadulf interposed.

'That the three killings had happened on the night of the full moon.' The steward spoke to him with a little more courtesy than before. 'I think it was young Gabrán, the woodsman, who first realised this and told our late Brehon Aolú . . .'

'He did,' intervened Becc in confirmation. 'But he was not taken seriously until Liag pointed it out. That was after the second body was discovered. But the fact that he felt it was significant was no secret. Liag knows about these things. He teaches our young about the stars and the moon. Though what Adag says is true. In spite of young Gabrán, and then Liag, the fact that the killer struck at the full of the moon only became generally realised after the body of Ballgel was found.'

Fidelma considered for a moment before resuming her questions.

'So Ballgel left for home and some time later the abbot also left?'

'That is so,' agreed the steward. 'Then I went to bed, for I knew my lord Becc's other guests would be staying the night.'

'That will be all for the moment, Adag,' Fidelma said with finality.

Adag glanced to his chieftain and Becc made a quick gesture of dismissal with his hand.

Fidelma waited until he had gone and then turned to Becc.

'We will see the families of the other two victims tomorrow, but perhaps we should start with the reclusive apothecary. As he examined all three bodies, he might be able to tell us something of significance. Remind me of his name. Liag?'

'Indeed. It is Liag,' Becc confirmed. 'I'd better send Accobrán with you as your guide, for these woods are wide and dark and deep. Liag dwells on a hillock by the river that is hard to find and he does not welcome visitors, especially strangers.'

'If the man is a recluse,' Eadulf pointed out, 'then it sounds as if you should be considering finding another apothecary to minister to the needs of the people here. Is there no apothecary at the abbey?'

Becc nodded. 'Indeed there is. But Liag is one of our community. He is not as reclusive as, perhaps, we have implied. He even accepts pupils.'

'Pupils?' mused Fidelma. 'Ah yes. You said he taught your young. Does he train them in the art of being an apothecary?'

Becc shook his head. 'As I have said, he teaches them star lore.'

'Star lore?'

'The symbolism of the sun and moon, of the gods and goddesses that rule them, and . . .' Becc stopped and looked uncomfortable. 'I do not mean to imply that he teaches anything that is contrary to the New Faith. But he is a repository of knowledge of the ancient beliefs and legends. He is a good apothecary. My people believe in him and have faith in his cures.'

'For a hermit who dislikes visitors to be relied upon to tend the sick and injured is, indeed, a sign of his ability,' Eadulf remarked. 'What makes him attract such loyalty?'

Becc smiled knowingly. 'His ability to cure. It is said that he is descended from those who were possessed of thorough knowledge. Those who practised the healing arts long before the coming of the New Faith.'

'Then we shall look forward to meeting him,' Fidelma assured the chieftain, as she rose to her feet. 'And now . . .'

'I will get Adag to show you to your quarters. I think your baths should be ready.' Becc took the hint. 'Afterwards, please join us in a small feast that has been prepared to welcome you to the land of the Cinél na Áeda.'

Later, as Fidelma and Eadulf, having washed away the dust of travel, eaten and imbibed well in the feasting hall and been entertained by poets and harpers, were preparing for bed, Eadulf succumbed to a contented smile. 'Well, this distant cousin of yours – Becc – seems an amiable chieftain. He dwells in a comfortable and pleasant fortress.'

'That may be,' Fidelma replied and it was clear that she was far from sharing Eadulf's content. 'But remember why we are here, Eadulf. There is an evil in this place. An evil which strikes savagely at young women at the full of the moon. Do not let the pleasant food, or company or surroundings, coax your senses into a false complacency. That evil that lurks in the dark forests round here can strike . . . and maybe not just when the moon is full.'

Chapter Four

The autumn morning was bright and crisp, without any mist. The shapes of the hills and trees were sharply defined and the colours of the countryside were still lustrous with browns and reds streaking through the multi-shades of green. It was only in the morning light, when they had finished breakfasting, that Eadulf had looked out of the window which gave an overview of the fortress and realised that Rath Raithlen was not small at all. It was a complex that covered nearly a hectare, enclosed by triple ramparts. He tried to work it out in Irish measurements but gave up. Brought up among farmers, he estimated that a yoke of oxen would probably take more than two days to plough the area. It was large by comparison to the fortresses and strongholds he had seen previously. It compared even with Cashel.

The ramparts were typically built along the contours of a hill that rose 80 metres or more, overlooking other smaller hills in all directions. Through the surrounding valleys ran a series of streams, some worthy of being called rivers, such as the one that twisted around the foot of the hill on which Rath Raithlen stood. There were woods as far as the eye could see, although now and then smaller raths or fortresses could be made out atop adjoining hills. It was a rich-looking and fertile countryside, in spite of the oncoming grip of autumn which had the leaves changing colour but not, as yet, falling.

Within Rath Raithlen itself, apart from the chief's hall and adjoining buildings, were several streets and alleys crowded with artisans' workshops and several residential buildings. Eadulf assumed these were the habitations of the chieftain's retinue. He realised that the walls of the fortress encompassed an entire village with several forges, saddle-makers' shops and even an alehouse. Rath Raithlen must be a prosperous place.

'I had not realised that the Cinél na Áeda were so wealthy,' Eadulf remarked to Fidelma when she suggested that they go down to the courtyard and prepare for the morning's work.

'The scribes maintain that this was the capital of the Eóghanacht before our ancestor, King Conall Corc, discovered Cashel and made his capital on the Rock,' Fidelma explained. 'I told you that Becc, my cousin, was grandson of King Fedelmid, which is the masculine form of my name.'

'It is an impressive place,' agreed Eadulf, looking around him as they went out into the courtyard before Becc's hall. 'I see many memorial stones with inscriptions on them but they are carved in Ogham which I cannot decipher.'

'If we have time, I shall teach you the ancient alphabet,' Fidelma assured him. 'When I was little and visiting here, I was told that they marked the tombs of great rulers of ancient times.'

'What puzzles me is the number of forges in the rath. I saw them from the bedroom window. Only a few seemed to be used, though. Why does Becc need so many?'

'This used to be a centre of metal working. The whole area is rich in metals: copper mines, lead and iron, even gold and silver. The Blessed Finnbarr, who was born at the abbey of which we have spoken, was the son of a metalworker.'

Eadulf frowned as he dredged a memory. 'I have often heard you talk of Magh Méine, the plain of minerals. Is this it?'

'That is not far from here, to the north-east. This countryside has a similar mining tradition.' She broke off as Accobrán, the handsome young tanist, emerged from a doorway and came across to them. He greeted them pleasantly and seemed more accommodating than he had initially been on the previous evening; more helpful and friendly. Fidelma still felt a distrust of his charm. He asked whether they wanted to go on horseback to visit the people they needed to question. Hearing that none was located more than twenty-one *forrach* from the fortress – a distance of no more than two kilometres – Fidelma decided that they should walk. It would be a chance to examine the countryside and possibly explore the places where the three victims had met their deaths.

Accobrán led the way through the ramparts, beyond the last great wooden gates, and turned down the hill. They followed the broad path for a short while and then the tanist turned off into a thickly wooded area through which a very narrow path twisted between the trees.

'Old Liag, the apothecary, dwells within these woods,' Accobrán informed them, speaking over his shoulder as there was only room for them to walk in single file with the growth towering on either side. 'He is usually to be found along the banks of the Tuath. That is the river that runs around the hill here.'

'It is an odd name for a river,' Eadulf commented. He liked to improve his knowledge of the language of Éireann whenever he could. 'Doesn't the name simply signify a territory?'

The young tanist smiled briefly. 'One of the septs of our people, south of here, was ruled by a chieftain named Cúisnigh and his district was called Tuath an Chúisnigh. Soon the original name of the river that divided his territory was forgotten. People referred to it as the river that runs through the territory of Cúisnigh and gradually even that was foreshortened into the "territory river" or Tuath. It is as simple as that.'

Fidelma had other things on her mind than to listen to his folklore.

'If this apothecary, Liag, is so reclusive, how do we make contact with him without fear that he will hide at our approach?' she enquired.

Accobrán tapped the bone horn that was slung at his belt. 'He is not really so reclusive. I will simply blow my hunting horn when we near his *bothán* and he will know that it is the tanist of the Cinél na Áeda who seeks him.'

The woods had become very dense indeed, a compressed mixture of thick-trunked oaks, lofty holly trees and alders and yews, as if someone had taken a handful of seeds and thrown them indiscriminately about so that they grew in a mixed profusion. Accobrán seemed very much at home as he conducted them through the woods and guided them easily along the twisted path. Suddenly he halted, turned and indicated a small area like a glade to one side. Fidelma's keen eye had already discerned that it had been lately disturbed by a human presence. The grass and shrubs had been trodden down, ferns had been bent and branches broken, showing signs of several people's having moved about the little area.

'That is where they found Ballgel's body, lady.'

Fidelma frowned as she inspected the area. 'Was this Ballgel's usual path home?'

The young tanist shrugged. 'I would not have thought so. A young girl does not usually take to this forest path alone at night. However, it is a short cut to her aunt's *bothán* where she lived. There is no denying that. The safe way would have been to follow the main track, which goes around the hill beyond the abbey, but this one would take some time off her journey. Perhaps if she were in a hurry she might have decided to chance it.'

'Chance?' Eadulf asked. 'That sounds as if she would know that some danger lurked here?'

Accobrán regarded him with a serious expression. 'Wolves and other animals, which would normally shun people during the day, sometimes haunt the woods at night and are not above attacking humans, especially if they can smell fear in them. There are some wild boars here that are very aggressive if disturbed.'

'You think that Ballgel would have exuded such fear?' Eadulf asked reflectively. 'Surely, if she grew up here she would have known the local dangers and not been fearful. Fear is usually to be reserved for the unknown.'

'She was young, Brother Eadulf. A girl. What young girl is unafraid of the woods in darkness?'

Fidelma smiled softly. 'Apparently Ballgel was not afraid to venture along this path on her own . . .' She paused thoughtfully. 'Or maybe she did not start down this path alone or of her own accord?'

Eadulf, who had been examining the ground, shook his head. 'There is no sign that anyone was compelled unwillingly along the path to this point. Obviously, several people have been here, presumably to recover her body. Surely, if she had been waylaid on the main path and killed there or dragged to her death here, there would be signs of a struggle. It appears to me that she came along this path willingly.'

'Or she might have been unconscious or dead,' pointed out Accobrán, 'then she would not have been able to struggle. She could have been carried here.'

'That is true,' agreed Fidelma. 'But, if so, there ought to be have been some sign of that such as deep tracks in the earth showing someone was carrying a heavy weight. However, the movement of the people who found the body has destroyed any useful traces. But I am inclined to believe that she did come along here of her own accord. She might even have known her killer.'

Accobrán grimaced indifferently. 'That sounds like speculation. I did not think a *dálaigh* would indulge in speculation.'

Fidelma regarded him seriously and answered, 'A *dálaigh* does not make judgements on speculation alone, but it behoves anyone considering or reflecting on a set of possible events to theorise or make conjectures to see if the evidence fits the known facts. Let us move on, for I do not think we shall find much in this spot to help us. It has been too long since the event and too many people have trodden here, including animals – I think I see the marks of a wild boar of which you spoke.'

Accobrán hesitated a moment but then turned and continued to lead the way. The path rose over the lower slope of a tree-strewn hill and then began to descend again. After a while the trees and the undergrowth began to thin as the path opened out. There were even a few grassy glades into which the sun penetrated. The tanist pointed ahead.

'The river is a short distance away and that rise on our right is called the Hill of the Sacred Tree. That is where Liag, the apothecary, dwells.'

There was a small wooded hillock rising before them to the right, almost sheltering in the shadow of the large, spreading hill whose footings they had crossed with its thickly covering forest of oaks and alders.

'Then perhaps you had better announce our presence,' Fidelma suggested.

Accobrán unslung his hunting horn, licked his lips, paused a moment and then gave three short blasts.

'If he is nearby, he will know that we need to speak to him,' he said, and resumed his steady pace towards the rise. The sound of running water now came to their ears, announcing a stream gushing over a stone bed. The trees thinned even more and they were able to see a moderate-sized stretch of river to their left.

'That is the Tuath. It flows around the base of the hill on which Rath Raithlen is situated and then it moves south from here,' explained the tanist.

They reached the base of the small rise and now they could see a wooden building amongst the trees near its top. The trees grew thickly and protectively around it.

'Identify yourselves!'

The shout startled them. Fidelma looked in the direction of the sound but could discern nothing in the dark shadows among the trees.

'Strangers, identify yourselves!'

The voice was male, strong and vibrant; a voice that seemed used to command.

Accobrán glanced at Fidelma before he raised his voice in answer. 'It is Accobrán the tanist, Liag. I bring some friends who wish to speak to you.'

'Your friends, not mine. Who are they and what do they seek?' came the uncompromising response.

'I am Sister Fidelma,' cried Fidelma. 'With me is Brother Eadulf.'

'I have no need of religious here in my sanctuary.' The voice was still unresponsive.

'We do not come as religious. I am a *dálaigh* and come representing the authority of the law.'

There was a silence and it seemed the speaker contemplated this information for a moment. Then a shadow seemed to detach itself from the trees. It was the figure of an elderly man clad in a woollen robe dyed saffron. He wore a silver chain around his neck and he had long snow-white hair that was fixed in place with a headband of green and yellow beads. A leather strap across one shoulder supported a satchel, which Eadulf recognised as the traditional apothecary's *lés* or medicine bag. In his right hand he carried what looked like a whip.

'Come forward, *dálaigh*. Let me see you who call yourself lawyer rather than religieuse.'

Fidelma moved a little way up the path, motioning the others to remain where they were. The man's face was etched with deep lines of age but his eyes were icy blue like glittering stones. He regarded Fidelma with deep suspicion.

'You seem young to be an advocate of the law,' he finally observed.

'And you seem old to be the only trustworthy apothecary in this area,' replied Fidelma solemnly.

The old man indicated the whip-like object in his hand. 'You recognise this?'

She nodded quickly. 'The *echlais* is your badge of office, showing that you are a lawful physician.'

'That is so. I hold the authority of my profession. I am no mere herb doctor.'

'I did not think you were.' She moved a hand to her *marsupium* and drew forth the rowan wand of office that her brother had given her. 'And do you recognise this?'

The old man's eyes widened slightly. 'The wand of office of the Eóghanacht, kings of Cashel, rulers of Munster, descendants of Eber Fionn, son of Golamh, the soldier of Spain who brought the children of the Gael to this place. I see the stag emblem and recognise it.'

Fidelma returned it to her *marsupium*. 'I am, as I have said, a *dálaigh* and sister to Colgú, king of Cashel.'

The old apothecary was silent for a moment.

'Why have you come to me?' he demanded at length.

'My companion and I are charged to investigate the deaths of the three girls who were killed here.'

The suspicious look still did not leave the old man's face.

'By whom charged?'

'By my brother, Colgú, king of Cashel, and by the invitation of Becc, lord of the Cinél na Áeda.'

The old man grimaced. 'One Eóghanacht name is good enough for your authority, Fidelma of Cashel. Let you and your companions sit awhile. I can offer you *miodh cuill*, the cool hazel mead that I distil myself.'

Fidelma seated herself on a fallen tree trunk and gestured for the others to come forward and do likewise.

Liag the recluse set down his bag and moved a short distance to where a spring was gushing over some rocks. He reached forward and tugged on a leather thong that appeared to be hanging in the water. As it came out they saw that a jug was tied to the end of it. It had been cooling in the crystal splashing water. The old man took a pottery bowl from his apothecary's bag and poured some of the liquid into it.

'I am afraid you will have to share,' he said without sounding apologetic. 'I neither expect nor encourage visitors.'

'Then we will not keep you long,' Fidelma assured him, accepting the bowl from him and taking a sip for politeness' sake before handing it on to Eadulf. The mixture was too strong for her and even Eadulf gasped a little as the first drop of the fiery liquid hit his throat. He coughed and hurriedly passed the bowl to Accobrán, who seemed more used to the strong liquid.

'I understand that you examined the bodies of the girls who were killed here during the last two months. You believed that all three were murdered.'

'I take my calling seriously, Fidelma of Cashel,' the old man said, seating himself before her.

'I am sure you do.'

'I know the law of Dian Cecht, so do not try to question my ability.'

'Is there a reason why I should do so?' demanded Fidelma so sharply that the old man looked startled for a moment.

'None,' he replied defensively.

'That is good. For I see no need to bring in the medical laws of Dian Cecht. I am here not to question your findings but to seek facts.'

The old man had composed himself and gestured for her to proceed.

'I am told that you examined all three bodies,' she repeated.

'That is so.'

'And I am told that you guided people away from the original idea that some animal had attacked the first of these poor women. Tell me why.'

Liag spoke thoughtfully. 'I could understand why such a notion sprang to mind. The first of the victims . . . Beccnat, was her name . . . was horribly mutilated. It was difficult to see from the dried blood and there was some decomposing for the body must have lain out in the woods for two or three days. It was only when the body had been bathed for the funeral rites that I realised that while the flesh was badly ripped, the wounds were not made by teeth but by the jagged edge of a knife.'

'And this was so in the other two cases?'

'It was so.'

45

'Tell me.' Fidelma hesitated, trying to formulate the question carefully. 'Was anything removed from the bodies?'

Liag was puzzled by the question. 'Removed?'

'Were the bodies intact apart from the mutilations?'

'No physical part was missing,' confirmed the old man, realising what she meant. 'Do not look for some ancient ritual here, Fidelma of Cashel. The three girls were simply stabbed to death by some madman.'

Fidelma looked up quickly. 'A madman? Do you choose your words carefully?'

'Who but someone with a demented soul could have done such a deed?'

'Do you subscribe to the idea that a lunatic is loose within the community, striking at the full of the moon?'

'I believe that is self-evident. Examine the time of the last killing, for example. It took place upon the Badger's Moon.'

Eadulf frowned and leant forward quickly.

'The Badger's Moon? What is that?' he demanded.

Liag turned to him in disapproval as he heard his accent.

'A Saxon? You surely travel in strange company, sister to King Colgú of Cashel,' he said to Fidelma. Before she could reply, he had turned to Eadulf. 'The October full moon is called the Badger's Moon, my Saxon friend. It is so bright that, according to the ancients, it was said that the badgers dried the grass for their nests by its light. The October moon is a sacred time and the light of the Badger's Moon shines benevolently on all who accept its powers . . . or so the ancients thought.'

Eadulf shivered slightly. He had converted to the New Faith in his early manhood and still remembered the superstitions of his pagan background.

Old Liag smiled appreciatively at his reaction. 'The ancients said the moon goddess, whose name must not be uttered, cleansed the earth at the time of the Badger's Moon, especially if one sacrificed a badger to her and ate the meat.'

'I have heard that you teach star lore,' Fidelma observed. 'So you know all about the legends associated with the full of the moon?'

Liag appeared indifferent. 'Such legends are our cultural birthright. We should all know the stories told by countless generations of our forefathers. It has fallen to my lot to impart these tales to the young of the Cinél na Áeda, is that not so, Accobrán?'

The young tanist flushed momentarily. 'You are a good teacher, Liag. Your knowledge is unsurpassed. But sacrificing a badger . . . I have not heard that. Surely badger's meat was said to be one of the delicacies favoured by Fionn mac Cumhail? In the ancient tales, it is recounted that one of Fionn's warriors, Moling the Swift, was charged to bring him such a dish.'

Liag did not contradict him.

'I have also heard it said that the Blessed Mo Laisse of the Isle of Oaks, in Uí Néill country, wore a hood of badger skin which is now cherished as a relic on the island,' Fidelma added softly.

Liag laughed cynically. 'I do not understand why those of the New Faith revert to worshipping objects while claiming not to do so. Veneration of the cross, holy objects and icons . . . what is the difference between that and the veneration of anything else?'

The comment elicited no response from anyone.

Fidelma waited a moment or two and then asked Liag: 'While examining the bodies, did you see anything other than the jagged wounds that you felt was unusual, something that might lead you to speculate on who the author of the attacks might be?'

The apothecary shook his head. 'Only that which I have told you.'

'Accobrán has shown us where Ballgel was found. Where, in relation to that site, were the other bodies discovered?'

'Beccnat's body was at a spot called the Ring of Pigs. It is a small stone group further up the hill.' He indicated the tall wooded slopes behind them. 'It overlooked the abbey. Escrach was discovered almost at the same place.' The old man suddenly rose. 'And if this is all the question you have to put to me . . . ?'

Fidelma rose awkwardly in surprise at the sudden termination of the conversation, as did her companions.

'I may need to speak to you again,' she called after him as he turned abruptly away.

Liag glanced back at her in disapproval. 'You have found me once, sister of the king. Doubtless, you may find me again, but there is nothing in your questions that could not have been answered by the words of others. If you wish to waste your time, that is your affair. I have better things to do with mine. Therefore, if you come again have more pertinent questions or you may not find me willing to play the host and squander precious time.'

The old man strode away, leaving Fidelma gazing at his vanishing figure in amazement.

'A man who has no manners,' muttered Eadulf sourly.

Accobrán grimaced wryly. 'I did warn you that Liag was a person who prefers his own company. He does not obey the accepted rules of behaviour in the society of others.'

'You did forewarn us,' agreed Fidelma. 'But in one thing Liag did speak the truth. Every question I put, I could have heard the answer from others. The one thing that was necessary, however, was to hear them given in the mouth and manner of Liag. Eadulf knows my methods. It is always important to hear the individual witness rather than rely on hearsay.'

Eadulf glanced at her in surprise. 'And did you learn anything?'

Fidelma smiled softly. 'Oh yes. Yes, indeed. And perhaps, Accobrán, you could now lead us to the father of the first of these sad victims, Lesren the tanner.'

Accobrán was looking more perplexed at her words than Eadulf but he shrugged. 'Lesren's place is but a short distance along the river, lady. It is upstream under the hill on which Rath Raithlen stands.'

As Accobrán started to walk ahead Fidelma reached forward and placed her mouth close to Eadulf's ear.

'Mark this spot well, Eadulf,' she whispered. 'We may have to return here alone.'

Once again the path Accobrán took was narrow and difficult even though it ran as near the river as was possible. For most of its length trees and underbrush grew all the way down to the banks, which were crumbling and unsafe. They were reduced to moving in single file once again. Eadulf had come to realise that Becc's country was very hilly indeed.

'That hill Escrach and Beccnat were found on,' Fidelma suddenly asked, 'I seem to recall that it had a name?'

Accobrán nodded. 'It is a wooded and hilly area which is called the Thicket of Pigs. The same name applies to the hill.'

Fidelma remembered that Becc had mentioned the name.

'The killer seems to strike in the same place,' she reflected.

Eadulf, behind Fidelma, said: 'Is that significant? After all, it seems that we are dealing with a madman whose killing would be random.'

'Perhaps you are right. But, perhaps, the choice of place has not been entirely random.'

Eadulf was about to question her further but she turned to him with an impassive expression that he knew well. She wanted to say no more on the subject for the moment.

They had walked for some distance when the narrow path suddenly joined a broader stretch of track along which the banks of the river became shallow and sloped into a shingle-like beach which ran into the river bed itself. Fidelma had heard them before she saw them. The sound of children is always shrill enough to be heard even above the rushing waters. Two boys were crouching in the shallows, apparently intent on examining something in the river.

'Local lads, fishing,' Accobrán explained brusquely to Fidelma and Eadulf and would have walked on.

'Not fishing,' Fidelma corrected. She turned aside and moved towards the riverbank. 'What luck, lads?' she called.

They turned. Two tousled-haired youngsters of about eleven or twelve. One of them, who held a metal pan in his hand, shrugged and gestured towards it.

'No luck at all, Sister. But Síoda claimed that he had found a genuine nugget the other day.'

'Oh? Who is Síoda?'

'A lad we know. That's why we came down here. Although he won't tell us exactly where he found it. So far, we haven't seen anything, just mud and stones.'

'Well, good luck, lads.'

Fidelma rejoined Eadulf and Accobrán on the main path. Eadulf was frowning.

'What are they doing?'

'It is what we call washing the ore,' Fidelma explained. 'Sometimes metals like gold are washed along the river bed. You place the sediment in a pan, as those boys are doing, and wash it with the hope of finding a gold nugget in the bottom of your pan.'

Accobrán laughed loudly and somewhat bitterly. 'It has been a hundred years, back in the time of the Blessed Finnbarr, since gold was last discovered in these hills, lady. Those boys will be there until the crack of doom if they are intent on finding gold nuggets.'

'You do not think that they spoke the truth when they said a boy called Síoda had made such a find?' Fidelma asked with interest.

'If a child found a nugget in that river, it will be *sulfar iarainn*.'

Eadulf frowned, for while he recognised the word 'iron' he did not understand the exact meaning of the Irish term.

'Iron pyrites,' explained Fidelma. 'Fool's gold, for it looks like gold but is not and many a fool has thought that he had struck lucky by picking it up.' She turned to Accobrán. 'Are you knowledgeable about such matters?'

The young tanist shrugged and shook his head. 'This was once mining country and the Cinél na Áeda grew rich and powerful through it. Now the gold and the silver are all worked out and we have only copper left, and some lead to the north of here.'

He turned and began to lead the way again. Here the wooded area was not so oppressive and now and again they came to small patches of cleared land bordering the river which had been sown with crops of corn and wheat.

'We will find the house of Lesren the tanner not far now,' called the tanist.

Indeed, a curious smell had come to Eadulf's nostrils. An acrid smell, as of bad cooking. He sniffed suspiciously until his senses told him what it was. They turned through a bordering treeline into a wide stretch of clearing that ran for some distance along the river. There was a small comfortable-looking *bothán*, a cabin built of logs with smoke curling from a chimney. There were several small outhouses, and all around the buildings were a score of wooden frames on which were stretched animal skins. Heavy iron cauldrons hung on chains over two large fires, their contents bubbling and smoking as a youth stirred them. It was the acrid smell from these that had assailed Eadulf's nostrils. He saw a man using a stick to drop a section of skin into the cauldron and presumed that this was part of the tanning process.

At one of the great wooden frames on which a hide was stretched, a thin, wiry-looking man in a leather apron was standing poking in an examining fashion at the taut skin.

'Lesren!' called Accobrán.

The man turned with a frown of annoyance. He had small, quick dark eyes in a face whose expression reminded Fidelma of a pine martin. Suspicious and fearful. His rapid glance took them all in before he returned his gaze to the young tanist.

'What do you want of me, Accobrán?' he snapped. 'Am I not busy enough?'

Eadulf exchanged a glance with Fidelma. The man was obviously not going to be helpful. No one of the Cinél na Áeda seemed kindly disposed towards strangers, so far as they were able to tell.

'I have brought a *dálaigh* to ask questions of you, Lesren.'

The tanner's dark eyes swivelled to Eadulf. '*Dálaigh?* That man is a foreigner.'

'Do you have objections to foreigners, Lesren?' demanded Fidelma sharply.

'None, woman, if they do not interfere in my business.'

Accobrán swallowed and was about to explain who Fidelma was when she cut him short.

'It is I who am the *dálaigh*, Lesren. I am come to ask some questions about your daughter.'

'You?' The tanner seemed amused. 'A young woman?'

'This is Fidelma of Cashel,' put in Accobrán. 'Sister to King Colgú,' he added *sotto voce*.

The tanner blinked but his unfriendly expression did not change. 'If you are here to ask me about Beccnat's murder, I will tell you who killed her. It was Gabrán.'

Accobrán expressed his impatience. 'We made inquiries, Lesren. You know that. Gabrán was nowhere near Rath Raithlen on the night your daughter died.'

'So you say.'

'I only say what the witnesses say. The fact is that he was staying twelve miles away.' The tanist's voice indicated that he had told the story a hundred times before. 'Aolú, our late Brehon, agreed that he was innocent of your claim.'

'If you claim that Gabrán slew your daughter,' Fidelma added. 'Are you also saying that he killed the other two girls as well?'

Lesren raised his chin stubbornly. 'I say that he killed Beccnat. That is what I say. I told her to beware of him and his thieving family.'

'Those words are harsh and have harshness in the saying of them,' Fidelma reproved him. 'I would caution you against calling people thieves. You know the law and the penalty that falls upon those who tell false tales about others. It could even lead to the loss of your honour price, *súdaire*.' She laid a soft stress on his title as a means of reminding him of the standing in society he could lose.

Eadulf knew that everyone in the five kingdoms of Éireann, from the lowborn to the highest, was possessed of an honour price. The High King himself was rated at the value of sixty-three cows while a provincial king, such as Fidelma's brother Colgú, held an honour price valued at forty-eight cows. In the time that he had been in this land Eadulf prided himself on having learned to judge the honour price of most people and concluded that a tanner would be valued at four cows. The cow was the basis of the currency, with a *séd* being the value of one cow while a *cumal* was that of three cows. Smaller coins like a silver *screpall* or a *sicil* were divisions of the value of a cow.

At first Eadulf had not been able to understand the honour price system and vainly tried to equate it with the caste system of his own people. He soon realised that there was a fairness in its structure that had much to do with the system of punishments for crimes. The whole basis of the law system was compensation and rehabilitation. To maintain a standard throughout the kingdoms, each person was ascribed an honour price that was based on the job they did, and not on who their parents were. Fines were assessed on the honour price of the one transgressed against. If a man killed a master builder then he would have to pay the master builder's family compensation to the value of twenty cows, together with a fine to the court. If he could not afford it, and his own

51

honour price was less than the value of twenty cows, then he would lose his honour price and all civil rights, and would have to work to compensate the family and the court. He became an 'unfree' man, a man without any rights – a *fuidhir*.

There were two types of 'unfree' person, depending on the seriousness of the crime. While a *daer-fuidhir* had no rights and could not bear arms, a *saer-fuidhir* was entitled to continue to work his own land or follow his own professional calling – within reason. He was expected to pay taxes. If, by the end of his life, he had not provided the required compensation and rehabilitated himself into society, then the punishment did not fall upon his wife or children. Every dead man kills his own liabilities, said the Brehons.

As a foreigner in Éireann, Eadulf was classed in law as a 'grey dog', *cú glas*, which actually meant one who was an exile from overseas. Thus Eadulf, no longer an emissary of the Archbishop of Canterbury, was without legal standing and had no honour price. Even married to Fidelma he would have remained without an honour price had not Colgú and Fidelma's nearest relatives recognised the union and approved it. Being accepted by Fidelma's family, Eadulf was also accepted as having an honour price that was half that of Fidelma's. But there were restrictions that someone of his culture found onerous and almost offensive. He was not entitled to make legal contracts without Fidelma's permission and she was responsible for any debts or fines that he might incur. Neither was he allowed to have any legal responsibility in the rearing of their son Alchú. That was Fidelma's responsibility alone. For Eadulf, his position as a 'grey dog' was a bitter legal concept in spite of the fact that, in reality, Colgú treated Eadulf as both friend and equal.

What Eadulf found astonishing was that Fidelma's people saw many matters that his culture would not even call transgressions worthy of severe punishment – if one could call fines and loss of rights a punishment. In Saxon society, death and mutilation and slavery were considered just punishment for the entire range of social and political transgressions, whereas in the *Bretha Nemed* the Brehons decreed that if a man kissed a woman against her will, he would have to pay her full honour price. If a man tried to indecently assault a woman, then the *Cáin Adomnáin* set the fine at the value of twenty-one cows.

Truth was taken seriously in law. The *Bretha Nemed* stated that if a person wrongfully accused another of theft, or publicised an untrue story that caused shame, it required the payment of the victim's honour price. Hence he could understand why Fidelma was now giving the tanner a fair warning.

Lesren, however, would not be warned.

'What I saw is the truth. Ask Goll, the woodcutter, if you do not believe me. Ask him why he had to pay me a fine of one *screpall*. I will say no more on the matter until you have done so.'

'One *screpall* is no great sum to pay,' muttered Eadulf.

'A transgression of the law is great enough, no matter the outcome,' snapped the tanner.

'And what Brehon imposed this fine?' asked Fidelma.

'Aolú.'

'And Aolú is dead,' muttered Accobrán.

Fidelma sighed impatiently. 'Am I to believe that you disapproved of your daughter's relationship with Gabrán because of his father, Goll, and this matter of the fine that you have mentioned?'

Again the chin came up aggressively. 'It is reason enough.'

'What did Beccnat have to say about your disapproval? She was seventeen and beyond the age of choice. She had the right to decide her own future.'

Lesren's features wrinkled in a scowl. 'She was my daughter. She refused to abide by my decision and look what happened to her. If only Escrach had not broken with Gabrán, he would not have pursued my daughter.'

'Escrach?' Fidelma glanced at him with quickened interest. 'What do you mean?'

'Gabrán was paying her attention until she made it clear that she was not interested in him. I warned my daughter not to encourage him.'

'Daughters have rights once they reach the age of choice,' Fidelma admonished him.

'Daughters also have duties,' replied the tanner angrily. 'I had to chastise Beccnat when she spent nights away from home. Even to the end she refused to obey and those last three nights she spent away from home – well, I feared she would pay for it and she did. Gabrán was to blame.'

'You are a stubborn man, Lesren,' Accobrán broke in. 'Gabrán was nowhere near here when your daughter died. No amount of accusations against Gabrán's father will alter the fact that this can be proved by witnesses. And even with your prejudice, you cannot blame the deaths of Escrach and Ballgel on Gabrán. Why would he kill them and for what reason?'

'To achieve what he has clearly done with you . . . to put you off his scent. To make it seem that there is a maniac at large here. I do not believe in maniacs. I will affirm it at every opportunity I am given. Gabrán killed my daughter.'

'But why? For what reason would he have killed her? They were to marry.' Fidelma's voice was quiet but her question cut like a knife with its logic.

Lesren stared at her.

'Why?' he repeated slowly, as if the question were new to him.

Fidelma was firm. 'He wanted to marry Beccnat. I have been told that your daughter was going to marry Gabrán in spite of your objections. What reason would he have to kill her?'

For a moment Lesren hesitated, seeming to gather his thoughts together.

'Because,' he said quietly, 'some days before her body was found, she told me that she did not want to cause her mother and me any upset. She said that she was not going to marry Gabrán. She said she had discovered that he was using her. She realised that he was not a suitable choice of husband. Then she went out and never came back. She went to tell Gabrán of her decision to break off her relationship. I know that he killed her because of it.'

Chapter Five

Fidelma had become aware of a woman who had approached them during this conversation and now stood quietly at Lesren's side. It was evident that she had been attractive in her youth. Although grey now streaked the blackness of her hair, her light-coloured eyes, the fairness of the skin and the comeliness of her features were not diminished by age. However, she carried herself with a careworn air. Although Lesren made no attempt to introduce her, Fidelma knew instinctively who she was.

'Are you the mother of Beccnat?'

'I am Bébháil, Sister.'

Lesren turned with a sarcastic sneer towards his wife. 'This is the king's sister, woman. A *dálaigh*, come to snoop about Beccnat's death.'

The woman blinked and hung her head. The thought crossed Fidelma's mind that it was in shame at her husband's boorishness.

'You have heard your husband state that Beccnat had changed her mind about marrying Gabrán and went out a few nights before she was found dead with the intention of telling him so. Were you a witness to your daughter's change of mind?'

The woman glanced nervously at her husband and then nodded hurriedly. Her eyes were suddenly tear-filled and she was clearly still distraught at the return of the memories.

'So the girl told you both of her intention and then left?'

'It is as my husband has said. I can say no more.' The woman called Bébháil moved hurriedly to the *bothán*, closing the door behind her.

Lesren smiled bitterly.

'Are you satisfied now, *dálaigh*?' he sneered.

Fidelma returned his gaze with a stony expression. 'Far from it. You are still forgetting one thing. Whether your daughter changed her mind or not, whether Gabrán had motive or not, Accobrán has stated that Gabrán was proved to have been twelve miles from here on the night of her death. But do not be concerned; I shall check that out. I shall satisfy myself of the facts.'

'Do so, *dálaigh*. I am waiting for justice.'

'Have no fear. Your wait for justice may not be long. I shall be returning here.'

Once they were out of earshot, Eadulf said quietly: 'He was lying, I am sure of it. Lying about his daughter changing her mind. The wife was clearly frightened to say anything in front of him.'

'I have no doubt that there was some tension between them,' agreed Fidelma. She glanced at Accobrán in curiosity. 'Does he really have such a hatred of Gabrán and his family? What about this fine imposed by Aolú on the boy's father – Goll?'

The young tanist shrugged. It seemed a normal appendage to his speech.

'There has been some enmity between Lesren and Goll for years. I would not have thought there was sufficient cause to bring it to this. Accusations of stealing are one thing, but of murder – triple murder – are something else.'

'What do you know of this accusation that Gabrán's father is a thief? Presumably this was the reason why a fine was imposed?'

Accobrán shrugged. 'I know little about that. I have heard stories. For the truth you must consult Becc, for he was sitting in judgement with Brehon Aolú at the time.'

Fidelma paused thoughtfully. Then she said: 'If we have time now, I would like a word with this Gabrán and his father.'

Accobrán glanced up at the sky. 'It is past noon, Sister. I would advise that we return to the rath for refreshment. I understood that you also want to see Seachlann, the father of the victim Escrach, and go to the abbey too today. Becc told me that you wanted to meet the strangers there. Goll and Gabrán work the woods on the far side of the river. I doubt whether we will find them before nightfall if we are to fulfil all your wishes.'

Fidelma did not seem perturbed. 'There is no immediate hurry. We will continue with the plan and if we cannot see Gabrán and Goll today, we will see them tomorrow. But since you remind me – what of Escrach? Was it true that Gabrán was having a relationship with her?'

Accobrán smiled easily. 'She was an attractive girl. The Cinél na Áeda have a reputation for the attractiveness of their women. He was a healthy youth. It would not be surprising in this community. Marriage and children come along before youth is lost for ever.'

'Yet you, I believe, are not married, tanist of the Cinél na Áeda,' Fidelma pointed out.

Once again the young man's features broke into a disarming smile. 'Alas, I have spent many years away following the gods of war. A warrior would be wrong to take a wife, for many a widow is the outcome. I have only recently settled down to learn the duties that my cousin and our *derbfhine* have bestowed on me.' The young tanist was suddenly thoughtful. 'I suppose that you are not expecting anything serious to happen until the next full moon?'

Fidelma regarded him speculatively. 'Do you believe that there will be another attack then?'

Accobrán's handsome features twisted in a grimace. 'What has happened three times can surely happen a fourth.'

'So you share the belief of Liag that there is a lunatic abroad? That the killer is motivated to his deeds by the full of the moon?'

Accobrán pursed his lips in a cynical smile. 'It is a more logical explanation than the story Lesren would have you believe. To be honest, I confess that I have little liking for Gabrán. He can be an arrogant youth at times. I do believe, however, that old Liag is right. What other explanation can there be?'

'We have yet to hear Brocc's reasons for accusing the strangers and have yet to hear what the strangers say in answer to them,' pointed out Eadulf. 'It is best not to draw a conclusion until we have gathered in all the evidence.'

He felt Fidelma's eyes on him and coloured a little, knowing that he was paraphrasing the words with which she had often reproved him.

'That is true,' agreed the young tanist. 'And the sooner we return to the rath to eat, the sooner we can start out again to get answers to those questions.'

He lost little time in leading the way back up the hill on a steep path to the towering walls of Rath Raithlen.

At the midday meal Becc joined them. The chieftain smiled wryly when the subject of Lesren and Goll was raised.

'Maybe I should have warned you about Lesren and Goll.'

'Is this feud so serious, then?' Fidelma asked.

'It depends how you define the term serious. If, as Accobrán tells me, that idiot Lesren is still accusing Goll's son of the murder of his daughter and, thereby, of the other murders, then it may turn out to be serious for Lesren. I am aware of the law against spreading malicious falsehoods.'

'Tell me, how did this quarrel start?'

Becc reflected for a moment or two. 'I supposed it started many years ago. Lesren was married before he married Bébháil, you know.'

'He had a wife before her?' Eadulf asked unnecessarily.

'Indeed he did. She divorced him. The woman was called Fínmed.'

He paused to make the next sentence significant. 'Fínmed is now the wife of Goll, the mother of Gabrán.'

Eadulf sat back with a faint hissing sound as he tried to stifle the whistle of surprise, which would have been considered bad manners for a guest at table. Fidelma glanced at him in reproof.

'There are several grounds whereby married couples may divorce under our law, Eadulf,' she explained for his benefit. She turned back to the chieftain. 'What was the cause in this case? Was it one of the categories where no one is judged to be at fault? Where each went their separate ways without blame?'

Becc shook his head immediately. 'The divorce of Lesren and Fínmed fell into the other category where blame was clearly judged by the Brehon. Fínmed left Lesren's house with full compensation and her *coibche*.' He glanced at Eadulf. 'The *coibche* is the bride price which the husband may give to his wife or her family.'

'I know about the *coibche*,' replied Eadulf softly.

Becc had the goodness to blush. He had forgotten the relationship between Fidelma and Eadulf. In fact, Eadulf had spent some time studying the *Cáin Lánamna*, the laws of marriage, with Colgú's Chief Brehon. He knew that if a wife left her husband, and the fault lay with her, then this *coibche*, or gift of goods or money, must be returned to the husband. However, if the wife was not at fault when the couple split up then she took the *coibche* with her and half of any wealth accrued during the period of the marriage.'

'What was the cause of the divorce?' asked Fidelma.

'Lesren was a violent man,' Becc explained. 'He used to drink and beat Fínmed. As you know, the right of immediate divorce is allowed to a woman who is struck by her husband. Lesren had to pay a fine to her as well as her *coibche*. In spite of her entitlement to a marriage settlement as well, Fínmed refused to take anything more from him and left. Lesren was not even grateful that he had been let off lightly. He was angry and never forgave her. When she married Goll, the woodcutter, he was almost beside himself with rage.'

'But he married again,' pointed out Eadulf. To Eadulf, logic was logic.

'He did,' agreed Becc. 'He married Bébháil. Although one hears rumours, they seem happy and she bore him the daughter Beccnat but no other child.'

'What you are implying is that Lesren still harbours a grudge against his former wife and against Goll who married her?'

Becc sighed and inclined his head in a gesture of agreement. 'That is true. Fínmed married Goll a year before Lesren remarried. They had a son, Gabrán. It became clear, over the years, that resentment still flared between Lesren and Goll.'

'And what of this accusation by Lesren that Goll was a thief?' asked Eadulf.

Becc grimaced indifferently. 'That was a paltry affair. Merely spite. It seemed that Lesren found out that Goll had illegally felled a tree.'

'Illegally?' Eadulf frowned. 'The man is a woodcutter. How would he fell a tree illegally?'

'Woodcutters have to obey the law along with everyone else. Certain trees in certain areas cannot be cut down without the woodcutter's seeking the proper permission. There are trees which we call "chieftain trees", whose illegal felling causes fines to be imposed on the offender. It seems that Goll was under pressure to provide some ash wood. The ash is one of the chieftain trees. Unfortunately, he cut it down without seeking permission of my Brehon or myself.'

Fidelma glanced towards Eadulf.

'Technically, this would have been considered tree theft,' she explained before turning back to Becc. 'But if the fine, as I was told, was a *screpall*, it was not considered as a theft with intent.'

The chieftain agreed. 'Lesren discovered the act and reported Goll to Aolú. The Brehon had no option but to summon him before the court. The reason for Goll's haste was that someone had commissioned a chair to be made as a present. It is a tradition that a chieftain should sit on a chair of ash. Had Goll sought permission then the surprise of the gift would have been negated. He decided to take a chance and cut down the tree. The act had been committed and could not be uncommitted. So Goll was fined the nominal sum of a *screpall*.'

'Did Goll know that it was Lesren who reported him?' asked Eadulf.

'Of course. Lesren had to appear before Aolú to give evidence.'

'So that fact did not endear Lesren to Goll?'

The chieftain grimaced with dry humour. 'Within a week, Goll had his revenge. As you may know, the bark of the apple is used to help with the tanning process. But bark may not be removed from trees within certain months called "killing months". That is when the removal of the bark may lead to the death of a tree. Goll saw Lesren removing the bark of an apple tree during a killing month. He reported him. Now Lesren had to appear before Aolú, charged on the witness of Goll. I had a word with Aolú and we both decided to even matters up by fining Lesren a *screpall*. Both sides were even and Aolú and I thought that would be an end of the matter.'

'But the feud continued?'

'It did. And then came the unforeseen circumstance. It seems that Goll's son and Lesren's daughter fell in love with one another. When Lesren was informed, there was nearly a battle here. Goll was more philosophical about the situation, although far from happy. My impression, however, was that all the hate emanated from Lesren.'

'None from Goll?' asked Fidelma. 'Are you sure?'

'It was Lesren who forbade Beccnat to marry Gabrán even though she was over the age of choice and there was no legal impediment to the marriage's taking place.'

'But Lesren claims that his daughter had changed her mind and, on the occasion of their last conversation, she told her father that she had decided not to marry Gabrán and was going to tell him,' Eadulf pointed out.

Becc raised his eyebrows in a look of astonishment. 'This is the first time that I have heard of it. Are you sure?'

'We are sure only in that this is what Lesren told us,' said Fidelma.

'It provides Gabrán with a motive conceived out of the anger of rejection,' explained Eadulf.

'This might well be. But Aolú, my Brehon, was still alive, although infirm, when the accusation was made against Gabrán. Accobrán was asked to check where Gabrán was and discovered that he was at the coast some twelve miles or more away from here. There were plenty of witnesses to that fact. So, if the girl had changed her mind, she would not have been able to tell Gabrán before her murder.'

'Lesren's wife supported his version of events,' murmured Eadulf.

'The man is not merely a fool, he is a wicked one,' replied Becc. 'Why his wife continues to put up with his abuse, I do not know. As I have said, surely Lesren cannot accuse the boy after the evidence that was gathered by Accobrán? Then there are the other murders. Brocc has convinced everyone, except Lesren, that the strangers in the abbey are to blame for all of them.'

Fidelma sighed deeply. 'There is much fear and distrust here, Becc. It is like peering into an impenetrable mist filled with swirling dark shadows. But it is early days yet. We still have many people to speak to and if Eadulf has finished eating, we should make another start.'

Eadulf hastily swallowed the remains of some fruit he was nibbling and sprang up. He did not notice that Fidelma was smiling at him.

'That's Seachlann's mill, lady.'

Fidelma and Eadulf had been following the young tanist down a winding pathway towards the riverbank for the second time that day. This area was rather like the clearing in which the tanner's buildings were placed except that the trees surrounding it were sparser than at Lesren's place. Dominating the area was a round watermill with a series of large pedals powered into motion by the force of the river. A short distance from the mill, by the fast-flowing waters, they saw a man seated before a small open fire. He was middle-aged, thickset and muscular but rough-looking, with a shaggy black beard and woolly hair. He held a basket before him that he extended over the fire, turning it and tossing the contents with his two hands.

Fidelma caught Eadulf's puzzled frown and smiled.

'He is drying *graddan*, wholemeal, in the *criather*, that is the basket he holds over the fire,' she explained. 'The dry grain will then be taken to the miller to grind. Do they not process the grain in similar fashion in your own land?'

Eadulf shook his head. 'Not exactly in the same way. Surely you can dry only a little grain in that fashion?'

'Oh, we also have a large oven, a kiln' – the term she used was *sorn-na-hátha* – 'in which we roast larger amounts of grain. The method this man is using is only for small amounts.'

'Why doesn't that little wooden sieve catch fire?' asked Eadulf.

'The bottom is made of bone, the *fabra* of a *míl-mór* or whale,' she said with a smile. 'The bone can scorch but not burn.'

The man at the fire heard their approach and now set aside his basket and rose slowly to his feet, a scowl on his unpleasant features. It did not imply that they were welcome.

Accobrán turned his head towards Fidelma and said quietly: 'The man is Brocc, the brother of the miller. This is our local trouble-maker.'

'What do you seek here, Accobrán?' came Brocc's gruff voice before they had closed the five- or six-yard distance between them. He took a few paces from the fire and they saw he had a pronounced limp. Fidelma recalled that this was the man whom Becc had shot in the thigh with his arrow. 'You have no cause to pester me with your presence unless you wish to imprison me again.'

Unperturbed by the man's surliness, the tanist laughed easily.

'I shall not pester you, Brocc . . . just so long as you are not stirring up trouble. We are here only to see your brother, Seachlann the miller.'

At the sound of their voices another man had emerged from the mill and stood before the door with his leather miller's apron covering his slightly corpulent figure. He stood, legs apart and hands on his hips. The resemblance between the newcomer and Brocc left one in no doubt that he was a brother. He was obviously older than Brocc and of a less muscular build.

'What do you seek of me?' he demanded, raising his voice without leaving the door of the mill. He was gazing at Fidelma and Eadulf as he spoke. 'I have little need of visits by religious with my daughter's murderers being harboured in the abbey.'

Accobrán introduced Fidelma and Eadulf. Brocc responded with a sarcastic chuckle.

'So you are the *dálaigh* whom our chieftain went to Cashel to fetch?' he demanded of Fidelma. 'A religieuse! And you have come here to protect the abbey?'

Fidelma turned a brittle expression on him. 'I am a *dálaigh* and uphold the law no matter who transgresses it. If you cannot remember that fact, Brocc, I suggest that you at least remember that I am sister to Colgú your king. I would also remind you that you have your freedom only on good behaviour.'

Brocc opened his mouth slightly as if to reply, saw the cold steel of her eyes, shrugged and remained silent.

'What do you want of us, lady,' the miller asked in a slightly more respectful tone.

'To learn more about your daughter, Seachlann, and the circumstances of her death so that I can resolve the matter of her killers.'

The miller waved them forward towards the mill. 'We can be seated more comfortably inside.' He paused and glanced towards his brother. 'That grain still needs to be prepared for the grinding,' he added sharply.

Without demur, Brocc limped back to the fire and his unfinished task.

Seachlann stood aside as they entered the mill. It was surprisingly light inside, the sun streaming through the apertures which served as windows.

He motioned them to sit on sacks that were presumably filled with grain or flour and took a similar seat himself.

'Careful, my friend,' he said suddenly as Eadulf made to seat himself. 'That sack is too near the shaft and I would not like you to have an accident.' Eadulf moved away to another sack and the miller smiled towards Fidelma. 'You see, lady, I know the "Rights of Water" from the *Book of Acaill*.'

'I hear that your brother is not so aware of the law, Seachlann,' replied Fidelma. Then she turned to Eadulf who had been puzzled by this exchange. 'Seachlann refers to a law relating to the fines and compensation for accidental damage or injury to persons in a mill,' she explained. 'It is the section we call "Eight Parts of a Mill", areas where accidents can happen and for which the miller is responsible in law. Each area is where the machinery of a watermill can damage the unwary.' She glanced back to Seachlann. 'It seems that you are a conscientious miller.'

In spite of being seated, Seachlann seemed to draw himself up with an air of momentary pride.

'I am a *saer-muilinn*,' he said.

Eadulf realised that a millwright was of higher professional status than a *muilleóir* or miller, which had been the title used by Fidelma. A millwright also designed and constructed the mill and did not simply operate it. Fidelma now inclined her head in acknowledgement.

'So let us return to the reason why we have come to you, Seachlann.'

The millwright's brows came together in a wary frown. 'Are you really here to learn the truth or merely to protect those of the cloth which you share?'

Fidelma decided to make allowance for Seachlann as the father of one of the slaughtered victims.

'My oath is to serve truth and justice, Seachlann. Truth must prevail though the sky falls on our heads or the oceans rise to engulf us.'

For a moment or two the millwright sat gazing at her as if measuring the value of the words in the expression of her face.

'What do you want to know, lady?'

'Tell me about Escrach and what happened on the night of her death,' invited Fidelma.

There was a pause and then Seachlann sighed.

'Escrach was the youngest of our children. She was only seventeen years of age. She was young and in the bloom of her youth. We knew how she would blossom for that is why we named her so.'

Fidelma knew that the name Escrach meant 'blooming' or 'blossoming' but made no comment.

'My wife and I had great hopes for her. Having reached the age of choice we had hoped that she would marry and . . .'

'I believe that Escrach and Gabrán were serious about each other at one point?'

The miller looked surprised for the moment and then shook his head. 'They were childhood friends, that's all I know. Escrach was friendly with many of the local boys and girls. Beccnat and Ballgel for example. They all went to the old one to learn of the ancient wisdom. A lot of our youth used to go to hear the tales. Gabrán and Creoda for example.'

'The old one?' queried Eadulf.

'Liag the apothecary. He teaches star lore.'

'Ah yes. Who is Creoda?'

'A youth who works at Lesren's tannery.'

'So Escrach was not a girlfriend of Gabrán?'

'It was Beccnat he was to marry. We are a small community. I do not think Escrach was friendly with anyone at Rath Raithlen in that way. We were going to send her to my brother, who is a miller at the seaport that is called the Stone of the Woods. He had told us that he could make a desirable match for Escrach.' There was a sudden catch in his voice and he hesitated. Then his voice resumed in a harsh tone. 'Whoever killed our child, killed my wife that day.'

Fidelma was startled by the statement and glanced towards Accobrán.

'You did not tell me that . . .' she began.

'But this is not so,' admonished the tanist defensively. 'Your wife is alive, miller.'

Seachlann laughed angrily. 'I do not mean a physical death. Since Escrach's death, my wife sits in front of the fire. She does not move. Her mind is dead to the world about her. The shock has reduced her to a living death. If you must have proof, I will take you and show you the shell of my wife.'

'Can you tell us the circumstances of Escrach's death as you know them?' intervened Fidelma gently.

'I can never forget them. It was the night of the full moon of last month. Escrach should never have been out on her own. But she had been visiting my mother's sister, her great-aunt, who lives just a short distance away along this river, beyond that hill you see to the south.'

'The hill which you call the Thicket of Pigs?' interrupted Eadulf.

'Just so. She should have returned earlier but I knew that the old woman was not well and supposed that Escrach had stayed as late as she could. The next morning, when she had not returned, I immediately took the route across the Thicket of Pigs to my aunt's *bothán* and found no trace of her along the path. When my aunt told me that Escrach had not even been there, I could not understand it. Had she lied to me? I retraced my steps down through the woods. Along the path I met Goll, the woodcutter. He was looking shocked and told me to prepare myself. I knew what he meant. He had been going into the woods about his day's work and not far from the path, near the stone circle . . .'

'Which you call the Ring of Pigs?' Eadulf intervened.

This time the millwright did not acknowledge him. '. . . Goll had found Escrach's mutilated form.' Seachlann swallowed hard. 'It was either a madman or wild beasts that destroyed her young life, lady. After Liag had made his examination, we brought home her poor body for burial and since then her mother has not moved nor spoken.'

There was a silence.

'Why is it that you believe the religious strangers in the abbey are responsible?' queried Eadulf, returning to practical matters.

Seachlann raised his head to stare at him with a hostile gaze. 'You seek to protect them? You are one of them yourself. You speak our language but your accent is foreign.'

'Brother Eadulf is my companion, an emissary at the court of Cashel. He is here to help me uncover the truth, not to hide it,' interrupted Fidelma snappishly. 'What he asks is a valid question. He asks it in my name.'

Seachlann stood up, moving to the door of the mill. 'Brocc! Come here and answer this *dálaigh*'s question.'

A moment later, Brocc entered and glanced about him.

'What question must I answer?' he demanded in surly tone.

'We have heard what your brother has to say about what he knows of the circumstances of the death of Escrach,' Eadulf said. 'What we have not heard is why you are convinced, and have convinced him, that the murder was carried out by one of the brethren visiting the abbey.'

Brocc turned angrily to his brother. 'I knew it. They are here to protect those at the abbey.'

Fidelma was about to respond when the millwright held up his hand.

'I believe that the sister of our king is here to see justice done, Brocc. She has given me her word as a *dálaigh*. She also vouches for the Saxon stranger.'

'And the abbot vouches for the strangers at the abbey!' snapped Brocc. 'Why should we believe her any more than the abbot? These religious are all in the same service, owing no allegiance but to one another.'

'That is not true, Brocc,' Fidelma reprimanded him. 'If you do not accept my word then accept your brother's.'

Brocc chuckled sarcastically. 'My brother is a good man. He believes the best of people and can be easily fooled.'

Seachlann shook his head sadly and showed no anger at his brother's words. 'Whether I am fooled by these words or not, Brocc, what is the harm in telling them the truth? Why withhold the evidence of your eyes now?'

Brocc sniffed in irritation. 'My word was not accepted before, why should it be accepted now?'

Fidelma leant back on her seat so that she could examine Brocc by the sunlight that shone through the breaks in the mill's wooden walls.

'In matters as grave as this, Brocc, it is not simply a person's word that is scrutinised, otherwise we might all make accusations against people we do not like and have them punished simply because we say it is so. We need more than words, Brocc.'

The burly man turned towards his brother with a sneer of triumph. 'See, Seachlann? Already my word is set at nothing.'

Fidelma exhaled angrily. 'Words are cheap, Brocc. We are concerned with truth. How can we judge your word as truth if you will not utter it?'

'My own chieftain shot and maimed me. Was he interested in the truth?' cried Brocc.

'He was. And he was interested in the law and the observance of the law. You were taking the law into your own hands. You had become judge and executioner of the law and it was the law as you thought it should be given. Now, enough. I shall not argue longer. Either tell me why you accuse the people at the abbey or I will see to it that you are brought before a Brehon on a charge of spreading malicious stories as well as inciting riot.'

Brocc blinked at the harshness in her tone.

'The murders began when the three strangers arrived at the abbey,' he said.

Fidelma waited impatiently.

'The three strangers are not like us. They are not men.'

'What do you mean?' countered Eadulf. 'If they are not men, what are they. Beasts, spirits – what?'

'Go to the abbey and look upon them, that is all I say. Come back and tell me if they are men as we know them.'

'You are being mysterious. Whatever you think of these religious is not the point,' Fidelma said. 'Tell me how you know that these strangers are the murderers of these girls, specifically the killers of Escrach. I do not want to know circumstantial matters; I do not want to hear about coincidences; I want to have facts, no more nor less.'

Accobrán the tanist, who was clearly bored with the whole proceedings, rose and stretched. 'Just tell the *dálaigh* why you believe the strangers had a hand in the murder of Escrach and we can make an end to this matter.'

'Why?' A crooked smile spread over the face of Brocc. 'Why? Because I saw the murderer!'

Chapter Six

There was shocked silence in the mill room.

Accobrán the tanist was the first to recover.

'You have never said this before, Brocc,' he said accusingly. 'You have never said that you actually saw the murderer.'

The heavy-featured man returned his look defiantly.

'I was never asked before, tanist of the Cinél na Áeda. I know what I know. Did you think that I would go to the abbey for no apparent reason?'

'Others certainly thought that you did,' replied Fidelma quietly. 'Most people believe that you were simply prejudiced against the strangers. Your own words seemed to imply that you were. Now for the first time you say you saw the murderer.'

Brocc's sneer was comment enough on what he thought of other people.

'So tell us, Brocc,' Eadulf took up the questioning again, 'tell us about this murderer and why you did not come forward to explain your evidence before. You saw the murder but you let your brother go looking for his missing daughter. We were told that it was Goll the woodcutter who found the body. Explain all this, for I am confused.'

Fidelma glanced appreciatively at Eadulf. The discrepancy between Brocc's actions and the story he now told was clear.

Brocc was not put out by the question.

'I said, I saw the murder*er* not the murder,' he said with emphasis.

Eadulf shook his head slightly, as if bewildered. 'Now what are you saying? How can you see the one without the other?'

'You'd better tell us your story in detail,' instructed Fidelma slowly and deliberately. 'Make it simple and clear. I do not want to play some game of semantics.'

Brocc scowled. 'I have no understanding of what you are saying.'

'I want no word games. Either you saw the killer or you did not. Which is it?'

'On the day Escrach was killed, I was doing some trade up on the River Bride, to the north of here,' Brocc replied. 'My brother will confirm it. By the time I returned, it was night. I was coming over the hill we call the Thicket of Pigs, which you can see from the doorway here, and the moon was full.'

'As a matter of clarification, as I am a stranger here, where were you heading?' asked Fidelma.

'To my *bothán*, which is on the edge of the clearing here.'

'Had you known that Escrach was supposed to be visiting her aunt and have taken the path over the same hill?'

'Not at that time,' replied Brocc.

'So you came across the hill?'

'The path I was following came over the shoulder of the hill, overlooking the abbey below.'

'Where is that in relation to the place where Escrach's body was found?'

'Escrach was found among some boulders, a ring of rocks, which is further up the hill on the same side. They are called the Ring of Pigs.'

Fidelma motioned him to continue when he hesitated.

'There is little else to tell. I came over the hill and I saw one of the strangers, one of those from the abbey.'

'What was he doing?' demanded Eadulf curiously.

'What was the stranger doing? Why, nothing. Just sitting there at the Ring of Pigs. His face was towards the moon. I should have known that this was unusual. I gave him greeting but he did not even reply to me. There was something sinister about the man. Just sitting there on the hillside in the moonlight, as if bathing his face in the light of the moon.'

'So what did you do?'

'I said a quick prayer and hurried on home to my cabin. It was the next morning that I heard that Escrach's body had been discovered.'

There was a silence as Fidelma considered what she had been told.

'From what you say, you saw this stranger seated on the hill. You did not see Escrach. However, the next day Escrach's body was found at the same spot. Is that a fair summary?'

'Exactly as I told you.'

Fidelma sighed. 'It raises questions that need to be asked. But there is no evidence that Escrach and the man met, far less that the man killed her. The law requires evidence not theories. And did you tell your brother this story? You did not arouse the people to march on the abbey on that same day, did you? Why did you wait a month until another young girl had met her death before you acted?'

Brocc shook his head like a large shaggy dog. 'I did not tell my brother. Not then. It was only after Ballgel's death last week that I realised the significance of the full of the moon. Only with Ballgel's murder on the night of the Badger's Moon did I realise that there was a killer among us striking on each full of the moon. It was then that I suddenly realised what I had seen . . . the stranger sitting on the hillside bathing in the rays of the moon. Only then did it become obvious to me.'

'Did you go to the abbey and identify the stranger?' demanded Fidelma, still sceptical.

Seachlann intervened in support of his brother. 'After Brocc had told me what he had seen that night, we all went then. The people went to demand that the strangers be handed over.'

'Was that when you all attacked the abbey, when Brocc, here, was shot?'

'It was.'

'Why did you demand that all the strangers be handed over for punishment? Why not demand to see the strangers, identify the one you saw and ask for an explanation?'

'The strangers are all alike,' interposed Seachlann angrily. 'They are all as guilty as each other.'

'That is not a sound philosophy,' pointed out Fidelma.

'You have not met them.'

'Then we will do so presently,' Fidelma assured him. 'But what you are saying is that you are not an eyewitness to Escrach's death or, indeed, any of the deaths. When you saw the stranger in the moonlight he was alone.'

'No man without evil intention would be sitting on a hillside in the full of the moon, just sitting and staring at the moon,' protested Brocc.

'There are many reasons why people do things that, to an outsider, may seem odd behaviour,' Eadulf assured him. 'Would it not have been better to have sought explanations rather than attempt to visit violence on the man . . . indeed, on him and his companions whom you did not see? The man might have a good enough reason for being on the hill at that time.'

'What reason?' sneered Brocc.

Eadulf smiled thinly. 'Exactly! None of us knows if reason there be. And we should find out before leaping to conclusions. Escrach's body was found at the same place, but where is the evidence that Escrach was even on the hill at the same time as the stranger?'

Seachlann shook his head in disgust. 'You speak like all religious. A honey tongue coaxing us away from seeing things as they are.'

'You should not fear truth, Seachlann,' snapped Fidelma. 'False tales are eventually discovered so we have no cause to protect that which is untrue.'

Eadulf nodded swiftly. 'May I suggest this? Perhaps Brocc will accompany us to the abbey. It is high time that we spoke to these strangers against whom so much suspicion and anger are directed. Then Brocc can tell what he saw in front of the stranger and the stranger, whichever one of the three it was, can present his reasons if he has any. Is that not a better, civilised way to proceed than running armed into the abbey baying for blood?'

The tanist Accobrán, who had sat quietly for a long time, rose with a positive smile. 'Well said, Brother Saxon. That sounds an excellent idea. Do you object to this, Brocc?'

The millwright's brother hesitated and kicked at the ground.

'Whatever way gets to the truth,' he growled in annoyance.

Fidelma looked relieved.

'It is only the truth that we are all wanting to find, Brocc,' she said quietly but firmly.

The abbey dedicated to the Blessed Finnbarr, nestling in the shelter of the tall hill about which they had heard so much, was not large. A wooden wall or palisade surrounded several buildings dominated by a large wooden chapel. The gates were shut and two stern-looking Brothers stood sentinel at a watchtower. Only when Accobrán was recognised did one of them shout down and the gates swung inwards.

A young, anxious-looking religious, a thin, wiry individual with fair hair and features, came out to greet them. He saw Brocc and immediately scowled at the millwright's brother. Brocc stood slightly behind the tanist as if seeking shelter. The young man's glance encompassed them all and then he addressed himself to the tanist.

'*Deus tecum*, Accobrán. What brings you here – and in the company of that man?' He indicated Brocc.

'God be with you, Brother Solam. I bring the *dálaigh* from Cashel,' Accobrán said. 'This is Fidelma of Cashel and her companion, Brother Eadulf.'

The young man turned to Fidelma and Eadulf and smiled shyly in greeting. 'Fidelma of Cashel?' He almost stuttered in his nervousness.

'This is Brother Solam, the steward of the abbey, lady,' Accobrán announced.

The young man was bowing nervously to Fidelma. 'Fidelma of Cashel.' His voice was breathless. 'Who has not heard of you?'

Fidelma looked positively embarrassed at the young man's obsequiousness.

'I should imagine that a great many people have not,' she assured him with a serious expression, although something sparkled in her eyes. 'We have come to see Abbot Brogán.'

'I will inform him of your presence directly, lady. Please enter.' Brother Solam hesitated a moment and glanced suspiciously towards Brocc and then at Accobrán. 'Who will be responsible for the good behaviour of that man?'

'I will,' said the young tanist, shifting his hand ostentatiously to the hilt of his sword. 'The brethren need have no fear of him while I am here.'

They followed Brother Solam into the courtyard beyond the gates as they swung shut behind them.

'Please wait here a moment, and I will inform the abbot,' Brother Solam instructed them.

'Only Brother Eadulf and I want to see the abbot initially,' Fidelma told him. 'Accobrán and Brocc can wait here.'

'It is warm at the smith's forge,' the Brother volunteered, indicating across the courtyard, where there was a seat and some shelter.

'Good enough,' agreed Accobrán. 'Let me know when you require our presence, lady.'

Brother Solam frowned slightly, not understanding. Fidelma did not enlighten him of the proposal that she had discussed with Accobrán on their way to the abbey, and in a moment he hurried away.

A few minutes later, he was showing them into the presence of Abbot Brogán.

The abbot was still a handsome man in spite of his age and he welcomed them with a grave smile and courtesy.

'This is an honour, Sister Fidelma. I have heard much of your work. I am told that even in Tara your name is known.'

'I have done some small service for the High King,' Fidelma acknowledged, as the abbot then extended his hand to Eadulf.

'Welcome also, Brother. Forgive me, I find difficulty pronouncing Saxon names. They seem so difficult. Yet I have heard of you. You were at the great Council of Whitby, I believe?'

'You have been well informed, abbot,' said Eadulf.

'Well, I am pleased that you have both accepted Becc's invitation to come to Rath Raithlen. There is much evil in this place and panic has seized our people so that they forget all sense of proportion and shame and even attack us, the religious.'

'Brother Solam has probably told you that we have brought Brocc, the millwright's brother, with us?'

The abbot inclined his head gravely. 'Indeed. And he has told me that the tanist Accobrán attends him with his sword, so we are not alarmed.' He waved them to seats and asked Brother Solam to fetch wine or mead in accordance to their preference.

'I am told that the abbey shelters three strangers, and that it is fear of these strangers that cause the people to attack you,' began Fidelma.

'Alas, people always fear the unknown, and hate is born out of that fear,' said Abbot Brogán, after a pause to allow Brother Solam to distribute the beverages.

'We would agree,' Fidelma acknowledged. 'Our task in coming here today is simply to assure ourselves that there is no other cause for the three visitors now under this roof to be suspected of involvement in the three deaths.'

Abbot Brogán stared at her for a moment in surprise. 'Then you would have me send for the strangers to question them?'

'That would be for the best,' Fidelma said softly.

The abbot turned to his steward and gave orders for the strangers to be sought out and asked to attend him.

'How long have you known these men?' Eadulf asked.

'They came here two months ago,' the abbot responded. 'I am not sure that I can say that I *know* any of them. They arrived here from Molaga's house on the coast. They had been saved from a shipwreck, recovered and expressed a wish to study here. We have a library which some are envious of.' He smiled when he saw Fidelma look surprised. 'It is true that we are a poor community. No more than twenty of us at this house. But we have saved many wand-books and manuscripts which is our wealth and our claim to respect among the larger houses.'

'So these visitors are strangers from beyond the seas?'

Abbot Brogán smiled broadly. 'That you will see for yourselves.'

Just then Brother Solam entered again and stood aside, holding the door open.

'The three guests are here, lord abbot,' he intoned solemnly.

Three tall men entered the room, dwarfing the rest of the company. They were lean and muscular and wore their simple undyed white woollen robes with elegance, like royal apparel. Each wore an ornate crucifix of silver on a chain which was unlike any Fidelma had seen before, even in Rome. Their faces were strikingly handsome, their eyes watchful, but Fidelma found their expressions unfathomable, as if they had purposely eliminated all emotion from their features. They halted in a line before the abbot and, as if at a hidden signal,

all three inclined their heads in deference at precisely the same time
with one brief movement. They were physically intimidating but both
Fidelma and Eadulf could not hide their momentary surprise at the
ebony blackness of their skins against the white and silver of their
apparel.

'You summoned us, lord abbot?'

It was the man in the middle who spoke. He used the language of
Éireann, although his tones were heavily accented.

'I did. This is Fidelma of Cashel, sister to our King Colgú. She is
what we call a *dálaigh* – a judge of our law courts.'

Fidelma was about to intervene to make the interpretation more
accurate but realised that the abbot was speaking in very simple terms,
doubtless so that the foreigners would understand.

The tall stranger spoke rapidly to his companions and all three turned
towards Fidelma. This time each man laid his right hand upon his breast
and all three bowed in unison towards her. She felt slightly embarrassed
but decided to rise from her seat and reply in kind.

'This is my companion, Brother Eadulf of Seaxmund's Ham,' she
said, to complete the introductions.

The three bowed again, but this time without the hands placed on
their breasts.

'Let us all be seated,' she suggested.

Chairs were brought forward for the three strangers. When they were
seated, Fidelma glanced towards Abbot Brogán.

'Do I have your permission to continue?'

The abbot made a quick gesture of assent.

Fidelma turned back and addressed herself to the stranger who
seemed to be the spokesmen.

'Do you all speak the language of my people?' she asked.

The man's expression did not change. 'I have learnt only a little
of your language. My knowledge is limited. My companions do not
speak it.'

'What language do you speak?'

'Our language is called Ge'ez. It is the language of the kingdom of
Aksum.'

He spoke with some pride. Fidelma had to confess to herself that
she had never heard of either the language or the country. The stranger
saw her look of dismay, and still without a change of expression said:
'While I have a limited knowledge of the language of your people,
we all speak the language of the Greeks, and a little Latin, as well as
several of the other languages which border our country.'

Fidelma felt relief. Greek was the language of the original movement of the New Faith, the language of the sacred texts. She had studied it for many years and delighted in reading the ancient philosophers of Greece in their original tongue. She knew that Eadulf also had command of the language and she glanced apologetically at the abbot.

'Would there be any objection to continuing this conversation in Greek, that we may more quickly discover the information I require?'

The abbot shifted uneasily in his seat. 'My knowledge of Greek is confined to the Holy Scriptures and may scarcely be competent to comprehend such a conversation. Nevertheless, I am content that you should continue as you wish, Fidelma of Cashel.'

Fidelma sat back, glancing briefly at Eadulf to assure herself that he had no objections.

'That is good,' she said, switching to Greek 'Now let us introduce ourselves properly.'

The leading member of the trio inclined his head. 'I am Brother Dangila and my companions are Brother Nakfa, on my left, and Brother Gambela, on my right.'

'And are you all from this kingdom called Aksum?'

'We are.'

'Can you tell me where this kingdom is?'

'It is a land beyond Egypt, situated between the Red Sea and the Atbara River. Have you not heard of Aksum's great port Adulis with its churches and palaces? Adulis gives to the world gold, emeralds, obsidian, ivory and spices.'

Fidelma shook her head slowly. 'I know nothing of the lands beyond Egypt. I have not heard of Aksum. Are there Christians in your land?'

For the first time the expressions on the handsome faces before her softened and almost broke into smiles.

'Know this, Fidelma of Cashel, that it was well over four centuries ago that our King Ezana ordained that Aksum would be a Christian kingdom. We were the first kingdom in the history of the New Faith to become Christian. It was Frumentius from Syria who taught Ezana and brought light to us, for we are the true descendants of the Hebrews and David was our king. It is among us that the Ark of the Covenant resides in which the *Decalogue* is kept.'

Fidelma was hard pressed not to allow her features to stare in amazement at the words of Brother Dangila. The *Decalogue* was the religious and moral guidelines that God had given Moses on Mount Sinai.

'Your kingdom sounds most fascinating and on some other occasion

I would hear more of it. But I am here in my official capacity,' she said regretfully.

Brother Dangila inclined his head slightly. 'If I have interpreted correctly, you are a judge as well as being sister to the king of this land?'

'It is so. When the laws of this kingdom are transgressed, my role is to inquire into the matter and discover who is the culprit.'

'We understand.'

'As you are aware, there have been three young women killed near this abbey.'

'We have realised this,' Brother Dangila replied. 'Outside, the people believe that we have been the cause of these unfortunate deaths. We are blessed that Abbot Brogán has protected us within the walls of his abbey.'

'Why do you think the people outside believe that you are responsible for the deaths?'

Now, for the first time, Brother Dangila smiled broadly. 'You have looked upon us, Fidelma of Cashel. Therein is the reason.'

'Explain.'

'I would have thought no explanation was needed to one of your intelligence. Are we not physically different from you and your people?'

'I cannot deny that. But, being so, why would that make you suspect?'

'Come, diplomacy is not needed. Dogs bark at people they do not know.'

Fidelma responded with a smile. 'So, you say that you are accused because it is obvious that you are strangers?'

Brother Dangila held out an arm and pushed back its sleeve to reveal bare flesh.

'Hold out your arm, Fidelma of Cashel, and place it next to mine.'

She did so, also drawing back her sleeve.

The black and white skins were side by side.

'Need we say more about the differences? Ignorance breeds prejudice, prejudice breeds fear, fear breeds hate.'

Fidelma grimaced and withdrew her arm.

'It is a sad fault of man,' she agreed. 'Nevertheless, I am constrained by law to investigate this matter to the point where evidence must be the deciding factor. My people have an old saying – the lie will pass away and the truth will remain.'

Brother Dangila sat back. 'Ask of us what you will.'

'Let us start at the time of the last full moon, when the girl Ballgel was killed. Where were you and your fellows that night?'

'Here in the abbey,' came the swift reply.

'And were there witnesses to this?'

'Brother Dangila looked swiftly at his fellows in turn before returning his unfathomable gaze to her.

'We were in the guests' dormitory, having retired to bed after the midnight Angelus, and we did not stir until the morning Angelus bell,' he said.

'That is not exactly true.'

For the first time, Brother Gambela spoke. A soft, almost feminine voice. Brother Dangila swung round, a slight irritation on his face.

'Not exactly true?' queried Fidelma. 'Explain, please, Brother Gambela.'

'I could not sleep immediately and while I can testify that my companions fell asleep on retiring I could not. My mouth was dry and so I went in search of water in the hope that I would settle to sleep after a drink to quench my thirst.'

'And did you find water?' asked Fidelma.

'I went to the kitchens and drank my fill and then returned to bed.'

'What time was this? Did anyone see you?'

'I do not know. It could not have been more than an hour after midnight. And, yes, someone saw me.'

'Who?'

'I did.' It was Abbot Brogán who spoke. 'I returned from Becc's feasting some time after midnight. I think I left the chief's fortress shortly after midnight and it would take me no more than half to three-quarters of an hour to walk back to the abbey. I entered and saw Brother Gambela coming from the direction of the kitchen and we bade one another a good night.'

'Last month, at the time of the full moon, the girl Escrach was killed. Where were you all then?'

'I believe that we were all in the abbey once again that night,' replied Brother Dangila.

Fidelma paused, looking from one to the other of the bland expressions on the faces of the three men.

'Is that so?' she asked quietly.

'You doubt it?' demanded Brother Gambela.

'How would you answer if I were to say that someone saw one of you on the night that Escrach was killed, sitting on the hillside that rises above the abbey? Sitting on the hillside and staring up at the full moon?'

The expressions on the three faces did not alter. They continued to be bland and unresponsive. For a moment or two in the silence, Fidelma felt that there was going to be no response. Then Brother Dangila spoke.

'We would answer, who is the someone who claims such a thing and which one of us does he claim he saw?' he replied softly. 'Even if it were true, when is sitting on a hillside regarding the stars in their courses considered a crime? Is this someone claiming that the murdered girl was seen in the company of whoever it was who was seen sitting on the hill?'

'A logical reply,' acknowledged Fidelma, feeling that the strangers were very astute. Turning to the abbot, she said, 'Let Accobrán bring Brocc in.'

The abbot rang his silver handbell.

After a quiet word with Brother Solam, Accobrán came in escorting the sullen and resentful Brocc who glowered angrily at the company.

'Now, Brocc, repeat your story before this company,' Fidelma instructed before she turned to the three strangers and added in Greek: 'If there is anything that you are unclear of, I will translate for you.'

The three sat impassively while Brocc went through his story. Curiously, in their quiet, dignified presence, Brocc seemed to be drained of his aggression, of his bravado. He spoke softly, almost politely.

'Last month I was returning home having conducted some business with a merchant on the River Bride. It was midnight as I came over the hills towards Rath Raithlen. I was crossing the Thicket of Pigs about that time. It was at the full of the moon and very bright. Suddenly I saw a figure seated at the Ring of Pigs on the hillside along which my path lay. It was a figure of a tall man, sitting on a rock. He did not see me. He was gazing up at the moon with an extraordinary expression on his face.'

'Did you speak to him?'

'I did. "What are you doing here, stranger?" I asked. I called him stranger for indeed I recognised him not.'

'Did he reply?'

'He did not, and I doubt whether he even knew the meaning of my words, for he was one of these fierce-looking strangers from beyond the seas whose skins are black. He was clearly not of our people.'

'Was he alone or with someone?'

'He appeared to be alone.'

'And you saw no one with him? Are you certain?' pressed Fidelma. Brocc replied with a positive gesture. 'I did not.'

'On this we must be firm so that the one you accuse may answer?'

'I did not see anyone with the stranger,' Brocc admitted sullenly. 'But I believe he was not alone.'

'The stranger would only have to answer to what you actually saw and not what you believed,' Fidelma pointed out sharply. 'However, you say that you spoke to him and he did not reply. What did you do?'

Brocc swallowed nervously. It was a new side to his character which Fidelma and Eadulf had not seen before. He was a man embarrassed.

'A fear seized me,' he admitted. 'I feared that he was a phantom, a spawn of the devil. He said nothing but the moon bathed his face, making it grey and awesome. He turned his face slowly to me and his eyes sparkled with a fierce fire. I turned and ran. It was the next morning when I heard that Escrach had been killed. As you know, it was not until Ballgel was murdered that I realised the significance of what I had seen. Then I tried to warn people about the strangers.'

'You told me that the person you saw was one of these strangers. Do you still make that claim?'

'Of course I do.' Something of his old aggressiveness rose again in his manner.

'Well, the three strangers are seated before you. Which of them was it who was seated in the moonlight?'

The three men sat impassively gazing upon the man.

Brocc scarcely bothered to examine them. He spoke directly to Fidelma.

'I cannot tell one set of their dark features from another. They appear all the same to me. I could not say which one it was. It is your job to make one of them confess.'

Fidelma snorted in irritation. 'I will tell you clearly what my job is, Brocc. My job is to interpret the law. The *Berrad Airechta*, which is the law of witnesses, is very precise. You come to me here as a *fiadu*, that is "one who sees". You can only give evidence about what you have seen or heard and you must be prepared to swear an oath in support of that evidence. You say that you saw a man. You claim that it was one of these three men seated before you. But which one? You cannot say. It is not up to these men to deny your accusation, it is up to you to prove it. So, Brocc, do you accuse one of these men, and if so which one do you accuse? Speak!'

Brocc shrugged his bull-like shoulders. 'I tell you that I cannot tell them apart. I saw one of them. That is all I can tell you.'

Fidelma exhaled softly. Her mouth was set tightly. She turned to the tanist.

'Accobrán, would you please escort Brocc from the abbey. Wait outside for us.'

Brocc turned angrily towards her.

'So, you religious are all alike. You take their word in preference to mine?' he cried.

Fidelma returned his sneering gaze impassively.

'In law, Brocc, you have no word to take. You make no specific accusation that can be entered in law. I am here to assess facts, not accusations without substance.' Fidelma dismissed him with a gesture of her hand and, without a word, Accobrán, rather roughly, propelled Brocc from the chamber.

Chapter Seven

When the door closed behind them, Fidelma turned back to the three Aksumites, who continued to sit impassively as if oblivious of what had just occurred.

'Have you anything to say in answer to Brocc's accusation?' she asked quietly. There was a silence. They did not speak. Then Fidelma added: 'The law does not oblige you to speak, but it might help our investigation. The sooner we can clear this matter up the better it will be for everyone.'

'There is nothing to answer, Sister,' Brother Dangila replied shortly. 'You have already pointed out that the man made a claim against one of us but cannot say against which of us he is making it. Even if the claim were true, what does that prove? It does not prove what he ultimately asserts – that one or all of us were involved in the deaths that have occurred in this place.'

Fidelma had to admit that Brocc, as an eyewitness, was useless. He could offer no evidence of identification.

'So you claim that you were all in the abbey on the night of the full moon?'

Brother Dangila sighed softly.

'We sleep and study in this abbey,' he replied quietly, without responding to her specific question.

'And on the night of the previous full moon when Beccnat was slain?' Fidelma asked wearily. 'Can you remember that night and where you and the others were or what you were doing?'

'We hardly ever move from the abbey,' Brother Dangila replied in his quiet, dignified tones. 'We have been applying ourselves to our studies here and trying to learn your language from the brothers of this community. Certainly, we are not disposed to wander abroad during the times of darkness lest we meet fear and prejudice on our path; the fear and prejudice which you have shown exists by bringing that man to confront us.'

'Your studies?' queried Fidelma, frowning at his explanation.

'Is not your land a centre of learning?' smiled Brother Gambela, having apparently grown confident of his ability to communicate in Greek. 'The knowledge that we garner here will stand us in good stead when we return to our people.'

81

'Is that why you came to this land?' Fidelma decided to change tack.

Brother Dangila shook his head. 'Our story is a long one, and, perhaps, it is tedious in the telling.'

'It will grow less tedious if you start,' Fidelma solemnly assured him.

'Very well. If you wish to hear our story, I will tell it. We three are, as I have said, Aksumites. We are not from Adulis but from the interior of the kingdom. But we were summoned to Adulis for there was to be a conference between representatives of the Christian communities in Malqurra and Alwa, which border the kingdom. We had not been in Adulis before and were intrigued by the sights of the great city. We went down to the quaysides on the river to examine the ships that trade from all corners of the world. It was our undoing, for we were attacked and knocked unconscious, and when we awoke we were in a ship's hold and out on the sea. Slave trading is one of the profitable means of commerce for those who have no conscience in our part of the world.'

He paused as if to reflect before continuing.

'An eternity of suffering seemed our lot until we arrived in a strange port and were taken ashore. Our treatment was harsh but the Lord guided us and kept all three of us together. We eventually realised that we had been taken to Rome itself. Rome, a city that has proclaimed itself the centre of the Faith we cherished. But there was no sympathy there even though we were followers of the Christ. Indeed, as we were taken in chains through the city, we called out to the people that we, too, were Christians. When they heard that we were Aksumites, they jeered us and denounced us as non-believers and heretics.'

Fidelma frowned in puzzlement. 'Why so?'

It was Brother Gambela who answered in his more stilted Greek. 'We proclaim the monophysis of the Christ. We are taught that Christ had a single nature rather than a double nature.'

Fidelma's eyes lighted in understanding. 'Ah, I have heard of the Council of Chalcedon when this matter was discussed and Rome expelled those who believed that Christ was of a single nature.' She turned to Eadulf, adding, 'Hence the Greek words *mono* and *physis*. Rome believes that Christ was both divine and human. These were the two natures. The Council of Chalcedon said it was heretical to proclaim that Christ had only one nature.'

Brother Dangila was shaking his head. 'We never believed in monophysis as it was portrayed by the Chalcedon Council. We Aksumites argued that Christ was perfect in his divinity and perfect in his humanity but his divinity and humanity were united in one nature – that is, the nature of the incarnate word. Did not the Blessed Cyril of Alexandria say that human and divine natures were united in one, without mingling, without confusion and without alteration? Those two natures were not separate. Perhaps the pontiffs of Rome conspired to misconstrue our teachings as a punishment for the refusal of our Church to obey them or be politically influenced by them.'

'Harsh words,' muttered the abbot reprovingly.

'Truth is often bitter,' replied Brother Gambela.

'So let us finish the story,' intervened Fidelma, seeing they might be entering dangerous theological territory. 'You were slaves in Rome, you say? And no one would raise a hand to help you?'

'That is true,' Brother Dangila agreed. 'We were used as labourers to load cargoes into the ships that docked along the river in Rome. Then we were sold to a Frankish merchant and forced to work as crew on his ship which undertook a long and terrible voyage from the Middle Sea and through a narrow strait, which we were told was called the Pillars of Hercules. Then came a terrible voyage along the coast of Iberia. A great storm came up and our ship was driven away from the coast, off its course. The captain began to panic and believed that we were going to be driven to our doom over the edge of the world.' The Aksumite smiled lopsidedly. 'The man believed that the earth was a flat shape and the horizon marked the edge over which none may venture. This idea we found a quaint teaching. Is such a belief current here?'

Fidelma shook her head. 'Our astronomers have long taught that the world is spherical, Brother Dangila. Martialis writes that even in the days of our pagan ancestors, the Druids taught us that the world was in the shape of a ball.'

Brother Dangila nodded approvingly. 'This captain was from a country called Frankia and seemed uncertain how to navigate his ship once we lost sight of land. While he and his crew panicked, we three prayed. The ship foundered in that terrible storm but God smiled on us for we three were among several who were then washed ashore into this kingdom. Your people fed, clothed and gave us hospitality. We were made welcome and made even more welcome when we revealed that we were of the Faith. Your people did not condemn us because we were Aksumites—'

Brother Gambela interrupted. 'We were blessed when we discovered that the followers of Christ in this kingdom do not slavishly follow the dictates of Rome but retain many of the original rituals and the teachings of the early Faith just as we have done. We felt that God had ordained our journey for a purpose – that we were meant to learn here and take back that knowledge to our people. From the place where we were washed ashore we were taken to an abbey called the house of Molaga where we spent some time.'

'Yet in spite of these adventures, or rather misadventures, you appear in clothing and with ornaments that are of your own country,' Eadulf suddenly pointed out with suspicion, speaking for the first time in what had been, for him, a long period of silence. His knowledge of Greek was less than his knowledge of Latin and he had been struggling to follow the nuances of the conversation. 'How were you able to keep those crucifixes of valued silver during your slavery?'

Brother Dangila turned to him, not in the least put out by his question. 'These robes were woven here on our instruction. But you are right; Aksumite silversmiths made these crucifixes. Alas, we cannot claim them as our own. The abbot of the house of Molaga gave them to us. They were apparently part of some spoils taken from shipwrecks. We noticed them when staying with the abbot and identified their provenance. The charitable man felt it just that we should have them.'

'After staying at the house of Molaga, what then?' asked Fidelma.

'Then we came here, to this abbey, where we have applied ourselves to our studies.'

'Out of interest, may I ask what these studies are?' enquired Eadulf.

It was Brother Nakfa, not having spoken before, who surprised everyone by suddenly speaking in reply. His voice was low and soft and yet his tone was quite musical, making his Greek sound like an incantation rather than speech.

'We are interested in the way you perceive the heavens. Interested in the interpretation that you give to the sun, the moon, the stars and their courses across the sky. We have discovered that within your land dwell many learned men who have studied and written on such matters. Our people pride themselves on their knowledge of the heavens and the celestial beings but we did not think to find others beyond our known world who have pondered such matters.'

Brother Dangila added: 'We have found the works of a learned brother named Augustine . . .'

Here Abbot Brogán, who had been following the Greek conversation with a frown of concentration, muttered: 'He means Brother Aibhistín who dwells on Carthaigh's Island. Aibhistín has devoted his life to studying the heavens.'

'But specifically the moon and the tides,' added Brother Dangila, 'which is of great importance for he has clearly observed that the *astrorum splendidissimum*, that most splendid of the heavenly bodies, the moon, governs the tides of the oceans and is therefore one of the great mysteries of the universe.'

Brother Gambela raised his head a little, his face, like his companions', lighting up with enthusiasm.

'We discovered, while we were at the house of Molaga, that this abbey possesses a copy of *De Mirabilius Sacrae Scripturae* in which the good Brother Augustine speaks of the importance of the moon. He argues that it was at the full moon that the Passion of Christ took place . . .'

Eadulf suddenly leant forward with a suspicious frown.

'You Aksumite brothers seem extremely interested in the full moon,' he said pointedly.

Brother Dangila turned to him with a disarming smile. 'What person can ignore the full moon and its consequences?'

'Its consequences?' Fidelma spoke sharply, suddenly alert to a possible significance in his words.

'Isn't that why you are interested in these deaths, Sister?' countered Brother Dangila impassively. 'I am told that your people place great weight on the fact that these local deaths have occurred at the full of the moon.'

'What consequences do you speak of, Brother Dangila?' demanded Fidelma, feeling that the impassive face of the Aksumite hid more than he was revealing.

'The flood tide begins three days and twelve hours before the full moon, and after completing its course it comes to an end after an equal length of time. This fact is according to your scholar, the Brother Aibhistín. Now if the tides are drawn into such intensity at the time of the full moon, then how much are the emotions of man so roused to flood and ebb? Is there not liquid that flows within our bodies that might respond to the moon as does the liquid of the seas?'

Fidelma pursed her lips thoughtfully.

'It is possible,' she admitted. 'And so, with such interests, one of you might have been seated on the hillside making observations that night of the full moon when Brocc happened to come along.'

Brother Dangila's mask almost slipped into a grin, but only for a moment.

'That is also possible,' he answered gravely.

'And was any of you doing so?'

'We have dealt with that matter, Sister. Let us avoid playing such games as catch as catch can.'

Fidelma knew that she would be unable to move forward on the matter and so she tried another tack.

'Do the local people here know that you have this interest in the moon and its behaviour?' she queried.

Brother Dangila stretched his arms in an eloquent gesture of indifference. 'We have made no attempt to hide our studies. Abbot Brogán is well aware of our interests.'

The abbot nodded swiftly in confirmation. 'It is so, Sister Fidelma. The brothers here have never hidden from me, nor anyone in this abbey, their passion for examining the celestial bodies.'

'But if this be known,' Eadulf pointed out, 'then it would add to the suspicions of the local people. The sight of one or other of you seated on a hill making observations of the moon would fuel such suspicions. Surely you should now explain the reasons for this, to avoid mistrust? I think this is what you are telling us. That Brocc did see one of you on the hill and that this was what you were doing. Why not tell us who it was? We will hear your explanation.'

'In our land of Aksum we have a saying that it is only lack of knowledge that makes people suspicious,' Brother Dangila replied gravely. 'The local people would not have your knowledge of why we study the celestial orbs. So if it was admitted that one or other of us might – and I only say might – have been on that hillside examining the full moon, then they would not understand and our admission would be fuel for their suspicions.'

Fidelma conceded the point. 'There is truth in that, Brother. However, Publilius Syrus points out that suspicion begets suspicion. They are already suspicious and it would be better to quell that suspicion before it outgrows our ability to do so.'

Brother Nakfa suddenly rose from his seat in a smooth unhurried motion which a moment later was copied by his companions.

'Sister, we are in your hands,' Brother Nakfa assured her solemnly. 'We have told you what we know of the matter you inquire into. We know little except that these deaths came at the full of the moon, and because we are strangers, alien in the colour of our skins as well as language and demeanour, and because we are studying the celestial motions, so we are suspects in these terrible crimes. All we can offer in defence is the truth. If we can offer nothing else, then we would seek permission to return to our studies.'

Fidelma found herself rising with a feeling of irritation. She disguised her feelings with an expression equally as bland as the three men's.

'There is nothing more I need ask of any of you at this moment,' she agreed reluctantly.

The three tall strangers bowed in unison and moved silently from the room. When they had gone, Fidelma resumed her seat.

Abbot Brogán was looking troubled.

'I fear that instead of dispelling suspicion, Sister Fidelma, they have ignited thoughts that were not there before,' he observed.

Fidelma was thoughtful. 'The purpose of questioning, Abbot, is to provoke new thoughts and possibilities. And it is my duty as a *dálaigh* to ask questions. It would be better for the three strangers if they could be more specific about where they were on the nights of the full moon. I am inclined to believe Brocc when he says he saw one of them but his evidence is useless if he cannot be specific about which of the three he saw. As Eadulf says, we can consider the strangers' interest in the study of the heavens once the matter is admitted. However, by not admitting it, they merely create suspicion.'

Abbot Brogán was unhappy and said so.

'Brother Dangila was correct when he said that even if Brocc's testimony was true, it did not mean that whoever he saw was responsible for the slaughter of any of the girls,' Fidelma pointed out. 'So do not fret on that account. You are acting correctly in continuing to offer them hospitality and refuge from the anger of others. Yet I find your guests most intriguing, Abbot. I shall certainly return to question them further.'

'Well,' the abbot replied, rising to escort his guests to the door, 'I would keep a careful watch on Brocc, for what he has tried once, he might try again.'

'Even with his wound?' asked Eadulf.

'A flesh wound, soon healing. Brocc is someone who lives revenge. And he has a friend, a smith called Gobnuid at Rath Raithlen. Gobnuid was among those who tried to attack the abbey. The two might plot some mischief.'

'Gobnuid? I seem to have heard that name but I can't place it. No matter. We shall take heed of your warning, Abbot Brogán,' Fidelma assured him.

Accobrán was waiting outside for them but there was no sign of Brocc, who had apparently departed back to his brother's mill.

The hour was growing late when they left the abbey and Fidelma decided that it was not worth while making a further journey across the valley to find Goll and his son Gabrán. It looked as though Accobrán was thankful for this, for he excused himself almost immediately they returned to the fortress and headed towards the stables. It was not long before they saw him ride out.

Eadulf wanted his evening wash immediately. He had grown used to the Irish custom of having a bath every evening, although it had taken some time, for he had found it strange both to wash in the morning and then to bathe in the evening. Fidelma decided to stroll around the rath by herself before having her own wash. While the October day was gloomy and growing dark, it was still early and there were sounds of activity through the fortress. She could hear the smash of metal against metal that showed that some of the forge workers were still hard at work, and a thought stirred in her mind. She made her way towards the sound, which came from a group of buildings towards the back of the rath.

A smith was busy shaping a metal pot in the glowing charcoal of a fire, holding the tongs in one hand while the other pounded the soft metal with a flat hammer. A few people were passing by and now and again someone would acknowledge him, but he would only grunt a reply without looking up. He did not look much like the way one might imagine a smith. He was a thin, wiry individual, with fox-like features. But the thin arms and torso, the taut muscles, belied strength greater than his appearance suggested. His glistening body was clad in a sleeveless leather jerkin and breeches.

Fidelma stood and watched him, admiring the dexterity of his work. She waited until he turned to plunge the pot into his water bucket before speaking. She had to pause for the hiss and cloud of steam, which arose as the metal cooled, to evaporate.

'Good evening, smith.'

He glanced at her and tossed his strands of sandy hair back from his face. In spite of his thin, foxy appearance, his expression was pleasant. His bright blue eyes were close set in a deeply tanned face which enhanced their colour and made them appear brighter than they were.

'Good evening to you, lady.'

She raised an eyebrow. Usually strangers addressed her as 'Sister'. That he called her 'lady' implied knowledge.

'You know who I am?'

The smith grimaced pleasantly. 'Doesn't everyone in the rath know that you are a *dálaigh* and sister to the king at Cashel?'

Fidelma sighed. She supposed it was natural that everyone would know the reason for Becc's journey to Cashel and the identity of those with whom he had returned.

'You are working late, smith,' she commented.

'I had need to finish this pot for Adag the steward. But I am done now.'

He took out the cold metal from the water barrel, placed it on the shelf, and began to return his tools to the rack.

'When I was here many years ago as a young girl, there were numerous forges working in this rath,' Fidelma reflected. 'There do not seem to be so many now.'

The smith smiled briefly.

'Not so many,' he agreed. 'Our mines used to make this rath one of the great metal-working centres of the kingdom. First the gold ran out and then the silver and now there is little left. There is still a lead mine over at Dún Draighneáin. That's but a short ride from here.'

'I hear that copper and iron are still produced in fair quantity,' Fidelma pointed out.

'Indeed, lady, but not enough to bring the Cinél na Áeda back to the prosperity they once had. Our gold and silversmiths used to turn out work for the High Kings in distant Temhair but they do so no more. I started out as an apprentice to a silversmith. We turned out many a bejewelled chalice for the abbeys in the district. Now, I shoe horses, and turn out ploughshares and metal pots.' He grimaced towards his forge with a wry expression. 'Ah, if only someone would find another rich gold vein or a silver mine . . . but that's a forlorn hope.'

Fidelma laughed softly.

The smith frowned with curiosity.

'What amuses you, lady?' he demanded.

'Today I came across two small boys sitting in the river . . . what do you call it? The Tuath? The boys were panning for gold.'

The smith shook his head. 'A child's game, no more. There's been no gold found in that river since our chieftain's father was a small boy.'

'Well, they did tell me that one of their fellows had found a gold nugget there.'

The man glanced up in surprise.

'Who found such a thing?' he asked sharply. 'Did they say?'

'The name of the child? They called him Síoda.'

The smith was chuckling grimly. 'Of course, it would be young Síoda.'

'Do you know him?'

'I know him well enough. He's the son of Becc's shield-bearer. In fact, it was only a few days ago when the young scamp came running to me proclaiming that he had found gold and asked me to buy it from him.'

He suddenly turned and reached up to a shelf and took something down. Then he held out his palm towards Fidelma. A piece of metal the size of the top of a man's thumb. It glistened with a yellow tinge.

Fidelma frowned.

'It looks like gold,' she hazarded.

'Iron pyrites. It is not worth anything.'

'Fool's gold?'

The smith nodded appreciatively at her knowledge. 'Fool's gold, indeed, lady. I gave Síoda something to assuage his disappointment. So I wish the two lads you saw the best of luck, but they may sit there until the crack of doom and not come near to finding a grain of gold in that river, nor anywhere else round here.'

'Until the crack of doom . . .' sighed Fidelma reflectively.

The smith turned for a moment as his forge fire began to hiss, some manifestation of the coal causing a blue flame to shoot out of it. Fidelma seized the moment to pick up a sharp implement and scrape at the metal and examine the golden glint the scratch caused. As the smith turned back to her, she handed it back to him.

'It is a shame that the Cinél na Áeda have fallen on lean times,' she said. 'But metal apart, this is a rich land and the people will not starve. You have trees in abundance, well-watered fertile soil, and some good grazing. Also you are only twelve miles from the seaport at the house of Molaga.'

'True enough, lady,' agreed the smith, replacing the metal on his shelf. 'People have to adapt to new conditions, for nothing lasts for ever. We have a saying: even the road to Temhair has turnings and twists.'

Fidelma smiled appreciatively. Then she became serious as she remembered the purpose of her exploration of the rath.

'There is no need to tell you why I am here, smith.'

'No need at all,' agreed the smith. 'Becc brought you here to investigate the strangers at the abbey.'

The word he used for 'strangers' was actually a legal term – *murchoirthe*, which literally meant one thrown up by the sea. It was an interesting term for the smith to use as it also implied that the person so referred to was one who might have been a criminal beyond redemption who had been punished by being set adrift on the sea and subsequently washed ashore. Everyone had previously used the term *deorad* or outsider, which was also a legal term but implied that the outsider had a legal standing. Fidelma hid her interest at the smith's choice of word.

'So, do I take it that you believe Brocc is right when he accuses these strangers?'

'Have you spoken with Brocc?'

'Of course.'

'And have you seen the strangers?'

'I have.'

The smith shrugged indifferently as if he had made a case.

'So what is your conclusion?' prompted Fidelma.

'They are not men as we know men. They are alien and ugly to us. Like the nocturnal animals, they are dangerous being let loose near our womenfolk at the full of the moon. Brocc's word is good enough for me. They should be driven from our land or punished for what they have done. Only Becc's interference saved them. Oh yes, lady, I admit that I was one of the crowd that went to the abbey to demand their punishment and visit it upon them if no one else would.'

Fidelma pursed her lips in disapproval. 'Then you must know, smith, that your action is not condoned in law. What if you had killed or injured the strangers?'

The smith laughed and his prejudice was made clear.

'A *murchoirthe* is without an honour price in law. Brocc told me that much. So there would be no fine or compensation to pay.'

'Indeed? Brocc should have told you that the abbot had taken the strangers in and given them hospitality. In law, therefore, the strangers are judged as having half the honour price of the abbot.' She glanced at his forge. 'I doubt whether your forge would raise the amount of compensation.'

She turned angrily away. Her anger was directed at the blind prejudice that the smith had displayed. She was about to storm away when she hesitated and turned back to the man. She realised that her anger was as destructive as the prejudice itself. She should be able to understand the origin of his prejudice and by that understanding seek to overcome it instead of allowing her anger to increase his righteous belief in his cause.

'What is your name, smith?'

'Gobnuid,' he replied defiantly.

She had begun to suspect this was his name, having remembered what the abbot had told her. It was ironic that she had met him when she merely wanted to ask any smith about the possibility of gold in the area.

'Then heed some advice, Gobnuid. Let not fear of that which is different create hatred in your soul. Hatred is but a weak man's vengeance for being intimidated and made fearful by what he does not understand.'

She still felt anger but now controlled it and made an effort to keep her voice even. Anger was going to be no way to discover truth at Rath Raithlen, and there was enough anger, hate and prejudice here without adding to it. She remembered where she had first heard Gobnuid's name. It had been from Sirin the cook.

'I believe that you knew Sirin's niece, Ballgel?'

The smith shrugged.

'Who did not know her in Rath Raithlen?' he responded. 'We are a small community.'

'Indeed you are. I have heard that there was some friction between you.'

Gobnuid stared at her in annoyance. 'Who says this?'

Fidelma's eyes fell on his nervously clenching hand. 'Is it not true then? You asked her to dance at the feast of the Blessed Finnbarr and she refused. You were angry and displayed your anger to all there.'

The smith's mouth compressed into a thin line. 'It was not anger at the girl. It was anger at those silly youths with whom she consorted. They decided to mock my age and looks because I dared asked her to dance with me. My anger was aimed at them.'

'So you felt no animosity to the girl when she refused?'

'I was upset to hear of her death. I had warned her that the night sky could be treacherous.'

Fidelma stared at him.

'What makes you say that?' she demanded.

'Ballgel and the others, they were all going to Liag who filled their minds with silly tales of the moon and the stars. Brocc told me that Escrach was so full of Liag's silly stories that she was going to consult with the strangers.'

Fidelma tried to hide her amazement. 'Consult them about what?'

'About the powers of the moon. Liag told Escrach that the strangers had the power of knowledge and knew many things of the moon's properties. That is why I believe the strangers should be driven from here.'

Fidelma swallowed hard. So Liag knew about the Aksumites' interest in star lore?

'Tell me, Gobnuid. You say that Liag taught star lore to Ballgel and to Escrach. Who else did he teach it to?'

'To many over the years. Even I often went to sit and listen to his stories.'

'So boys went as well?'

'Even Accobrán our tanist,' agreed the other. 'But remember that the strangers had the power of knowledge and knew many secrets of the moon. That is evidence enough for me that there was evil afoot in the abbey.'

Fidelma shook her head. 'Not evidence at all. Remember that, Gobnuid the smith. Remember, I am concerned only in getting to the truth. Let no one try to pre-empt the decision of my investigation, otherwise the law will be made clear to them and the punishment will fit their transgression of it.'

She had walked a short distance from the forge when some instinct made her glance back. Gobnuid was apparently examining something in his hand with a frown of concentration. It sparkled in the glinting light of the forge fire. It was the nugget that he had told her was iron pyrites. Fidelma turned and hurried away.

Eadulf glanced up as Fidelma entered the guestroom. He had already bathed and dressed ready to attend the evening meal in Becc's feasting hall.

'You'll have to hurry,' he began and then saw her expression. 'What has happened?'

'I have just had an interesting conversation with a smith called Gobnuid. There is certainly fear and prejudice against the strangers in this community. I fear that it will not be enough to exonerate them to say that there is no evidence that they are guilty. It must be demonstrated that they are innocent.'

'Do you really think that they are innocent?' Eadulf demanded.

Fidelma looked sharply at him. 'Thought has nothing to do with it. Where is the evidence?'

Eadulf's eyebrows rose at her sharp tone. 'I would reserve my judgement on their innocence or guilt until I have heard all the evidence. So far there are many questions that remain unasked, let alone unanswered.'

Fidelma compressed her lips for a moment and then slumped on the bed, realising that, perhaps, she was being too sensitive. Of course, Eadulf was right. Was she now beginning to see prejudice where there was none?

'The Aksumites as good as admitted that one of them was on the hillside that night,' went on Eadulf. 'The fact that Brocc could not identify which one of the three is no absolution of guilt. It is, however, an admission of lying and why do people lie? Only when they have something to hide.'

Fidelma sighed deeply. 'You are right, Eadulf. I am sorry if I was sharp. It is a matter that we must deal with in our search for the truth. But blind prejudice is something I cannot deal with.' She rose suddenly as she realised the growing lateness of the hour. 'I must bathe. Go to Becc's hall and tend my apologies. Say that I shall be there directly.'

Chapter Eight

It was after they had broken their fast on the next day that Fidelma decided that they should find Goll and his family. This time she told Accobrán that they would travel by horse because the previous day's walking had been quite exhausting. While the distances had been short, the hilly terrain and small woodland paths had been tiring. The young tanist went off to arrange for their horses to be saddled. While he was doing so, Fidelma and Eadulf took the opportunity to examine the high watchtowers that marked the gates in the triple ramparts of the fortress.

'Impressive,' Eadulf commented as he peered up at the constructions.

Impulsively, Fidelma suddenly made for the doorway to one of the towers.

'Let's climb up and see what view we can gain of the terrain,' she called over her shoulder. 'It will help us get a good perspective of the countryside about.'

With a suppressed groan, Eadulf followed, for he was the first to admit that he had no head for heights. Inside the wooden tower, ladders ran from floor to floor, and Eadulf counted five levels before they emerged on a flat roof. It was bathed in the soft October sun. Eadulf blinked nervously at the scene that unfolded below him. The woods spread like vast carpets of green in all directions, criss-crossed by silver lines that marked the run of rivers through the valleys. And faintly to the north and west he could make out the distant shadows of mountains.

'A beautiful countryside,' Fidelma was saying, stretching languorously in the early morning sunlight. Although it was autumn, the sun was growing quite warm. Eadulf could feel it through his clothing. He stood nervously near the hatch through which they had ascended rather than venture to the edge of the tower where Fidelma stood looking down towards the territory they had traversed yesterday. Whether he looked down or whether he looked outwards across the hills from this high point, Eadulf felt an uncomfortable sensation. It was a sense of losing his balance; that he would fall off the earth into the void of the sky. He felt the sweat stand out on his brow.

Fidelma had not noticed his discomfort and appeared to be making calculations of distance as she surveyed the wooded countryside.

'Come and see, Eadulf,' she urged. 'No wonder there are so many names of places in this area with the word *garran* in them.'

Eadulf tried to concentrate, to focus on what she was saying rather than the dizzy view beyond.

'*Garran?* What does that mean?' he asked absently, knowing full well its translation.

'A wood of small size or an avenue through trees,' replied a male voice at his feet. It was a thin, wiry man with a thatch of sandy hair, whose head and shoulders had appeared through the hatch.

Fidelma swung round and her eyes widened a fraction as she recognised the smith named Gobnuid.

'Exactly so. In your own Saxon tongue, Eadulf, you have the word *gráf*, I think.' She pronounced it 'grove'. 'It means the same thing.'

Eadulf, nodding, was attuned to the hostile glance that she gave the newcomer.

'The land of groves. It seems appropriate.'

'I have been sent to tell you that your horses are ready, lady,' Gobnuid announced, having climbed onto the roof to join them. 'Accobrán the tanist is waiting below for you.'

'Thank you,' Fidelma said, her voice distant. 'We were admiring the beautiful countryside around here. It certainly is best seen from this high vantage point.'

'None finer,' the smith agreed, glancing around as if examining the landscape for the first time.

'In what direction is the *bothán* of Goll the woodcutter?'

'To the south-west, beyond the Thicket of Pigs and across the river.'

Fidelma glanced towards the dark green of the treetops that spread across the hills in the direction Gobnuid had indicated.

'It appears that it will be a pleasant ride,' she observed.

The smith nodded absently.

'Perhaps it is time you should be leaving, lady? Accobrán is waiting below,' he repeated.

'Perhaps you are right,' replied Fidelma softly.

'After you, lady.' The smith stood aside from the hatch.

Eadulf said quickly: 'I'll go first.' In truth, he was glad to leave this high, unprotected place. Without awaiting a reply, he climbed onto the ladder, hoping that Fidelma would not observe his haste to be gone, and began to descend. Fidelma followed him with the smith bringing up the rear.

Eadulf was halfway down the first ladder when he felt the rung on which he had placed his foot give way with a sudden crack. Had his fear not been making him hold the ladder so tightly, the surprise of the breaking rung might have precipitated him off the ladder and could have sent him tumbling the five floors down the ladder well. For an eternity he hung by his arms, his feet waving into space as they sought for a support.

He lowered himself a rung by his arms, and his foot finally found the support of the rung below the one that had snapped.

'Are you all right, Eadulf?' came Fidelma's concerned voice from above him.

'I've been better,' Eadulf breathed after he felt secure. 'One of the rungs snapped under my foot. Come down carefully, I'll guide you over it.'

He waited until she came further down the ladder.

'Right,' he called. 'The next rung is now missing. Lower yourself by your hands and feel for the next rung.' He paused as she did so. 'That's it. Your foot is on the rung. Come on down.'

Fidelma did not do so at once. As she passed over the broken rung, reaching it at eye level, she paused and examined it carefully while Eadulf stood impatiently on the landing. As she came down level with him, she asked anxiously: 'Are you sure that you are all right?'

He nodded. 'I'd better lead the way down again.' He smiled. 'There could have been a nasty accident. The wood snapped.'

Gobnuid came down quickly to join them. He looked nervous.

'Accident?' He picked up on the word. 'I think you are right. Some of the wood is rotten and in need of replacing.'

Eadulf glanced from Gobnuid to Fidelma with silent curiosity. He could sense something of the tension between them. Accobrán was waiting outside the tower when they emerged. He saw that something was amiss.

'What happened?' he demanded.

'One of the rungs was rotten,' replied the smith almost defensively. 'No one is hurt.'

'Eadulf was lucky that he had a good grip,' added Fidelma, 'otherwise things might have been different.'

Gobnuid vanished towards his forge and Fidelma saw the look of anger on Accobrán's face as he looked after the smith. It seemed that he was on the point of following him, but a stable lad brought forward their horses.

'What made you send Gobnuid up to fetch us?' Fidelma asked the tanist. 'A smith has more important things to do than act as a messenger. The stable lad could have summoned us.'

The young tanist shrugged.

'Gobnuid was here. He had to shoe my mare this morning, lady,' he replied almost defensively. 'He volunteered to run up to get you.'

Accobrán dismissed the stable lad and began to mount his horse. 'Fidelma and Eadulf followed his example and they were soon trotting out of the gates of Rath Raithlen.

It was a pleasant ride along the forest tracks and, as if by mutual agreement, they rode in silence for most of the way. Eadulf was bursting with questions but he knew Fidelma well enough to remain silent when he saw her preoccupied features.

They passed over the wooded hill, the strangely named Thicket of Pigs, and crossed the River Tuath by a ford where the water gushed over a bed of pebbles. Suddenly, in mid-stream, Accobrán halted and pointed to the hills that rose before them. Solemnly, he intoned: 'A forest in full colour. The sigh of myriad leaves whispering to the listening heavens. Even great cities appear as muddy hovels to the venerable shady groves that were old before the first brick was placed on brick.'

Fidelma was startled out of her silence because the verse Accobrán had just recited was in Greek.

'I did not know you spoke Greek,' she commented.

The young tanist shrugged. 'A little of Greek, Hebrew and Latin, for I spent some years at the house of Molaga thinking to become one of the religious before I realised that my hand was better suited to hold a sword than a stylus. I spent some time serving my uncle Becc in the campaigns to prevent the Uí Fidgente raids on our territory.'

'And thus you were elected tanist, Becc's successor?'

'Ten months ago,' confirmed Accobrán with a smile. 'Now, while Becc enjoys the prestige of chieftainship, I enjoy the hard work of riding through the territory to ensure that order is kept and no one has cause to complain.'

Fidelma glanced at him with a slightly raised eyebrow. 'Do you resent that?'

'Resent? Accobrán seemed surprised at the idea. 'Of course not. That is the task I undertook. When I am elderly, and I am chieftain with a tanist, it will be his task to do as I do and my reward to do as Becc does. That is in the way of things. Brother Eadulf, there' – he indicated Eadulf with a nod of his head – 'does not resent the tonsure he wears. He would not have become a religious if he did not want to wear the garb and perform the duties that go with the job, would he? No more do I resent the duties that are incumbent on me as tanist.'

They continued on their way through the dark woods, climbing steadily along the forest pathway through the thickly growing trees.

A loud shout from nearby caused them to abruptly rein in their horses.

There came the sound of something being struck, a crack, and then an awesome tearing noise. It was as if a mighty army was coming crashing through the trees. The horses shied nervously and Eadulf, not the best of horsemen, nearly took a tumble. He managed to regain control more by desperation than with skill.

'What the devil . . . ?' he began. 'Are we under attack?'

Accobrán was laughing and he patted his horse's neck to calm its nervousness.

'Not the devil, Saxon. It is just a tree being felled nearby. By law, the *gerrthóir*, the woodcutter, must give a cry of warning before the tree falls.'

The sound of an axe biting into wood now came to their ears.

'Through here,' called Fidelma, guiding her horse expertly in the direction of the sound.

They soon emerged in a clearing where a young man was working on a newly felled holly tree, hacking at its branches. He paused as he saw them, straightened up. He was scarcely out of his teenage but handsome, tanned with fair hair and blue eyes. He seemed to carry an air of boyish innocence with him. As he examined them and recognised Accobrán, a frown crossed his features.

'I did give a warning cry,' he said defensively.

Fidelma halted her horse before him and smiled down at his belligerent features. He was hardly more than eighteen or nineteen years of age.

'So you did,' she replied pleasantly.

The young man shifted uneasily, axe held loosely at his side. He stared at Fidelma and Eadulf with a glowering, suspicious look.

'Don't worry, Gabrán,' called Accobrán, moving his horse alongside Fidelma. 'We are not here to remonstrate with you.'

Gabrán glanced up at the tanist and Fidelma noticed that his suspicion gave way to a momentary expression of intense dislike. Then he seemed to control his features into a mask of indifference.

'What is it you want, Accobrán?' His voice was icy. Fidelma realised that there was no friendship between these young men. Then Gabrán's gaze suddenly returned to Fidelma and his eyes widened. 'You must be the king's sister – the *dálaigh* of whom people are talking.'

'Who talks about the *dálaigh*, Gabrán?' asked the young tanist in irritation. 'More importantly, what are they saying? It is not courteous to gossip about the sister of the king.'

When the boy answered he spoke to Fidelma and not to Accobrán. 'It is only the usual gossip.' He was guileless about protocol. 'We were in Conda's *bruden* last night and we heard about the *dálaigh*'s arrival.'

'Conda's tavern is by the little fort on the other side of that hill,' the tanist explained with irritated embarrassment as he raised a hand to indicate the direction. 'The Hill of Crows, we call it.'

'Well, such talk is natural.' Fidelma smiled. She was no great believer in meaningless etiquette. 'It would be amazing if my arrival was not talked about. So,' she looked down at the young woodcutter, 'there should be no need to explain why I have come to see you and your parents.'

The young man frowned again. 'No need to explain why you should come to see me. Doubtless, Lesren is still making terrible accusations about me. But why do you have to bother my mother and father? They have suffered enough from his vile tongue.'

'I simply need to clarify some matters, that is all. Is your *bothán* near here?'

'Not far. The track here leads up to a standing stone and you have to turn across the hill. Our place is a short distance away.'

'Then let us proceed there, for the sooner we have talked, the sooner we can resolve matters,' Accobrán suggested. 'Swing up behind me, Gabrán, and it will save you a walk.'

He reached down one arm but the young woodcutter shook his head.

'I have my tools to collect and bring with me. It is more than my life is worth to leave them lying about in the woods. My father would flay me.'

'Then we will wait until you are ready,' Fidelma announced. 'Your father is right. Tools are valuable. Sometimes tools are more precious than gold. Is that not so, Accobrán?'

The tanist sniffed disdainfully. 'I know nothing of the value of an artisan's tools. My tool is this!' He clapped his hand on the hilt of his sword. 'That, certainly, is precious.'

Gabrán lost no time in gathering his tools in a leather bag, which he then slung across his shoulders. He turned back to the horses but hesitated.

'There is more room behind Eadulf,' suggested Fidelma diplomatically. 'He is not laden with a warrior's accoutrements.'

The woodcutter took Eadulf's extended hand and swung up behind him within a moment. Leading the way, Accobrán allowed his horse to walk along the path through the woods. A standing stone stood where the track turned at a right angle and began to rise more steeply up the hill.

They soon came upon a large wooden building which appeared to be the home of Goll the woodcutter. Piles of logs and stacks of newly cut timber and and planking stood around the clearing in which the *bothán* was constructed. There would have been no need to ask the occupation of the person who dwelt there.

A woman appeared at the door and then called to someone behind her. She stood aside and a man took her place, bearing a strong resemblance to Gabrán. The youth swung down from Eadulf's horse and walked swiftly towards them.

Fidelma and Accobrán dismounted. Eadulf followed and took the reins of all three horses, tying them to a stake set in the ground for just such a purpose, before joining them before the door of the *bothán*, where Gabrán had already explained who his companions were.

'You are welcome here, lady. I am Goll, the *gerrthóir*. This is my wife, Fínmed. We have heard that you have come at the behest of our chieftain, Becc, and we have heard why you have come. Nevertheless, I believed that Lesren's outrageous claims had long been disproved and that suspicion now lay with the strangers at the abbey.'

'Lesren continues to voice his accusations against Gabrán,' replied Fidelma calmly, 'and it is my duty to hear and judge the merits of all accusations and the evidence for and against.'

'But the Brehon Aolú said . . .'

Fínmed moved forward nervously with a warning glance at her husband to still his protest.

'Will you and your companions come into the *bothán*, lady, and take a little mead with us? Then the facts may be discussed in more comfortable conditions than on the threshold.'

Fidelma gave her a look to show her appreciation. Fínmed had a pleasant face. She was still a handsome woman but what was more appealing than simple regularity of feature was the gentleness and kindness that could not be disguised in her eyes and around the corners of her mouth.

'You are very kind, Fínmed. We are pleased to accept your hospitality.'

Goll's wife conducted them inside and seated them before a pleasant log fire while she fetched the jugs of sweet honey mead.

'Now, lady,' she said, after they had all savoured the first mouthful, 'how can we help? You must know that there is enmity between Lesren and our family. You must also know of what passed between us before Aolú gave judgement.'

'I have heard the story and that is why I wanted to meet all of you to clarify matters,' replied Fidelma. 'I should like you to tell me how you perceive the causes of this enmity.'

'Easy enough,' Goll said roughly, trying to disguise his obvious irritation at being reminded of the events. 'It goes back to the time when my wife Fínmed was wed to Lesren. The man was a beast. He beat her and she divorced him.'

Fínmed pursed her lips, glanced at Fidelma and nodded. 'It is true. The man was drunk most of the time. He beat me and so I left him.'

'I understand that you were awarded compensation and left the marriage with you *coibche*?' Fidelma said.

'That is so.'

'My wife was also entitled to the *tinól*, which she took, and the *tinchor* which she refused to claim,' Goll pointed out.

The *tinól* was a kind of wedding present to the bride from her friends, of which two thirds went to the bride and one third to her father. If the bride was at fault, the husband could claim the bride's share. The *tinchor* was the bride's wedding portion of household goods, considered as a joint property. These awards clearly demonstrated that the fault for the break-up of the marriage, at least in law, lay with Lesren.

'You claim that Lesren has held a grudge ever since?' asked Fidelma.

'He has.'

'So how did you feel when your son told you that he was in love with Lesren's daughter?'

Goll and Fínmed exchanged a quick glance of embarrassment and then Fínmed replied.

'It would be foolish,' she said, choosing her words carefully, 'to pretend that we approved – at first, that is. We disapproved on principle. Then we met the girl and she seemed untainted by her father's moods. She was a pleasant enough girl who, in other circumstances, we would have been delighted to welcome into our house. We eventually accepted that Gabrán had the right to take his own path in life and so, for his sake, we made her welcome. Then, as I say, she was welcome for her own sake.'

Goll was in agreement. 'It was Lesren who started this feud with me from the moment I married Fínmed. I avoided the man. However, when Gabrán announced his intentions, Lesren really became a nuisance to me.'

'A nuisance?' Eadulf asked quickly. 'In what way?'

Gabrán had been standing silently by his mother. The matter was apparently painful to him. Now he spoke.

'If anyone killed Beccnat, it was Lesren. She hated him and he used her like an animal in the same manner as he used her mother, Bébháil.'

'I presume that when you say Lesren killed Beccnat you are not making the claim literally?' demanded Accobrán, astonished.

'He killed her spirit. He killed her childhood and youth. That is what I mean,' replied Gabrán defiantly.

'Let us come to that later, Gabrán,' Fidelma said. 'In what way did Lesren became a nuisance to you, Goll?'

'He began to spy on me and reported me to Aolú, the Brehon at Rath Raithlen, for felling the ash tree. I know. I was in the wrong. I was fined a *screpall* for the illegal act. I have no complaints as to the judgement. It was the pettiness of Lesren that I felt anger over. That's when my thoughts turned to revenge; I just wanted Lesren to know that two could play at that game. I had heard he was bark-stripping at the wrong time. I set to watch him in the woods and that's when I saw him stripping apple-tree bark during the killing month.'

'And he, too, was fined before the Brehon. Did that bring an end to this childish feuding?'

Goll shook his head. 'Lesren went insane with anger. He tried everything to turn Beccnat from my son. He told appalling stories about my wife.'

'Did you report this to the Brehon Aolú?'

'Of course, I did. Aolú told me to forget it.'

Fidelma looked shocked. 'Aolú, a Brehon, told you to forget that someone was spreading lies about you?' There was an incredulous tone in her voice.

Eadulf was again reminded that verbal assaults on a person were treated with the utmost seriousness under the law. That a judge would advise such assualts to be ignored was the reason for Fidelma's shock. She had already warned Lesren the previous day that his words might be seriously interpreted. A victim's entire honour price might be the fine involved against the person who spread such tales.

'Aolú, the Brehon, told me not to pursue this matter. He said that he would have a quiet word with Lesren and put a stop to it.'

'Did it stop?'

Goll grimaced. 'Lesren lost no opportunity to spread lies and rumours about us.'

'Beccnat was very upset,' interposed Gabrán, who had been quiet since his outburst. 'She told me that life was becoming unbearable with her father, and her mother was too weak to do anything about the situation. Lesren dominated Bébháil. We decided that we would elope.'

Fínmed nodded quickly. 'We supported our son in this matter. It was not illegal.'

'I know,' agreed Fidelma. There were two forms of legal marriage that involved a girl's eloping with a man without the consent of her kin. 'So when was this elopement to be?'

Gabrán looked pained for a moment or so. 'As soon as I returned from the coast.'

'You were at the coast when Beccnat was killed?' enquired Eadulf.

'He was staying at the house of Molaga,' Fínmed said swiftly.

'And Beccnat was in total agreement with this plan?' Fidelma pressed. 'She did not tell you that she had changed her mind? That she no longer wanted to marry you?'

'You have been listening to Lesren,' snapped Gabrán angrily.

'I just want to clarify all the facts,' Fidelma was unperturbed by his anger.

'Everything was well when I last saw Beccnat,' Gabrán said with quiet vehemence.

'And when was that?'

'About two days before the full moon.'

'Why did you go to the coast?'

It was Goll who replied. 'There was a wagon of holly wood that had been bought by the abbot at the house of Molaga. It was specially cut for the new altar that was being constructed in the chapel there. I was going to take it but there was much work to be done here. So Gabrán said he would drive the wagon to the coast. Rather than returning with an empty wagon and the payment from the abbey, he decided to return with some goods that we needed to purchase. The ship with these goods had not arrived and so my son waited a few days until it put into the port. By the time he returned, it was a few days after the full moon.'

'Is that so?' Fidelma demanded sharply of Gabrán.

The young man nodded.

'So you returned – when?'

'Two days after . . . after . . .'

The boy had a catch in his throat and his mother rose from her chair to put an arm round his shoulders.

'And, of course, this was checked when Lesren made his accusation against you?' Fidelma went on, as if ignoring the boy's emotion.

Her matter-of-fact voice seemed to quieten the boy. He nodded slowly.

'Ask Accobrán there,' he replied. 'Aolú asked him to confirm my story.'

'Which I did, as I have already told you, lady,' the tanist pointed out. 'Gabrán was at the house of Molaga over the period of the full moon. Aolú accepted that.'

'Lesren is a beast,' Fínmed interrupted in a slightly shrill tone. 'An evil beast that he would descend so low as to suggest . . .'

Gabrán patted his mother's hand for she was not able to finish. Her voice had choked with emotion.

'Aolú has pronounced that I could not have . . . have done what Lesren claimed I did,' he insisted.

'Nevertheless,' Goll added, 'this evil beast Lesren has continued to spread his lies. Aolú is dead and as you are now acting as our Brehon, I want his mouth closed and compensation paid to me for his wickedness.'

'I am only a *dálaigh*, not a Brehon,' Fidelma pointed out. 'Nevertheless, I hear you. When this investigation is concluded, then action shall be taken against all who have not told the truth.' She turned to Gabrán again. 'I believe that you knew the other girls who were killed – Escrach and Ballgel?'

The youth nodded sadly. 'The Cinél na Áeda is not such a large population that there are strangers among them, lady. I knew Escrach. We were childhood friends and more recently I would often take grain to her father, the miller, for grinding. Ballgel I did not know so well.'

'We knew all the girls and their families,' Fínmed added, a little defensively. 'As my son says, we are not such a large community. Why do you ask?'

'I am wondering if there was some common factor between them as to why they should become victims,' replied Fidelma.

Goll rubbed his chin thoughtfully.

'If you were to ask me, lady, the common factor was that they were alone in the woods at night when the moon was full,' he replied quietly.

'All the mothers of the Cinél na Áeda have instructed their daughters to remain inside their homes during the hours of darkness,' Fínmed said.

Fidelma pursed her lips thoughtfully for a moment. 'A difficult policy when the feast of Samhain is fast approaching and the hours of darkness are getting longer.'

'Apparently, people believe a maniac stalks the woods.' Eadulf addressed himself to Goll. 'Who do you think is responsible for the tragic deaths in these last few months?'

The woodcutter hesitated, staring at the floor.

'You suspect the strangers?' pressed Eadulf quickly. 'Those at the abbey?'

Goll sighed and shook his head. 'I have no knowledge of those strangers. I have heard that Brocc favours the idea that they are responsible. He has been able to persuade others.'

'Others such as Gobnuid, the smith at Rath Raithlen?'

'Such as Gobnuid,' agreed Goll.

'And you?'

'All I know is that there is someone who is . . .'

It took Eadulf a moment to translate the phrase *do bhíodh tinn lé goin an ré* as someone suffering from lunacy; someone affected by the power of the full moon.

'And that someone not being one of the Cinél na Áeda?' suggested Fidelma. 'We are back to the strangers.'

To her surprise, Goll shook his head.

'You have a suspicion who it is?'

'I am not like Lesren. I would not spread a story for the sake of spreading a story. All I know is that it is easy to find a person who forsakes the New Faith, who lives a life following the old ways and thus knows the forbidden names of the sun and the moon. I objected when my son went with the others to learn of such things.'

Fidelma looked thoughtful and when Eadulf, who was puzzled by the woodcutter's words, opened his mouth, she turned and frowned quickly at him. He shut his mouth.

'I understand you, Goll,' she said quietly.

She rose from her seat and the others followed her example.

'Thank you for your hospitality.' Fidelma smiled at Fínmed. 'I am hoping that we will soon clear up this mystery and end the misery that you and your family must be suffering from the stories that Lesren has spread.'

The woman returned her smile sadly. 'I am afraid my son has suffered much for my first mistake.'

'Your first mistake?' Fidelma frowned.

'The mistake was that I ever married Lesren. My excuse was that I was young and innocent and did not realise that youthful handsomeness could disguise a personality that was selfish and brutal. I feel sorrow – not so much for myself, for I have discovered a loving husband now and have a loving son – but for Bébháil. She has to suffer marriage to Lesren and, as an additional curse, she now has to bear the loss of her only child, her daughter Beccnat.'

Fidelma laid a hand on the woman's arm in a gesture of sympathy.

'You have a great heart, Fínmed, that you are able to allow a corner of it to feel sympathy for the suffering of Bébháil. But remember that if life was unbearable for her, she could have done as you did. Divorce is within her power also. So perhaps she is content with her lot with Lesren, for they have been seventeen or eighteen years as man and wife. But, truly, the loss of a child is a great tragedy for any mother, and in feeling sorrow for her on that account I would join you.'

They were riding away, down the slopes of the Hill of Crows, when Eadulf, who had been silent with his thoughts awhile, finally spoke.

'Whom did Goll mean, Fidelma, when you asked about the person he suspected?'

'I have to respect his wishes, Eadulf. He did not wish to name names. But it is a name that has crossed my thoughts and one that I shall keep to myself. For in naming names, you have a power to destroy if it is done in injustice.'

She noticed that a sulky look of irritation crossed Accobrán's features for a moment. Then he asked: 'Where do we ride to now, lady?'

For the first time in the many investigations that she had undertaken, Fidelma realised, with some surprise, that she did not know what her next move was going to be. She had pursued all the obvious avenues and each had led to a dead end. Goll had prompted her about one person she had a passing suspicion of, but it would not do well to approach that person with as little knowledge as she currently possessed. She needed more information first. One thing Fidelma had learned was that alerting someone to your suspicions when suspicion was all you had to offer was to provide them with time and opportunity to lay in alibis and defence. No; she was not going to go down that path yet.

'Lady?' Accobrán was prompting, thinking that she had not heard his question. He was looking sharply at her and in that moment she suddenly realised that she was neglecting to clarify a point that had previously worried her.

'You do not have a friend in young Gabrán,' she observed to the tanist. 'Why is that?'

Accobrán flushed at the unexpected question. 'That is a personal matter.'

Fidelma pursed her lips in disapproval. 'I must be the judge of that, Accobrán.'

'I can assure you—'

'As a tanist,' Fidelma cut in, 'you should know something of the law and the powers of a *dálaigh*.'

Accobrán exhaled swiftly. 'Very well. Gabrán suspected that I was seeing Beccnat behind his back.'

Fidelma raised her brow in momentary surprise. 'And were you?' she said calmly.

The tanist flushed and shook his head. 'Beccnat was an attractive young girl. I believe we danced once or twice at some *féis*, a feasting, but nothing more. I think young Gabrán was jealous, that is all. I have also danced with Escrach and even Ballgel, come to that.'

'And that is all there is to it?' asked Fidelma.

'That is all.'

'You should have told me of your relationship with Beccnat before,' she rebuked him.

'There was no relationship.'

'Except that you knew and danced with her. And Gabrán believes that there was more to it.'

Accobrán gave a snort of indignation. 'There was no more to it.'

'We have already discovered, Accobrán, that more often than not suspicion is a stronger provocation to action than the truth.'

The tanist looked at her with surprise mingled with uncertainty. 'Do you mean . . . ?'

'When I speak I try to make my meaning clear,' she snapped.

There had been silence for a few moments when Fidelma decided that she wanted to speak with Brother Dangila again.

Chapter Nine

Fidelma left Eadulf and Accobrán on the road to Rath Raithlen and in spite of their strenuous protests she proceeded by herself the short distance to the abbey of the Blessed Finnbarr.

'It is midday,' she had pointed out to a perturbed Eadulf. 'What harm can come to me at midday when we are looking for a killer who strikes at the full of the moon and the next such moon is not for some weeks yet?'

Accobrán had agreed with Eadulf's protest.

'I am responsible for your safety while you are in the territory of the Cinél na Áeda, lady,' the young tanist had argued. 'I should stay with you at least.'

'There is nothing for either you or Eadulf to do,' she replied. 'I shall go to the abbey alone and shall return to the fortress thereafter. And, if it mattered, I shall be back well before sunset.'

It was only after some more cajoling of Eadulf and then using her authority over Accobrán that Fidelma found herself alone on the track to the abbey of Finnbarr again. In fact, as soon as Eadulf and Accobrán were out of sight, Fidelma gave her horse its head and nudged the animal into a canter, feeling the cool wind on her face. She smiled in genuine pleasure. She had learnt to ride almost as soon as she could walk and, unlike Eadulf who was still a nervous rider, enjoyed the synchronisation of rider with the muscular and powerful beast. For Fidelma, there was little to match the thrill of a gallop or a canter. She had been so long cooped up in Cashel, confined with her child, that she rejoiced to be out in the open again and feeling free. Fidelma had always been a lover of solitude. Not all the time, of course, but now and then she needed to be alone with her thoughts.

She felt a sudden sense of guilt.

During the last few days she had not thought once of little Alchú. Did that mean that she was a bad mother? She halted her horse and sat frowning as she considered the matter. She remembered something that her mentor, the Brehon Morann, had once said when judging the case of a neglectful father. 'For a woman, giving birth to a child is the path to omniscience.' Ever since the birth of Alchú she had been having disturbing thoughts, thoughts which troubled her because she found she did not agree with her teacher. Fidelma had not felt her wisdom increase nor felt any of the joys that she had been told by her female relatives and friends should have been forthcoming. She felt vexed. It was as if she saw Alchú almost as a bond that ensnared her – a curtailment of her freedom rather than something which enriched her. Did she really desire the sort of freedom that she was now experiencing?

What was it Euripides had said? Lucky the parents whose child makes their happiness in life and not their grief, as the anguished disappointment of their hopes. Why didn't she feel those emotions for little Alchú that she had been told to expect? It was not that she did not care about the child, nor feel anything at all, but she had been told that the birth of her child would be an earth-shattering event, one which would change her. It had not. Maybe it was this lack of the fulfilment of the expectation that was the problem and not the relationship with her baby.

A sudden anger at her own complex feelings came over her and she kicked viciously at her mount's belly and sent it speeding once more along the track. This time she let the horse have its head completely. The wind sent her red-gold hair streaming out behind her and she raised her face into the welcoming coolness with a sensual smile of pleasure. Was it not Brehon Morann who had declared that a gallop on a bright, fresh day was the cure for all the evils that assailed the mind?

It was some time before she eventually decided to halt the animal and turn it, blowing and snorting, to walk gently back along the track, for she had ridden well past her proclaimed destination in her sudden delight at the freedom of the gallop. She was, at least, feeling some sense of equilibrium as she rode towards the gates of the abbey. The subject of her motherhood and her emotions had been dispelled and her mind was now able to concentrate on the matter in hand.

As she approached the track to the abbey, under the shadow of the hill, she was suddenly aware of a lumbering great wagon being pulled by two horses making its slow progress down the track towards her. The man hunched on the driver's seat seemed very familiar. She frowned for a moment and then recognised him.

'We meet again, Gobnuid,' she called.

The smith scowled as he drew abreast of her. Fidelma glanced at the wagon. It seemed packed with hides.

'Transporting hides does not seem a task for a smith,' she said. 'You appear to be doing several jobs that are unsuited to your profession – messenger and now wagon driver.'

Gobnuid shrugged his broad shoulders. He did not rise to her sarcastic bait.

'I take on whatever tasks there may be when there is no work for the forge,' he said sourly.

'Where do you sell the hides?' she asked.

'They eventually go down to the coast, to the house of Molaga or to the abbey of Ard Mhór where they make leather goods.'

'You are taking them all the way there?'

'I am only taking them to the Bridge of Bandan. From there they will go by river boat to the house of Molaga on the coast.'

It struck her as odd that his usual reticence had given way to a desire to answer her questions.

'Do they fetch a good price?'

Gobnuid pursed his lips sourly. 'Whether they do or not, my fee for transporting them is the same.'

'So they are not your hides?'

'I am a smith, not a tanner.'

Fidelma was curious. 'So you are transporting the hides for Lesren?'

Gobnuid gave a gruff laugh. 'Not for Lesren. I would do little for that son of a . . .' He paused. 'No, these hides belong to my lord Accobrán. Now, I need to be on my way.'

He flicked the reins and the cart began to move off, leaving deep tracks in the mud of the road. Fidelma stared at the tracks for a moment or two and then turned her horse again towards the abbey. She wondered why Gobnuid had been forthcoming with information. It was unlike his previous attitude and she was certain that he had been responsible for the so-called accident on the ladder that morning. She had not told Eadulf but she had clearly seen the way a sharp knife had cut into the rung of the ladder. There was no rotten wood there. The rung had been almost severed so that it would break under any heavy weight.

Brother Solam came to the gate to meet her as she swung down from her horse. She noticed that he had been standing with another religieux who had the dust of travel on him and had the reins of his horse still looped over his arm. The youthful steward of the abbey greeted her respectfully.

'If you seek Abbot Brogán, Sister, you will have to wait awhile. He has gone to his cell to meditate. At such times, we are not allowed to disturb him.'

'Then do not do so, for it was not the abbot that I particularly wanted to see,' she replied.

Brother Solam was frowning over this when the other religieux left his horse and came quickly forward. There was a smile of greeting on his owlish features. Fidelma could not place him. He was a dark, lean-featured man.

'Sister Fidelma? Fidelma of Cashel?' the man asked. Even before Fidelma affirmed the fact, the man continued: 'I am Túan, the steward of the house of Molaga. I was at the abbey of Ardmore when you were staying there last year. I don't suppose you remember me . . . ?'

Fidelma rejected the polite impulse to say that she did. It interested her to hear that the man was from the house of Molaga.

'Have you just arrived?' It was asking the obvious but she wanted to deflect from talking about an unremembered previous meeting.

Brother Túan indicated that he had. 'Brother Solam was just telling me of the problems here and that you had arrived to resolve them.'

Fidelma decided that her original purpose in coming to the abbey could be delayed a moment or two longer and she glanced about. In the courtyard was a bench under an apple tree, conveniently by the warmth of the abbey blacksmith's forge. She indicated it.

'Let us sit there awhile, for I would seek your opinion, Brother Túan.' She turned to Brother Solam with a bright smile. 'Will you forgive us, for a moment?'

Still frowning, Brother Solam was clearly unhappy. But he simply said: 'I will attend to the needs of Brother Túan's horse. Do you want me to stable your own mount?'

'There is no need. I do not plan to stay long.'

Brother Túan and Fidelma seated themselves on the bench beneath the shade of the shrub-like tree with its spiny branches. There was still fruit on it.

'I suppose you have heard some details about what has been happening here?' Fidelma asked without further preamble.

The steward of the house of Molaga grimaced. 'They say that there is a lunatic abroad, Sister. One who strikes at the full of the moon.'

'And do you know that a young woodcutter named Gabrán has been accused by the father of one of the victims?'

'That was found to be false,' replied Brother Túan immediately. 'You must have been told that on the night of that murder, at the full moon of that month, the Month of Greenflies, this youth Gabrán was staying at the house of Molaga?'

Fidelma smiled at the confirmation. 'And you can personally confirm that?'

'I can indeed.'

'Can you be so sure?'

Brother Túan thrust out his chin, a little defensively. 'I am the *rechtaire*, the steward of the abbey, and it is my duty to know and record what passes from day to day. Would I not know the month and the full moon? I remember well that moon and I remember well the young boy's stay because, and I tell you this in confidence, Sister, two of our brothers had to carry Gabrán back to the abbey. He had been found drunk and senseless in a dockside tavern. It seemed that it was his first time away from his parents and he had fallen in with bad company. It had been fortunate that he had left the money the abbey owed his father in our keeping until he started for home. He was robbed but, thanks be to God, he did not lose much.'

Fidelma was thoughtful. 'He did not tell me this story when I saw him this morning and questioned him with his parents.'

Brother Túan grinned broadly. 'Are you surprised? I imagine that he would scarcely have told his father and mother. A young man's foolishness. He will learn by it. I have told you this in confidence only to assure you that I can fix the date in my mind as to when young Gabrán was at the house of Molaga. He arrived in the daytime and that evening of the full moon he was drunk. I would not wish the young man to get into trouble with his parents but, as steward, I recorded the events for our records. However, you may be assured that there is no way that Gabrán could have been anywhere near where the girl was killed on that night.'

'Thank you for this information, Brother. I will keep the young man's secret. Has Brother Solam also told you about the suspicions held of the three strangers here?'

A dark frown crossed Brother Túan's features.

'Tales have reached us at the house of Molaga about this,' he confirmed.

'I am told that these strangers first sought refuge at the house of Molaga.'

'Sought refuge? That is not entirely accurate. A slave ship foundered in a storm off our coast. Parts of the ship came ashore in the mud flats in the tidal estuary below the abbey. Some fishermen found the three strangers manacled to one another and attached to a spar. They were more dead than alive. They were fished out of the mud flats at low tide and brought ashore to our abbey.

'As fate would have it, some of our community have a good knowledge of Greek and this was the only language we had in common with the three strangers. Communication was established and we found that they were religious followers of the Christ from some far-off land – a place called Aksum.'

'Were there any other survivors from the ship?' Fidelma asked.

'A few. They were mostly Franks and they immediately took service on a Frankish merchantman which was in the bay.'

'You offered the strangers refuge?'

'We did so. We released their manacles and nursed them back to health, for they had clearly been badly treated. They stayed awhile with us, learning something of our language and telling us about their country and how the Faith reached them. Our scriptor took down many of the things they told us and, in return, they questioned him about our land, our culture and our learning. We even had some artefacts from their country. Some silver crucifixes which our abbot gave them as gifts to commemorate their safe delivery from the sea.'

'I understand that they have become very interested in the work of Aibhistín of Inis Carthaigh.'

Brother Túan smiled slightly. 'When they heard about the work Brother Aibhistín had done on the moon and its effects on the tides, they became very excited. Indeed, they seemed to find it impossible to concentrate on any other subject. Brother Dangila, in particular, was fascinated by the work relating to the studies of the moon and the stars. He devoured a lot of the works we had, such as Abbot Sinlán's chronology and the astronomical tracts of Mo Chuaróc of Loch Garman.'

'I believe that Brother Dangila was told that it was here, at the abbey of Finnbarr, that Aibhistín's work on the moon and tides was kept?'

Brother Túan surprised her by shaking his head. 'No one at the house of Molaga told Brother Dangila that for the simple reason that no one there knew. We all knew of Aibhistín's work but no one knew where the manuscript was kept.'

'How did Brother Dangila learn of its whereabouts then?' queried Fidelma.

Brother Túan rubbed his jaw thoughtfully. 'I suppose it must have been from Accobrán.'

'The tanist?'

'The same. I did not realise that he was knowledgeable on such matters, though, of course, he had studied for a time at Molaga. He is a good man. A fine warrior. Without the likes of him the Uí Fidgente might have asserted their power over Cashel a long time ago and the Eóghanacht might have been destroyed.' Brother Túan suddenly flushed. 'I mean no disrespect to your brother, Sister.'

Fidelma raised a shoulder and let it fall in a quick shrug. 'It is well known that the Uí Fidgente have plotted for many years to gain power in this kingdom. They have often made attempts to displace the descendants of Eoghan at Cashel. There is nothing disrespectful in telling the truth. But what were you saying about Accobrán?'

'Accobrán was staying at the house of Molaga some ten weeks ago, just about the time of the feast of Lughnasa . . . no, let me show you that I am precise as to days, for I know that as a *dálaigh* you require precision. It was the day after the feast when Accobrán arrived at our abbey. He met the strangers and spoke with them several times and the next thing I knew they announced that they had decided to come here to the abbey of the Blessed Finnbarr to continue their studies of the astronomical manuscripts. They left for this place soon after Accobrán returned here. He must have been the one to tell Brother Dangila the manuscript was here.'

'A few days after the feast of Lughnasa? And some days later the first slaughter of a young girl, Beccnat, took place,' muttered Fidelma reflectively.

Brother Túan looked uneasy.

'Are you saying . . . ?' he began.

Fidelma made a motion with her hand. 'I am merely contemplating the facts, Brother Túan, and that is a fact. Tell me, what do you think of the strangers? I mean their general demeanour and so on.'

'Think?' Brother Túan shrugged. 'They certainly have a profound knowledge. They are polite and considerate. They are aloof and keep themselves to themselves. I would not say that they are easy to get to know. It is easy to find prejudice against them.'

'Why so?'

Brother Túan looked unsettled. 'Well, they are so different from us.'

'You speak of the blackness of their skins?'

Brother Túan made an affirmative gesture.

'Let us forget the colour of their skins and judge them as we should judge everyone – on the content of their character.'

'It is well said. Would that everyone were capable of rising above their fears of things and people that are different. I only say that this is the reason why people will judge the strangers harshly: because of their fear.'

'Say they were strangers but, in appearance, no different from us. What would you say of them then?'

'Intelligent, learned, but hard to get near. There is an aura of suspicion about them. Their fixation on star lore makes them subject to further suspicion in the light of the conditions surrounding the killings here.'

Fidelma did not mention that Brocc had claimed he had seen one of the strangers sitting gazing at the moon on the night that Escrach was killed or that the strangers had refused to identify which of them it was. That was the thing that made Fidelma suspicious of the strangers and, indeed, brought her back to the reason why she had come to the abbey.

'Thank you, Brother Túan. You have been most helpful.'

She rose from the bench and he with her.

'I am pleased to do whatever I can to help.'

'Will you be staying here long?'

'A few days. I have come bearing letters from my abbot to Abbot Brogán. I shall have to wait for answers before returning to the coast.'

He bade her farewell and went off to the main building of the abbey. Fidelma caught sight of Brother Solam walking back across the courtyard. She waved him forward.

'I have finished with Brother Túan,' she began.

The young steward interrupted her before she could go further. 'I am glad, Sister. I had need to speak with you.'

Fidelma was slightly puzzled at the man's apparent coyness. 'About what matter?'

'Why, the matter that you are investigating.' He glanced round in a conspiratorial way. 'It is this matter of the full moon that worries me.'

'Why would it worry you, Brother Solam?' she asked, guiding him back to the spot that she and Brother Túan had vacated and motioning him to be seated next to her. 'Come, speak what is on your mind.'

'Well, there has been much talk about the strangers, and claims that they might be attracted to the night skies and the moon . . .'

'And it is the strangers that you wish to speak of?'

To her surprise, Brother Solam shook his head. 'Not. I am afraid it is of someone who is close to our chieftain, Becc. And I tell you this in confidence. I would not like it to be known that I have told you.'

Fidelma pursed her lips. 'Brother Solam, I cannot make any promises to you. If you have material evidence of wrong-doing . . .'

Brother Solam shook his head.

'It is not that, not that,' he said quickly. 'It is no more than a report of suspicious behaviour.'

'Well, if it turned out to lead to the guilty party then your anonymity could not be maintained. You would be called to appear before a Brehon and take an oath to support your evidence.'

Brother Solam was silent for a while and then he nodded slowly. 'It is something that does not allow me to rest easily and I must tell you or live with a feeling of guilt. I have tried to keep this secret to myself but am unable.'

Fidelma struggled to keep her patience in the face of the moralising tone of the steward. 'Very well. Proceed with your story.'

Brother Solam paused for a moment or two before continuing. 'It was when the moon was at its fullest last month. It was the night that Escrach was killed. I was returning to the abbey across the lower slopes of the Thicket of Pigs. It was approaching midnight. In fact, as I came along the road I heard the chime of the midnight Angelus from the abbey bell.'

'What took you out so late?'

Brother Solam leant forward confidentially. 'I have a brother who lives over at the Pass of the High Wood, not far from here. I had permission that day to go to visit him. That I did and I was late returning.'

'Very well. Go on.'

'As I came along the road, I saw a figure approaching. That is, the figure was heading up the hill.'

'And did you identify this figure?'

'Of course. It was Escrach.'

Fidelma started. Of the people she expected Brother Solam to identify, she had not anticipated the name of Escrach. She had been sure that the young steward was about to confirm that he had seen Brocc crossing the hill.

'Are you saying that you saw Escrach at a time which must have been shortly before her death?'

Brother Solam lowered his voice in affirmation. 'That is why I have kept it to myself all these weeks.'

'Did you speak to one another?'

'Of course. I asked her what she was doing so far from her home and so late at night. She laughed at me. You know how insolent the young can be? Then she told me not to worry for she knew where she was going and whom she was meeting. Those were her very words.'

Fidelma waited while the steward paused and appeared to sink into his own thoughts.

'What then?' she prompted after a few moments.

Brother Solam raised his head. 'Oh, then she went on her way, up the old track.'

'Up the old track? Up the hill? Which led where?'

'The old track eventually leads to the cave complex on the top of the hill. Only I presume she did not make it for I understand that her body was found below that, near a stone circle we call the Ring of Pigs. If only I had stopped her.'

'Much power in that word "if". You might not have been able to prevent what followed. Tell me, did you see anyone else – did you see Brocc, for example? Or anyone else?'

117

'Brocc?' The steward was clearly startled. 'What would he have been doing on the hill?'

'Or anyone else?' repeated Fidelma.

Brother Solam nodded quickly. 'And that is what troubles me.'

Fidelma regarded his expression closely.

'Whom did you see?' she asked sharply.

Not for the first time in the conversation, Brother Solam leant towards her in a conspiratorial manner. Fidelma could smell a faint odour of onions on the man's breath and moved slightly backwards in distaste.

'You must promise that you will treat this information with prudence.'

Fidelma compressed her lips in irritation.

'I treat all information with prudence,' she replied. 'But you must realise how important this information is. You are speaking of someone who, if not the killer, may have been the last person to see Escrach alive.'

Brother Solam raised an arm in a curious gesture as if attempting to apologise. 'You see, it is a matter that has caused me disquiet and I would like what I have to say treated with caution, in case of misinterpretation.'

'Leave interpretation and circumspection to me. If the information warrants their use than I will judge how and when they should be used. Now what is this thing that causes you such anxiety?'

'Escrach had left me and continued up the old path. I continued down the hill on my way towards the abbey.'

'I am following,' Fidelma said when the man paused again.

'I was nearing the abbey when I heard the sound of a wagon coming along. The moon was bright and I could see the dark bulk coming up the track. I do not know what made me turn aside from the path and seek shelter among the trees that lined the pathway. I think it was the sight of one of the two men who were seated side by side on the driver's seat.'

'What sort of wagon was this?'

'It was a normal *fén*, a common rough wagon with solid wheels drawn by two oxen. Why do you ask?'

'Detail is everything, Brother Solam. You tell me that you see a cart and hide from it. Something disturbs you. What is this cart like? Does it have solid wheels or spoked wheels?'

'I told you, it had solid wheels.'

'Exactly. And solid wheels indicate that the owner might not be as wealthy as someone with a spoke-wheeled wagon. You have described a wagon that is quite ordinary. And you said that it was the sight of one of the two men that made you hide from its passing?'

Brother Solam nodded. 'I did not recognise the passenger. I admit that. But I did recognise his robes.'

'Robes?'

'The man was one of the three strangers who reside in the abbey.'

Fidelma blinked. It was the only sign she gave that she was surprised by the revelation. So, Brocc had been right. One of the strangers was out on the hillside that night.

Brother Solam was continuing: 'I saw the white robes that the Aksumites wear and noticed that the man was tall and his features were dark.'

'And you say that he was a passenger on this wagon? Who was driving the wagon?'

'This is what causes me disquiet.'

Fidelma stared at him. 'The sight of one of the guests from your abbey abroad that night on this wagon did not disquiet you? But you express disquiet at the sight of the driver. Who was that driver? Tell me plainly.'

Fidelma's angry expression caused Brother Solam to swallow hard and then continue hurriedly.

'The driver of the wagon was the tanist.'

Fidelma's eyebrows shot up. 'Accobrán?'

'Indeed, it was the tanist Accobrán,' affirmed the steward.

There was a silence for a few moments and then Fidelma gestured for Brother Solam to go on with his story.

'As I say, I was disturbed and this was the reason I did not make my presence known. What was the stranger doing abroad in the night? What was Accobrán doing at that hour driving a common wagon in which the stranger was a passenger? These questions assailed my mind. As the wagon approached, it being a clear night, I overheard snatches of their conversation. They spoke in Greek. The strangers seem proficient at that language and it is the language in which we communicate with them in the abbey.'

'You speak Greek?' asked Fidelma, resorting to that language.

'I can construe Dio Chrysostom, Hippolytus, Diogenes Läertius, Herodotus of Halicarnassus—' he replied in the same tongue.

Fidelma interrupted his recital. 'And what did you hear of this conversation?'

'The stranger was saying that the signs were auspicious. That as the daughter of Hyperion and Theia had power over that night, so would she cast her spell over Endymion once more.'

'And did you know what was meant by that?'

'I know only the Greek of the Christian texts. What was being referred to was some pagan concept to which all good Christians should shut their ears.'

'Presumably you did not shut your ears?'

'Accobrán replied that while Selene dominated the night there was much work to be done, for soon Eos would interrupt their labours and the sacrifice of the night must be made before that time. That was all I heard because the wagon went by and disappeared up the hill in the direction in which Escrach had gone.'

'You know what Selene represents?' queried Fidelma.

'I know that she was the goddess of the moon among the pagan Greeks.'

'Indeed. Selene was the daughter of Hyperion and Theia and she was the moon goddess. Her sister was Eos, goddess of the dawn. Selene fell in love with Endymion, the human king of Elis, and rather than watch him wither and decay she caused him to fall into sleep in a cave so that he would remain for ever young.'

Brother Solam stared at her in awe. 'I do not have your learning, Sister. Yet I knew that they were talking about the moon that night.'

'What then?' prompted Fidelma. 'What did you do?'

'Then I returned to the abbey.'

'You did not report this to the abbot, nor tax either the strangers or Accobrán to find out what they had been doing?'

'I did not.'

'Yet the very next day, Escrach was found murdered on that hill. When that news reached you, why did you not report this matter to Abbot Brogán?'

Brother Solam shook his head. 'I am a coward, perhaps. But how was I to be certain that my own life was not in danger if I revealed what I had seen and heard that night? Feelings have been running high against this abbey and its brethren. I could not reveal that I was alone on the hill or spoke with Escrach that night. If a stranger was involved in her slaughter and I came forward as the only witness, perhaps my life might be forfeit to them. Then there is the fact that Accobrán was driving the wagon and talking of the work they had to do by the light of the moon. He was the one who talked of "the sacrifice of the night". I remember his words clearly. I might not have your knowledge of the literature of the Greeks but I know the language well enough.'

Fidelma sat in thought for a moment and then sighed. 'You have been most helpful, Brother Solam. I will keep what you have said between us until I believe it can prove useful. I will not repeat our conversation to anyone except Brother Eadulf who assists me. I can vouch for his discretion. Dismiss any anxiety that you have.'

Brother Solam looked relieved and broke into a speech of gratitude but Fidelma cut him short by holding up a hand and rising from the seat.

'Thank you for being so honest, Brother Solam. Now, I wished to have another word with Brother Dangila.'

'Brother Dangila?' The steward stood up, looking uncomfortable. He glanced nervously about him. 'I said I did not recognise who the stranger was that night.'

'It is not about your story that I wish to see Brother Dangila. I came to see him on another matter.'

Brother Solam continued to look worried.

'I do not know . . .' he began.

'Is there a problem?' Fidelma asked, puzzled by the look of guilt on his face.

Brother Solam licked his lips nervously. 'Brother Dangila is not here.'

Fidelma examined the man closely. 'Not here? Where then?'

'Brother Dangila insisted that he needed exercise and demanded permission to leave the abbey for a walk.'

'If I recall correctly, Abbot Brogán had ordered that the three strangers should remain within the walls of the abbey until matters were resolved. People have tried to kill him and his companions because they think that they were responsible for the killings here. If nothing else, Brother Dangila's life could still be in danger if he is found wandering the countryside. It was your duty to prevent the stranger's putting himself in the way of harm.'

Brother Solam grimaced helplessly like a small child being told off unjustly. 'I did try, Sister. But it is hard to argue with Brother Dangila. He insisted on taking a walk.'

'Was the danger properly explained to him? You should have told me immediately. If Brother Dangila is found alone and unprotected . . .' Fidelma lost no more time but turned to where she had left her horse. 'Which way did he go?' she called as she mounted up.

'He has often gone to the hillside there,' Brother Solam said, pointing to the shadowy Thicket of Pigs rising above the abbey. 'He has often . . .'

But before the words were out, Fidelma had mounted and sent her horse into a canter along the path from the abbey and through the woods up the hillside track in the direction the steward had indicated.

It was simply irresponsible on the part of Brother Solam to allow the man to wander on his own, especially in view of what had recently happened. Such lack of thought infuriated her. She gave the horse its head and allowed it to follow the ascending track through the trees, climbing the hill at its own pace. She found that the trees quickly thinned and soon she emerged on the bald bluff not far up the slopes. There were some boulders there, grey stones, as if some ancients had hauled them there with the intention of building a stone circle but then abandoned the idea, leaving the stones lying in confusion, the circle half finished. She saw Brother Dangila immediately, a tall still figure seated on one of the stones, his chin resting on a cupped hand, the elbow balanced on his knee. He seemed to be staring into space.

However, he turned at the sound of her blowing mare as it clambered upward towards him. He rose and awaited her. His features were impassive.

When she slid from her horse, he greeted her in his accented Irish. 'Blessings on you, Fidelma of Cashel.'

'It is not wise to be out alone, Brother Dangila,' she replied in Greek without preamble. 'The people are still afraid and we are no closer to resolving the matter of culpability. You should not have strayed beyond the boundaries of the abbey.'

Brother Dangila inclined his head gravely.

'I thank you for your concern, Fidelma of Cashel,' he replied, now using Greek. 'The God of Solomon will watch over me. I do not fear.'

Fidelma looped the reins of her horse around a small shrub, turned to one of the stones which lay lengthwise and seated herself. The tall Aksumite resumed his previous position and regarded her without curiosity.

'The abbot gave me assurance that you would not wander abroad from the abbey so that your safety would be guaranteed until this matter was resolved.' she said irritably.

'Is it solely in concern for my safety that you have come seeking me?' he asked. There was a faint smile on his lips, which seemed to imply a hidden knowledge. For a moment, Fidelma felt awkward. Her eyes suddenly focused on his white woollen robe.

'You are not wearing your beautiful silver crucifix today,' she observed.

Brother Dangila's hand went immediately to his neck. He hesitated and then he nodded gravely. 'I must have left it in the dormitory. Have no fear. It will be safe, for I believe I know where I left it. As I said, is it concern for me that has brought you hither?'

'It is true that I wanted to speak to you anyway. So much was left unsaid when we last spoke.'

An eyebrow lifted in interrogation was the only motion of the man's features that indicated a reaction.

'Are these the stones called the Ring of Pigs?' she asked.

'I believe that is the local name for them,' replied the other gravely. 'The stones do look like a litter of piglets around a sow.'

'And this is where . . . ?' She left the question unfinished.

'So I am told.'

She waited a few moments and when the man did not speak she asked: 'Do you often come to sit on this hillside and meditate?'

'It is in the nature of my people to contemplate the works of the God of Solomon from whose seed my people descended,' replied Brother Dangila. 'Is it not written in the Book of Psalms – "When I look up at Thy heavens, the work of Thy fingers, the moon and the stars set in their place by Thee, what is man that Thou should remember him?"?'

The words of the psalm sounded beautiful in his Greek.

'So you come at night to look upon the moon and the stars?' she countered quickly, trying not to get diverted.

Brother Dangila glanced at her with a smile. 'You have a quick mind, Fidelma of Cashel.'

'I presume that you were the one seen by Brocc that night?'

'Have I admitted as much? Whoever Brocc saw, he must identify. Until he does, there is no more to be said.'

'He is not able. You know that as well as I. What troubles me is that Escrach's body was found close by here the next day, and before that the body of a girl called Beccnat.'

'I give you my word that I did not kill them,' came the quiet tone of the other.

'Let us make a hypothesis then.'

'Which is?'

'Brocc concludes that someone sitting looking up at the night sky was probably doing so for a sinister purpose, especially on the night of the full moon, and especially on the night when a young girl, his niece, was killed.'

'What stirs this man Brocc's thoughts is that which is within him,' replied Brother Dangila. 'I am not responsible for what thoughts he has.'

'You might contend, though, that there is another, innocent explanation. Let us continue to hypothesise and see what innocent explanation there can be.'

The Aksumite reflected for a moment in silence and then shrugged.

'Let us say that the man might have been someone like myself, sitting gazing at God's creation, and measuring the stars in their journeying across the heavens. His concern was what happened in the sky and not what happened on the earth. He might argue that he heard and saw nothing and, after a while, he went his way – in innocent ignorance of any evil-doing.'

'You and your comrades are much concerned with the passage of the stars across the heavens?'

'It is an ancient science, Fidelma of Cashel. Your people are adept at it, or so we have discovered. It may be – and we shall continue to hypothesise,' he interspered with a smile, 'it may be that what we have read in your ancient books, we might like to check with the practicality of the star map that God provides at night.'

'Were you always a contemplative religieux?' she asked abruptly.

For the first time the features of the Aksumite dissolved in a broad grin.

'I was thirty when I decided to join the religieux and thirty-three when I was enslaved and sent to Rome.'

'What were you before?'

'I worked in the great gold mines – King Solomon's mines.'

'Gold mines?'

'In the shadow of Ras Dashen, our highest peak,' confirmed Brother Dangila. 'It was from Aksum that the great treasure temples of Solomon were supplied and King Solomon's fabulous wealth was accumulated. Menellk, the son of Solomon by the Queen of Sheba, became our ruler. Our mines still supply the wealth of Aksum. My father was a mineworker and I followed him in his work. But I was not satisfied, and from one of the Holy Fathers who lived on the slopes of Ras Dashen I learnt more than how to spot a rich vein of gold or copper. I learnt Greek and a few words of Latin and I read some of the holy texts. I left the mountains and went to Adulis and the rest I have told you.'

Fidelma was thoughtful. 'I would like to know exactly how all three of you decided to come to the abbey of Finnbarr.'

'I thought I had told you. The answer is simple. The abbey holds the works of your scholar Aibhistín and we wanted to study them, having seen references to his work in other tracts.'

'Indeed, you have told me this before. How did you know that they were here?'

'At the house of Molaga we learnt much about your culture and the fact that you, too, were fascinated by the courses of the stars in the heavens. Exactly as I say, we saw references to Aibhistín's work. By some happy coincidence, a man from this place was staying in the house of Molaga and we spoke with him. It was he who persuaded us to come to the abbey.'

'Oh? Was it one of the religious from the abbey?' She decided to test out what Brother Túan had told her.

'It was not,' Brother Dangila said at once. 'It was the young man . . . the prince, I forget what you call him in your own language. Accobrán is his name.'

'He told you that the works of Aibhistín were held in the abbey?'

'He did. We owe him much for that information. They are fascinating works, especially the tables on the moon and the tides. I have never seen another treatise that concisely explains the tides in relationship to the phases of the moon.'

Fidelma exhaled softly.

'You seemed troubled, lady,' remarked Brother Dangila astutely.

'If young girls had been slaughtered in your land, Brother Dangila, in the way they have been slaughtered here, would you not also be troubled?'

The tall man inclined his head.

'It is of little use to you, lady, but I would take an oath by the power of the Ark of the Covenant, which shelters in the nameless holy place of my land . . . I would take an oath that my comrades and I had nothing to do with these terrible killings in this place. Yet I would say that in my own land, we, too, would be suspicious of strangers in similar circumstances.'

'An oath is of little use. While I might believe you the people here do not.'

'They are fearful because the colour of our skin is different.'

'More important, it is because you are strangers to this place and people are afraid of strangers. Are your own people, in Aksum, not afraid of strangers?'

'Perhaps some are. Aksum stands at a crossroads of many cultures and many religions, lady. We have learnt to live in harmony with most of our neighbours whatever they look like and whatever language they speak or whatever god or gods they follow.'

'That surely sounds like an ideal place to dwell,' agreed Fidelma, a little sarcastically. 'Yet if you have learnt to live in harmony with all your neighbours, how is it that you were taken, with your fellows, and sold as slaves?'

Brother Dangila shook his head with a slight smile. 'Even in the Garden of Eden there was a serpent.'

'There is much wisdom in your words, Brother Dangila.'

'We are taught in the sayings of Solomon that there are seven things the Lord God hates: a proud eye, a false tongue, hands that shed innocent blood, a heart that forges thoughts of mischief, feet that run swiftly to evil, a false witness telling lies, and one who stirs up quarrels between brothers.'

'Words of wisdom are meaningful in any language,' agreed Fidelma.

'One cannot be responsible for the dark thoughts of all one's brothers and sisters. There are many in Aksum and along the seaports trading in human cargoes. Many owners of slaves are members of the Faith. In our world, Sister, there are many ways of becoming a slave. Sometimes people sell their children to escape debts. Then some people sell themselves into slavery to escape the insecurity of life or to seek a position in life. I was unlucky. My companions and I were kidnapped. Unfortunately we were in the wrong place at the wrong time. However, a bishop of the New Faith in Rome bought us.'

'Ah, and he tried to set you free?'

Brother Dangila laughed uproariously. 'He was a slave owner. No freedom for us. He preached the words of Paul of Tarsus to us. "Every man should remain in the condition in which he was called. Were you a slave when you were called? Do not let that trouble you but, even if a chance of liberty should come, choose rather to make use of your servitude." He only decided to sell us to the Frank when we became too rebellious and attempted to strike for liberty. Perhaps you would like to see our backs where the leather whip lacerated us for our impertinence in believing that we should be free men?' He acknowledged Fidelma's momentary look of distaste. 'I will not inflict the sight on you, Fidelma of Cashel. It is my cross to bear. As I have already told you, that is why we were on the high seas bound for some God-forsaken place called Frankia when the ship foundered and we found refuge on your shore.'

Fidelma was sad. 'While our law refuses to allow men and women to be bound in servitude, transgressors often lose the rights to be as free men and women. Sometimes, unscrupulous merchants have been known to gather up people and sell them overseas to where the use of slaves is the way of life. I have been to the Saxon kingdoms, to Rome and even to Iberia, so I have seen something of the world beyond these shores. It is not a good world.'

'You would do well to remember that this land is not separated from the rest of the world but shares the sins of humanity in equal proportion,' commented Brother Dangila drily.

Fidelma smiled wanly. 'Well spoken, Brother Dangila. You are right, and you remind me of our frailty and, indeed, of my task. Let us return to the hypothesis that we were discussing.'

'I will not change my views.'

'I do not ask that. I am simply going to work on the hypothesis that it was you that Brocc saw. You see, Brocc was not the only person abroad on this hillside that night who will be called to witness.'

Brother Dangila regarded her with a stony expression. 'Let that witness also come forward and make identification. If so, we may drop this game of hypothesis for I was told that a Brehon only went by what was a proven fact.'

'Let us say that I am speculating. I also speculate that your defence would be that you were merely looking at the stars out of your interest in such matters.'

'As you please.'

Fidelma turned in seriousness towards him. 'Then let me add this warning, Brother Dangila. If my speculation is found to be false in any point then I can become as a bolt of lightning striking a tall oak. No matter how tall the oak, lightning can be a powerful force. I think you understand me.'

'You have made it clear, Fidelma of Cashel. You are a woman of firm belief and courage. I admire you for it.'

Fidelma was about ask why Brother Dangila had been in Accobrán's wagon when there was a sudden cry from the edge of the woods. The next moment, a horse bearing Accobrán, sword in hand, came bounding out of the trees. A second horseman was following close behind. Eadulf was maintaining his seat with difficulty.

Brother Dangila sprang up. To Fidelma's surprise, the tall Aksumite made to place himself before her in a protective attitude, ready to defend her from the attack.

'Wait!' cried Fidelma, grabbing hold of Brother Dangila's hand in which a sharp throwing knife had appeared. Then she shouted to the oncoming tanist. 'Put up your sword! Stop, I say!'

Accobrán drew rein, slid from his mount and stood, sword still in hand, ready to threaten Dangila. Eadulf came to a halt beside him and half tumbled, half dismounted from his own horse.

'What does this mean, Accobrán?'

'Are you all right, lady?' demanded the tanist.

'Of course I am,' replied Fidelma in annoyance. 'What are you doing threatening Brother Dangila with your sword? Sheathe it, I say. I am in no danger.'

Accobrán's eyes were filled with suspicion.

'How long have you been here with Brother Dangila?' demanded the tanist, still not obeying.

Fidelma shook her head. 'Long enough to have a talk.' She glanced at Eadulf, who had recovered his composure and now came to her. 'Eadulf, can you explain this behaviour, since Accobrán will not?'

Eadulf had relief etched into every feature of his face as he grasped her hand.

'We were worried for your safety . . .'

'Why? I do not understand. Did I not tell you that I would be safe?'

'Lesren has been found . . .' Eadulf hesitated as if trying to find the right words.

'Been found? For God's sake, explain!'

It was Accobrán who finally answered. 'Lesren the tanner was found a short time ago. His throat has been cut.'

Chapter Ten

After Brother Dangila had been escorted back to the abbey, Fidelma accompanied Eadulf and Accobrán to the tannery of Lesren by the banks of the river. It was Eadulf who cynically pointed out that Fidelma might have come on Brother Dangila after he had killed Lesren. The hill overlooking the abbey was but a half-hour's walk from the tannery where Lesren's body had been discovered.

'I do not discount any fact, Eadulf,' Fidelma replied, 'but why on earth would Brother Dangila want to kill Lesren?'

Eadulf opened his mouth and then, as he thought about the question, shut it.

'The death of Lesren would be a significant development,' Fidelma said, after a pause.

'I do not understand, lady.' Accobrán was frowning.

'If the killing of Lesren is part of this pattern of killings, then we must reconsider our popular theory.'

Seeing their incomprehension, Fidelma motioned to the blue autumnal sky above them.

'When was the body found?' she asked.

'A little after midday.'

'And when was Lesren last seen?'

'Just after the noon meal and . . . oh.' Eadulf cut himself short and then sighed. He flushed in embarrassment. 'His death could not be ascribed to any lunatic killing. It is out of sequence with the killings at the full moon.'

'Exactly so.'

Eadulf suddenly hit his balled fist into the cupped palm of his other hand as a thought struck him. He forgot he was on horseback and the horse shied nervously as the movement tugged on the reins. He struggled to bring the animal under control.

Fidelma regarded him with amusement.

'Gabrán! The boy had good reason for killing Lesren. There is the possibility that, after our visit this morning, Gabrán might have been so angry that he went to have it out with Lesren.'

The thought had already occurred to Fidelma. The boy had certainly been angry that Lesren was still accusing him of the death of Beccnat.

Accobrán seemed impressed. 'I think Brother Eadulf's suggestion is worthy of investigation.'

'Certainly, nothing should be discounted,' Fidelma said. 'But we know that Lesren's accusation was false, so Lesren's death is not part of the pattern of killing.'

'I suppose that motive can be ascribed to Fínmed as well,' sighed Eadulf as he thought more about the matter. 'All three, Goll, Fínmed and Gabrán, felt an anger and hatred towards Lesren which might be a motive for this crime.'

'On the other hand, there may be no connection with any of these matters at all,' Fidelma reminded him. 'We must consider this development very carefully. But, as yet, I have heard no details at all. You have still to tell me how you came by the knowledge of Lesren's death.'

It was Accobrán who explained. 'After we left you, we had just returned to the fortress when one of Lesren's workers came to find me. It was he who reported the matter. So we rode to check whether it was true. Lesren's body was at the edge of the woods just behind the tannery. Seeing that we could do nothing further for the man, thinking that you might be in danger, we came straight away to find you.'

'And the man who found the body?'

'We left him looking after it and rendering what comfort he could to Bébháil, Lesren's wife.'

They had joined the road which stretched along the riverbank and came once again to the collection of wooden buildings that constituted the tannery of Lesren. The drying hides were still stretched on the frames about the buildings but there was no sign now of anyone working at the framing or the dyeing.

'Where is the body?' Fidelma demanded, as they halted outside Lesren's *bothán*, and dismounted.

Accobrán indicated the edge of the wood. Even before he spoke, a man appeared from the cover of the trees and waved to them.

'That is Tómma, Lesren's assistant. It is he who reported the death and he whom we left looking after it,' the tanist explained, waving back to the man.

'Am I to presume that Tómma left the body unattended when he came to tell you at the fortress?'

'He told us that he and Creoda had discovered it and then he called Bébháil. She said she would stay with the body while Tómma came to the fortress to find me.'

They left the horses hitched to the rail outside the main building and Accobrán led the way towards the waiting man.

'Where is Bébháil?' asked Fidelma, glancing quickly around. There was no sign of the woman. Accobrán shrugged by way of reply.

As they neared Tómma, Fidelma saw that Lesren's body was lying on its back by the edge of the trees. It was stretched out in repose as if waiting for burial. In fact, it was clear that someone had carefully laid Lesren's body out on the grass, straightening the limbs and folding the arms across the chest. Indeed, as Fidelma peered closer she realised that the corpse had already been washed.

Fidelma suppressed a hiss of irritation. She knew that clues could have been destroyed in the process. She glanced angrily at the man who stood there.

'Did you do this?' She indicated the body and then, realising that her question was open to misinterpretation, she added: 'Did you lay the body out and wash the limbs?'

Tómma was a man of about the same age as Lesren but with curly black hair. He looked surprised at her question and shook his head rapidly.

'Not I, Sister. It was Bébháil who did this.'

'You should have stopped her,' admonished Eadulf, who realised what was passing through Fidelma's mind. 'Where is she now?'

'Resting in the *bothán*,' Tómma replied. 'The woman was in shock and it would be pointless to rebuke her for ministering to her dead husband.'

'You were right to treat her gently, Tómma, but this makes my task the more difficult,' Fidelma said with a tightness in her voice which showed that she was still annoyed. She bent down and began to examine the corpse. There was little she could tell at first glance.

'Do you recall how the body was lying when you first came upon it, Tómma?' she asked. 'And how did he die? In fact, what were the circumstances of your finding his body?'

The man shuffled his feet uneasily. 'It was just after midday. There was only drying to be done and Lesren had sent most of the other workers back to their homes. That was the last time I saw him alive, Sister. I went home but I was to return this afternoon to help Lesren and Creoda take the bigger skins down from the frames—'

'Creoda? What is his position?'

'He is one of the young workers at the tannery. I called at his cabin on my return here, so we came together. Lesren was nowhere to be found and so I went to his *bothán*. Bébháil was there but said she had not seen her man since the midday meal. Creoda and I went looking around to see if we could find him.'

'And you did?'

'We found him.'

'And he was dead?'

Tómma hesitated and looked unhappy. 'Not quite.'

Fidelma raised her head to look squarely at him. 'You mean that he was alive?'

'He was dying and delirious.'

'Did he say anything?'

The man hesitated again. 'He was muttering something. All I heard was the name Biobhal.'

Fidelma frowned. 'Biobhal? Not Bébháil? Was he asking for his wife?'

'He was not. The name was clearly Biobhal. I remarked on that to Creoda, for Lesren died while uttering it. I know of no one by that strange name.'

'Where is this Creoda, by the way?'

'He returned to his *bothán*.' Tómma paused and gestured apologetically. 'Creoda is barely eighteen years old and lives nearby. I suppose with what has happened he was naturally fearful, and . . .'

'No matter. We will see Creoda later. Where may we find him?'

Tómma indicated with his hand. 'Westward, along the river track. His *bothán* lies back in the trees about twenty-five yards from the river. If you head in that direction, you can't miss it.'

'Very well. Now, where was Lesren lying when you found him?'

'He was just here by these trees. He was lying there but in a more untidy fashion. The legs spread out, one under his body. The arms stretched out – so.' He demonstrated with his own arms.

'And, when he had muttered this name that you say you do not recognise, you knew that he had then died?'

The man considered for a moment. 'I was fairly sure. Blood was everywhere. Creoda had run off. So I went to fetch Bébháil. She told me to run to the fortress.'

'When did she start to clean the body?'

It was Eadulf who answered Fidelma. 'When we left Tómma and Bébháil, she had not begun.'

The assistant tanner nodded. 'Liag told her that she could do so after the tanist and this brother had ridden off to bring you here.'

Fidelma was genuinely startled. 'Liag the apothecary? Was he here? How does he come into this drama?'

She glanced at Eadulf and Accobrán but their astonished looks gave the answer to her question. Liag's arrival was news to them.

'As soon as the Saxon brother and our tanist had left, Liag came out of the woods and examined Lesren,' explained Tómma. 'He instructed Bébháil to begin the funereal ministrations.'

Fidelma almost cursed the apothecary under her breath. 'And she did so?'

'As you can see.'

'You do not know when Liag arrived here?'

Tómma shrugged. 'All I know is that I was here alone with Bébháil when he appeared from that woodland path and that was after the tanist and the Saxon brother had left.'

Fidelma found herself having to undo the clothing of the corpse in order to make her examination. It became obvious that Lesren had been stabbed several times, judging from the wounds about the neck and chest. The jagged wounds spoke of a frenzied attack with a blunt knife. The wounds were not the clean cuts which one might expect from a hunting knife or – the thought came unbidden into her mind – a physician's scalpel. Lesren had been stabbed twice in the back of the neck, once in the throat and once in the chest.

She stood up and shook her head slowly. It was useless trying to learn anything further from the corpse. Fidelma gave only a cursory glance around but it was obvious that there were no signs of the discarded weapon or any other significant item, and too much movement had taken place after Lesren's death for there to be any meaningful clues.

'Let us find Bébháil,' she said. 'You'd best stay here, Tómma. Make sure that no one does anything further with this corpse until I say so.'

When they were out of earshot of Tómma, Accobrán moved to her side and said with quiet vehemence: 'Upon reflection, there are only a couple of real suspects in this case. I think I should go to apprehend them.'

Fidelma glanced at him, knowing what was in his mind but wishing him to make his thoughts clear. 'Who may these suspects be?'

The tanist gestured in impatience. 'As we have already discussed, lady. Who but Goll or his son Gabrán? Having heard how Lesren still accused Gabrán, and the hurtful contempt in which he held that family, I know what I would do if I was filled with youthful pride and anger.'

'What you might do does not mean that someone else has done it.'

'I believe the killer of Lesren will be found at the woodcutter's homestead.'

'You may well be right, Accobrán,' agreed Fidelma. 'However, I shall conduct my investigation in my own way, adhering to the priorities that I have set.'

They found Bébháil sitting in a chair before her hearth. She looked up, dry-eyed but with pinched, strained features, as they entered. Then she turned her gaze back to the embers of the fire.

'It is sorrowful to me to be in life after Lesren has departed from this world,' she muttered.

Her voice was wooden, without feeling. Fidelma glanced at her companions and motioned them to withdraw, for she felt it best if she talked to the widow by herself. When they had done so, she seated herself opposite the woman.

'Bébháil, I am sorry to ask these questions, but if we are to find the killer of Lesren, then they must be asked. When did you last see your husband?'

The woman stared at her for some time as if not recognising her. It took several times of asking before she formed a proper answer. Lesren had had his midday meal and gone outside to continue his work. Some time later, Bébháil did not know how long, Tómma had called to say he and Creoda were looking for Lesren. They had gone off to search. Then Tómma had returned with the news of their discovery. She had stayed with the body while Tómma had gone to find Becc or Accobrán at Rath Raithlen.

Fidelma listened intently as the woman confirmed Tómma's account.

'Where was Liag during this time?' she asked quickly.

Bébháil blinked. 'The apothecary?'

'He was here, wasn't he?' pressed Fidelma.

'He came after the tanist had ridden off with your Saxon companion.'

'How was that?'

'Tómma and I were with the body when Liag suddenly emerged from the woods nearby. There is a small footpath that comes through the woods near where Lesren was found.'

'Where does the footpath lead?'

'Up to Rath Raithlen, to the fortress.'

'Did Liag seem surprised to see the body?'

'Surprised?' The woman frowned and gave a quick shake of her head. 'Liag never expresses surprise.'

'What did he do?'

'He examined Lesren and said that he was dead. Then he told me that I ought to lay out the body before the limbs grew cold. That I should prepare the body for the funereal rites.'

Fidelma's lips thinned. 'So it was on the specific instructions of Liag that you washed and prepared the body?'

'It was.'

Fidelma wondered what had motivated Liag. Had he purposely set out to destroy evidence or had he done so from ignorance? She tried to put the questions to the back of her mind because there would be no answers until she spoke to Liag.

'During the time between Lesren's leaving the *bothán* and the finding of the body, did you hear or see anything unusual?'

Bébháil shook her head. 'I knew nothing until Tómma called me.'

'You were not aware of anyone else here or around the tannery during this time?'

'No one.'

'Have you any idea who might have done this?'

Bébháil regarded her with large, dark eyes.

'My husband was not a man who was well liked, lady,' she said softly. 'You must already know that he had several enemies. However, I will not lift a finger to point in any direction.'

Fidelma was quiet for a moment or two. Then she said, 'Have you ever heard the name of Biobhal spoken? It sounds very similar to your own name, I know. But it seems your husband was calling it out when he died.'

Bébháil frowned and shook her head rapidly.

'There is no one in these parts who has such a name,' she said simply. 'Biobhal? Are you sure that he was not calling out my name?'

'Tómma was sure and apparently Creoda also heard it.'

'I know of no such name, lady.'

Fidelma gave her a smile of reassurance. 'I have done with my questions. Can I do anything for you, Bébháil? Can you call on anyone to come and be with you? Is there anyone who is able to make the funeral arrangements for you?'

'I have a sister who lives nearby. Tómma will fetch her for me.'

Her voice was low and measured and still without emotion. Fidelma rose, reached forward and laid a comforting hand on the woman's shoulder.

'I will ask the tanist to do so. Tómma should stay here until your relatives arrive so that you are not alone.'

'Alone?' Bébháil sighed. 'Ah! Let the days of lamentation begin for my man was alive and now is dead. Cry and clap your hands and sing the *Nuall-guba*, the lamentation of sorrow.'

'It shall be done with all ceremony, Bébháil,' Fidelma assured her solemnly in answer to the ritual instruction of one who has suffered the death of a near one. She called for Accobrán to come in to receive instructions from Bébháil.

She was about to turn from the room when she caught sight of a small piece of glinting polished metal standing on a table. She frowned and took it up in her hand. It was heavy and there was a glint of metallic yellow about it.

'You appear rich, Bébháil,' she said quietly. 'This is a large gold nugget.'

'Let me see!' Accobrán demanded, reaching out his hand and taking it from her. He seemed abruptly curt. He turned it over for a moment or two and then put it carelessly back in place. 'It's only iron pyrites – fool's gold,' he said. Was it relief that Fidelma heard in his voice?

'Ah,' Fidelma said softly. '*Non teneas aurum totum quod splendet ut aurum.*'

Bébháil continued to sit without moving as if she no longer saw nor heard them.

Outside, Fidelma told Tómma what was intended and while she was speaking to him Accobrán followed her out and informed her that he had agreed to undertake the task of arranging the funeral obsequies.

'I'll also alert Bébháil's sister and her family,' he agreed. 'When can the funeral go ahead, lady?'

'As soon as custom allows,' replied Fidelma. 'There is nothing more to be learnt from the body. Eadulf and I will meet you at the rath on your return.'

Accobrán raised an eyebrow. 'Your return? Return from where, lady?'

Fidelma was already moving back to her horse with Eadulf trailing in her wake. She mounted up quickly.

'We will have a word with this youth Creoda and then I want to see Liag to find out how he just happened to be passing by here. Perhaps he noticed something.'

Accobrán looked uncomfortable. 'I should go with you. I have told you that he—'

'Don't worry,' Fidelma interrupted him. 'Eadulf and I will find the way. You concentrate on finding the sister of Bébháil.'

She knew well enough that Accobrán had not meant that they needed to be guided to Liag's hermitage but that he was worried for their safety. However, she had begun to feel that she had now had enough of being chaperoned. She needed freedom to continue her own investigations now she knew the lie of the land.

Side by side, she and Eadulf rode silently along the bank of the river, retracing their route of the previous day towards the place where Liag dwelt. Accobrán stood staring after them a few moments before he mounted his own horse and rode off in the opposite direction.

After a while, Eadulf said: 'We should have asked Accobrán for his hunting horn. Didn't he say that he had to use it to summon the hermit?'

Fidelma glanced at him with amusement. 'If our upraised voices do not summon Liag then nothing will.'

Eadulf grimaced without humour. 'What do you think the old apothecary was doing so close to the tannery?'

'That is what I hope to find out.'

'And destroying evidence?' added Eadulf.

'The question has occurred to me,' she replied quietly.

Eadulf fell silent. It was obvious that Fidelma had considered all the matters he had wondered about.

It was not long before they spotted a log cabin through the trees.

'This must be Creoda's *bothán*,' Fidelma said as she turned her horse towards it.

They were some distance away when a youth emerged and called shrilly: 'What do you want here?' He was clearly nervous.

'Are you Creoda?'

The youth was clad in a tanner's traditional leather apron. He wore a sharp leather-worker's knife in his belt and had one hand on the handle. His features displayed his anxiety. He regarded them with suspicion.

'I am Creoda,' he replied. Then he seemed to relax. 'Ah, you are the *dálaigh*. I saw you at Lesren's tannery yesterday.'

Fidelma and Eadulf dismounted.

'We have come to ask you a few questions about Lesren,' Fidelma told him.

The boy thrust out his lower lip in a grimace. 'Lesren is dead.' He jerked his head towards Eadulf. 'He was there with the tanist. He saw the body.'

'I know. We have come from the tannery.'

'I can tell you little more.'

'I just need to hear your version of the events.'

Creoda hesitated before commencing his story. 'I had finished my noonday meal when Tómma called for me. We went to the tannery together. There was some work for us to do but everyone else had been sent home. We arrived at the tannery but there was no sign of Lesren. We asked at the *bothán* but he was not there and so we went looking for him. We found him by the edge of the woods. That is all.'

'I gather that he was still alive,' said Fidelma.

'Alive? Aye, barely; alive but rambling.'

'What did he say?'

'Tómma was bending down by him. He will tell you.'

'We would like to know what you heard – just to clarify things.'

Creoda pursed his lips. 'Nothing that made sense. I heard some snatches of words and a name . . . it was indistinct. Tómma turned to me and asked me if I had heard the name before.'

'What was the name? And had you heard it?'

Creoda shook his head once more. 'Tómma clarified the name for me because, at first, I thought he was calling for his wife, Bébháil. But the name was apparently Biobhal. It is not a name that I know or have heard the like of here.'

'Biobhal,' repeated Fidelma. 'Are you sure that was the name?'

'I asked Tómma to repeat it. I have never heard of its like,' affirmed the tannery worker.

'Then we will trouble you no more,' Fidelma said gravely, turning to remount her horse.

'Will you find this killer who threatens our peace, Sister?' demanded the boy. 'Three of my friends have been slaughtered by this moonlight maniac and now comes the death of him who was training me in the art of tannery.'

Fidelma glanced back at the youth.

'Lesren was killed in the sunlight,' she said pointedly.

The youth blinked as if he had not considered this.

Fidelma waited for a while and then said: 'Yet you have reminded me. You knew all the girls who have been killed. Did they know each other well?'

Creoda pursed his lips in a sullen expression. 'They were great friends, the three of them. Thick as thieves and no secret safe with any of them but was shared between them. Or, at least, that is my opinion.'

'And didn't you also attend old Liag's instruction on star lore?'

Creoda inclined his head. 'I did.'

'And who else attended?'

'Gabrán came with Beccnat, of course. They were always together and, in spite of Lesren's disapproval, I heard that they were going to marry.'

'Who else?'

'Escrach. I liked Escrach very much . . . I had hoped that . . .' He shrugged. 'Anyway, Escrach tried to comfort Gabrán after he returned from the coast when it was found that Beccnat had been killed. Escrach was a kindly girl. She and Gabrán had been friends from childhood. Then, of course, Ballgel attended and sometimes Accobrán the tanist.'

'Accobrán?' Eadulf was surprised. 'He is several years older than all of you.'

Creoda grimaced.

'I am not sure whether he was interested in star lore or in Beccnat,' he said bitterly. 'I know Gabrán did not like the way that the tanist sought her out at feastings to dance with him.'

'Did she protest at his attentions?' asked Fidelma.

Creoda sighed and shook his head. 'The tanist had an eye for girls. I think he and Gabrán quarrelled over Beccnat because he danced with her at some festival. But Accobrán was not the oldest to attend Liag's classes. That smith – Gobnuid – he came along a few times.'

'I am interested in what Liag taught in these sessions,' Eadulf said. 'He taught about the moon and the stars? What in particular?'

'The old lore, the old names of the stars and what their courses meant, the moon and its powers . . . you must know the sort of thing? Perhaps if Liag hadn't taught so much about the moon then the girls might still be alive.'

Fidelma raised her eyebrows.

'You ought to explain that,' she suggested.

'Liag was always going on about knowledge meaning power. There was no need to fear the darkness of the night for if you possessed the knowledge of the secret names of the moon then you could control her. The night held no secret for Liag and he taught that power came at night.'

Eadulf frowned. 'Power came at night?'

'Had he taught that there were things to fear at night, Beccnat, Escrach and Ballgel might never had ventured forth,' Creoda said. 'Had they feared, then they might still have been alive.'

'Where fear is, knowledge and safety are not,' Fidelma reproved him.

Creoda stared at her for a moment and then, almost pleading, asked: 'Will you find out who has done this evil?'

'I will find the person responsible,' Fidelma replied gently. 'On that account you should have no fear.'

They remounted and retraced their route back to the main path.

'Are we still seeking out Liag?' asked Eadulf after they had ridden some way in silence.

She nodded absently, apparently lost in thought. Eadulf did not interrupt her and they rode on without speaking. They came to the spot where they had seen the two boys panning for gold on the previous day. At first they thought the river and its banks were empty, but a loud *plop* caused them to glance to where a rock overhung the riverbank.

A small boy was sitting on the rock and had obviously just thrown a stone into the water for he held another in his hand. At first they thought that it was one of the boys they had seen on the previous day. He was about twelve years old with fair hair and small limbs, and his clothing was not dissimilar to the other boys'. Some passing thought in the back of her mind caused Fidelma to ease her horse to a halt where the track passed close to the overhang. Eadulf looked at her in surprise and also halted.

'A pleasant day, boy,' she called.

The boy stirred and seemed to notice them for the first time. His expression was morose.

'The day may be pleasant but not so all that passes in it,' he replied sullenly.

Fidelma's eyes widened a little and she chuckled in appreciation at the other's words. 'You sound like a philosopher, my boy.'

He put down his stone and put his arms round his knees. 'I have heard the old ones say it when things go wrong for them.'

'And what is going wrong for you on this bright day?'

'Gobnuid made fun of me.'

'Gobnuid the smith?' Fidelma frowned.

The boy nodded. 'I brought him something I thought valuable and he laughed at me.'

'Is your name Síoda?'

The boy scowled immediately.

'What do you know of me?' he demanded defensively. 'Has Gobnuid been spreading the story—'

'I heard from your friends that you had discovered some metal,' Fidelma interrupted.

'I thought it was gold,' the boy affirmed, his mood swinging again to gloom. 'Gobnuid said it wasn't. He gave me a coin for it but I thought I would be really wealthy.'

'*Ad praesens ova cras pullis sunt meliora,*' said Eadulf.

The boy glanced at him as if he were stupid. 'He's a foreigner, isn't he?' he asked Fidelma.

Fidelma smiled.

'It is a Latin saying that eggs today are better than chicken tomorrow,' she explained. 'In other words, a coin in your pocket is better than the promise of riches to come. It's good advice.'

The boy sniffed. 'I was sure that the metal was gold.'

'Did you find it in this river?' Fidelma asked.

'I did not.'

'I saw two other boys panning for gold here yesterday. They seemed to believe that you had found the gold in the river here.'

The boy laughed bitterly. 'I told them that I had found it in the river when I thought it was valuable. I didn't want them to find out where I had really discovered it. Now I don't care. I am not going to be wealthy.'

'So you did not find the metal in the river?' Fidelma sought clarification.

The boy shook his head. 'I found it on the Thicket of Pigs. There are old mines there.'

'The Thicket of Pigs?' Fidelma's brow creased a moment.

The boy pointed across to the hill in front of them. 'It is really the wooded area on top of that hill, but the entire hill is now called by that name.' He confirmed the knowledge they already had.

'Should you be in the mines at your age?' demanded Eadulf. 'Surely it is dangerous?'

The boy regarded him with a frown.

'There are many metal workings around here,' he said. 'My father worked in them when he was not much older than I am. They are abandoned now. We all play in them. The boys from the area, that is.'

'So, you were playing in the mines on the Thicket of Pigs when you found the metal?'

The boy sniffed.

'I was not playing but exploring,' he corrected grandly.

Fidelma smiled briefly. 'Even so, you should have a care. My companion is right. It is very dangerous to play . . . to explore disused mine workings.'

The boy sniffed again and returned to his contemplation of the river. Fidelma bade him farewell but he did not bother to respond and so she and Eadulf rode off.

'Why were you interested in where the boy picked up his fool's gold?' asked Eadulf, in a reproving tone, after they had ridden some distance. 'We should be concentrating on other matters.'

Fidelma glanced at him. 'I am interested in the fact that the piece of metal which Gobnuid showed me, the piece he said the boy had found, and which he assured me was fool's gold, was real gold. I have handled both metals before and know the difference. I tested the nugget at Gobnuid's forge. It was gold.'

Eadulf stared at her for a moment before replying. 'You mean that this smith, Gobnuid, cheated the boy?'

'Certainly he told him an untruth.'

'Why would he do that? Just to make some money?'

Fidelma did not reply for a moment. Then she said, 'That is what I would like to find out. The girls met their deaths at the Thicket of Pigs. Could there be a connection?'

A silence fell between them again before Eadulf finally said: 'How long do you think we will remain here?'

Fidelma's eyebrows rose quickly. Her eyes widened. 'Here? In these woods?'

'No, at Rath Raithlen, away from Cashel.'

'When we have been asked to investigate a matter such as this, do we not usually remain until we have a resolution, Eadulf?' she asked, puzzled.

'Before there was not a little one awaiting our return,' he replied. 'You have not mentioned Alchú once since we left Cashel.'

The corners of Fidelma's mouth suddenly tightened.

'Because my son's name is not always on my lips, it does not mean to say that he is not in my thoughts,' she snapped. Her sudden anger was born of guilt that until that very morning Alchú had actually been entirely out of her thoughts.

'We have not discussed *our* son since we left Cashel.' Eadulf spoke softly but with emphasis on the change of personal pronoun.

Fidelma flushed guiltily. She knew that Eadulf was justified but, in her guilt, she became more defensive.

'Is there need to discuss him? He is safe at Cashel with Sárait. We have other more pressing business to attend to.'

Eadulf's jaw was determined. 'He is barely a month old. You have already given him up to a wet nurse. I learnt enough about such matters, when I studied at the great medical school of Tuam Brecain, to know that allowing the baby to suckle at your breast returns the mother's body to health and helps the love develop between the child and the mother instead of—'

'This is not the time nor place to criticse my ability as a mother, Eadulf,' she snapped.

Eadulf controlled a spasm of anger. 'I am not sure that I understand your moods, Fidelma. Ever since the child was born you have become a changed person.'

'Are we not allowed to change, then?' She knew well what he meant for she had been questioning her motivations of late. 'Some people would be better off for a change!' She was growing irritable and the irritation lay in the knowledge that she was in the wrong and Eadulf had every right to discuss the matter. 'If you are so worried about the child, why don't you ride back to Cashel and leave me here to resolve this problem?'

Eadulf blinked a little and then he shrugged.

'*A verbis ad verbera*,' he sighed. The Latin quotation meant 'from words to blows' and described a discussion that spilled into anger.

Fidelma opened her mouth to reply hotly and then she sighed. She leant forward from her horse and placed a hand on Eadulf's arm.

'*Non sum qualis eram bonae sub regno Cinarea*,' she said contritely.

After a moment's reflection, Eadulf remembered the line from Horace. 'I am not what I was under the reign of good Cynara.' It was used to signify a change of character and behaviour. He made to reply but Fidelma raised a finger to her lips. Her expression was suddenly penitent.

'Let us say no more at the present, Eadulf. Do not press me further until I am ready. Ever since Alchú came into this world I have felt strangely disturbed. It is as if my mood changes from moment to moment for no apparent reason.'

Eadulf looked concerned. 'You did not tell me this before?'

She smiled thinly. 'You should have noticed.'

'I did but did not think that you were ill . . .'

She shook her head. 'It is not an illness of the body. When I consider my actions with reason, I perceive myself as if some irrational fever has overtaken me. Sometimes I fear for myself. Yet it is only when I think of the baby, Eadulf. My logic remains when I concentrate on other matters. This makes me fear even more.'

Eadulf ran a hand through his hair as if to massage his mind into some line of positive thought. 'I seem to recall . . . I was told that sometimes, after a birth, a mother can feel unhappy—'

'I have resolved to see old Conchobhar when we return to Cashel,' Fidelma intervened sharply. 'Until then, let us speak about this no more.'

Conchobhar was chief apothecary at Cashel as well as an astrologer.

Eadulf realised that it was pointless to pursue the matter further. They rode on silently, entering the thickness of the woods where the trees grew close together down to the riverbank. They tried to keep the river to their left as they rode along but the track twisted and turned and once or twice they had to retrace their path to follow another route. But suddenly they emerged along a stretch which both Fidelma and Eadulf recognised.

'There's the hill,' muttered Eadulf as they halted in a clear space by the river. 'What was it that Accobrán called it?'

'Cnoc a' Bhile,' replied Fidelma.

'That's it. Hill of the Sacred Tree.' Eadulf sighed. 'I think I have heard that such a tree relates to the habitation of the pagan gods.'

'Bile was a sacred oak, according to the old ones, and when Danu, the divine water of heaven, flooded down it nurtured the oak and produced acorns and out of each acorn grew one of the ancient gods and goddesses. That is why the old deities are called the Tuatha de Danaan, the children of the goddess Danu.'

Eadulf looked uncomfortable. 'I thought Bile was a god of darkness and death from the underworld.'

Fidelma shook her head. 'Some of the New Faith who came here from Rome have viewed the old deity in that form. Our people still hold the great tree sacred and many of our chieftains are inaugurated under its branches, for it was symbolic of our kings, a place of origin of all the people. It is sacrilege to cut a sacred tree although the chief or king's rod of office might be cut and carved from a branch of the tree to give him power. A few centuries ago the High King carried such a wand of office cut from a sacred ash tree. The tree was called Bile Dathí and it was classed as one of the six wondrous trees of Ireland.'

Eadulf frowned. 'I thought that you said Bile was an oak tree?'

'Language changes. Now any tree regarded as sacred is called by that name. Bile has also long been seen as a divine personification, a god who the ancients belived ferried souls along the sacred rivers, or by sea, to the Otherworld.'

Eadulf felt uncomfortable. He had grown to manhood before he had converted to the New Faith, and was still trying to deny his pagan past. Fidelma seemed more comfortable in the ancient lore of her people even though the people of Éireann had accepted Christianity several centuries before. But now a memory stirred.

'I passed through Londinium once,' he said reflectively. 'It is mainly deserted these days but once it was a thriving Roman city.'

'I have heard of it,' Fidelma responded gravely.

'The Welisc, who called themselves Britons, once dwelt there and continued to do so even when Rome ruled the city.'

Fidelma nodded, frowning slightly as she wondered what Eadulf was getting at.

'I know the Welisc shared many ancient gods and goddesses with the Irish.'

'This is true. What is your point?'

'Near where I was staying was an ancient gate called Bile's Gate which opened onto the great river Tamesis which flows past the city. An old man told me that in ancient times, when people died, their heads were severed from their bodies and taken through the gate and ferried downriver. Not far away a confluence called Welisc Brook emptied into the Tamesis and here the heads were thrown into the river with various items like swords, shields and so on. A terrible pagan custom.'

Fidelma smiled and nodded. 'Not so terrible. The ancients believed that the soul dwelt in the head and to honour the dead they often removed the heads – which freed the souls – and deposited them in their most sacred places. It is fascinating that there is such a reminder of the ancient custom in the heart of what is now the land of the Angles and Saxons.'

Eadulf shook his head sadly.

'*Semel insanivimus omnes*,' he said. 'We have all been mad once. I do not know whether people should be reminded of such things. It is a hard enough job to convert them to the true Faith without referring to the old one. We learnt that last year, didn't we?'

Eadulf was obviously thinking of how many of the Saxon kingdoms had recently converted back to the old gods of the forefathers. Sigehere, king of the East Saxons, on the very borders of Eadulf's own country of the East Angles, had reopened the pagan temples after the plague of two years before.

'You cannot build the future by ignoring the past or trying to destroy past knowledge. But we all make such mistakes. I view with sadness the account by the Bishop Benignus, who became the successor of the Blessed Patrick at Armagh, when he wrote that Patrick burnt one hundred and eighty books of the Druids in his attempts to convert the people to the New Faith. The destruction of knowledge, any knowledge, does not provide a sure foundation for the future.'

'You surely cannot disapprove of the destruction of the pagan faith when you are sworn to proselytise for the New Faith?' Eadulf was aghast.

'What I am saying is that mankind's folly should be destroyed by laughter, not by creating martyrs. That is the tradition of our satirists and why our laws have strong punishments for those who satirise people without justification. *Castigat ridendo mores*.'

Eadulf pondered.

'They correct customs by laughing at them?' he hazarded.

Fidelma smiled. 'In other words, laughter will succeed where threats, punishments and pious lectures will not.'

Eadulf sighed. 'It is an interesting philosophy. I am sure there is an argument against it.'

'Tell me, when you have discovered it. In the meantime, let us continue with our task.'

They moved their horses on at a slow walking pace towards the tree-covered hill where they had previously met Liag.

'We'd better raise a shout,' muttered Eadulf, glancing around nervously. 'He might try to avoid us.'

Chapter Eleven

Liag, the apothecary, had emerged from the trees behind them. He appeared as he had on their previous meeting, with his saffron-dyed woollen robe, the snow-white hair held in place by the green and yellow bead headband and the silver chain around his neck. The elderly apothecary still carried his traditional apothecary's *lés*, the satchel containing his cures and implements, and the *echlais*, his whip-like wand of office.

'You seem startled to see me, Fidelma of Cashel.' He smiled thinly. He did not even acknowledge Eadulf.

'You came up behind us quietly,' returned Fidelma, dismounting from her horse.

Liag raised his eyebrows in a bland expression. 'Did you not hear my approach? When I was young, one was taught to attune one's ears to the sounds of the forest. One was taught to hear the lizard avoiding the hungry eye of the kestrel, the badger slinking through the undergrowth and the stoat splashing homewards. Hark!' The old man tilted his head to one side and cupped a hand to an ear in an exaggerated stance.

Eadulf glowered in annoyance. He had succeeded in dismounting from his nervous beast and was tying the reins to a bush.

'You don't mean to tell me that you can hear anything?' he sneered.

Liag turned to Eadulf. 'I hear a rat grab a lizard by its tail and the sound of the lizard's cry as it sheds its tail to fool the predator while it scurries off to its nest, for this is the month it sneaks into hibernation.'

Eadulf regarded the bland expression on the face of the old recluse and was not sure whether he was being made fun of or not. 'I can hear nothing.'

'Exactly so, Brother Saxon. Exactly.'

Fidelma regarded the apothecary cynically. 'If you can hear such things, Liag, then you should be able to answer some simple questions.'

The elderly man's eyes narrowed suspiciously.

'It is said that those who ask questions cannot avoid the answers,' he replied softly. 'But it is not every question that is deserving of an answer.'

'A good response. If your ears are so attuned, then you surely heard the death cries of Beccnat, of Escrach and of Ballgel.'

The apothecary's cheek coloured hotly at the sarcasm. 'I do not claim omniscience. I do not hear all that passes in the forests. Had I been near to where they perished . . .' He lifted a shoulder and let it fall eloquently.

Fidelma's lips thinned. 'Then I presume that you heard the death gasp of Lesren? I understand that you were close by when he died?'

Liag's brows came together in a frown. 'Who said I was near?'

'So you do know that Lesren has been killed?' Eadulf pointed out quickly.

'I do not deny that,' replied the apothecary.

'You emerged from the forest when Bébháil and Tómma stood by the body of Lesren?'

'But Lesren was dead, my Saxon friend. In fact, so far as I could tell, he had been dead for some time.'

'What were you doing there?' asked Eadulf.

Liag wore a droll expression. 'In case you have not perceived it, Saxon, if I crossed the hill of Rath Raithlen and returned in this direction, my path would pass through the forests that surround Lesren's tannery.'

'And you were crossing the hill and just happened to be passing at that time?' said Fidelma.

'I happened to be passing the tannery at that time, *dálaigh*,' he responded with irony in his voice. It was the first time he had chosen to address her by the title of her profession and it was clear that he was being sardonic.

'Where had you been?'

'Rath Raithlen is the only place of importance on that hill.'

Fidelma hid her surprise. 'Everyone says that you are a recluse, Liag. That you dwell in the forests and shun the outside world. Are you telling me that you were visiting the fortress of the chieftain?'

'I believe that is exactly what I told you.'

Fidelma tried to stifle her irritation. 'Why this change of character, Liag?'

'There is no change of character. Whether I wish to see people or not is my own affair. I rule my life, not other people. If I want to see them, I see them. If I do not, I shall not.'

'Are you saying that some business or some desire drew you to the chieftain's fortress?'

'Some business drew me there,' affirmed Liag.

'You are not being helpful,' Fidelma replied impatiently.

Liag was amused. 'I thought that I was obeying the law that says that one must answer the questions of a *dálaigh*. I am replying to your questions.'

Fidelma knew that the apothecary was right. He was answering her questions but to a minimum level.

'Will you tell me what business took you to Rath Raithlen?'

The old man considered.

'I had need to see a smith,' he replied.

'Gobnuid?' The name shot out of Fidelma's mouth, catching the apothecary by surprise. He was the only smith at Rath Raithlen that Fidelma knew. She thought it worth throwing out to see if it would force Liag into more explicit answers. He merely nodded affirmation.

'What was the nature of your business?'

'I cannot see that it bears any relationship to your inquiries, Fidelma of Cashel. Anyway, Gobnuid was not at his forge so I returned.'

'Gobnuid has left Rath Raithlen driving a wagonful of hides to some river merchant. What was the nature of your business?'

Liag half closed his eyes as if the information surprised him, but he recovered in a split second.

'Even a recluse who lives in the forest by himself sometimes has need of a smith. I had some knives and axes that needed sharpening.'

Eadulf glanced at Fidelma.

'And these knives and axes . . .' he began, but Liag's features were wreathed with his mocking smiling again.

'I am afraid that I was returning to my home after taking them to the smith. I was not carrying the sharpened implements. I left them at Gobnuid's forge so that he might attend to them on his return. I did not use them to end Lesren's life, if that is what you wish to imply, my Saxon friend.'

'You might find this matter amusing, Liag,' Eadulf said irritably, 'but a man lies dead and also three young women. Corpses are not matters of amusement.'

The old man's eyes were like gimlets. Cold and sparkling. 'Indeed, they are not, Brother Saxon. Neither are accusations made by some stranger in this land.' He jerked his head in Eadulf's direction.

'Brother Eadulf is making no accusations,' Fidelma interposed. 'Neither am I. We are seeking information, that is all. If there is an accusation to be made, it will be couched in terms so direct that no one will misunderstand it. Now, tell us your account of what happened. You were returning home when . . . ?'

For several moments the old man stood staring into Fidelma's eyes, his own cold eyes challenging. Fidelma did not waver. Her features were fixed. It was Liag who finally shrugged and accepted defeat.

'I came through the woods, at first thinking to skirt round Lesren's tannery. I do not particularly like Lesren and his workers. I noticed that there was a strange stillness to the place. Usually, Lesren has several people working for him, boiling the noxious brews for his tanning and stretching the skins to dry. In the stillness I heard a woman's sobbing.'

He paused for a moment.

'Go on,' prompted Fidelma, still feeling irritable with the man.

'I found both Bébháil and Tómma standing by the corpse of Lesren. I decided that the woman was so distraught that she might need my help. It seemed that Tómma was unable to calm her.'

'And?'

'I managed to calm her but Bébháil seemed to be unsure whether her husband was dead or not. I made an examination and realised that not only was he dead but that he had been dead some time.'

'How did you know that?' demanded Eadulf.

Liag looked pityingly at him. 'The body grows cold after a while.'

'Why did you advise Bébháil to wash the body and prepare it for burial?' demanded Fidelma abruptly.

Liag replied immediately. 'It seemed to me that in her emotional state she needed something to do which would awake her to the finality of the situation. It would be wrong to allow her to think that her husband might be somehow resuscitated. It was an act of charity to get her to concentrate her mind . . .'

'An act of charity that probably destroyed all the clues to Lesren's killers,' pointed out Fidelma.

Liag stared at her thoughtfully and then shook his head. 'I doubt it. There was nothing I could see that would have constituted a clue.'

'Ah, as well as hearing lizards in flight, I presume that you are also a trained *dálaigh*?' Eadulf sneered.

Liag looked at him. A spasm of anger distorted his features for a moment and then he seemed to relax and smiled broadly.

'You have a right to be angry, my Saxon friend. I have been unkind to you and that is unworthy of me. You have been unworthy in return. Let us make an end to it. I am competent enough as an apothecary to say that there was nothing about the corpse that could lead to the killer.'

Eadulf swallowed in annoyance at the condescension in the other's tone, but he could not think of a suitable response.

'Tell me, Liag, having now observed all four deaths in this place, have you discerned any similarities between them?' queried Fidelma.

'Only in as much as all met their deaths by a knife – and a knife that was jagged and blunt.'

'If that was the only similarity, what were the dissimilarities?' Fidelma pressed.

Liag shot her an appreciative glance. 'I would say that there was a distinct difference between the way the first three victims came by their deaths and the way that Lesren came by his.'

'How so?'

'The first three victims were, of course, young girls. They were savagely attacked and mutilated. The fourth, Lesren, was a male. While there was savagery in the number of wounds he sustained, being stabbed several times in the neck and chest, there was no mutilation. Indeed, Tómma told me that Lesren was still alive when he reached him and was able to breathe a few words that did not make sense.'

Fidelma nodded slightly.

'He was able to breathe a name,' she conceded.

'A name that makes little sense, if Tómma has reported it correctly. It may well be that the wounds inspired some delirium. Who knows what passed through his mind in the last moments before death?'

'You are a man of knowledge, Liag,' Fidelma said. She spoke simply, without sounding as if she was paying the apothecary any compliments. 'You must know about the old days when gold and silver were worked in this area.'

Liag inclined his head a little, although he was clearly puzzled by her apparent change of subject. 'I have some knowledge. The ore raised here was rich and excellent and was once produced in abundance. Now, alas, gold of such quality is only found in the eastern mountains of Laighin.'

'Did Lesren ever work in the mines?'

Liag shook his head quickly. 'Never. What makes you ask that?'

'Do you recall who, according to the ancients, first brought gold to Ireland?'

The apothecary looked surprised. 'Is this to be a discussion on our ancient lore and history? Well, it was Tigernmas, the twenty-sixth High King of Éireann, after the coming of the children of the Gael. He first smelted gold in this land. During his reign it is said that golden goblets and brooches were plentiful and that his chief artificer was Uchadan.'

Eadulf was also regarding Fidelma with a bewildered frown at her seeming irrelevant line of questioning. She seemed momentarily disappointed at Liag's answer.

'I have heard it said that the mines here are all in disuse now.'

'You have heard it said correctly, lady,' agreed Liag. 'There are some lead workings not far from here but the old wealth is gone.'

'I suppose things would greatly change if the precious metals were found again?'

Liag grimaced distastefully. 'They would indeed change, but probably not for the better. For myself, I prefer the quiet and peace that solitude and a degree of indigence brings. Wealth brings greed, greed brings hate, and crime spreads—'

'Crime such as murder?' snapped Eadulf, losing patience with the conversation. 'Have not such crimes already been visited on your idyll, master apothecary?'

Liag's mouth tightened as he turned on Eadulf. 'You are direct, Brother Saxon. There is no denying that you come to the point with a directness that others might not use. Yet I prefer my idyll, as you call it. The place is not responsible for the evil in men's hearts. There is an old saying that wealth does not improve character but always changes it for the worse.'

Eadulf was about to open his mouth to retort when Fidelma moved forward to her horse, unloosening the reins.

'Thank you for your time, Liag. We have much to do and must now return to the rath. But one question more. When was it that you were asked to examine the body of Beccnat?'

The apothecary looked surprised. 'On the morning after the full moon. I thought that was understood.'

'And both Escrach and Ballgel were also examined on the morning after the full moon?'

Liag confirmed it.

'Thank you once again, Liag. You have been most helpful.'

Liag did not respond but stood motionless as they mounted their horses and rode away. Once out of earshot and sight of the old apothecary, Eadulf learned forward to Fidelma.

'Why are you so interested in the mines? What has gold to do with this case?' he demanded, perplexed.

'Perhaps I should have mentioned to you earlier that it is interesting that the subject of gold often appears in this case. Now, if the name that was on Lesren's lips really was Biobhal, then it becomes of particular interest.'

'How so?' demanded Eadulf.

'Because there has been only one Biobhal that I know of. It is the name of a character out of our ancient times. The ancients say that long, long ago, before even the children of the Gael came to these shores, there were many invaders of our land. Partholón, the son of

Sera, who had killed his father in the hope of obtaining his kingdom, led one of the invasions. But he was driven into exile and he and his followers came to this very kingdom of Muman. Partholón is said to have introduced ploughing into the kingdom and cleared plains and established agriculture and built hostels. Then a plague descended on the land and he and all his people were wiped out.'

Eadulf was looking baffled. 'So what of this Biobhal?'

'Biobhal was one of Partholón's followers. He it was who is claimed as having discovered the first gold in the kingdom.'

Eadulf smiled in amusement. 'That is a story for old folks and young children told before a blazing hearth on a winter's night. I see nothing relevant.'

Fidelma gave a patient sigh. 'I am not arguing the relevance of it, Eadulf. To anyone who is blessed with knowledge of the legends of the old ones, the name of Biobhal is synonymous with gold in this kingdom. I just wonder why Lesren would die with that name on his lips?'

Eadulf shrugged indifferently. 'Well, now I know why you asked Liag your question, but he did not seem to know who Biobhal is. He mentioned someone called Tigernmas.'

Fidelma nodded with a frown.

'Indeed, that is curious,' she agreed. 'He would surely know the name Biobhal but he chose to name Tigernmas. Tigernmas was certainly the High King in whose reign it is said that smelting of gold began in Ireland. But the ancient story tells that Biobhal discovered gold in the land. Yet Liag claimed not to recognise the name which Tómma said Lesren had on his dying breath.'

'I can't see any connection,' repeated Eadulf.

'Nor I. We have much talk of gold. I want to see this Thicket of Pigs.'

'The place where the young boy found his fool's gold?'

'The place where he found genuine gold and was fooled out of it by Gobnuid the smith,' corrected Fidelma.

'Very well,' agreed Eadulf. 'But what shall we find in some disused mine in this Thicket of Pigs that will help us solve these killings?'

'Who knows?'

Eadulf stared at her and then shrugged. 'Are you saying that you see a link with the deaths of Beccnat, Escrach and Ballgel?'

Fidelma did not reply. Silently, Eadulf admired her. It was her ability to remember all the salient facts that constituted Fidelma's exceptional ability as an investigator and solver of conundrums. But he could see no relation at all between the gold and the murders.

He was aware that Fidelma was glancing about her and peering up at the sky through the canopy of trees. Abruptly she pointed to a track which led directly away from the riverbank.

'Follow me, Eadulf.'

She turned her horse along the narrow path and Eadulf was forced to follow her.

'What is it?' he demanded. 'Where are you heading?'

'We should be able to strike through these woods to join the main track and then head westwards towards the summit of the Thicket of Pigs.'

Eadulf was at once anxious. 'But we have only a short while of daylight left. What can we achieve in that time?'

Fidelma glanced over her shoulder.

'I am not a prophet, so I cannot answer your question,' she said waspishly.

Eadulf fell silent. He realised that his questions were interrupting some thought process and antagonising her.

They rode on for a while, the path narrowing to a cutting through which it was difficult for their horses to pass even in single file. Then, at last, they burst out of the woods onto the main track which led from the distant gates of Rath Raithlen, beyond the turning to the abbey of the Blessed Finnbarr, and south-west over the wood-covered hill that was called the Thicket of Pigs. They continued on until the track began to rise sharply up the hill. Trees, shrubland and rocks spread in all directions around them with nothing to indicate any mines or metal workings at all. Fidelma looked in vain for some signs. Only someone who knew the area would be able to spot them.

Fidelma felt disappointed. However, she was not so egocentric that she refused to admit that she had, perhaps, made an error in trying to find the location of the metal workings without anyone to guide them. She halted her horse and gazed around. There was a chill in the air now and the skies were darkening in the east. She let out a sigh of irritation.

Eadulf knew better than to state the obvious but it seemed his diplomatic silence agitated her just as much.

'You can observe that I was too enthusiastic, Eadulf,' she said sharply.

Eadulf lifted a hand in a gesture of peace and let it fall.

'A search is always the better for a guide when it is made in a strange land,' he quoted quietly.

Fidelma pressed her lips together in annoyance. 'Then we'd best return to the fortress and when we come back it will be with a guide.'

She was about to turn back along the track when they heard a loud whistling sound and a moment later a dog came bounding out of a thicket close by. It was a small hunting hound, not a wolfhound but a short, bristle-haired dog. It skidded to a halt, placing its paws apart and uttering a growl before letting loose a series of yapping barks.

The whistle came sharply. Then they heard a voice calling.

A moment later a young man appeared out of the cover on the slope just below them. He came to a halt as he caught sight of them. It was quite easy to see what the man was. On his broad shoulders he carried the carcass of a dead boar. He balanced it with one hand while his other held a bow of yew. His quiver of arrows hung from his belt alongside a great hunting knife. His clothes were of finely worked buckskin. His hair was auburn and fell to his shoulders though fastened by a band around the forehead. He had fair features and a ready smile.

He stood for a moment in indecision and then snapped sharply to his still barking hound. 'Quiet, Luchóc!'

The dog immediately sat down, looking contrite.

'God be with you, Sister, and with you, Brother,' the young hunter greeted them. 'Pay no mind to my dog. He is more bark than bite.'

Fidelma responded with a smile.

'A strange name for a hunting dog, master huntsman,' she replied.

The young man nodded. 'Good mouser? Aye, I'll grant you that it is an odd name for a working dog. But, in truth, the poor hound is better at catching mice than catching game.'

'But you do not appear to have done too badly,' Eadulf pointed out, indicating the boar slung on the man's shoulders.

To the huntsman smiles seemed to come naturally.

'A family will not go wanting for the next several days,' he agreed. 'You are obviously strangers in this district.' The words were a statement, not a question.

'Indeed we are,' replied Fidelma. 'Do you know this area, the Thicket of Pigs?'

'I live on the far side of the hill there. I have done so all my life. But if you seek anyone other than myself, the place has been deserted these many years. They say the place was populated even in my grandfather's time, but it is so no longer.'

'They tell me there are metal workings there,' Fidelma said.

The huntsman chuckled. 'It is not in search of precious metals that two religious have come to this countryside, is it? I heard talk of a *dálaigh* and her companion staying with our chieftain, Becc. I suppose that you are that *dálaigh*?'

'It is because of our investigation that I want to know about this hill and its mines.'

'Well, there are deserted metal workings a-plenty, and some caves, but they are dangerous, Sister. It is not a place to go without fore-knowledge.'

'You say that you dwell near here?'

A slight cast of suspicion came into the young man's eye. 'I do say so, Sister. And I pay allegiance to Becc, my chieftain.'

'And your name is . . . ?'

The quiet authority of Fidelma's voice caused the young man to respond, even unwillingly, to her questions.

'I am Menma the hunter. And, as I have told you my name, pray, what are your names and from what place do you come?'

'I am Fidelma of Cashel, Menma. This is my companion, Brother Eadulf.'

The young hunter sighed. 'Then the talk among the Cinél na Áeda is true – the king of Cashel has a sister who is a famous *dálaigh*.'

'We are proof of it, Menma,' Fidelma assured him.

The young man dropped the carcass of the boar on the ground and bowed respectfully. 'I am sorry for any discourtesy, lady.'

'There has been none,' Fidelma assured him. 'You are right to be suspicious of us in view of what has transpired in this place in recent months.'

The hunter grimaced in agreement. 'The lands of the Cinél na Áeda are not so large that I did not know those three girls. My wife was a friend to Escrach. It is a bad business.'

'A bad business, indeed,' agreed Fidelma. 'Tell me, Menma, do you know the mine and caves on this hill?'

'Well enough, lady.'

She glanced up at the sky. 'The hour grows late and it will soon be dark. However, should we want to go exploring there, would you be willing to serve as our guide?'

'Willingly, lady. But the Thicket of Pigs is quite deserted. The mines are long closed.'

'It is not people that I go in search of,' Fidelma assured him. 'I want to see something of the area, of the deserted mines. Are there mines near a spot called the Ring of Pigs?'

To her disappointment, he shook his head. 'None near. But there is a cave above the Ring that used to be worked for gold. That is deserted and dangerous.'

'If we wished to go exploring that cave, say tomorrow or the next day, how might we find you?'

The young man pointed to the far side of the track. 'There is a path through those trees. A short distance along the path you will come across my *bothán*, lady. If I am out at the hunt, my woman will be there. She will show you how to find me by blowing three times on the horn that is hung by the hearth. When I hear its call, I will return. It is a signal that my wife and I have long arranged in case of need.'

'You are a thoughtful man, Menma,' observed Fidelma.

'I would rather worry without need, lady, than live without heed. They have an old saying in these parts, that one should never test the depth of a river with both feet.'

'There is wisdom in that,' Fidelma agreed.

The young man bent and picked up the dead boar and flung it across his broad shoulders as if it weighed nothing. He smiled up at them, each in turn.

'I will await your call then. Safe journey back to the fortress of the chief.'

He raised the hand that held his bow in farewell and turned with a sharp call to his dog, which bounded swiftly after him. Within a moment he had disappeared through the trees in the direction of his home.

'Now we shall return to Rath Raithlen,' Fidelma said, turning her horse back along the track.

Eadulf turned with her. 'I still cannot understand what you expect to find among the deserted metal workings, even with a guide such as Menma.'

He was expecting some caustic response but Fidelma's features softened a little.

'In truth, Eadulf, I am not sure what I expect to find. Maybe nothing at all. It's just that I have this nagging thought that there is some mystery that is mixed up with gold. Remember the ladder in the tower of the fortress, which had been damaged so that one of us might have fallen to injure or kill ourselves?'

'You suspected that Gobnuid the smith was responsible.'

Fidelma looked at him in surprise. Sometimes she felt that she underestimated Eadulf's perceptive qualities.

'I did. Gobnuid had tried to tell me that the piece of real gold which Síoda found here was simply fool's gold. Why?'

Eadulf pulled a wry face. 'What makes you sure that it has something to do with the death of the three women? Have you not considered that this is but a wild goose chase?'

'Their bodies were found near here,' Fidelma pointed out.

'But does that signify anything? There are lots of places near here. The abbey, for example. The place of the apothecary, Liag.'

'And there is Lesren's last word . . .'

'A name . . . which could be anything. It was a name that certainly did not strike a chord in the mind of Liag when you questioned him. I think that you should—'

'Hush!' Fidelma suddenly snapped, holding up her hand, while hauling on the bridle with the other. Her horse snorted in protest.

'What . . .' began Eadulf.

Fidelma was pointing down the hill to the oncoming gloom.

They had followed the track where it passed over the brow of the hill, overlooking the valley where, below and to the left of them, lay the buildings that constituted the abbey of Finnbarr. Some distance below was a clearing among the trees. Eadulf could just make out two small figures hurrying across this clearing. One was more obvious than the other for it was a tall figure and it was clear that it was clad in long white robes. They were visible for no more than a few moments before they vanished into the darkness of the trees beyond the clearing.

Eadulf cast a puzzled glance at Fidelma.

'What was that all about?' he demanded.

'Did you recognise anyone?' she asked.

'I did not.'

'I did. It was Gobnuid the smith. Back rather early from his trip. Did you not recognise the other, Eadulf?'

'How could I recognise anyone?'

'Think, Eadulf! The tall figure with white robes!'

Eadulf knew what she was getting at. 'It could have been one of the three strangers at the monastery, I suppose. But which one? I have no idea. They were too far away.'

Fidelma was in agreement. 'Yet it was one of them. But why would Gobnuid and one of the Aksumites be out together on this desolate hill at dusk?'

Eadulf gave a negative shake of his head. 'To be honest, I can understand nothing of this. Never have I been so totally baffled by a mystery . . . by a series of mysteries, in fact.'

Fidelma was defiant. 'The more the mystery deepens, the greater the challenge, Eadulf. I am determined not to let this overcome me. The Brehon Morann, my mentor, once said that no object nor puzzle is mysterious. The mystery is the eyes and what they perceive. So when the eyes see a mystery do not use the eyes to understand it.'

Eadulf smiled somewhat sceptically. 'The heart always sees before the head can see?'

'Exactly so. We will solve this mystery yet.'

It was growing dusk when they finally reached the gates of Rath Raithlen. A stable boy came running forward as they rode in and took charge of their horses as soon as they had dismounted. They noticed that there was some movement in the fortress. Brand torches were being lit to dispel the darkness and suddenly Becc appeared at the doorway of his great hall and came forward to greet them.

'I am glad to see you back safely, Fidelma. Accobrán was worried that you had gone off by yourself.'

'I had Eadulf with me,' she replied shortly, glancing around. 'What is the excitement about? Where is your tanist?'

'Gone,' replied Becc with satisfaction. 'He's gone in chase of Lesren's killer.'

Chapter Twelve

Fidelma stood for a moment, staring at the chieftain of the Cinél na Áeda as if she had not heard him.

'Lesren's killer? Does that mean that the identity of the killer has been discovered?'

'A farmer came into the rath not so long ago and said that he had encountered Gabrán on the road. The young man was heading for the coast and told the man that he was going to find a ship and sign on as one of the crew.'

Fidelma glanced quickly at Eadulf, her face a mixture of surprise and irritation. Then she turned back to Becc.

'Did this farmer say any more?'

Becc nodded. 'The young man as good as admitted that he was fleeing from justice. Anyway, Accobrán has taken some warriors and will take the road to the coast. They should be able to overtake him soon enough and bring him back for trial. At least we have solved one murder. Maybe Gabrán will be the means of solving the others. Perhaps Lesren was right after all?'

'The boy may be stupid,' replied Fidelma in an exasperated tone, 'but to run away does not mean to say he is responsible for any deaths.'

Becc regarded in her astonishment. 'But the very act of running away proclaims his guilt.'

'A stupid act, I warrant you, but not a proclamation of guilt,' replied Fidelma. 'It can also imply fear. Let me know immediately Accobrán returns.'

Then, motioning Eadulf to follow, she led the way to their chambers. Once inside the room, she closed the door with a sharp thud behind her.

'The stupid, stupid boy!' she exploded.

Eadulf stood observing the anger on her features as she began to pace the room. 'You really think that he is innocent?'

Fidelma did not even bother to answer the question.

'I fear for the boy's life now,' she said quietly. 'Remember there is enmity between him and Accobrán.'

'But that is all on the part of Gabrán,' replied Eadulf. 'A silly suspicion that Accobrán was trying to seduce his betrothed.'

Fidelma did not say anything for a moment. Then she said softly: 'Let us hope that if Accobrán and the boy meet up on the road, they may come back to us living and not as corpses.'

There was no further news of the tanist and his pursuit by the time they retired for the night.

The next day, as the early grey October light filtered through the windows, Fidelma was already at her morning ablutions. In the distance she could hear the tolling of a bell, presumably from the abbey of the Blessed Finnbarr. She found Eadulf waiting for her in the kitchen of Becc's great hall where they normally broke their fast. He had been up and washed before her.

Becc came in while they were finishing their meal and looked uneasy.

'Accobrán came back in the middle of the night,' he announced without preamble. 'He overtook Gabrán.'

Fidelma was immediately concerned.

'I asked you to inform me immediately Accobrán returned,' she replied sharply. 'Is the boy alive?'

Becc blinked in surprise at the abruptness of her tone.

'Accobrán brought him back for trial, cousin. Not for execution,' he said defensively.

'So the boy is in good health?' she insisted.

'He may be bruised a little but he should not have resisted his capture.'

Fidelma's features were immobile. 'No, he should not – especially when he is innocent of the murder of Lesren.'

Becc showed his irritability. 'You will have to present the evidence to prove it then.'

'That I shall do,' Fidelma replied. She made to rise, and paused. The distant bell from the abbey was still tolling. 'What is that bell sounding for?'

The chieftain looked surprised, as if hearing the bell for the first time. 'It will be for Lesren's funeral.'

Fidelma sprang to her feet with an exclamation. 'I had forgotten the funeral in all that has transpired. Eadulf, come. We must attend it.'

Eadulf grabbed a piece of cold meat and some bread and went quickly after her as she headed for the door. On the threshold she halted with such abruptness that Eadulf bumped into her. She was looking back at Becc.

'Are you not coming?' she demanded.

The chieftain had seated himself at the vacated table.

'I was never a friend of Lesren or of his family. He was a good tanner, that is all. Accobrán has gone there to ensure all is as it should be. But it would be insincere should I attend.'

Fidelma had not waited for the chieftain to finish. She was through the door and instructing their horses be saddled and brought without delay.

'I don't understand why you want to attend this funeral,' Eadulf protested, trying to finish his bread and meat.

'At funerals one may gather information,' she replied mysteriously.

It did not take them long to reach the abbey. A few other stragglers were hurrying in answer to the bell's summons and it was still tolling as the gatekeeper admitted them and pointed to the chapel.

Lesren's body had been taken to the abbey chapel and it was here that the funeral obsequies were to take place. As Fidelma and Eadulf entered the chapel, they found it surprisingly crowded with many from Rath Raithlen. They immediately saw Accobrán, and by his side Adag the steward. Fidelma nudged Eadulf and indicated that Gobnuid the smith was also there. There were many others who had probably traded with the tanner or were relatives of Lesren and Bébháil. Bébháil herself sat at the front of the chapel with a woman who looked remarkably like her. Fidelma remembered that the widow of Lesren had a sister who was to have been summoned to look after matters. There was Tómma close by. Even a frightened-looking Creoda was standing just behind Tómma. Among the religious, however, the three strangers were not present. There was no reason why they should be and, indeed, Abbot Brogán told Fidelma afterwards that he had thought it wise that they should not attend in case of trouble.

The congregation was subdued by the ominous tones of a new bell. The solemn baritone of the *clog-estechtae*, or death bell, which was always rung to mark the death of a Christian, replaced the tenor of the summoning bell. The religious who were gathered began to sing their requiem, the *écnairc*, an intercession for the soul's repose. Members of Bébháil's household had probably watched over Lesren's body for the entire night. Eadulf knew all about the custom. In some cases, he knew, the relatives and their guests indulged in the *cluiche caintech* or funeral games that preceded the *fled cro-lige*, the feast of the deathbed.

The body had been wrapped in a *recholl*, a winding sheet, and placed on a *guat* or wooden bier. Eadulf wondered whether the body had been accompanied to the chapel by the wailing cries of the relatives, and hired mourners who wept aloud in a strange fashion called the *caoidneadh* accompanied by the slow clapping of hands, said to emphasise despair.

When the prayers and psalms were over, the bier was lifted by four men and carried out of the chapel. Fidelma and Eadulf followed the mourners as they moved behind the bier. Outside, a grave had been dug and the body was gently lowered into it while the women set up cries that, although Eadulf had heard them before, made his blood run cold.

Then, to Eadulf's surprise, a man came forward with an axe, and broke up the bier. The pieces were thrown into the grave. Seeing his puzzled look, Fidelma leant close and whispered: 'It is the custom to destroy the bier, for if it is left whole then the evil demons, the fairy folk, might use it to carry off the corpse on their nightly excursions. The bier is destroyed so that the corpse might obtain peace.'

Eadulf thought it not the time or place to comment disapprovingly on the continuance of a pagan ritual as part of a Christian ceremony. Then he saw that everyone was lining up before a Brother of the Faith who stood next to a great pile of broom. Each person was handed a branch of broom and took it to the grave and dropped it in.

'This is just to protect the body from the clay,' explained Fidelma. 'But each person who drops the broom in does so as a sign of respect.'

When this was done, the grave was closed. Bébháil's sister held up her hands and the lamentations stilled.

'The *Amra* – the elegy – will be spoken by my husband.'

A man, looking every inch a farmer, came forward. He appeared very uncomfortable. It was clear that he was unhappy at the task he had been asked to perform. He spoke in a swift, mumbling tone.

'We have interred the body of Lesren who was married to my wife's sister.' He hesitated and coughed. 'Lesren was a tanner. He was a *súdaire*, a craftsman, whose worth was well known to all who are here today. He now lies beside his daughter, Beccnat.' He paused again and sniffed. 'Beccnat was killed, even as he was, and so this is the second time in as many months that the *laithi na canti* – the days of lamentation – have been visited on us who were related to Lesren. Sorrow is the load we must bear.'

Yet again he paused and looked across to Bébháil who stood, dry-eyed and stony-faced, supported by her sister on one side and Tómma on the other. He set his jaw as though he had made up his mind to follow through an unpleasant task.

'There is little I can say. I cannot pretend I liked Lesren or made him welcome at my threshold. But I suffered him for the sake of my sister-in-law. He was not a good father; he was not a good husband. But they are truly good who are faultless. I will not call praise on him, for that would be insincere, false and pretending. I will say only this –

he was my wife's sister's husband and I am sorry that his passing has made her a widow.'

Eadulf studied the faces of those around him with surprise, expecting some to react at this curious elegy. It seemed that no one wanted to articulate any criticism for what had been said. More important, Bébháil was standing with her face devoid of emotion. Eadulf realised that few people could have liked Lesren in the community. That fact caused him some consternation. He wondered how many had a motive to kill Lesren. He realised that it was not just Goll and his son. Lesren had made enemies of many people. He wondered if Fidelma was relying on this fact to defend Gabrán.

The people had begun dispersing from the graveside. Accobrán was approaching them with a smile of satisfaction.

'Have you heard the news, lady?' he began, seeming pleased with himself. 'The news about my capture of Gabrán?'

Fidelma did not match his smile.

'I shall go to see him shortly,' she said. 'While the boy was stupid to run away, I do not believe he was guilty of Lesren's murder.'

Accobran's jaw dropped in surprise.

'Not guilty . . . ?' He shook his head in disbelief. 'Well, I think he was, and guilty of Beccnat's murder as well.'

'Yet you were the one who found the evidence to prove otherwise,' pointed out Eadulf quickly.

Accobrán flushed. 'Perhaps he fooled me. Perhaps he was not at the house of Molaga on that night of the full moon.'

'I spoke to Brother Túan from the house of Molaga.' Fidelma cut him short. 'You were not mistaken. He was there at the night of the full moon.'

The young tanist looked glum. 'Well, at least he showed his guilt of Lesren's death by running away.'

'He showed his fear of being blamed for it,' Fidelma pointed out. She turned and made her way across to where Bébháil was standing with her sister and Tómma.

Tómma greeted her with a grim smile. 'The tanist has told us that young Gabrán has been caught and imprisoned for Lesren's death.'

Fidelma examined the downcast features of Bébháil for a moment before replying.

'He has been captured because he was running away. If he were guilty, it would be stupid to run away and draw attention to himself. There has been too much innocent blood shed in this place for another innocent to have his life destroyed.'

Tómma frowned and cast a nervous glance at Bébháil. 'But the tanist said . . .'

'I am returning to the fortress to question Gabrán. I am hoping that the innocent will go free and that the guilty may come forward.'

She returned to Eadulf, aware that Bébháil had taken an involuntary step after her and that Tómma had reached out a hand to stay her.

Accobrán accompanied them as they rode back to the fortress. Fidelma and Eadulf went immediately to the place where Gabrán had been confined. Fidelma gently declined the tanist's offer to attend the questioning of the youth. She wanted to speak with Gabrán without Accobrán there.

The young woodcutter rose as they entered the dark stone cell in which he had been confined. He had a cut across one eye and a bruise on his cheek.

'You have done a stupid thing,' Fidelma told him after a moment or two.

The boy shrugged, trying to be indifferent. It was clear that he was nervous.

'I did not kill Lesren,' he said quietly.

'Is running away designed to make us believe that?' she asked, motioning Eadulf to shut the door so that they would not be overheard. He did so.

'What else could I do? No one here appeared to believe that I did not exact revenge for what Lesren was saying about me.'

'Who told you that?'

'Why, Creoda said—'

'Creoda? And he said – what?'

'That everyone believed that I had killed Lesren because he accused me of murdering Beccnat. I knew I had to leave.'

'You should place your trust in the law.'

'Law and injustice are often the same thing,' the boy replied quickly. 'I often heard old Aolú say as much before he died.'

'That may be true, but it is the interpretation of the law which balances the account.' Fidelma indicated that the boy should reseat himself on the wooden bench that served as a bed. Then she took a chair while Eadulf stood by the door. 'When did you first hear of Lesren's death?'

'I was returning home from cutting wood.'

'And Creoda told you?'

The boy nodded.

'Is Creoda a friend of yours?'

'I know him.'

'Did he tell you to run away?'

'He advised it.'

'So you ran away at Creoda's behest. Did you not think that you were doing a foolish thing, if you were innocent?'

Gabrán was regarding her thoughtfully.

'You do not think that I am guilty?' he whispered. There was no disguising the sudden hope in his voice.

'I think that you were panicked into flight to make you appear guilty.'

'Then you think Creoda is guilty?'

Fidelma shook her head. 'However, first we must demonstrate that you are not.'

There came a rap on the door and Accobrán came in. Fidelma glanced up with a frown of irritation.

'I am in the middle of questioning Gabrán,' she began.

'It is Bébháil and Tómma come to see you, lady. They insist on seeing you immediately. Also,' he glanced at Gabrán, bent close to Fidelma's ear and whispered, 'the boy's parents have arrived.'

Fidelma sighed in resignation. 'Very well. Tell them that I will join them in a moment.'

She waited until he departed and the door was closed again before she glanced back to Gabrán.

'You do not like Accobrán, do you?'

The boy raised a hand to his bruised face. He returned her gaze levelly for a moment or two and then shrugged.

'I have reason not to.'

'Why?'

'The answer is simple. Knowing Beccnat to be in love with me, he tried to separate us.'

'You will have to explain that.'

'A month or so before Beccnat was murdered, there was a *féis* at the chieftain's hall. Accobrán insisted on dancing with Beccnat.'

'Insisted?' Fidelma picked up on the word. 'He was forcing his attentions on her?'

Gabrán sniffed and nodded quickly.

'How did Beccnat respond to that?'

The corner of the boy's mouth drooped. He said nothing.

'Did she raise objections? Accobrán is a handsome man,' she added.

Gabrán looked up angrily. 'She was flattered at being asked to dance with the tanist. That was all. I suspect that after the *féis* he tried to see her again. But, as I told you before, Beccnat and I were in love . . .

we were going to marry in spite of the story Lesren was spreading around.'

'But you suspected Accobrán tried to meet with Beccnat secretly?' queried Fidelma. 'Tried or succeeded?' she added sharply.

'Tried,' the boy responded immediately. 'I trusted Beccnat. I did not trust Accobrán.'

'Very well.' Fidelma rose to her feet. 'I'd better see what Lesren's widow wants. We will continue this shortly.'

Bébháil and Tómma were waiting for them in the chieftain's hall with Accobrán. Becc was out hunting and not expected back before evening. Accobrán rose quickly and came to her. In a low voice he explained that Goll and his wife had been taken to an antechamber to await them so that they should not confront Bébháil.

The tanner's widow and Tómma had risen awkwardly as they entered and Fidelma, having acknowledged Accobrán's arrangements, walked across to them and motioned them to be seated again.

'I have little time,' she began, feigning irritation. 'Tell me what brings you here. I presume that you have something to tell me about Lesren's death, Bébháil? Have you persuaded Tómma that he should let you tell me the truth now?'

Tómma half rose from his seat, his eyes wide.

'How could you—' he began.

Fidelma motioned him to silence with a cutting gesture of her hand.

'It is no trick. I saw that Bébháil wanted to speak to me at the funeral but you prevented her. I will not put words in your mouth. I now presume that you are persuaded to tell me the truth of what happened between Lesren and yourself.'

Tómma sunk back again, his face grim. He lowered his head as if resigned to what was to follow. Fidelma turned to Bébháil with an expectant expression. The woman was dry-eyed and in firm control of her faculties.

'What I did was wrong,' she began. Then she fell silent again. Fidelma did not say anything but continued to wait patiently until she continued. 'I could not stand the life any more. I did love him once. But love departed even before Beccnat was born.'

Fidelma regarded her with sympathy.

'And what did you do that was wrong?' she said encouragingly.

'I killed him,' she said simply.

Eadulf let out a noisy exhalation of breath and Accobrán gave a little moan of astonishment. Fidelma did not glance in their direction, keeping her eyes on Bébháil. She turned to Tómma.

'It was stupid to lie to me.'

The tanner shrugged helplessly. 'I had to. I could not tell you that Lesren was telling me that Bébháil had struck the blow that killed him.'

'The name he spoke was Bébháil and not Biobhal. How did you think of such a name? Biobhal, I mean.'

'It was the only thing that came into my head. You see, while Lesren was mumbling away about Bébháil, Creoda was standing at my side. I could not gamble on the fact that he might have heard what Lesren was saying. I turned to him and pretended that I had heard the name Biobhal just in case. I could pretend that he had misheard the name, as it was so similar. He readily accepted that Biobhal was the name he had heard.'

Fidelma's lips were pressed firmly together to hide her annoyance. 'I swear, Tómma, that your false information led me astray for a while. You chose a name that could have had some pertinence.' She turned back to Bébháil. 'What you have to confess is very serious, Bébháil. The most serious offence under our law is to deprive another person of his life. You are confessing to a killing. You had best tell me the story from the very beginning.'

The widow appeared calm and implacable. 'It is a simple story, lady. It is one that is as old as the relationship between men and women. I was young. I was beguiled. Lesren was an attractive man. An artisan. A *súdaire* – a tanner. I knew he had been married before but he had told me all manner of bad stories about Fínmed. I married him.' She paused and gave a quick, meaningless smile. 'His stories were untrue, as I soon found out. My life has not been happy.'

'There was a redress for your situation in law,' pointed out Fidelma. 'The law allows for separation and divorce.'

'I stayed for many reasons. I suppose my daughter was the chief reason but perhaps I am only making excuses. I should have left after poor Beccnat was murdered. Yesterday, he began abusing me again. It was then that something seemed to snap within me. I grabbed a kitchen knife and—' She broke off and gave a helpless sob.

'Are you pleading self-defence?' demanded Accobrán harshly. He seemed to be trying to take command of the situation, perhaps in an attempt to make up for his treatment of Gabrán.

'Of course she is!' snapped Tómma, moving closer to Bébháil and putting an arm protectively around her shoulders. 'Can't you see how ill this woman has been treated by that beast? If you want proof, lady,' he added, turning to Fidelma, 'ask her to go with you into the next room and show the blemishes that Lesren made on her body.'

'Is this true, Bébháil?' Fidelma asked gently.

The woman did not raise her eyes but merely nodded. Fidelma was quiet for a moment or two.

'This crime of *fingal*, kin slaying, is the most horrendous in our laws,' she reflected.

'Heavy sanctions are made against the perpetrators,' added the tanist sharply. 'You will have to face a harsh punishment.'

'But,' Fidelma's voice suddenly snapped like a whip, irritated at being interrupted by the young man who knew little of the law, 'the law recognises that there are circumstances in which the killing of another person is justified. It is not a crime in kill in battle, no crime to kill a thief caught breaking into your house with the intent to steal or render harm to you. The *Cairde* text also shows that it is permitted to kill in self-defence. Had you brought this matter before me while Lesren still lived, you would have received an immediate divorce and not only half his property but also a considerable recompense. The laws are clear on the protection of women from men, even husbands, and abuse, whether physical or verbal, is treated seriously. You should have pursued that course in law. You did not and your suffering coalesced into a point where you struck back. I cannot pretend that it was correct to kill him but that you did it in self-protection is a defence that must be taken account of.'

They waited in silence while she pondered the matter.

'It is clear that there has to be a hearing. I must sit in judgement on this matter with the chieftain of the Cinél na Áeda and the abbot. Come back to the Great Hall when you hear the evening Angelus bell striking at the abbey.'

Tómma seemed unhappy but Bébháil inclined her head in agreement.

'It shall be as you say, lady,' she said.

Fidelma gave her a brief smile of encouragement. 'That you have come forward voluntarily with this confession, Bébháil, also stands you in good stead before judgement. Had you not done so, I might have been tempted to waste many days pursuing a wrong path.'

She swung round on Tómma with a frown.

'You stand in greater peril than Bébháil,' she said sternly.

The assistant tanner shuffled his feet uneasily but did not reply.

'The *Din Techtugad* says that to give false witness is one of the three great crimes that God avenges most severely. A person who is a *gúfiadnaise* loses his honour price.'

Eadulf was not sure of the legal word she had used and he was glad when Tómma asked her to explain.

'A person who bears false witness. What made you pick on the name Biobhal?'

Tómma shrugged. 'As I told you, it was the only name I knew which sounded like Bébháil. I had to think of something to confuse Creoda in case he had heard Bébháil's name.'

'But where had you come across this name before? It is unusual, not one that a tanner might readily know.'

Eadulf realised she was stating a simple fact, and not being condescending. There was a purpose behind the question.

Tómma thought for a moment, as if trying to remember in order to answer Fidelma's question. 'It was old Liag who told me some story. I can't remember what about but Biobhal was in it somewhere.'

Fidelma could not help meeting Eadulf's eye.

'Liag told you the story. Are you sure?' she insisted.

'I am sure. I am sorry that I misled you, lady. I did it only to protect Bébháil.'

'And did you tell Creoda to advise Gabrán to flee?'

'I told Creoda that everyone thought Gabrán was the culprit. He took it on himself to advise Gabrán as he did.'

The woman moved forward eagerly. 'Tómma has been my friend these many years. When I told him what I had done, he was afraid for me and tried to protect me. You must not blame him.'

Accobrán snorted indignantly. 'The law is the law.'

Fidelma ignored him and smiled in gentle reassurance at the woman. 'All things will be taken into account, Bébháil. You and Tómma must be in the Great Hall this evening and you must be judged accordingly. But remember, Tómma, that there is always a consequence to our actions. The Gospel of the Blessed James says "How great a matter a little fire kindles." A word spoken in innocence can do great harm. Remember that.'

The assistant tanner nodded and, taking Bébháil by the arm, left the room.

Accobrán was angry at their departure. 'They should be imprisoned. You are too lenient, lady. I do not understand. You are a *dálaigh* but do not follow the law as it is laid down.'

Fidelma regarded him coolly. 'Sometimes it is better to follow the spirit of the law than the syntax of the law. What do you wish, tanist? An eye for an eye?'

'The woman confessed to the murder, the man to being her accomplice – yet you have allowed them to go free!'

'Hardly free. They must return here for judgement.'

Accobrán laughed scornfully. 'Do you expect them to do so? What Gabrán did, so can they.'

Fidelma was serious. 'Gabrán fled from fear. These two do not fear the consequences of what they have done. Why would you expect them to flee? It is our law and custom that truth is more important than action. Our laws were written for the obedience of fools and the guidance of the wise.'

'I don't understand.'

'That is why I am the *dálaigh* and you are the tanist. You have much to learn before you take the chieftain's oath.'

Accobrán glowered. His pride stung. 'I accept that I am no lawyer. One thing I do not understand was why you seemed more concerned with the man's lying to you than with the woman's crime of murder.'

'The woman killed from fear. I think it is obvious that she was telling the truth about her crime. The law makes allowances for that and though she will be judged to owe compensation and fine for the crime they will probably be cancelled out by the hurt committed by her husband Lesren upon her. But giving false evidence, telling a lie, is something that is abhorred by the law. Is there not an ancient saying that the gods love not a lying tongue? While truth may be bitter, nevertheless truth is great and must prevail.'

'You seem concerned that Tómma misled you with this name Biobhal. Why would such a name mislead you?'

'We thought Biobhal . . .' began Eadulf, caught Fidelma's eye, swallowed, and managed to regain his composure before the tanist turned to regard him questioningly. 'We thought Biobhal was the name of the murderer,' he ended lamely.

'Well, it's not a Cinél na Áeda name,' replied Accobrán.

'Probably not,' Fidelma agreed, dismissing the subject. 'Didn't you say that Goll and his wife were also waiting to see me?'

The tanist gave a nod of assent and moved off to summon them. Eadulf waited until he had left.

'I presume that you did not want him to know about your idea that there is some connection about gold?'

'You presumed correctly,' she replied quietly.

'But with Tómma's confession that he spoke the first name that came to mind which sounded like Bébháil, you must surely have to change your mind about any such connection?'

Fidelma was serious. 'The more I think about it, the more I am not so sure. Let us keep this matter of the gold to ourselves for the moment, Eadulf. There are some things here that I find intriguing.'

'You were not surprised that Lesren was killed by his wife.'

'I suspected it. I suspected that it was a matter entirely unrelated to the deaths of the three young girls.'

Eadulf grimaced. 'I don't see how.'

'I felt instinctively that young Gabrán could not have had anything to do with Lesren's death. It was obvious from the day we met Lesren and Bébháil that there was tension between them. But Liag's chance appearance and the use of the name Biobhal distracted me. Those matters threw a doubt in my mind.'

'You are too hard on yourself.'

'I know when I am at fault.'

'Having seen and recognised your fault, do you not always advise that one must move on without dwelling on it?'

Fidelma smiled benevolently at him. 'That is true. Sometimes, Eadulf, you know when to say the right thing to help me.'

'Then what is our next move?' he replied brusquely.

'As I planned before. I want to see this Thicket of Pigs before I do anything else.'

'You can't really think that there is some connection to the murders of the young girls other than the fact that the place provided the location where they were attacked?'

'I can't think so logically,' replied Fidelma shortly. 'But I will be honest and say that I have some instinct. It is like an itch and I fear that I must scratch it or go mad. Remember how we saw one of the strangers and the smith, Gobnuid, on the hill? I would like to speak more to Gobnuid but I do not think that he will be in much of a mind to reply to my questions until I have some information to give weight to my interrogation.'

Eadulf suppressed a sigh. He had seen Fidelma presented with many difficult cases but he had never seen her attempting to show confidence while being so ill at ease. He was reminded once again that Fidelma seemed to have become a different person from the self-assured, confident *dálaigh* he had fallen in love with. It had all changed with the birth of little Alchú. There was no denying that, even though he felt guilty in returning to those thoughts he had been turning over in his mind in recent days.

He had heard stories of women who had given birth to babies and then, by all accounts, seemingly altered their very personalities, becoming victims of moods of black despair or varying temperament. The apothecaries at Tuam Brecain, the great medical school he had attended, said it was one of those mysterious feminine conditions that was released by childbirth. He racked his memory to recall what else they had said.

The idea was that the condition was induced by a state of blood deficiency. The heart, according to the apothecaries, was the powerhouse of the mind and the heart governed the blood. When the heart's blood became deficient then the mind had no sustenance and became anxious and depressed. This caused the woman's mind to become filled with negative thoughts, so that she felt anxiety, depression and fatigue, and was unable to cope and mentally restless and agitated.

Eadulf compressed his lips tightly.

There was a treatment they prescribed. He wished that he could remember it. Even if he did recall it, he realised it would be difficult to get Fidelma to take any medication. His eyes brightened suddenly when he remembered what the treatment was.

At that moment, Accobrán came through the door with Goll the woodcutter and his tearful wife, Fínmed. Eadulf turned quickly with a muttered apology to Fidelma, begging to be excused, and made for the door, taking Accobrán by the arm.

'Tell me, tanist, do you have a dyer in the fortress?'

Accobrán looked astonished.

'A *dathatóir*?' he murmured.

'Indeed,' snapped Eadulf. 'There is surely a *dathatóirecht* in the fortress, a place where fabrics are dyed?'

'Well, if you can find the smith's forge on the east side of the fortress, within the walls, you will see the shop of Mochta nearby. He not only tends to the clothes of the chieftain, but also . . .'

Eadulf did not wait to hear any more but was already hurrying away. Accobrán stood shaking his head as he looked after the Saxon. Then he turned back to where Fidelma was greeting Goll and his wife. The woodcutter's face was grim.

'I have come to tell you that my son is innocent,' he said belligerently. 'Furthermore, I am here to declare that I shall undertake the *troscud* until my son has been released without blemish on his character.'

Fidelma tried to hide the smile that rose unbidden to her lips and she drew her brows together as she tried to concentrate. It made her features express harsh resolve.

Fínmed moved forward, her hands imploring. 'My husband is indeed resolved, lady. I have argued with him. But we both know that Gabrán is not guilty of that with which he is charged. He tried to run away in a moment of weakness, of fear, because—'

Goll snorted in derision. 'Words will not release him. I am prepared—'

'To go without food and water until he is released,' supplied Fidelma. She knew the *troscud* well for less than a year ago she had been forced to face a difficult situation in which a chieftain threatened the *troscud* against a people who had no idea of the significance and symbolism of the act. She gave a hiss of breath denoting her irritation.

'Listen to me, Goll. Listen well, woodsman. The *troscud* is a course of last resort. To starve to the point of death and to death itself is a weapon not to be used as a mere whim. Do you think if your son were guilty that it would be moral to secure his release by such a means? The consequence of the action would fall on you.'

Goll's jaw came up aggressively. 'I know my son to be innocent and I will not be swayed from my intention.'

Fidelma shook her head sadly. 'Fínmed, I will address myself to you. You are more sensible than your husband and your son; indeed, more sensible than many here. Take your husband and take your son, Gabrán, and go home. There is hot blood in your men, Fínmed. Too much reaction and too little thought.'

Fínmed and Goll stood staring at her as if they had not understood what she had said.

'Did I not make myself clear?' Fidelma demanded. 'Take Gabrán and go home. He has not been accused of any crime except the mistake of not believing the inevitability of justice.'

She turned and quickly left the Great Hall before realisation hit them.

Chapter Thirteen

Eadulf easily found Mochta's shop not only from Accobrán's directions but also from the pungent odours of the dyes.

What was the flower he wanted called in Irish? He thought it was *brachlais* something or other. In his own Saxon it was called a wort – those of the New Faith called it the wort of John the Baptist because it was said to bloom on that day in June which was celebrated as the Baptist's birthday. It was the flower that the old apothecaries of Tuam Brecain had said was good for the condition he suspected Fidelma was suffering from. The trouble was that it only appeared in the summer months, otherwise he would have gone looking for it in the abundantly endowed countryside. He knew that there was only one place in which he might find some stored for the winter months, apart from an apothecary's shop. The plant was used to dye cloth.

Mochta, the dye-master, greeted him warmly.

'Greetings, Brother Saxon. I know who you are and why you are come to this place. I saw you and the king's sister the other day. What can I do for you?'

Eadulf told him.

'St John's Wort?' He looked thoughtful. 'I use it. Most certainly I use it. I take a purple dye from the flower heads and extract a yellow dye from the plant tops. A useful plant for a *dathatóir*. But why would you have need of it?'

Eadulf leant forward eagerly. 'Accept that I have a use for it also, my friend. If you would sell me some of the plants, what price would you put on them?'

Mochta rubbed his chin.

'What use would you have for such a plant?' he demanded again. 'I swear that you are not going to indulge in the business of mixing dye.'

Eadulf laughed quickly. 'That I am not, *dathatóir*. But plants are useful for other things apart from mixing dyes.'

'Ah, I see. Are you by way of being an apothecary, eh?'

'I have studied the art but am merely a herbalist rather than one who pretends to the medical skills.'

Mochta stroked his nose with a forefinger as he considered the proposition. 'I can sell you a bunch for a *screpall* but certainly no more, for I have need for these colours soon.'

'A bunch will do well enough,' Eadulf agreed.

The Angelus bell had tolled its last chimes that evening when people began to gather in Becc's great hall. Eadulf, taking an unobtrusive seat at the back of the hall, observed that most of the people were those who had been in attendance at the funeral that morning. There were also several of the religious from the abbey.

Bébháil and Tómma had been brought in to sit in front of those attending, facing the chieftain's chair. Immediately behind them was a group of people whom Eadulf recognised as relatives of Bébháil come to support her. At either side of the chieftain's chair of office were several other seats.

Accobrán entered bearing a staff of office which he thumped on the ground three times calling for quiet. Then Becc entered, followed by Fidelma and Abbot Brogán. The chieftain took his seat with Fidelma on his right hand side and the abbot on his left, with Accobrán seated on the abbot's left.

Becc turned to Fidelma and motioned for her to proceed.

'This is a sad matter,' Fidelma began softly. 'Thankfully, it is a simple one. Bébháil has confessed to the unlawful killing of her husband, Lesren the tanner. The obstruction of justice by giving false testimony has been confessed to by Tómma. Bébháil and Tómma have described the circumstances of this crime from their view. Your chieftain and I have discussed these circumstances in the presence of the abbot and the tanist. We are all agreed on a resolution to this matter.'

She paused and glanced down to where Bébháil and Tómma were seated with pale faces and eyes downcast.

'The crimes being confessed, all that now remains is the announcement of the penalties. Does either of you have anything to say as to why we may not now impose such penalties upon you?'

The widow of Lesren shook her head quickly while Tómma looked up. He seemed about to open his mouth to say something but his companion laid her hand on his arm and he dropped his gaze again.

'Very well. To the crime of *fingal* as charged against Bébháil, we have taken into account the circumstances of this act. The *Cairde* text, as I have already indicated to those who have confessed, takes into account that it is permitted to kill in self-defence and the text is clear – every counter-wounding is free from liability. We have fully taken into account that Bébháil was driven to a point where she was not in control of her actions and, in this condition, she killed Lesren. So she leaves this court without penalty as to that killing. However' – Fidelma said the word quickly as the audible murmur began to gather throughout the hall – 'we must impose a small fine for the delay before which she confessed the matter to me, which wasted time and could have led to a potentially harmful situation. For that Bébháil must pay her chieftain two *screpalls*.'

Bébháil was in tears now but smiling through them. It was a small sum for a tanner's widow to pay. Members of her family were gathering round and patting her on the back.

Fidelma turned to Tómma, who had clearly been surprised and happy about the lightness of his companion's punishment, and called for silence.

'Tómma, I am afraid it is you who have committed the more serious of the offences that has to be judged this day. I have told you that a false witness is deemed beyond God's forgiveness. If we do not have truth, then we have nothing. For this false testimony you must pay the consequences.'

Bébháil was clutching her companion's hand now and she raised her tear-stained face to Fidelma. 'But he did it for my sake, to protect me, lady. He was willing to perjure his soul to protect me. Can you not find mercy . . . can you . . .'

Fidelma regarded her coldly, causing her to hesitate and fall silent.

'The law cannot admit to justification for lies,' she replied firmly. 'But as judges and interpreters of the law, we have taken into account the circumstances as, indeed, we must. But still the law demands its price for lies.'

Tómma patted Bébháil's hand in pacification.

'I am ready to answer to justice, lady.'

'You will lose your honour price for a year and a day. In token of which you will pay a fine of that honour price.'

There was quiet in the hall as people tried to reckon up how much this would mean. Fidelma smiled grimly at their puzzled expressions.

'Tómma, I believe that you are of the class that is not yet possessed of any land handed down from your father or family. You are of the *Fer Midbad*.'

The tanner nodded slowly.

'You have been in this position for fourteen years?'

'I have.'

'Then your honour price in accordance with law is the value of a heifer cow of one year in age, which is four *screpalls*. Can you pay that sum?'

Tómma swallowed as he felt the relief surge through him. 'That I can, lady.'

'A year and a day from now, providing you give no further cause for legal action, your honour price will be returned to you.'

There came some muted cheering in the hall among those who had nursed a dislike for Lesren and had been sympathetic to Bébháil. The relatives were now leaning forward and congratulating both of them. No one argued that the judgement was harsh. No one took any notice of Accobrán's stern remonstrance to be silent. Becc glanced at Fidelma, smiled and shrugged.

'Let us leave them all to their moment of relief,' Fidelma said, rising from her seat. 'In their joy they have failed to remember that we still have a murderer to find.'

Fidelma and Eadulf paused to rest their horses on the brow of the hill and looked down the road along which the *bothán* of Menma the hunter lay.

Eadulf was irritable since his attempts to make Fidelma swallow a draught of the potion he had prepared from an infusion of St John's Wort had come to nothing. She had instructed him to throw it away and no amount of cajoling could make her even taste it.

'This is a waste of time,' he said crossly.

'I have never known you to have a feeling about an investigation that is not based on logical deduction from tested information,' he replied moodily. 'Usually, it is information that I have neglected to assess.'

Fidelma shook her head immediately.

'I have no more information than you have,' she replied firmly.

'Very well.' Eadulf was almost surly. 'You do not convince me. I know you too well. Let us find Menma and explore this place, whatever it is. You will obviously explain it to me in your own good time.'

They halted in front of the log cabin that was Menma's home. Before they dismounted, an attractive young woman with shoulder-length corn-coloured hair came out. She was wiping her hands on a cloth and looked from one to the other with a frown and then smiled abruptly.

'You must be the lady Fidelma and her companion. My man Menma told me about you yesterday. Have you come in search of him?'

Fidelma bent across her horse's neck with a smile. 'We have. Are you Menma's wife?'

'I am. My name is Suanach, lady.'

'Is it an inconvenient time to come in search of your husband?'

'Not so, lady. I will call him.'

She went to one of the wooden beams of the porch, where hanging from a nail was a horn on a leather thong. The girl took it, tried a few experimental breaths and then blew into it, long and loud. While the sounds echoed away, she replaced it and stood for a moment or two with her head to one side. Eadulf started to say something but she raised a finger to her lips to stop him. A moment later, the sound of another horn echoed through the forest.

Suanach smiled at them. 'He is not far away. He will be here shortly. Will you dismount and come in and take some mead?'

Eadulf was still in a grumpy mood and about to refuse when Fidelma assented. He realised that he had almost broken an essential rule of etiquette, for when hospitality is offered it must never be refused, even if accepted only in token form.

They were sitting at the table in the cabin and the drinks had been poured when the door opened and Luchóc came bounding in, yelping and sniffing suspiciously at them. Menma came in immediately behind the dog and greeted them.

'I recognised your horses outside. Sit, Luchóc! Sit!'

'We have come to ask if . . .' began Fidelma.

'. . . if I can show you the caves on the Thicket of Pigs?' Menma smiled. 'I recall our conversation. I will, indeed, escort you there. When will you be ready?'

'We are ready—' began Eadulf but was cut short by a surreptitious kick under the table from Fidelma.

'We are ready after we have finished sampling Suanach's excellent mead,' she ended for him. 'Then we should start with that cave you mentioned which is on the hill above the Ring of Pigs.'

The ritual of hospitality ended, Fidelma and Eadulf followed Menma and his dog on horseback up the forest-covered hill. Menma did not ride, but preferred to jog up the slope, and with such agility and stamina that he was able to keep in front of their horses. The animals had to walk, blowing and snorting as they ascended the rise. Fidelma soon realised that riding was a mistake and eventually, as they came to a clearing not far from the summit, she halted and dismounted. Eadulf, with a little prayer of thanks, followed her example.

'It is probably best to tether the horses here in this glade and continue on foot with you,' she said to Menma.

The hunter acknowledged her suggestion with a smile.

'It is not really the terrain for horses,' he assented, but that was as close as he came to criticism. He pointed towards the top of the hill, which was still fairly well obscured by the trees. 'That is what you seek. The old mine has its entrance near the summit.'

'Why is this place called the Thicket of Pigs?' Eadulf asked as they began to ascend on foot. He was looking around in bemusement at the oak and alder groves that stretched across the hill on either side. 'Why would anyone name it so?'

'Have you not heard the tale of Orc-Triath, the King of Boars?' asked Menma with a smile.

Eadulf disclaimed knowledge.

'The boar was one of the prized possessions of the fertility goddess Brigid, daughter of the Dagda, Father of the ancient gods and goddess of Éireann.'

'According to the old story, this boar represented a powerful Otherworld creature which symbolised plunder and destruction,' explained Fidelma.

'And many a huntsman has encountered the animal and not lived to tell the tale,' added Menma with apparent seriousness.

Eadulf raised his eyebrows in surprise. 'You really believe that?'

'It is not a question of belief but knowledge, Brother Saxon,' replied the hunter. 'This was the area, according to legend, where Orc-Triath roamed and ruled.'

'What is that place?' demanded Fidelma, pointing to where some grey limestone rocks rose on their right like some curious fortress among the trees. She did not wish to dwell on the ancient legends for she wanted to concentrate on her purpose in coming to this place.

'That stand directly above the Ring of Pigs? It used to be called Derc Crosda.'

Fidelma examined the great limestone outcrop with sudden interest.

'The forbidden place of darkness?' She translated the name. 'Meaning the cave, I suppose?'

'I should warn you that the mines are probably in a dangerous condition. They have long been abandoned,' Menma said earnestly.

'We will be careful. Let's see this cave.'

Menma called his dog to him and led the way through the thicket towards the rocky outcrop.

'This is what you are looking for, lady,' the hunter said, pointing.

The entrance into the cave was fairly large. It was clear that many people had used it in times past and even widened it with tools, for there were marks on the walls that showed the application of axes and hammers, splitting the rock.

Inside, the light that came into the cave showed the rubble of the entrance levelled onto a floor of sand.

'The dancing floor of the Síog,' explained Menma in hushed tones.

'The what?' demanded Eadulf.

'The fairies,' admitted the hunter. 'There is a legend that the fairies dance here, and that if you throw a stone onto the floor it will not remain there long, for the fairies clear the floor for their dances.'

Eadulf sniffed in disapproval. 'It seems this whole hill is riddled with legends.'

Menma did not seem perturbed by his cynicism. 'Of course it is, Brother Saxon. Each crack and crevice of the land is filled with a thousand years of life and experience. Do not your own people have such a folklore?'

Fidelma had turned impatiently. 'Can we lay our hands on some torches? I would look further into this place. We should have thought to bring some with us.'

'I will do my best, lady. I should have brought lamps or a candle. I didn't think.'

Menma's best proved good, for it was not long before he returned with two substantial brand torches, which he had cut and made from dry grasses.

The cave revealed itself to be large, with several passages leading off. It was clear that the place had once been a place of work and there were even the remains of a forge and rotting bellows to one side.

'This was abandoned many generations ago,' Menma pointed out. 'I was told that it was once a rich mine.'

Fidelma peered around. A stalagmite with a hollow top stood in one corner. There was a small pool fed by drops from a dripstone on the wall above. A few blocks of stone almost concealed a fissure at the back and she immediately felt drawn to it.

'Careful, lady,' called Menma anxiously. 'There are many loose stones and objects here.'

Fidelma did not acknowledge him. She moved forward and began to squeeze through the fissure.

'Fidelma!' cried Eadulf in alarm. 'For heaven's sake, be careful!'

'This leads into another chamber,' her voice came back in reply, as she and her torch vanished. 'Come on.'

Eadulf exchanged a glance with Menma, who held the second torch. The hunter motioned him to go first. Gritting his teeth, Eadulf plunged into the darkness, turning sideways and trying to hold his breath as he squeezed through the narrow fissure. But a moment later he was, as Fidelma had said, in another chamber about the size of a wealthy chieftain's hall, with dripstones on the walls and several stalagmite columns on the floor, while the roof, in parts, was almost obscured by stalactites that were quite spectacular.

Fidelma was already crossing this dramatic chamber when Menma joined them.

'This way!' she called and disappeared into another passageway.

They could do nothing but follow.

The passage was not as narrow as the fissure and was tall enough to take a man walking at ease, but it led downwards. Eadulf could feel the incline. He had the impression that this passage was manmade, for it seemed rectangular and even in shape, with the sides of its walls as smooth as the floor.

'I hope we have enough light to find the fissure again to get back into the original cave,' he muttered anxiously.

Menma, coming behind him, did not reply but his muttered prayer suggested that he was clearly unhappy with Fidelma's heedless forward progress.

Suddenly the passageway ended and emerged into a high circular chamber in whose centre was a black pool of what looked like deep water. It was beautiful, with stalactites descending from the roof while stalagmites grew up from the floor at various points for a height of fully eighteen or twenty feet. What made it breathtaking was that the stalagmites and boulders were encrusted with a crystalline deposit which resembled small bunches of grapes.

'There are several galleries leading off over there,' Fidelma observed aloud.

Menma reached out a hand to hold her arm. 'Forgive me, lady, but you must go no further. We are not equipped to do so. These torches will last only a little while longer.'

Fidelma was reluctant but realised that Menma was making good sense.

'This part does not appear to have been worked for metal,' she said, looking round one more time.

'Maybe not,' agreed Eadulf. 'There was a lot of working up in the main cave. No one seems to have squeezed through the fissure to come as far as this.'

'It is time we were heading back towards the light,' insisted Menma again. 'These torches . . .'

Before they realised it, Fidelma had taken several quick steps towards the dark pool, bent forward as if to reach for something at its edge, slipped, and fallen into the black water with a splash. Her torch was extinguished and only the light of Menma's saved them.

'Quick!' cried the hunter. 'Pull her out. The water down here is icy.'

Eadulf had needed no urging. He dashed forward even as Fidelma was falling.

'Be careful!' Menma admonished him needlessly.

Eadulf had to watch his step on the slippery stone but he saw Fidelma splashing vainly, her breath coming in great visible gasps in the ice-cold air. He knelt down and reached out his arms to her. The water must be almost freezing for her face was very pale in the gloom. A flailing hand gripped his. He caught it and began to pull. It took several long seconds, seconds that seemed an eternity to him, before he was able to tug her from the dark wetness.

'No time to delay,' cried Menma. 'Quick, we must return to the main cave where there is more light and we can get some warmth.'

Half dragging, half carrying her, Eadulf followed the hunter as he hurriedly led the way back up the inclined passage into the hall-like chamber and straight across to the fissure.

At that point, his torch spluttered and gave out.

Eadulf, with the half-conscious Fidelma in his arms, found himself in total darkness and halted, unsure whether to continue or not. Menma's voice came out of the blackness not far away.

'I am at the fissure. Can you continue to come towards the sound of my voice?'

Eadulf hesitated but there was no other decision to make. 'I'll try. Keep talking.'

'This way, then. I can feel the opening and will be able to squeeze through it into the main cave. Can you reach me?'

Eadulf began to edge forward step by step, slowly, slowly . . . Menma kept talking and after what seemed a great age he bumped into an obstruction. Menma's voice came from his right.

'I think you are at the wall. Move towards me.'

A moment later Eadulf felt the hunter's outstretched hand. With Fidelma, now unconscious, hoisted over one shoulder, he found the opening to the fissure.

'Thank God!' came Menma's voice. 'I'll squeeze in first; you push her in and come behind. Between the two of us we should be able to drag her through to the main cave.'

It was easier said than done. It seemed the longest period of Eadulf's existence before a faint grey light began to replace the blackness and suddenly they were in the main cave with its hint of daylight coming from the distant entrance. Fidelma was still unconscious and Menma joined Eadulf in carrying her. Holding her on either side, they dragged her towards the entrance and out into the pale autumnal day.

'She needs to be stripped off and dried and have some warmth put into her,' Menma observed. 'The water of that underground pool is cold enough to cause frostbite. The sun is not warm enough. We'll have to get her to my *bothán* as soon as possible.'

'Let's get her to her horse,' suggested Eadulf. 'I'll ride with her and you can take mine.'

Menma was not one to waste words. He helped Eadulf balance Fidelma's inert form on his shoulder and they moved down the hill towards the clearing where they had tethered their mounts. By the time they reached it, the pain in Eadulf's muscles was almost unbearable. Menma helped him raise her body onto her horse once Eadulf himself had mounted. Eadulf immediately sent the beast into a canter, praying that his poor horsemanship would suffice to take him to the *bothán*. Menma was following close behind on Eadulf's mount. Luchóc, the hound, was barking, puzzled at the mystery.

Fidelma was still unconscious when they dismounted, and Suanach came out to greet them with a worried expression. Menma explained what had happened in terse tones and the woman immediately took charge of matters. Under her instructions, Fidelma was carried into the second room of the *bothán* that served as the sleeping quarters and laid on the bed. Suanach ushered the two men from the room while she began stripping her and wrapping her body in woollen blankets, rubbing warmth into her cold flesh. She called for Menma to bring a hot drink of *corma*, a strong ale, and then begin to heat water for bathing the frozen body. To Eadulf, it seemed an age before Suanach called him into the bedroom.

To his relief Fidelma was sitting on the bed, wrapped in blankets but conscious, and there was colour in her cheeks. She smiled almost apologetically.

'It appears that I owe you and Menma thanks for saving my life.'

Eadulf sat by her side and reached out a hand.

'What possessed you to reach out into that dangerous pool?' he demanded, trying to hide his concern in gruffness.

'I did not mean to overbalance into it,' she replied with dry humour. 'The rock was slippery. Anyway,' she held out a hand, 'this is what I saw. When I fell into the pool, I must have clenched it tight and my hand remained grasping it, for when Suanach revived me here she found it still clasped in my hand.'

Eadulf reached out a hand to take it. 'It's a piece of silver chain? Why risk your life for that?'

Fidelma glanced at him and shook her head.

'Examine it carefully,' she instructed.

He did so. It was a broken piece of finely wrought silver chain. He shrugged.

'What am I suppose to see?' he demanded.

Fidelma let out a breath of exasperation. She took it back.

'Have you ever seen such workmanship in these lands?'

Eadulf grimaced.

'I am not an expert on jewellery,' he replied defensively.

'Then by time everything will be revealed,' she said. 'I need to go back to that cave and explore further.'

Eadulf stared at her in surprise. 'I would have thought that you might have had enough of caves. You nearly died back there.'

'As I did not, it is a superfluous comment.'

'Well, at least you need to take things easy for the rest of today,' Eadulf said sternly. 'Do you know how long you have been unconscious?'

Fidelma brought up her jaw pugnaciously. 'People's lives are at risk here, Eadulf. Surely I do not have to remind you of that?'

'No, you do not. Nor do I have to be reminded that your life is at risk. It is my duty to prevent you putting yourself in harm's way.'

Eadulf's stubborn resistance matched Fidelma's when he believed himself to be right. She glowered at him for a moment and then suddenly relaxed, realising that what he said was true. She was in no condition to return to the cave that day. In spite of the compulsion to pursue the lead that she knew existed in the cave, it would have to wait.

There was a gentle tap on the door and Suanach entered with a bowl of steaming broth.

'You should have some of this soup and then rest, lady,' she said, with a reproving glance at Eadulf.

Eadulf rose immediately. 'I agree. You stay here and rest.' He glanced at Suanach. 'That is if it is all right with you?'

The hunter's wife agreed at once. 'Of course, the lady must stay here until she is recovered. At least she must stay for this night. She has been through a bad experience.'

Eadulf smiled in satisfaction. 'That settles it. I will ride back to the fortress and inform Becc of your intentions. Then I shall return here tomorrow morning.'

Fidelma looked at him suspiciously. 'Eadulf . . . you will go back to the fortress and . . . well, you will not go off on your own and do anything foolish? I think we may be facing some evil force that is even more dangerous than we think. I don't want you moving without me.'

Eadulf was reassuring. 'You have that broth and rest now. I'll return in the morning.'

He found Menma outside the hut rubbing down the horses.

'How is she?' the hunter enquired anxiously.

'Recovering and in good spirits,' Eadulf informed him. 'I shall be returning to Rath Raithlen to say that she is staying here this night, with your wife's approval . . .'

'Of course, the lady Fidelma will be our guest.'

Eadulf glanced at the sun, observing that it was still not far after midday. There was a whole afternoon that would go to waste.

'She wants to go back to the caves tomorrow,' he added quietly.

Menma looked astonished.

'The lady is tenacious,' he replied. 'What does she hope to find there?'

Eadulf did not reply but a thought was stirring in his mind. 'There are some hours before daylight ends. I wonder . . . ?'

Menma was looking at him expectantly and read his thoughts. 'Are you intending to go back yourself, Brother Eadulf?'

'If we had proper lamps to see with . . .'

'I have such lamps. When do you intend to go?'

'There is no time like the present,' Eadulf replied with confidence.

'Then saddle the horses again. We can ride back to where you left them before. It will save time. I will go to fetch lamps and some rope, for we might need it if you intend to explore the lower caves.'

A short time later they were approaching the familiar rocky outline of the Derc Crosda. Menma had brought oil lamps and two long pieces of stout hemp rope that they carried between them. He had left his small hound, Luchóc, behind at the *bothán*, feeling that the animal would be a hindrance in view of the expected cave exploration.

'What do you expect to find here, Brother Eadulf?' asked Menma as they reached the dark entrance leading into the rocky cavern. Eadulf had to confess that he did not know and that he was merely pre-empting Fidelma's exploration.

Menma lit the lamps and they moved through the main cave. This time Eadulf lost no time in moving to the fissure and into the next cave, finding the passageway and descending to the cavern with the circular pool. Things were much clearer now they had proper lights to see by. The stalactites and stalagmites were rather beautiful now they could view them properly. However, Eadulf had his mind on other things.

He walked to the edge of the pool and stood staring at the point where Fidelma had tumbled in. There were many times when he wished Fidelma was more open with her thoughts. What was the significance of the piece of silver chain?

Menma stood quietly behind, waiting patiently.

Then, moving around the dark pool, Eadulf suddenly realised that there were several tunnels leading off from this cave. He raised the lamp so that the light fell on their entrances and he saw that they appeared to be manmade.

'When was this mine worked out, Menma?' he asked.

The hunter shrugged. 'In my grandfather's day, or so I was told. Apparently, this was a rich mine once but like all mines it was eventually exhausted.'

Eadulf was frowning, trying to remember what it was that Fidelma had said about mining in the area. He was moving round the pool to examine the tunnels. One in particular caught his eye.

'I would have thought that this had been worked fairly recently,' he observed, pointing to the markings on the wall.

Menma came forward to examine it and whistled slightly in surprise.

'It does looks new,' he admitted. 'But I should imagine that down here things are better preserved than in the open.'

'Perhaps,' Eadulf replied, not convinced. He bent to examine the marks in more detail, holding the lamp close. 'Let's explore this one further,' he suggested, moving off without waiting for Menma's assent.

Unlike the cavern with the pool, the tunnel seemed extraordinarily dry and it was clearly hewn by men. It seemed to move upwards at a gentle angle and as it did so it narrowed and the roof grew lower so that soon they were crouching.

'We must be coming to a work face,' Menma hazarded. 'It will just lead into a dead end.'

Eadulf determined to press on to the end of the tunnel in spite of Menma's conviction that it was a waste of time.

Before the tunnel ended it opened into a small area six feet in width by six feet high and nine feet long. There were tools stacked in this manmade cave and lamps ready for lighting. Even Menma was forced to blink at the sight.

'This has not been deserted for any length of time,' Eadulf pointed out unnecessarily. 'Men have been mining here and recently.'

Something glinting on the rock face caught his eye. He moved forward, holding the lamp high. Then he took his knife from his belt and scratched at it.

'Fool's gold?' he queried.

Menma, at his side, shook his head wonderingly.

'I swear that is the real thing,' he said. 'My grandfather worked the mines before they were abandoned. I know something of this metal.'

He reached up a hand to touch it. Then, to Eadulf's surprise, he rubbed his finger on the glinting surface and placed the finger to his tongue. Finally, he nodded vigorously.

'It is a taste that you do not forget easily, Brother Eadulf,' the hunter sighed. 'It is genuine. You are right. It looks as if someone has been working the seam recently.'

Eadulf was deep in thought.

Could the boy – what had been his name? Síoda? – could the boy have taken his gold from here? But then Gobnuid had told Fidelma it was fool's gold. Not genuine. Fidelma had not believed it. And what had this to do with the deaths of the three girls? He shook his head. The conundrum was too much for him. He did not have enough knowledge even to consider the questions that now presented themselves.

'Is this what the lady Fidelma was looking for?' asked Menma, interrupting his thoughts.

'I believe so,' Eadulf replied. But why, he thought to himself. What possible connection could this working have to do with the investigation into the murders of the three girls?

'Are you absolutely sure that this is genuine gold?' he pressed Menma.

For an answer the young hunter reached for one of the tools that had been stacked at the side of the cave.

'It is easy enough to demonstrate,' he said. 'We will take a piece with us and show it to a smith. But I am positive it is real gold.'

He set to work on the rock face and within a short time had isolated a small round nugget, which he handed to Eadulf. Eadulf regarded it dubiously for a moment and then placed it in his *marsupium*.

'Now let us return to the daylight, while there is daylight,' he said, and noted the relief with which Menma accepted the suggestion.

It was not long before they were blinking in the pale autumn sunlight.

They had started to move down towards the tree line when Menma suddenly halted, laid a restraining hand on Eadulfs arm and placed a finger to his lips.

'What is it?' whispered Eadulf.

'A sound, a stone falling . . .' Menma whispered back. He turned, as if looking for something, and then pointed towards a clump of nearby trees and bushes. He hurried towards them with Eadulf on his heels. Eadulf allowed himself to be led into the cover of the undergrowth and followed Menma's example in crouching down for better concealment.

Menma was holding his head to one side in a listening attitude.

'Someone is coming up on the far side of the hill, from the direction of the abbey. I thought you might not want them to see us before you have seen them.'

Eadulf was just about to reply when the figure of a man came scrambling quickly over the rocks around the shoulder of the hill. He was moving swiftly, glancing behind him every so often almost as if he were being pursued. He reached the open area before the cave and stood hesitating for a moment. Then he turned. For a second or so Eadulf thought that he was going to make a beeline towards the undergrowth in which they were concealed. Then the man seemed to make up his mind and hurried towards a group of rocks that also gave cover at the side of the cave entrance. To Eadulf's amazement the man concealed himself behind them, but not before Eadulf had realised who it was.

It was Goll, the woodcutter, father of Gabrán.

Eadulf turned to Menma with a frown but the hunter placed a finger to his lips. He did not move from his crouching position but peered with a frown of concentration on his face in the direction from which Goll had first emerged.

Then Eadulf heard the sound of new movement.

A youth came into view. Eadulf was astounded as he recognised him. It was Gabrán. The father was hiding and observing his own son. Eadulf glanced at Menma and shrugged in order to display his bewilderment. The young man sauntered along the path and did not seem at all interested in the cave. He went quickly on and disappeared into the encompassing thicket of oaks and alders. They saw Goll begin to rise to his feet as soon as the boy passed out of sight. Then a strange thing happened. Goll dropped behind the rocks again.

Eadulf was about to say something to Menma but the hunter put a finger to his lips and pointed again.

A tall man came into view and it was clear that his objective was the cave from which Eadulf and Menma had recently emerged.

Eadulf's face fell in astonishment.

There was no mistaking the man – he was one of the strangers from the abbey. The tall figure of Brother Dangila, striding along with a comfortable, dignified gait, was unmistakable. He carried a bag of tools over one shoulder.

There was no hesitation until he reached the cave mouth. There he stopped and appeared to be doing something. It was soon obvious that he was lighting a lamp before moving inside.

After he had vanished, Eadulf glanced across to where Goll had concealed himself. There was no movement there. He turned to Menma and shrugged to indicate that he had no idea what was going on. He realised that Fidelma would want to know what was happening and it was obvious that neither Goll nor the stranger would be disposed to

Chapter Fourteen

Eadulf stared at the man but nothing now surprised him. He just wished Fidelma had confided in him about her suspicions concerning the cave. Perhaps the matter had nothing at all to do with the deaths of the girls. They watched as the thick-set figure of the blacksmith approached the cave entrance. He did so quickly, surely footed as if he knew exactly where he was going. At the cave entrance he halted and gave a sharp call, apparently announcing his presence. Then he disappeared inside.

Eadulf glanced across to the rocks where Goll still lay hidden. He noticed a movement behind the rocks that indicated the woodsman's presence and gave a quiet sigh of exasperation. He wished he had listened more carefully to what Fidelma had said about the mine. He could not see how it was at all relevant to the moonlight killings of the girls except that the bodies had been found in the vicinity. And what had Goll to do with it? He could not even think what questions to ask, let alone seek answers.

Menma gave a tug on his sleeve. The dark stranger, Brother Dangila, and Gobnuid were coming out of the cave mouth. Gobnuid was waving his hands in the air as if to help him explain something to the stranger. Brother Dangila extinguished his lamp and they both began walking slowly back down the hill in the direction of the abbey. Gobnuid was talking loudly but not loud enough for Eadulf to understand what he was saying. As soon as they were out of sight, Goll rose from his hiding place and began to follow them in a stealthy manner.

When they had all disappeared Menma rose. 'What now, Brother? Do we follow them?'

'We do not,' Eadulf replied. 'I need to report this to Sister Fidelma. Following them will not tell us anything. The stranger and Gobnuid seem to be heading back to the abbey. Goll appears to be merely watching them. The question that must be resolved is why?'

'That is true,' agreed Menma. He glanced up at the sky. 'Anyway, within the hour it will be dark. Let's get back to the horses.'

The horses were waiting patiently, tethered where they had left them. Menma led the way back down the winding track through the hilly woodland. They had progressed about halfway down the trail when they came to a fairly open stretch of hillside. Eadulf, lost in his thoughts, almost let his horse run into that of Menma, who had sharply halted.

'What—' he began, startled.

'Look!' Menma held out a hand.

Eadulf followed the line he was indicating to the woods at the bottom of the hill. Dusk was coming down, obscuring the clarity of his vision, but even so he could make out a rising plume of white smoke.

'It's coming from my cabin!' Menma suddenly yelled. 'My cabin is on fire!'

Without another word, he thumped his ankles into the sides of his mount. With a startled whinny, the horse leapt forward and began to canter down the hill. A sudden fear for Fidelma clutching at his breast, Eadulf followed swiftly in the other's tracks.

It seemed to take an interminable age to get down the hill. They had to slow their speed several times because of the steep descent in places, which threatened to precipitate both horses and riders in tumbling heaps down the hillside. They reached the main track to Rath Raithlen and crossed it, plunging on into the woods. As they neared the hunter's home they realised that the entire cabin was one gigantic bonfire. It was blazing from wall to wall, and as they rode up the roof fell in with a cascade of sparks and burning debris.

'Suanach!' yelled Menma, peering round in desperation for his wife. 'Suanach!' He flung himself from his horse and, for a moment, looked as though he was going to dash forward into the burning building.

Eadulf had dismounted and ran forward to grasp his arm. 'You cannot go in there!' He had to yell to make his voice heard above the crackling of the flames as they ate hungrily into the wood.

Menma halted, his eyes wide and staring.

Eadulf, too, was gazing in horror at the burning building. If Fidelma and Suanach had been inside then there was no hope for them. He moved backward and his heel hit something hard and metallic. He dragged his gaze away from the burning cabin and glanced down, finding, to his surprise, a discarded shield on the ground. He raised his eyes and began to look around.

There was something about the scene that did not seem right. The carcass of a dog was lying a short distance away, an arrow projecting from behind its shoulder. It was Luchóc. And now Eadulf saw there were boxes and garments strewn about, as if discarded in hurried fashion. He tugged at Menma's arm and pointed silently.

The young hunter stared, visibly shaken. Then he dropped to his knee by his dog and examined the arrow. He saw the shield that Eadulf had found, and swore vehemently.

'What is it?' demanded Eadulf.

'Uí Fidgente!' snapped Menma.

Eadulf shivered slightly. He was well aware of the rebellious clan of north Muman. He had had dealings with them before.* He also knew that they were a constant threat, challenging the authority of Fidelma's brother at Cashel and sometimes raiding his territory.

'You mean it is an Uí Fidgente raid?' he demanded.

There was no need for Menma to confirm the obvious. The hunter was examining the area, using his tracking skills.

'Probably about twenty men. At least, there were enough horses here to carry that amount.'

He was looking down at an area of churned-up earth. All Eadulf could see was a number of hoofprints.

'But Fidelma and your wife . . . ?' he began.

'I think they have been taken as prisoners. Look, a woman's footprint over the hoofprints.'

'I don't understand.'

'A woman was made to mount the horse here.'

'Both of them? Or one of them?' demanded Eadulf.

Menma pulled a face. 'That I cannot say . . .'

The rumble of many horses approaching caused Eadulf to swing round and Menma to run for his weapons.

A dozen horsemen broke through the surrounding trees, weapons in hand, and halted. Accobrán was at their head.

He caught sight of Eadulf and Menma. Even by the glow from the fire, which made a distorted reflection on his face, Accobrán was clearly surprised.

'We saw the smoke from the fortress and came to investigate. What's caused this? What are you doing here, Brother Eadulf?'

Menma took a step forward. 'Uí Fidgente! They have taken my wife and Sister Fidelma as hostages.'

'What?' Accobrán looked startled.

Menma quickly explained the evidence, the Uí Fidgente arrow and shield and the signs of horses.

'We must ride after them. How much start do you think they have, Menma?'

---

* see *The Subtle Serpent*, the fourth Sister Fidelma mystery

'A good half an hour, no more.'

'Then we may yet catch up with them. This is the first time they have raided our territory for years. Why now?'

Eadulf was mounting his horse and preparing to join Accobrán's men.

'Not you, Brother,' the tanist said sharply. 'I cannot risk you being slain or taken as a hostage. It is bad enough that the Uí Fidgente have taken the sister of King Colgú. For that, someone will surely pay a price.'

'But Fidelma—' Eadulf protested.

'Exactly so!' snapped Accobrán. 'I want you to ride back to the rath and tell Becc what has happened. Our people need to prepare just in case this raid turns into a major onslaught on the Cinél na Áeda. I would not put it past the Uí Fidgente to begin an undeclared war. If they are only a small raiding party, then we have a chance to overtake them and rescue the women. If not, then our people need time to prepare. Go back and tell Becc!'

Eadulf sat uncertainly on his horse but Accobrán ignored him and waved Menma and the others forward, following the tracks leading towards the north-west.

Eadulf realised that the tanist was right. Dusk had already given way to night. Someone had to warn the chieftain of the Cinél na Áeda about the possibility of an incursion by the Uí Fidgente. The chase of the raiding party was best left to the warriors of Accobrán.

He turned his horse and began to gallop quickly along the track towards the dark hill of Rath Raithlen, hoping his horsemanship was good enough to cover the distance without mishap.

A short time before, Fidelma had been drowsing comfortably. Her headache was gone and so was the intense feeling of cold. She felt warm and comfortable.

A hand suddenly clutched at her wrist, bringing her wide awake. She was staring into the pale face of Suanach.

'What's the matter?' She blinked rapidly as she struggled up. Her senses informed her that there was fear in the eyes of the wife of Menma.

'I went to the well for water. Several riders are coming this way. They carry an Uí Fidgente standard. The Uí Fidgente are not well intentioned towards our people.'

At the name, Fidelma had already sprung out of the bed and was hauling on her robe.

'We must hide,' she whispered.

'Truly,' agreed the woman. 'If you fell into their hands, lady . . .' Her eyes rolled at the idea for a moment.

There came the sounds of horses halting before the *bothán* and a voice calling harshly for the occupants to come forth.

'Too late!' cried Suanach. 'I must go and see what they want. You must hide.'

She knelt on the floor and removed the rug, revealing a wooden trapdoor. She pulled it up and pointed down.

'It is our *uaimh talún* – the sousterrain where we store food. Crawl along the tunnel as far as you can. It's a safe place to hide.'

They heard the door of the *bothán* crash open abruptly.

Fidelma did not waste time by trying to persuade Suanach to come with her. She dropped down into the tunnel and was immediately engulfed in darkness as the trapdoor was lowered and the hunter's wife replaced the rug.

'I'm coming!' Fidelma heard the woman call out to the intruder in the other room. She heard her footsteps cross the floor and then she decided to move further along the darkened tunnel just in case anyone found and lifted the trapdoor.

The tunnel was merely a crawlway. One could not stand in it but could progress only on hands and knees. It seemed to go on for ever, but then she reminded herself that space and time became meaningless when you were plunged into utter darkness. At least it was insulated with stone – she could feel the hard, smooth surfaces – and, above all, the tunnel was dry. She moved carefully along and soon aromatic smells came to her nostrils. She realised that this was where Suanach stored her herbs and mysterious items of food in bottles and boxes.

She sat with her back against what seemed to be a box and relaxed for a moment or two wondering whether Suanach had been right. The Uí Fidgente would surely not dare to raid this far south? And yet Fidelma knew just how brutal and rapacious they were. She sniffed in deprecation and, as she did so, caught a whiff of an acrid smell. It was a moment or so later that she realised just what it was.

Smoke!

She fought a moment's panic. Smoke was permeating along the tunnel. That had to mean that the *bothán* was alight. The raiders had set fire to the place. She could feel the smoke growing thicker as she began to breathe with difficulty. There was no chance of crawling back down the tunnel. There was no escape.

She turned and began to feel around her. Something that squeaked brushed by, then another and another. Mice! Mice were escaping the burning building. Again she almost panicked and then she realised that the mice were heading in one direction, away from the trapdoor through which she had come. She sought to control herself and move further along the tunnel.

It was not so much a light as a thin glowing line in the roof of the tunnel. Another trapdoor? Sometimes sousterrains had two entrances. Could Menma have built one that had an outside entrance? Would it be far enough away from the *bothán* to escape detection? Well, there was no other course but to find out. The smoke was growing thicker and she fancied she could feel an increasing heat blowing down the tunnel. Fear lent her strength as she scrambled over the boxes that lay in her path towards the chink of glowing light.

She pushed at the dark roof above her. It was wood! A trapdoor, indeed. But it did not move. Was it secured from the outside? She positioned herself under it, her back against it, and began to straighten up. It seemed immovable. But then . . . did it give a little? She pushed again with her back and felt it loosen. Something snapped. Then she heaved and found herself above the soil line.

She scrambled out with the quickness of a cat, crouching on all fours and looking round. She had emerged more than fifteen feet behind the *bothán*, from which smoke and flames were curling upwards. Fortunately, the raiders were all at the front of the building. She could hear shouting and laughter and the whinnies of their horses mingling in the commotion of the raid. She hoped that Suanach was not harmed, but her immediate need was to find shelter in case the raiders should venture around the back of the building. She remembered to push the trapdoor back into place and examined her escape route.

There was a distance of perhaps twenty or twenty-five feet from the place where she had emerged to the line of the surrounding forest. She rose to her feet and, crouching low, she ran headlong towards its shelter, praying that she was fully hidden from the raiders by the angle of the building and the heavy, swirling smoke.

No warning shout reached her ears before she plunged into the undergrowth, flinging herself flat beneath some bushes, and recovering her breath before she crawled to a vantage position where she could peer back to the *bothán* of Menma and Suanach. It was firmly alight and the smoke was rising in a tall spiralling column. Surely, she thought, the smoke would rouse those at the fortress and bring riders racing to investigate?

She had not escaped a moment too soon, for just then two horsemen came trotting their mounts round the corner of the building as if examining it.

'No sign of her husband. She must have told the truth when she said that he was away in the woods,' one man was saying in a loud, almost raucous tone.

His companion had a reed-like but sharp voice. He was waving his hand towards the cabin.

'The smoke will bring our enemies down on us soon. We should rejoin our companions before we are discovered.'

'And with our purpose unresolved?'

'What do we tell our chieftain?' demanded the second man.

'There is no need to tell Conrí anything.'

'Let us hope you are right and this hunter, Menma, follows his wife,' the other went on.

'He'll follow the bait sure enough. Suanach will lure him to us.'

'If we wanted to find him, surely all we had to do was wait here. I still fail to see why Menma is so important. There are others among the Cinél na Áeda who could supply the information.'

'The old merchant said that Menma knew all there is to know about the Thicket of Pigs. He would know what has been discovered there. If what the merchant said is right, then we would be able to avenge our defeat at Cnoc Áine by that usurping upstart Colgú.'

'We will not be able to avenge anything unless we leave this place before the warriors from Rath Raithlen arrive,' retorted the other.

The two riders turned and rode back to join their companions, leaving Fidelma trying to understand the meaning of their conversation. At least it seemed that Suanach was safe and merely taken hostage rather than perishing in the flames. But what was the mystery discovery at the Thicket of Pigs? Why would it bring the Uí Fidgente raiding deep into Eóghanacht territory? Who was the old merchant and what could Menma know?

There was no time to ponder more on the questions that assailed her. The only thing for her to do was to hurry back to Rath Raithlen and inform Becc. He would have to send warriors in pursuit to rescue Suanach if he had not seen the flames and done so already. Then she and Eadulf would have to go in search of Menma and find out more about this Thicket of Pigs. She was sure that the answer probably lay in the cave that she had wanted to explore. She was thankful that she had told Eadulf to go back to the safety of Rath Raithlen that afternoon. His life would be worth nothing to the Uí Fidgente.

She heard the horsemen leaving. There was nothing she could do to put out the flames of Menma and Suanach's home. The *bothán* had become a burning pyre. She rose and began to move through the woods, turning eastward at a tangent that she felt would intersect the main track to the fortress. She would probably meet Becc's warriors on the way.

Dusk was beginning to settle now. There was hardly any discernible path in the undergrowth and she had to twist and turn to find a way through. After a while she began to feel sorry that she had not gone by way of the main path from the *bothán* to the track. After all, the raiders had ridden in the opposite direction. But it was better to be safe than sorry, although her safety was a matter of speculation at the moment. She realised that she had become a little disorientated and she looked about, trying to figure out if she were going in the wrong direction. The darkness made such observation futile and the tall oaks and alders stretched skyward, blotting out the residual light which might have revealed the path.

When all seemed utterly hopeless, she realised that a natural path, perhaps a track used by generations of wild boar, had opened up to give an easier trail through the trees and undergrowth. She saw, even in the twilight, that several of the trees were dark on one side and stopped to reach out a hand to touch this shadow. It was damp moss.

Fidelma smiled.

That side of the tree was facing north. It was an old woodsman's trick to establish direction. She placed her back to the dry side of the tree and held her two arms straight at right angles to her body. Her left arm would indicate the easterly direction, the direction of the track.

She turned in that direction and nearly tripped over a long, slender branch. It was like a staff and perhaps someone had begun to shape it as such. She picked it up and realised it was a handy weapon. Feeling more secure, she began to push her way along another narrow path and it was not too long before she saw the open space of the track before her. She felt better. Although it was now dark, the moon and stars were out in a cloudless sky and there was some light along the road.

She estimated it would take about an hour certainly no more, of good walking to reach the fortress of Becc. She set out at a quick steady pace.

Barely ten minutes had passed when she heard a horse coming at a gallop. She moved quickly into the nearby bushes and held her staff ready. The moon gave light to a long stretch of the road behind her and she saw the black shadow of a horse emerge. Its rider seemed to be crouched in an awkward position over the beast's neck. Was it one of the Uí Fidgente who had discovered her flight and was trying to cut her off before she reached Rath Raithlen? Well, little time to debate the point. And she could use the horse.

As the beast drew near she leapt out screaming like a *bean sidh* – a woman of the fairy folk. The horse reared up on his hindquarters, lashing out with his forelegs at the air. The rider tumbled backwards and hit the road, lying still. Fidelma dashed towards the figure with upraised staff ready to strike.

The figure groaned and swore – a strange Saxon oath. Fidelma dropped her staff and stared down.

'*Nar lige Dia!* God look down on us!' she cried. 'Is it you, Eadulf?'

Eadulf groaned and shook his head, which he was holding in both hands.

'I don't think I ever will be me again,' he muttered. 'I am surely broken in two.'

'I am sorry. I thought you were one of the Uí Fidgente,' cried Fidelma. She was aghast as she bent forward and tried to raise him into a sitting position.

Eadulf blinked and attempted to focus in the darkness. Her saw her shadowy form, heard her voice, and realisation suddenly hit him. His senses returned in a rush. He struggled up.

'You were not captured by them?' he demanded incredulously, reaching out a hand to touch her cheek.

She shook her head with a brief smile, which he could not see in the darkness.

'As you can surely tell, Eadulf,' she replied waspishly to hide her relief. 'Otherwise I would not be here.'

'Accobrán and Menma with some men from Rath Raithlen have gone in pursuit of the Uí Fidgente,' he said, managing to scramble to his feet. 'We thought that you and Suanach were captured.'

'Suanach is their prisoner,' she confirmed regretfully. 'The Uí Fidgente were hoping to lure Menma after them.'

Eadulf seemed to have recovered his senses if not the feeling of his bruised body. He was puzzled.

'*Lure* Menma? I don't understand.'

'No more do I. But I overheard two of the Uí Fidgente speaking. It seemed that the purpose of their raid was to get information out of Menma. Information about some discovery on the Thicket of Pigs.'

'It seems a bit extreme to conduct a raid as far south from their territory as this in search of information. What sort of information?'

'Your guess is as good as mine, Eadulf. My immediate concern is for Suanach. She hid me in the sousterrain of the house while she went to confront the Uí Fidgente. That is how I managed to escape.'

Eadulf spoke with all seriousness. 'Let's hope Accobrán is as good a warrior as we have heard. Anyway, I think Menma is an excellent tracker and he will be able to follow the trail of the raiders.'

'In this darkness, I doubt whether he will be able to track them. Why are you not riding with them?'

'Accobrán told me to go back to the fortress and tell Becc just in case this is not a small raiding party but part of some larger attack on the Cinél na Áeda. Accobrán said that they saw the smoke from Rath Raithlen and he and his warriors rode to investigate. No one realised it was the Uí Fidgente. I was to inform Becc of the fact.'

'Accobrán said . . . ?' Fidelma suddenly realised the implication. 'Were you not at the fortress, then?'

'I went with Menma this afternoon to investigate the cave that you were so concerned with,' admitted Eadulf. 'We were returning to the *bothán* when we saw it in flames. We were there when Accobrán arrived.'

'You did *what*?' came Fidelma's sharp tone. 'You went back to the cave?'

'You were so keen to explore it that I felt I could save you the trouble. If there was anything of interest there, I felt that I could find it without you endangering yourself again.'

There was a pause while Fidelma digested the information. 'And did you find anything of interest?'

'*Dei gratia!*' Eadulf confirmed.

'Then you must tell me all as we ride.'

Fidelma looked round. The horse that Eadulf had been riding had trotted on a few yards and now stood nibbling at some bushes by the roadside. She started for the horse, felt for the reins in the darkness, and then turned to Eadulf.

'You mount first and I'll get up behind you.' Then she paused. 'You are sure that you are not hurt by your fall?'

'As you know, I have a thick hide.'

She imagined that Eadulf was grinning in the darkness and she nodded.

Eadulf had just finished his story as they came within sight of the gates of Rath Raithlen. Fidelma had been mostly silent during his recital, only intervening once or twice to clarify points.

Eadulf waited a while and then said: '*Quid nunc?*'

'Well might you ask what now,' Fidelma mused.

There came some shouting from the gates ahead as the lookouts spotted them in the darkness.

'Now,' she reflected on the question, 'now we shall tell Becc what has happened at Menma's *bothán* and then I must think awhile.'

In fact, Becc was waiting at the fortress gates for them with his steward Adag.

'Fidelma!' He came forward with arms outstretched. 'I am thankful to see you, cousin. When we saw smoke rising in the forest we were concerned. When Adag told me that you had not been in the fortress since this morning – you and Brother Eadulf,' he nodded quickly to Fidelma's companion, 'we grew very concerned.'

'Your concern should be for the wife of Menma the hunter,' responded Fidelma and quickly told him about the raid of the Uí Fidgente.

Becc was shocked. 'The Uí Fidgente raiding this far south? Adag,' he turned to his steward, 'send someone to spread word of this to the abbey and to the surrounding raths so that they may be warned and keep a careful watch.'

All was commotion within the fortress as the chieftain's orders were carried out. Meanwhile, Becc, having ordered that their horse be cared for, guided Fidelma and Eadulf back to his great hall and summoned a servant to bring wine and mead.

'How dangerous do you think the Uí Fidgente threat is?' he demanded of Fidelma after wine had been brought to them.

'The Uí Fidgente are always to be considered dangerous, Becc,' replied Fidelma. 'Since their defeat at Cnoc Áine, they have been waiting for another chance to rise up. Yet, somehow, I believe that this is a small raiding party in search of something specific. I don't think they were a war party. Merely scouts.'

'I don't understand.'

'They want some information. If they came in strength towards your territory, they would rouse the countryside. Someone would have seen the passage of their army. They could not take the easterly route because the Eóghanacht Áine stand in their path. If they came directly south they would encounter the Eóghanacht Glendamnac and if they tried to swing westwards and approach from that direction they would have to come through the Eóghanacht Loch Léin. No large army could come from the lands of the Uí Fidgente without an alarm being given by their very passage. Where an army cannot pass without being seen, a small raiding party can move with stealth and concealment. I think that this band is just such a party.'

Becc leant back looking relieved at her assessment. 'Still, even a small raiding party presents problems to me at this time. We do not have many young men trained and under arms at present. However, what do you think . . . what exactly are they after?'

Fidelma raised one shoulder and let it fall expressively. 'That I am unable to say.'

'You said that they were a scouting party. But what were they seeking?'

'Hopefully, Accobrán will overtake them and bring back prisoners so that we may question them. Only then will we know for certain.'

Becc was clearly worried.

'There is nothing else to do until the return of Accobrán,' Fidelma gently assured him.

Becc sighed in resignation.

'You will want to retire and refresh yourselves,' he said, rising. 'The evening meal will be ready in an hour's time.'

Fidelma and Eadulf rose with him. She was turning to the door when she swung back to look at the chieftain.

'I have a question, Becc. Do you have a *senchae*, an historian, in the fortress?'

'Several. It depends on what history you wish to know. There is the genealogist, the custodian of the history of my house; there is the teller of the ancient tales . . .'

Fidelma held up her hand. 'I am rather more interested in the history of the Thicket of Pigs.'

Becc raised his brows. 'I am afraid there is only one person who has stored that history in his mind. He might take some persuading to part with his knowledge.'

'Old Liag, the apothecary?'

Becc gazed at her in surprise. 'How did you know?'

'A guess, that is all,' she replied softly. 'We will join you for the meal within the hour.'

Chapter Fifteen

'Is there nothing that can be done until the return of Accobrán?' queried Eadulf, once they were in the seclusion of their chamber. 'I would have thought that there would be many things we could do. For example, what are we to do about Gobnuid? Brother Dangila and Goll also need to be questioned.'

Fidelma shook her head.

'You are impatient, Eadulf,' she replied quietly. 'I am not neglecting our main purpose in being here. Certainly, all being well, we shall continue our investigation in the morning. Now, show me the nugget that you and Menma found.'

Eadulf produced it from his *marsupium*. Fidelma examined it for a moment or two.

'I would say that Menma was right. It is genuine gold, just as the nugget that young Síoda found was genuine. Are you not intrigued by that?'

Eadulf shrugged. 'I thought our only concern was to find the killer of the three girls?'

Fidelma showed her disapproval.

'*Scintilla set potent*,' she said softly. 'Knowledge is power. You are fond of repeating that maxim, Eadulf.'

'I fail to see what a history of that hill has to do with the murders of the three young women. We know that a madman killed all three on the nights of the full moon. So I cannot see what the old mine has to do with anything except there is gold still there. In fact, I cannot see that we are making any progress at all in the matter of the murders.'

'Then you should remember another maxim – *perspicuam servare mentem*. If you keep a clear mind you will see the truth instead of being bogged down in irrelevancies.'

The next morning came with no news of Accobrán's pursuit and so Fidelma and Eadulf mounted their horses and went directly to Goll's cabin. As they entered the clearing before Goll's *bothán*, the door opened and Gabrán came out. The youth looked surprised to see them and stood scowling in the doorway.

205

'I thought that I was now cleared of suspicion,' he greeted them sourly as they rode up.

Eadulf was surprised at the boy's unfriendly manner after all Fidelma had done for him. Fidelma looked down at the youth.

'As you well know, you were cleared of suspicion in the death of Lesren. But we are still trying to account for other deaths.'

'I was cleared of Lesren's foul claims.'

Fidelma swung down from her horse and faced the belligerent youth.

'I am here to speak to your father,' she said in a sharp tone that made the youth blink and take a step backwards. 'Where may he be found?'

The boy hesitated and then motioned to one of the outlying sheds. 'He is at work there.'

'Thank you. And where is your mother?'

'My mother?' He frowned. 'She has gone to wash clothes down at the stream. Shall I call her?'

'It is Goll that we wish to see.' Fidelma turned to the shed that Gabrán had indicated. Eadulf, also dismounting, tethered their horses to the nearby pole and followed her, leaving Gabrán regarding them with his look of suspicion deepening.

The shed door was open and inside Goll was bent over a workbench. He was engaged in polishing a large piece of timber. Even Eadulf could recognise that it was a piece of red yew and carved with intricate designs.

'God be with you this morning, Goll,' Fidelma said as they pushed open the door and stepped inside. Goll looked up, startled.

'What do you want here?' he replied gruffly.

Fidelma chuckled in amusement. 'I swear, Goll, that I get the feeling from you and your son that you are not pleased to see the *dálaigh* who prevented a miscarriage of justice being visited on this family.'

Goll hesitated and then forced a grin. He laid down his polishing rag, took another cloth and wiped his hands.

'Forgive me. I was involved in my work.' He saw Eadulf peering at the carving. 'It is a lintel. The carved red yew is to ornament the replacement door of the chapel at the abbey. The abbot commissioned it some time ago. Forgive my lack of courtesy. I was not thinking. I am sorry. I am truly grateful for what you have done for my boy, Gabrán.' He laid aside the cloth and looked from Eadulf to Fidelma. 'How can I be of help?'

'I noticed that there is a bench outside,' said Fidelma. 'Let's go and sit awhile and I will tell you how you may help.'

Goll looked puzzled but nodded and followed them outside. Against the side of the shed, Fidelma had noticed a large bench and on this all three took their seats.

'What do you know of the Thicket of Pigs, Goll?' Fidelma began.

'The old hill? There is good wood growing on it. Oaks and alders.'

Fidelma smiled. 'That is a woodsman's assessment. You know nothing else about it?'

Goll shrugged. 'In ancient times it was said that a herd of supernatural pigs dwelt on the hill and were led by a great pig owned by the goddess Brigit. If anyone caught and killed and ate one of the pigs, it would reappear alive and well the next day. That is why the hill received its name.'

'So we have already heard,' Eadulf muttered.

'Do you often walk on the hill?' Fidelma asked suddenly.

There was no mistaking the reddening of Goll's cheeks.

'What do you mean?' he countered.

'I thought my question was clear.'

'Hardly ever.'

'Then let us be specific, Goll. It seems that yesterday's excursion on the hill was unusual for you. Is that so?'

Goll was silent for a while and then he shrugged. 'It was unusual.'

'What was your purpose in being there?'

When Goll still hesitated, Eadulf said: 'It is of little use to prevaricate. I saw you on the hill. You were seen observing someone.'

'You saw who I was following?'

'I did.'

'Then you should know why I was following them.'

'Let us hear the story, in your own words, Goll,' Fidelma said sharply. 'I do not have much time for guessing games.'

'What other purpose would I have but the same as your own, Sister? I know my boy was innocent of Lesren's charges. But someone killed Beccnat, also Escrach and Ballgel. I have become suspicious of the strangers, especially their leader. I do not know his name. But it is not the first time that I have seen him move surreptitiously about that hill. The more I listen to Brocc, the more he makes sense.'

'You mean that you believe that the strangers are guilty of the deaths of the three girls and you were following their leader yesterday in search of proof?'

'That is exactly what I mean. I knew that you had dismissed such an idea—'

'Then you knew more than I did,' snapped Fidelma. 'But I do not

207

work without evidence. Brocc would try and condemn a person without evidence. That is not how the laws of the Brehons work.'

Goll bent forward eagerly. 'Exactly. I went to find the evidence.'

'And did you?'

Goll shook his head reluctantly.

'From what I saw, I thought you were following your son, Gabrán,' observed Eadulf.

'Gabrán was on the hill, it is true. I thought the tall stranger was following him but he turned aside into a cave.'

'So you simply decided to follow the stranger to see if he would reveal anything to you. And did he?'

'Only that he seemed involved with Gobnuid the smith and they were interested in the old cave. It used to be an old mine working but it's long since been abandoned.'

Fidelma stood up suddenly. 'Thank you, Goll. But if there is any further investigation to be done, leave it to us.'

Fidelma decided that they should return to the fortress immediately in case there was any news of Accobrán's pursuit party.

There was. When they rode in they could see several horses were mingling in the courtyard and one of the warriors at the gate hailed them to say that Accobrán and his men had returned in good spirits. Fidelma and Eadulf made their way immediately to the chieftain's great hall.

Becc was sitting back smiling in his chair of office while to one side Accobrán was poised as if halfway through some story. Adag was there as well with several members of the chieftain's retinue. They glanced up as Fidelma and Eadulf entered. Accobrán smiled broadly.

'It is good to see you safe and well, Fidelma of Cashel. We heard that you had been hidden in Suanach's sousterrain during the raid. We examined it on our return but guessed that you had escaped the flames. Becc has now told us of your escape.'

Fidelma inclined her head in brief acknowledgement. 'And Suanach? Is she safe?'

'Safe and well and with Menma in the *forus tuaithe.*'

The 'house of the territory' was the name given to the building for the reception and treatment of the old, sick and injured.

'Don't be alarmed, cousin,' Becc said quickly, seeing the expression on her face. 'The girl is merely exhausted and a little shocked by the experience. She was anxious for your safety.'

'I would have no safety had it not been for her,' admitted Fidelma. 'The Uí Fidgente would not have treated one of our family well. I will see her in a moment. But, Accobrán, I seem to have interrupted you in the telling of your story. How did you fare in the pursuit and what prisoners have you taken?'

Accobrán shifted his weight and smiled wanly. 'I was saying that it was a good thing that we had Menma along with us as our tracker. The Uí Fidgente were devious. We could have lost their trail several times, but Menma was equal to the task.'

The tanist paused while Fidelma seated herself, and when Eadulf had done the same he went on with the story.

'We set off in pursuit at the time you returned to alert Becc,' he began again, initially speaking to Eadulf. 'It was dark by then and so we soon had to halt as we could see nothing. We waited until first light and then moved on again. The first part of the trek was easy as it lay through muddy woods. It seemed their leader knew what he was about because he soon took to the rivers and stony ground, which made tracking almost impossible. At least the dark had forced the Uí Fidgente to halt for the night as well. As I say, only Menma was able to keep us on their trail.'

'Did you get the impression that they were part of a larger body?' interrupted Eadulf. 'Were they trying to link up with a real invasion force?'

Accobrán shook his head. 'There were ten of them all told. We came on them just before midday when they thought they had shaken us off and had paused to rest. In their confidence that we were far behind, their leader was not clever. I placed my men in ambush positions.'

'Good,' Fidelma said approvingly. 'So you were able to take all of them prisoners?'

Accobrán dropped his gaze to the floor for a moment and made a dismissive motion. 'I am afraid I did not. Thanks be, however, Suanach was not injured in the fight which developed . . .'

Fidelma was frowning.

'How many did you capture?' she said quietly.

'None.'

'Not one of the ten was captured?' she cried, aghast. 'Not one of them injured?'

Accobrán was defensive. 'In battle, lady, it often happens.'

'It does,' agreed Becc amiably. 'I think that Accobrán has done well to bring Suanach home safely. One of Abbot Brogán's brethren is leaving this afternoon for Cashel and then will proceed to Imleach. He will take news of this matter to the king and doubtless Colgú will know what to do. Compensation must be forthcoming from the Uí Fidgente, and especially for Menma for the loss of his home and the insult to his wife. In the meanwhile, Menma may rely on the Cinél na Áeda to help rebuild his *bothán*.'

'It shall be so ordered, Becc.' Adag, the steward, nodded with satisfaction.

'With your permission then, my chieftain, I will wash the dirt from my body and take some refreshment before going to my rest,' the tanist said, preparing to leave.

'One question!' Fidelma's quiet tone stayed them as they were about to disperse. Everyone turned and looked expectantly at her. 'Did you discover the purpose of this Uí Fidgente raid?'

'Does it need a purpose?' queried Accobrán in amusement. 'They say that all the Uí Fidgente are cattle thieves and plunderers.'

'Does it not strike anyone that this is a long way to come in search of plunder – just ten men, passing through the lands of many rich clans before they reached here?'

No one responded. Fidelma tapped her foot impatiently.

'Does no one have an explanation to offer?'

Eadulf turned to her and opened his mouth but the look he received from her caused him to snap his jaw shut. He was about to point out that she had heard the Uí Fidgente discussing why they had come and for a moment he had not realised what she was doing. He had almost given away her intention to prise information from Accobrán.

'It is a pity that you took no prisoners in order to find out the reason behind the raid, Accobrán. You heard nor saw nor found anything to give you an answer to that question?'

'Nothing, lady,' vowed the tanist earnestly.

'Don't forget that Suanach was in their company for a long time. Perhaps she has some knowledge,' Becc pointed out.

'Then I must ask Suanach,' Fidelma said softly.

'An excellent idea,' Becc approved. 'And now let us allow Accobrán to rest and refresh himself after his exertions.'

When they were alone, Eadulf glanced apologetically to Fidelma. 'Why keep silent about what you overheard the Uí Fidgente say?'

'Come, let us speak with Suanach,' she said, without replying to his question.

The girl was sitting up having a bowl of broth with Menma at her side. They both smiled broadly as Fidelma and Eadulf entered.

'Well, this is a reversal of fortunes,' Fidelma greeted them. 'I seem to remember that last time it was I who was in bed being fed broth by you, Suanach. Are you injured?'

'No, lady. I am only a little tired for I have not slept this last night.'

'Then I am afraid that there is a question that I must ask of you, and of you, Menma, before I leave you to rest.'

'Ask away,' invited the young hunter.

'I will ask you first, Suanach. During the time that you were the captive of the Uí Fidgente, did they speak of the reason behind the raid?'

Suanach placed her bowl of broth on a bedside table and clasped her hands before her. She considered the question thoughtfully.

'One of them . . . no one mentioned any names . . . told someone to make sure that a trail was left so that Menma could follow them without difficulty.'

'They mentioned Menma's name?' interposed Eadulf quickly, confirming what Fidelma has already told him. 'They wanted Menma to follow?'

She nodded assent.

'Did they say for what purpose?'

'They wanted to capture him and ask him some questions.'

Fidelma turned to Menma with eyebrows raised in interrogation. The hunter shrugged before she said anything.

'I have no idea what they could want. I have neither friends nor enemies among the Uí Fidgente. I have been to their lands neither in peace nor in war. Why they would come hither to attack me, burn my home and kidnap my wife to lure me after them, I cannot begin to understand.'

'I heard snatches of conversation as we rode along.' They turned to Suanach who had spoken and waited expectantly. She went on: 'Nothing made any sense at all. One of the men mentioned something about a ship's captain. Something about the cargo at the house of Molaga. Then something about enough gold to finance a kingdom.'

Fidelma left out a soft breath. 'You say that these were snatches of conversation?'

'I can tell you no more than what I have said. I heard no more that made any sense.'

Fidelma turned to Menma. 'Does this make any sense to you?'

The hunter shook his head.

'Would it make any sense if I mentioned that the Uí Fidgente wanted to question you about the Thicket of Pigs?' added Fidelma. 'I, myself, overheard this.'

Menma's astonishment was not feigned. 'I do not understand it, Sister. What could I tell them that would be of value to them? Riches? Well, Brother Eadulf here will confirm that it was only yesterday that we discovered the old mine was being worked again.'

Fidelma turned back to Suanach. 'Was gold mentioned at all?'

She shook her head. 'Nothing more was mentioned in my hearing than what I have said.'

Fidelma tuned to Menma. 'Do you have any cause to go to the house of Molaga and speak with the merchants or captains of ships that put in there?'

'Now and again,' he admitted. 'I am known only as a hunter in these forests. I knew nothing about the working of the mine until yesterday so if you are saying that I mentioned it to some merchant who then told these Uí Fidgente . . .'

'I am not saying that,' replied Fidelma. 'I am not sure of the connection yet. There is something else which worries me. Accobrán says that the raiding party's tracks were hard to follow. Suanach hears one of them telling his men to make it easy for Menma to track them. The idea was to be able to capture you. These two views do not balance each other.'

Menma looked genuinely puzzled.

'Their tracks were easy enough to see. I suppose the tanist would like to make the chase sound more arduous and exciting than it was. We came on two sentinels waiting for us but Accobrán had them shot before they could raise an alarm.'

Fidelma said nothing for a moment and then: 'We will leave you for a while. I would not mention anything of this conversation to anyone.'

'Accobrán has already asked if I had overheard anything about the purpose of the raid,' Suanach said.

'And did you tell him what you told me?'

'I was tired and not thinking. It is only now that you have asked me that those snatches of conversation have come back to me.'

Fidelma compressed her lips a moment. 'In which case, I would say nothing further to anyone about this matter until I ask you.'

'I do not understand, Sister, but I . . . we . . . will do as you ask. Is it not so, Menma?'

Her husband nodded a little morosely.

'Then we will leave you in peace for the time being.' Fidelma hesitated a moment. 'Tell me, Menma, did you ever attend when old Liag was giving instruction in star lore?'

'Of course, when I was younger. So did Suanach.'

'Beccnat, Escrach and Ballgel also attended, I am told.'

'Indeed, but not in my day. They were all far younger than I was.'

'I think most people of the Cinél na Áeda learnt the ancient tales at the feet of old Liag,' added Suanach. 'He appears unfriendly and eccentric but he is really a nice old man.'

'Even our fierce tanist used to attend,' added Menma.

'And these tales of Liag's – were they no more than the folk stories associated with the ancient beliefs of what the moon and stars represented?'

'Of course. Liag was very particular,' Suanach replied at once. 'He used to tell us that knowledge was power and to know the hidden names was to possess a very dangerous knowledge . . .'

She broke off and Fidelma was just quick enough to see a warning glance from Menma. She turned back to the door.

'Thank you, Suanach. A special thanks for what you did for me. I am beholden to you. The Uí Fidgente are enemies of my blood and there is no need for me to say—'

'No need,' interrupted Suanach with an answering smile.

Outside, Eadulf was still puzzled. 'What was all that about? Surely the raiders were not looking for this gold mine . . . ?'

Fidelma turned to him and placed a finger to her lips. 'No word of the cave to anyone yet, Eadulf.'

At that moment the door opened behind them and Menma came out, drawing it shut. He looked troubled.

'I wanted to add something, lady,' he said quietly. 'I did not want Suanach to hear.'

They looked at the young hunter expectantly.

'You realise that Accobrán took no prisoners from the Uí Fidgente?'

'Indeed,' agreed Fidelma. 'I found that something hard to understand.'

Menma inclined his head. 'Accobrán had the bloodmist on him.'

It was an old term meaning to lose all sense in battle. The old storytellers told how the mythical hero Cúchullain could be engulfed by a battle frenzy when fighting and become possessed of what was known as the *ríastrad*, such a fury, such a battle madness, that he might slaughter friend as well as foe. The word literally meant an act of contorting but had become applied to the loss of control that a warrior might suffer in a battle fever.

Fidelma gazed at Menma in surprise. 'You mean that prisoners could have been taken from the Uí Fidgente?'

'I mean just that, lady. I have not seen a man in the grip of the bloodmist before. He killed three of the Uí Fidgente while they were attempting to surrender.'

'Thank you, Menma.'

The young man nodded and returned to join his wife.

Fidelma was quiet for a moment while Eadulf waited for her to comment.

'It is not a good sign for a tanist to lose control in battle. Yet often one hears of warriors doing so, for battle is a terrible experience.'

'But this was no battle,' pointed out Eadulf. 'To surround and capture less than a dozen men is not a task that should provoke such a condition in a trained warrior.'

'We must bear that in mind,' Fidelma agreed. 'Becc should be made aware of the fault, as should his *derbfhine* if Accobrán is to succeed to the chieftainship. Now where were we? Ah yes, no mention of the cave to anyone unless I say so.'

'Very well. But between you and me, what does it mean? Why would the Uí Fidgente be searching for that mine? They could not hope to work it and precious little gold would they be able to take before being discovered. I find nothing here that makes any sense at all.'

'You are right, Eadulf. But we do not have all the facts as yet. Just a few major pieces are beginning to come together, though I believe that I begin to see some sort of pattern emerging.'

'More than I do,' sighed Eadulf.

'Let us have something to eat. Then we will have to confront Brother Dangila and finally go in search of the wily Liag.'

Eadulf was in agreement. 'I understand the path we are going to tread with Brother Dangila but, frankly, little else.'

After their meal they were riding along the track to the abbey of the Blessed Finnbarr when a small boy nearly ran across their path, causing them to rein in sharply. The boy was Síoda.

'Hello, Sister.' The boy halted and greeted Fidelma with a grin of recognition.

'The very person I wanted to see.' Fidelma smiled down at him. 'How would you like to earn a *screpall*?'

The boy was definitely interested but regarded her with some suspicion.

'What do I have to do?' he asked dubiously.

She reached into her *marsupium* and pulled out the coin and held it up. 'Answer a question. Do you remember telling us about that piece of gold that you found?'

The boy pouted. 'The fool's gold?'

'I think that you told us that you found it on the hill near the Ring of Pigs?'

The boy nodded.

'But Gobnuid said it was fool's gold,' he said.

'He did,' agreed Fidelma. 'Can you be more precise as to where you found it? Was it in the cave that stands at the top of the hill, just above the Ring of Pigs?'

'It was not,' the boy replied.

Fidelma was disappointed. 'Where was it, then?'

'On the track. A little way down the old track that runs towards the abbey and past the Ring of Pigs.' The boy glanced round surreptitiously. 'Do not tell my parents that I was playing by the Ring of Pigs. I am not supposed to.'

'On the track to the abbey?' mused Fidelma.

'Are you sure of the place?' demanded Eadulf.

'It was where the track passes the old rocks.' The boy was scornful. 'I know it well enough. It was where I saw Accobrán shouting at Beccnat back in the summer. That was when I found the nugget.'

Fidelma stared hard at the boy.

'The place where you saw Accobrán shouting at Beccnat?' she repeated slowly. 'What was he shouting about?'

The boy shrugged indifferently. 'You know the way grown-ups are. One minute shouting, the next minute being all sloppy and kissing.'

'They were kissing?'

'I said so, didn't I?'

'And you are sure about the place?' Fidelma pressed him. 'And the time? Summer, you said. Was it about the feast of Lughnasa?'

'I have said so.'

'Did you tell Gobnuid where you found the gold?'

The boy shook his head. 'The fool's gold? Not exactly.'

'What do you mean – not exactly?'

'Well, when I thought it valuable, I did not want to let on about the place just in case Gobnuid went there and found any other pieces. I told him it was further down the hill, nearer the abbey.'

Fidelma smiled and handed the coin to the boy. 'You have no need to tell anyone of this conversation, Síoda.'

The boy grinned and tossed the coin into the air.

'What conversation, Sister?' he chuckled. Then he turned and ran off into the woods.

Eadulf regarded Fidelma with a degree of bewilderment. 'Does that help?'

'It shows that Gobnuid was not told of the real location of the boy's find. His knowledge of the cave came from other means. And it shows that Gabrán was right – something was going on between Beccnat and our handsome, bloodthirsty tanist. And it places them together at the spot where Beccnat was found and around the time she was killed.'

Eadulf was startled. 'Do you mean that Accobrán killed Beccnat?'

'We still do not have enough information. But everything helps when you are struggling to find a path in the darkness, Eadulf,' replied Fidelma solemnly.

Eadulf sighed impatiently.

'How do you even know whether such a path exists?' he asked in exasperation. 'I confess that I am less certain of things now than I was when we first came here. To begin with, we were confronted with the murders of three girls. Each killed at the full of the moon. Obviously it was the work of a lunatic, a maniac. Then we were sidetracked by the murder of Lesren by his wife. In a way, it did seem logical in that Lesren's killing was remotely connected with the murders. But now, with this raid by the Uí Fidgente and gold mines and so on . . . well, I haven't a clue what is going on.'

'I believe that our next port of call will put some of the pieces together,' she said.

'Brother Dangila?'

Fidelma inclined her head.

When they reached the abbey of Finnbarr Fidelma espied a familiar figure about to leave on horseback. She halted her horse and waited for the man to approach.

'Brother Túan, isn't it?'

The owlish-faced religieux halted and greeted her with a smile. 'Sister Fidelma. How go your inquiries?'

'I am encountering difficulties,' she confessed. Then, indicating Brother Eadulf, she introduced him.

'I have heard of Brother Eadulf the Saxon,' acknowledged the steward of the house of Molaga with a smile of greeting. Then he turned quickly back to Fidelma. 'So you are finding the path difficult?'

The corners of her mouth turned down a little in a wry expression. 'My mentor, the Brehon Morann, always said one should beware the easy path for there is more deception on the path that appears simple than on the path that appears difficult.'

'Doubtless, there is truth in that,' acknowledged Brother Túan solemnly.

'Speaking of paths, I am glad, however, that our paths have crossed again. You remember what we were speaking of last time we met?'

The round-faced man nodded mournfully.

'Remembrance does not make the facts better,' he said. 'Death before its time is a bad visitor.'

'You implied that it was Accobrán who encouraged the three strangers to leave the house of Molaga and come to the abbey of Finnbarr.'

Brother Túan nodded. 'I am glad that you said I implied it for it is true that I could not swear it as a fact. Accobrán left shortly after the feast of Lughnasa and returned here. The three strangers came here soon afterwards.'

'But you say that Accobrán did talk with them while he was visiting your abbey?'

'He did.'

'Do you know what their conversation was about?'

Brother Túan smiled wanly. 'I was not privy to all their conversations and the only one that I overheard was innocuous enough. That was why I could only suggest that it might have had something to do with their removing themselves from Molaga to come here.'

'What was it that you did overhear?'

'It was innocuous, as I have said. One of the strangers was telling Accobrán about the country that they came from and what he had done before joining the religious, that sort of thing.'

'Accobrán speaks some Greek, as I understand? And the conversation was carried on in Greek?'

Brother Túan confirmed it. 'Accobrán studied at the house of Molaga and has a rudimentary grasp of the language. Indeed, it was the only language that we initially had in common with the strangers. I am sure I have mentioned that fact. I tried to teach them a little of our own tongue.'

'Do you remember what Accobrán was doing in the seaport at that time?'

The steward rubbed his chin thoughtfully. 'I think he was conducting some trade on behalf of the Cinél na Áeda. He was looking for a ship to transport some goods. Hides, I think.'

'So he spent some time down on the quays among the merchants?'

'I suppose he did.'

'Sea trading is essential to the life of the house of Molaga. I don't suppose you remember what sort of ships put into the port at that time?'

Brother Túan chuckled ruefully. 'It would be a miracle if I did. There is quite a lot of trade that goes through the port at that time of year. In the summer months, especially at Lughnasa, sometimes ships have to wait outside the harbour until there is space to come in and unload or take on cargo. As steward I do make a note of ships that trade with us.'

Fidelma sighed softly. She had realised that it would not be easy but she had been hoping. Brother Túan regarded her disappointment with amusement.

'I am sorry if I cannot help. Truth to tell, of all those ships in and out of the port at that time I can only be sure of one. It was taking a cargo for the house of Molaga up to the abbey at Eas Geiphtine.'

Fidelma suddenly stiffened. 'To the abbey at Geiphtine's Waterfall? That's on a narrow creek of the River Sionnain. That is in Uí Fidgente country, isn't it?'

The steward seemed surprised that she knew the whereabouts of the abbey.

'The Uí Fidgente are not without religion,' he admonished her, misunderstanding her emphasis. 'We often communicate with the abbey there. I know Brother Coccán, who is head of the community, very well.'

'I am especially interested in the fact that this trading ship might have left Molaga for a port in Uí Fidgente country at the time when Accobrán was there. Are you absolutely sure?' she pressed.

Brother Túan was frowning, trying to understand her sudden interest.

'I know for certain that we sent a cargo to Brother Coccán. It was, indeed, at the time when the tanist of the Cinél na Áeda was there. He was looking for a ship to transport a cargo of hides to Ard Mhór. It was the same time that he was talking to the strangers.'

'Would you know if he spoke with the captain of this ship, the ship transporting a cargo to the abbey at Geiphtine?'

'It is possible.' Brother Túan examined her curiously. 'But Geiphtine is in the opposite direction to Ard Mhór. What is this about?'

Fidelma smiled and shook her head.

'It is not for you to understand. It is for me to gather information and so long as you answer my questions honestly then there is nothing to worry about, Brother Túan,' she said softly.

The steward gave an irritated sniff. 'I am sure that I have no wish to pry into the affairs of a *dálaigh*.'

'I am sure you do not,' replied Fidelma gravely. 'We do not have to hold you from your journey any longer. Thank you, Brother, for all the help you have given us.'

Brother Túan looked disconcerted for a moment and then shrugged.

'*Deus vobiscum*,' he muttered with a glance at them both and smacked his horse's flanks with his heels. He rode away without waiting for them to reply.

Brother Eadulf was regarding his disappearing figure with an air of bewilderment.

'Are you now trying to discover whether Accobrán was responsible for bringing the Uí Fidgente raiders into this territory?' he asked Fidelma after a moment or two.

'I already know that Accobrán was responsible, directly or indirectly,' Fidelma assured him. 'What I did not know until just now was the manner in which information reached the Uí Fidgente.'

'What information?'

Fidelma heaved a short sigh of impatience. 'The information about the Thicket of Pigs, of course.'

'You don't mean that the raid was something to do with the gold, do you?'

'I believe it had everything to do with the gold. But we must not let ourselves run before we walk. Ah, here is Brother Solam,' she said, spying the approaching fair-headed young steward. 'Now we will find Brother Dangila.'

A short time passed before the tall, dark figure of Brother Dangila joined them in the abbey garden and bowed gravely to each of them before accepting the invitation to seat himself on a bench before them. They had already taken seats beneath the apple tree in the courtyard for it was a warm day of late October and the sun shone out of a cloudless sky.

'I am told that you wish to speak to me again, Sister,' Brother Dangila said in his musical Greek.

'I do. How do you know Liag the apothecary?'

The man's face was impassive. He hesitated before responding.

'He is an old soul. I am sure his lives on this earth have been many,' the Aksumite finally replied. 'Perhaps we have encountered one another in a past life and past age.'

Fidelma made a quick, impatient gesture with her hand. 'Stick to this life, this time and this place.'

Brother Dangila looked steadily at her. 'Then in this life, at this time and in this place, I met Liag when I was out contemplating the great work of the heavens. It was an interest that we both shared. I have already told you that my comrades and I are fascinated by star lore. That is the reason why we came here, as I told you. We came to see the manuscripts of Aibhistín.'

'The *only* reason why you came here?' Fidelma said with emphasis.

For the first time a slight look of uncertainty crossed the man's bland features. He did not reply immediately.

'You told me that you had worked in the mines of your country before you became a religieux,' Fidelma pointed out. 'The gold mines.'

Brother Dangila gave a long sigh. 'You are very astute, Sister.'

'Leaving mining aside for the moment,' Fidelma went on, much to the bewilderment of Eadulf, who was trying to follow her line of questions, 'let me turn to another matter.'

'Which is?' asked Brother Dangila in mild surprise.

'Were you ever asked to instruct any pupils of Liag?'

'You mean those young ones who went to hear his teachings on star lore?'

'That is precisely what I mean.'

'I think you already know the answer. One young one, a girl, came seeking knowledge.'

'Her name?'

'I find your native names impossible to remember.'

'In what language did you communicate, then?' Eadulf interrupted. 'We are speaking to you in Greek since we share no other fluency.'

'I have said that I have some imperfect knowledge of your tongue. When the girl made clear what it was she wanted I was able to make her understand that I could not help her. We had not sufficient vocabulary between us for anything further.'

'In what language did you communicate with Liag?' asked Fidelma.

'The old one knows Greek. You must have known that?'

Fidelma shook her head. 'I did not. Yet it does not surprise me. Tell me, does the name Escrach mean anything to you?'

Brother Dangila shook his head.

'Did you ever see the girl who came to you to ask about star lore later? Say, on the night of the full moon last month?'

'I did not.'

'But that night of the full moon you were out on the hill.' She gestured towards the Thicket of Pigs. 'You were out with Accobrán.' It was a statement, not a question.

Brother Dangila returned her gaze but did not say anything.

'You realise that your involvement with Accobrán will have to be made public?' she asked.

'What is to be, must be. If I have transgressed your laws, then I am truly sorry, but I did not, nor did my companions, kill the girl or any other girl, as some of your people claim.'

Fidelma rose to her feet. 'I will inform you and your companions when the official hearing into this matter will be. Until then, I would once again advise – indeed, would urge – you not to leave the shelter of these abbey walls.'

Riding through the woods towards the riverbank, Eadulf was still confused.

'This mystery is getting beyond me. In the past, I could at least see the path that we had to tread. But this is one confusion after another.'

Fidelma glanced at him and smiled quickly. 'That is because we are faced with several mysteries rather than a single one. Yet, I believe, they intertwine one with another. I am confident that we are nearly at a solution.'

Surprisingly, they found Liag seated on a rock by the river with a fishing line in his hand. He barely turned his head as they rode up, dismounted, and tethered their horses to a low branch of a tree.

'Speak quietly, lest you disturb the fish,' he said as they came near.

'Are you seeking the Salmon of Knowledge, Liag?' Fidelma asked mischievously as she walked down to the bank and seated herself on a nearby boulder.

The old apothecary glanced up indifferently. 'I will settle for a trout, for the salmon is a noble fish. Yet I fear that it is a certain *dálaigh* who is in need of the properties of Fintan.'

Eadulf, not understanding the meaning of this repartee, felt excluded and demanded to know what they meant. Liag glanced over his shoulder and saw his bewilderment.

'A shared culture, my Saxon friend. That is all. Fintan was a great salmon who ate of the forbidden Hazelnuts of Knowledge before swimming into a pool in a great river to the north of here named after the cow goddess, Boann. The Druid Finegas eventually caught the salmon. By eating of the flesh of the fish he would imbibe all the knowledge of the world. So he began to cook it. But Finegas, being lazy, decided to have a nap and told his young assistant, a boy called Fionn, son of Cumal, to turn the spit but forbade him to eat of the fish. Fionn accidentally burnt his thumb on the flesh of the fish as he was turning the spit. He sucked his thumb and acquired great wisdom and grew up to be the most heroic leader of the Fianna, the bodyguard of the High Kings.'

Eadulf greeted the tale with a sniff of disapproval.

'It is no folk tale that we are interested in,' he snapped.

Liag glanced at Fidelma. 'Is it not?' he asked gently.

'In a way, it is,' said Fidelma. 'I have been interested to hear about your classes on folklore, the lore of the moon and stars.'

Liag nodded slowly. 'I thought you might be. I have taught these things to many generations.'

'Is it true that all three of the girls who were slaughtered attended your teachings?'

'Many others also attended.'

'Others such as Accobrán?'

'Indeed, Accobrán, Menma, Creoda, Gabrán and even their fathers before them. Others too numerous to count.'

'I believe that you shared a common interest with Brother Dangila? I had not realised that you spoke Greek.'

'One of my calling has to speak many languages, Fidelma, as you yourself do.'

'And your relationship with Brother Dangila?'

'An intelligent man, a man of wisdom of his people. We meet and talk of the moon and stars, for these are the maps of civilisation. Man raised himself from the earth by looking at the sky and found that it could tell him many things. When to get up and work and when to go to bed and sleep. As he watched the rolling map of the heavens he saw that it could tell him how time passed, when the seasons came, when to sow his seed, when to harvest it, when to expect warmth and when to expect coldness, when the days were growing longer and when they were growing shorter . . . all these things are written irretrievably in the sky if we would but look up as our forefathers used to do.'

It was a long speech for the old apothecary.

'So you shared this knowledge with Brother Dangila?'

'Our knowledge was different for our place in this world was different and our culture was different.'

'Did you tell Escrach to seek him out?'

Liag paused thoughtfully. 'Escrach was a promising pupil. She must not be judged by a comparison with her uncle Brocc. I did not advise her to seek out Dangila but I mentioned some of the wondrous things he knew. She went of her own accord. I was hoping that one day she would go to one of the secular colleges and be taught by—'

'By Druids?' Eadulf broke in disapprovingly.

Liag glanced at him with a smile. 'One who holds my beliefs is not going to recommend a school of the New Faith where the mind is limited to that which is pleasing only to narrow teaching. Escrach needed to spread herself into the wider world.'

'She could not communicate properly with Brother Dangila.'

'I was surprised when she told me that she had attempted to talk to Dangila.'

Fidelma looked quickly at him. 'You mean that she saw him and then she saw you afterwards?'

'Did I not make myself clear?'

'In relation to the day she died, when was this?'

'Several days before the full moon, if that is what you are asking.

No, Dangila did not kill her. She told me that she had been walking and saw Brother Dangila. She took the opportunity to approach him and attempt to ask him if he could expound on her knowledge of the moon's properties. Questions such as how the moon could move the great seas, the pounding tides along our coasts. She wanted to know. They had not sufficient common language to communicate such matters.'

'And she came and told you this some days before she was found dead?'

'That is so. I promised her that soon I would approach Dangila and bring him to our little group so that he might explain his views to all of us. I would be his translator.'

'Did she agree?'

'Of course. Some of the others were unhappy with the idea of inviting Dangila to our circle. They were afraid of him.'

'Of whom was your group constituted then?'

'Ballgel, Escrach, Gabrán and Creoda. I think I had made a mistake in overemphasising the power of knowledge to them. That our words for the moon and its manifestations as goddess and arbiter of our destinies belonged to us and not to outsiders. What I had meant was that the power to pronounce the names and contact the power directly belonged to the cognoscenti of all peoples. They had taken my meaning to be that it was a special preserve of the Cinél na Áeda. They voiced their resentment of any involvement in our group by Dangila.'

'I believe that Accobrán had been one of your group? You do not mention him. What was his view?' asked Fidelma.

'Accobrán was—'

The sound of a horn blast cut through the air in a long and almost plaintive tone. It came again, sounding more urgently. Puzzled, Fidelma raised her head.

'The sound came from Rath Raithlen,' muttered Eadulf apprehensively, glancing towards the hill which was obscured by the trees. 'What does it mean?'

'It is the sound of an alarm,' old Liag said, rising calmly and hauling in his fishing line. 'I have not heard it in many a year. Usually, it is blown to summon people to the fortress as the territory is under attack.'

Eadulf sprang to his feet. 'Uí Fidgente. I wager a *screpall* on it.'

Liag's face was grim as he turned towards his *bothán*. 'I fear that you will find no takers for that wager. After the raid of yesterday, retribution for Accobrán's enthusiasm may well be the result.'

Fidelma was already mounting her horse with Eadulf following her example.

Chapter Sixteen

'Our sentinels report a *sluaghadh* of the Uí Fidgente encamped on our borders,' Becc explained as Fidelma, followed by Eadulf, burst into the great hall and asked the reason for the sounding horn. The harassed chieftain was surrounded by several of his retinue. There was no sign of Accobrán among them.

'A *sluaghadh?*' Eadulf was not familiar with military terms and asked what was meant by the word.

'A war band,' explained Fidelma quickly. 'Is it reported how big this hosting is?' she asked, turning to Becc.

'Not large, but too large for us in our present circumstances. The sentinels report that it looks like a *lucht-tighe*, a house company of no more than four score warriors. However, I doubt whether we can muster a score of fighting men at this moment. I've sent for Accobrán and ordered the alarm to be sounded.'

'He did a foolish thing in not finding out whether the raiding party was an advance guard of a larger band,' Fidelma muttered. 'Now we know. Doubtless they are here to avenge their dead.'

Becc was clearly worried. 'What can we do? We are mostly farmers and woodsmen, with very few warriors left among us. If they are professional warriors then we are outnumbered.'

At that moment, Accobrán entered noisily. He had a grim look.

'Have you heard the news?' Becc demanded of him.

The tanist nodded curtly. 'I can probably raise thirty-five men to face them but of that number only a dozen have been under arms before. Perhaps we can delay them until we have sent out to other parts of our territory and raised more men.'

'Where are the Uí Fidgente now?' demanded Fidelma.

'No more than a mile from here, perhaps less,' replied Becc.

'We can find a place to ambush them,' Accobrán said. 'We can cut them down before they know it.'

'And if you don't surprise them?' queried Fidelma. 'Are you prepared to take the risk that you will leave your people defenceless? That is not a good decision for a tanist to make.'

'What is your proposal, Fidelma?' Becc asked quietly.

'Let us go and talk to them and discover what brings them here and

225

what, if any, are their demands. Then we may see if there is any means of ending this matter by talking rather than bloodshed.'

Accobrán laughed harshly. 'That is a woman's answer and not a warrior's way.'

Becc wheeled round on his tanist, his face grim. 'Remember to whom you are talking, Accobrán. And remember also that some of our great warriors were women. Scáthach was the one who instructed Cúchullain in the martial arts at her academy – was she not a woman? Was not Creidne a woman, one of the most relentless warriors of the Fianna? Did not Medb of Connacht choose a female champion, Erni, to guard her treasures? Here, among the Eóghanacht, was not Mughâin Mhór our greatest warrior queen? Shame on you, Accobrán, that you can forget your inheritance so quickly that you insult your own people by your thoughtless words!'

The tanist flushed angrily but was silent.

Becc turned back with an apologetic look to Fidelma. 'You are right, cousin. We should first seek the way of peace before resorting to the way of sorrow and bloodshed.'

'Good. Then perhaps—'

The door burst opened and Adag the steward came in breathlessly.

'Becc!' he gasped, without apologising for his entrance which contravened the etiquette of a chieftain's house. 'A rider has come to the gates of the fortress. He rides under the *méirge*, the banner of the Uí Fidgente.'

Accobrán had clasped his hand to his sword hilt and was moving to the door.

'I'll deal with this,' he shouted. 'Sound the alarm!'

'Stop!' cried Fidelma harshly. 'Have all your senses left you, Accobrán?' Having caught their attention, she turned to Adag. 'I presume this rider is a herald from the Uí Fidgente?'

Adag nodded swiftly. 'He is indeed a *techtaire* bearing a message to our chieftain.'

Fidelma looked at Becc with grim satisfaction. 'This saves us having to ride out and find the Uí Fidgente. Let us go and speak to this *techtaire* and find out what it is that his hosting seeks here.'

They left the chieftain's hall and moved to the courtyard, where a couple of Becc's warriors stood nervously, arms at the ready, before a horseman. The man was still seated in his saddle and carried nothing more lethal than a banner of red silk on which was a design of a ravening wolf. It was the symbol of his people. He wore his hair long and had a bushy sandy beard. His close-set bright eyes watched them approach impassively.

'I am Becc, chieftain of the Cinél na Áeda,' Becc announced as he came to a halt before the *techtaire*.

'I see you, Becc,' intoned the herald ritually. 'I am here as a voice of Conrí, King of Wolves, war chieftain of the Uí Fidgente.'

'I see you, herald of the Uí Fidgente,' replied Becc in return ritual. 'Why are you so far from your own lands?'

'I am told to say these words to you – Conrí enters this country with a *sluaghadh*, a hosting, more in sorrow than in anger. He has encamped at the place you call the Marsh of the Birch and will await you or your representatives there to discuss why he should leave the land of the Cinél na Áeda without spilling the blood of its people.'

Becc inclined his head. 'Why would your chieftain contemplate spilling that blood?'

'I have been told to say, should you ask that question, that our *sluaghadh* was on its way to the lands of the prince of the Corco Loígde, where we were invited to take part in the games.'

Fidelma knew that most of the larger principalities held annual games to prepare themselves for the three great festivals at Tailltenn, Tlachtga and Uisneach. It would not be unheard of for the ruler of the Corco Loígde to invite a band of young men from the Uí Fidgente to participate in the local games there. The herald was continuing.

'While we were passing near the borders of your land, a small foraging party from our *sluaghadh* went missing. We sent out scouts and they found the bodies of our men – all had been slaughtered. The arrows we found bore the marks of the Cinél na Áeda. Some of the party had been cut down by sword blows; many had wounds in their backs that spoke plainly of how they came by their deaths. Thus, chieftain of the Cinél na Áeda, was it decided that our *sluaghadh* would turn from its path to the Corco Loígde and enter your territory to demand an explanation. We will see whether that explanation allows us to continue in peace or whether it forces us to invoke the law which demands *dígal* – blood vengeance.'

Fidelma frowned. She tried to hide the fact that she was appalled that Accobrán had not even buried the slain Uí Fidgente but had abandoned the bodies to the elements and ravering beasts. She drew herself together.

'The futility of vengeance has been censured by the New Faith,' she pointed out in a sharp voice.

The *techtaire* glanced at her as if to dismiss her. 'Those of your cloth would say so. However, it is written in the *Crith Gablach* that the blood feud has legal standing and that a party of avengers may pursue such a feud in the territory of those who have wronged them.'

Fidelma smiled grimly at being lectured on the law.

'However, that law says that the *dígal* can only be carried out a month after the collapse of any attempt to negotiate compensation if culpability is proved,' she replied quickly.

The herald's features twisted in a sneer. He was about to speak when Becc said gruffly: 'Have a care, *techtaire*. It is a *dálaigh* of the courts who addresses you.'

The man blinked and hesitated for a moment. 'I am not here to debate points of law but to tell you the intentions of my lord, Conrí. He awaits you, Becc, or your representatives, at the Marsh of the Birch. Tell me, chieftain of the Cinél na Áeda, will he wait in vain?'

Becc shook his head immediately. 'You can tell your war chieftain that while it is improper for the chieftain of any *tuath* or tribe to come to him at his demand, nevertheless I shall send representatives to demand his withdrawal from our lands without the spilling of blood on either side.'

'Brave words. My part is now over. Your part has begun.'

The horseman wheeled swiftly about and rode off through the gates of the fortress.

'Let me send him back to his war chieftain with an arrow in him,' muttered Accobrán, his hand clenching on his sword.

Fidelma turned to him with a sour expression.

'Had you been a little less concerned with slaughter, Accobrán, then this confrontation need never have happened,' she snapped.

'And Suanach and even you might not be alive,' retorted the tanist.

Becc raised a pacifying hand.

'Let us confront the common enemy,' he said reprovingly. 'Fidelma, this Conrí is only a war lord and, as I am chieftain here, I cannot be seen going to him now that he has invaded our territory.'

'I should go as tanist!' said Accobrán quickly.

'Your going with your current attitude would guarantee more bloodshed,' said Fidelma waspishly. 'No, I shall go as negotiator.'

Becc looked horrified. 'But you are the king's sister. If it is not right for me to go and negotiate with a warlord, then how much less fitting is it for you . . .'

Fidelma shook her head. 'I am here as a *dálaigh*. Indeed, my relationship to the king might prove useful for the Uí Fidgente might then know that they may once again have to deal with Cashel. A memory of their defeat at Cnoc Áine might cause them to reflect on any precipitous action.'

'It is like presenting the Uí Fidgente with a hostage,' protested Accobrán in irritation.

'Better than presenting them with a dozen corpses still warm from the slaughter! The warrior's code respects the bodies of slain enemies.'

Accobrán flushed at her retort. Becc was worried and held up a hand to still any response from his tanist.

'I believe that you are right, Fidelma,' he said. 'But you cannot go alone.'

'I'll go with her,' interposed Eadulf quickly.

'But there should be a representative of the Cinél na Áeda present,' protested Accobrán. 'If she is to speak for us, how do we know what she will say?'

'Are you saying that I am not to be trusted?' Fidelma asked quietly. There was an ominous tone in her softly spoken words.

Becc moved forward hurriedly and laid a pacifying hand on her arm.

'Accobrán has fallen into the habit of speaking with impulsiveness. He did not mean that. Yet he does raise a pertinent point. Let Adag my steward accompany you and Brother Eadulf. Then everyone will be satisfied.'

Fidelma smiled in agreement. 'I have no objection if Adag is willing.'

The steward was not looking happy but he stepped forward quickly enough. His chubby features were firmly set.

'It is the will of my chieftain. I shall go with you, lady,' he affirmed.

'How will you proceed?' asked Becc, turning back into his hall. They followed him in while someone was sent off to the stables to order the horses to be saddled for them.

'I think that we will have to see what this Conrí's intentions are,' Fidelma said. 'We know that this foraging party came to the *bothán* of Menma and Suanach. They kidnapped Suanach, and burnt the cabin. That is hardly in keeping with the behaviour of what the herald described as a peaceful foraging party. For our part, we have to admit that these Uí Fidgente were all slaughtered instead of being made captive.'

Accobrán muttered angrily: 'Them or me. The choice was obvious.'

'Are you saying that the messenger was lying when he said that some of the bodies showed that they had been shot or stabbed in the back?'

'Back or front. An enemy is an enemy and we did right to slaughter the vermin.'

Fidelma compressed her lips for a moment.

'It might be that compensation will have to be offered for this slaughter, Becc,' she pointed out.

'Never!' snapped Accobrán, his voice rising in his anger.

'It is surely true, Fidelma,' Becc said, waving his tanist to be silent, 'that it is lawful to kill a thief caught in the act of stealing who does not surrender and threatens violence.'

'That is so, just as it is permitted that a death resulting from defending oneself against an attack is not subject to punishment. Everyone is entitled to self-defence. The problem is whether a case may be made out that a person who has been shot or stabbed in the back was a threat to the life of the person who killed him in this fashion.' She stared briefly at Accobrán who scowled back at her but made no reply.

'I think,' ventured Eadulf hurriedly, seeing the anger in the tanist's eyes, 'we had better leave any decisions on culpability until we see what the Uí Fidgente have to say.'

'Agreed,' sighed Becc in relief. 'In the meantime, I do not think it will harm us if we prepare the defences of this fortress.'

'That would be an obvious course,' agreed Fidelma solemnly. 'Also you might enquire how this war band came so near to Rath Raithlen without an alarm being raised. I thought you had ordered a watch yesterday?'

Becc glanced at his tanist. The young man flushed again.

'I called it off once we had returned here triumphant after pursuing and defeating the raiders.'

Becc did not say anything but his features were like granite as he turned to give instructions, ordering that defences be prepared as they rode out of the gates and down the hill. It was Adag who led them to the area called the Marsh of the Birch, which was scarcely an hour's ride away. There was no mistaking the area because they were soon in sight of an encampment marked by posts from which red silk banners bearing the wolf symbol fluttered. The wolf symbol was always associated with the Uí Fidgente. Watchful sentinels challenged their party and then allowed them to pass into an area sheltered by trees beside a small stream.

Several warriors stood about there and Fidelma had no trouble recognising the *techtaire* who had come to the fortress. He looked surprised as she and Eadulf, followed by Adag, dismounted and approached.

Two felled trees provided seats by the banks of the stream.

Fidelma made straight for one of the logs and took a seat, ignoring the astonished looks of the Uí Fidgente. Eadulf and Adag took a stand behind her. The half-dozen dumbfounded warriors looked at one another. No one said anything for a moment and then Fidelma announced icily: 'I am here to see Conrí. Let him come forward.'

Her natural hauteur and air of command confused them even more and again no one seemed to know how to speak to her.

Then a tall, well-muscled man, with a shock of black hair, grey eyes and the livid white of a scar across his left cheek, emerged from a nearby *pupall* or tent as used by military commanders in the field. He scowled as he saw Fidelma seated at her ease on the log and moved forward to face her.

'I am Conrí, King of Wolves, warlord of the Uí Fidgente,' he growled. 'You are arrogant, religieuse. You forget your manners.'

Fidelma regarded the man coldly.

'I am Fidelma of Cashel,' she replied in icy clear fashion. 'I am here as a *dálaigh*, qualified to the degree of *anruth*. Thus I may sit even in the presence of kings, thus I may speak before they do, and thus they must be silent until I have had my say. I am Fidelma of Cashel, daughter of Failbe Flann, sister to Colgú, who reigns in prosperity there.'

Conrí had taken an involuntary step backwards, his eyes wide. He glanced at his herald and Fidelma noticed the man spread his hands, palms outward, and shake his head as if disclaiming any knowledge.

A look of reluctant admiration spread over Conrí's features.

'You have courage, Fidelma of Cashel. I'll grant you that. Courage that you come with only two unarmed companions into the lair of the warlord of the Uí Fidgente, especially after your brother slaughtered my people on the slopes of Cnoc Áine two years ago.'

Fidelma looked at him levelly. 'You might recall that it was the hosts of the Uí Fidgente who began a rebellion and marched on the legitimate ruler of Muman. They were an armed host desperate for victory. They had only themselves to blame for their fate. As for the courage of my companions or myself, is courage needed here when we come at your own invitation, under bonds of the strict code of hospitality and the rules of the Brehons which no one can break with impunity? What danger can possibly be here for us?'

She threw the question at him in challenge.

Conrí stared at her for a moment and then his stern features dissolved in a smile. He moved to the second log and sat down opposite her.

'You are right, Fidelma of Cashel. There is no danger in my camp for you or any member of your party who comes here in the office of *techtaire*.'

'That is good. Now, perhaps you will tell me what brings you to this land?'

'Willingly. Although I would like to know why you are here and how you represent the Cinél na Áeda?'

'I came at the invitation of Becc, chieftain—'

'I know of Becc,' interrupted the warlord. 'What are you doing in his territory?'

'I am here as a *dálaigh*. There have been some unlawful killings among his people.'

Conrí pursed his lips sourly. 'Then we share a similar goal, for it is the unlawful killings of my men that bring me also into this territory.'

'I doubt that we share the same goal, Conrí,' Fidelma returned evenly. 'But tell me the details for, at this time, it cannot be accepted that the Cinél na Áeda are responsible for the death of your men.'

'That we must see.'

'I am told by your *techtaire* that your host was passing on their way to the games being held by the prince of the Corco Loígde.'

'That is true,' agreed the warlord.

'Why did this group of men, whom you so lament, leave your main body and cross into the territory of the Cinél na Áeda? And spare me the story claimed by your *techtaire* that they were merely a foraging party.'

Conrí regarded her with slightly narrowed eyes.

'Why do you doubt our word?' he demanded.

'Because I happened to be in the *bothán* of Menma and Suanach when your men rode up outside. This foraging party set fire to that place and took Suanach as a prisoner among them.'

The warlord let his breath out in one long sibilant sigh. His eyes narrowed. 'You were taken hostage?'

'Suanach hid me in the sousterrain because she feared that harm would befall me, being sister to the king. I escaped. She did not.'

There was a silence, then Conrí lowered his head slightly.

'You realise that this places your hosting in a bad position legally,' pointed out Adag, feeling that he should add something.

Conrí raised his head and glanced at the steward, but not angrily. 'My intention and the intention of the main body of my men is clear. We were passing down to the land of the Corco Loígde.'

'Your foraging party had come to that *bothán* seeking the woodsman, Menma,' Fidelma pointed out. 'Finding him not there, they kidnapped Suanach in order to lure him after them so that they might capture him. I heard them speaking to one another and that is what they said.'

Conrí was still looking uncomfortable.

'Why would they be seeking Menma?' demanded Fidelma. 'And

what was the attraction of the Thicket of the Pigs?' she added, leaning forward, the words spoken so softly that not even Eadulf and Adag could hear her.

Conrí started on his seat. 'You know of that?' His voice had lost its aggression.

'What game are you trying our patience with, Conrí?' She sat back and spoke normally.

Conrí glanced around for a moment and then he gestured to his *pupall*. 'One to one, Fidelma of Cashel. I am willing to tell you and no other. Will you come into the tent while I explain?'

Adag started to protest. 'It is not seemly, it is not correct protocol.'

'I am happy to dispense with protocol so long as we find truth at the end of the path,' Fidelma said, rising, and giving a reassuring nod to Eadulf.

There was a murmuring among Conrí's men but he silenced them with an angry glare. Fidelma followed him into his tent and he motioned her into the only camp chair while he took a seat on the edge of his bed.

'There is one thing that we must be clear about,' he began. 'I spoke the truth when I said that my men and I are on the way to the games at Corco Loígde. We had gathered at Geiphtine's Waterfall in our own land and thought to come by ship to the harbour of our hosts. But the captain of the ship we had hired was killed in a fight on the evening before we sailed. A stupid drunken brawl. We could not persuade the crew to fulfil the agreement.'

'Killed?'

'By one of his drunken crew. But before he died he spoke to Dea, who, as it turned out, was the leader of the foraging party. Dea was with the seaman when he died.'

'I presume that there was no suspicion that Dea was involved in the man's death?'

Conrí quickly shook his head. 'Dea was a good warrior but inclined to be headstrong. He commanded his own small company.'

'A company of ten men?' queried Fidelma.

Conrí made a motion of assent. 'As we came south, I noticed that Dea was growing more and more preoccupied. Then, as we approached the border of the territory of the Cinél na Áeda, he asked me if he could take his men on a foraging party. I will admit that I was suspicious of his intentions and asked him what was on his mind. Then he told me that the sea captain, just before his death, had spoken of new discoveries of gold in Becc's territory.'

'At the Thicket of Pigs?'

Conrí nodded morosely. 'You see, when our prince, Torcán, was killed fighting your brother at Cnoc Áine, we not only lost a lot of our youth but were forced to pay reparation for our rebellion both to Cashel and to the High King. It impoverished us.'

'How would the finding of gold in this land, where lawful Eóghanacht rule continues, have anything to do with you?'

Conrí grimaced wryly. 'Dea had an idea. But the first thing to do was to check whether the information was true or not. The captain said that he had picked up the information while his ship was in the port of the house of Molaga. A man who was trying to find ships to transport the gold approached him. He heard that the gold was found near a place called the Thicket of Pigs. The captain knew that there was a hunter called Menma who lived in that area and knew it well. The captain had an idea to return to the shores of the territory of the Cinél na Áeda and seek out Menma who must surely be able to identify the discovery. When he was dying, the captain simply passed the information on to Dea.'

Fidelma was silent for a moment and then she said, 'However, I repeat my question. Even if gold were found here, what use would it be to the Uí Fidgente?'

Conrí looked uncomfortable. 'As I said, we are improverished by the defeats inflicted on us.'

'They were just defeats against a rebellious people,' Fidelma reminded him.

'One may interpret our rebellion. But, anyway, it is true that we were defeated and impoverished. The captain had said the discovery of gold was still a close secret, known only to a couple of people and not even the chieftain of the Cinél na Áeda knew it. Dea's idea was that before the news was widely known, a powerful Uí Fidgente raid could carry off a sufficient quantity of gold to restore some power to our people.' He paused and then added, 'I swear that I knew nothing of this until the day Dea asked me to allow him and his men to go foraging. I would not dissuade him for I am not traitor to my own.'

Fidelma gazed into his features for a moment or two. 'Curiously, I am inclined to believe you. It is too bizarre a tale not to be the truth.'

'But then Dea and his men did not return and my scouts found their bodies. Surely, whatever the intention was, they should have been allowed time to surrender? They did not deserve to be slaughtered like animals, shot in the back with arrows, or cut down from behind. This is what has angered my warriors and me. I am determined to see reparation.'

'Conrí, you have told me your truth. For that I am grateful. I cannot accept any legal basis why your men should be compensated for they were found having burnt down an innocent person's home, abducted his wife and slaughtered his animals. Furthermore, their intention was theft. This Dea came to you and proposed no more than theft . . .'

'Dea was my brother,' Conrí replied in a hollow voice. 'That is why I cannot let this matter rest.'

'For that, I am sorry for you. But I represent the law not the spirit of vengeance. Let me make a proposal to you . . .'

Conrí looked at her with suspicion. 'I cannot return to my brother's wife and children without telling them that his death has been avenged.'

'I said that I do not represent the spirit of vengeance. However, you might be able to return to them and say that justice still prevails, for I know that your brother and his men were not given the opportunity to surrender.'

'Then what is your proposal?'

'Simply this. Stay encamped here, attacking no one, harming no one, and tomorrow I shall summon you and two others of your band that you care to nominate to attend the chieftain's hall at Rath Raithlen. You will be there under my personal guarantee of protection. There I shall reveal all the truths behind what has been happening in this troubled land. You will know the truth behind the deaths of your brother and his men and who was responsible. There is no need to wreak vengeance on the entire people just for the sin of a few.'

Conrí sat in silence for a while and then he shrugged. 'I am a reasonable man, Fidelma of Cashel. I know the Eóghanacht think all Uí Fidgente are mindless monsters, seeking only blood and booty. It is not so. We are an independent people, a proud people, bowing to nobody and accepting nobody as our lord. That brings us into conflict on many occasions. But we are, above all, just and fair-minded. I have heard what you have said. You, too, are just and reasonable. I will answer your summons to Rath Raithlen. My men are all warriors and like hounds that are straining at the leash to be among those that killed their kindred, so assure the Cinél na Áeda that if they try to trick us, their punishment will be that much harsher and bloody.'

Fidelma rose slowly and reached out a hand. 'I hear you, Conrí.'

The warlord rose and took her hand. They shook silently.

'We have made a good start, Fidelma of Cashel,' the man said as they emerged from the tent to face the waiting men. Eadulf and Adag stood with worried expressions on their faces while the Uí Fidgente were sulky and suspicious.

'Then let us hope the finish is good also.' Fidelma smiled.

Chapter Seventeen

At Rath Raithlen Fidelma consulted with Becc and made her plans for a hearing to be arranged for the next day at the noon hour.

That evening, before the meal, she realised that she had one more person to question and slipped out of Becc's guest hostel without consulting Eadulf. She made her way straight to Gobnuid's forge and found the surly smith still bent over his anvil.

'Well, Gobnuid, you are working late this night.'

The smith glanced up with a growl, but whether of annoyance or merely a greeting it was hard to discern.

'Did you deliver your hides safely?' Fidelma smiled.

The smith glared at her. There seemed to be some concern on his features.

'Why do you ask me that?' he demanded.

'Because you returned early from your trip. You could not have reached the Bandan river and returned so soon.' She perched herself on a small wooden stool that stood near the forge furnace and stretched comfortably in the heat.

Gobnuid scowled. 'If you must know, the wheel of my wagon broke and I had to do a makeshift repair and leave it with a friend for safety while I returned here to get a replacement.' He gestured to a wheel in the corner of his forge.

'It is taking you some time to return to your wagon,' observed Fidelma.

'You know full well that the Uí Fidgente raided and everyone was needed. Now I am told by the tanist that I am required to attend this meeting you have called in the Great Hall tomorrow. My business will wait until afterwards.'

'Do you often work for the tanist?'

The smith's brows drew together. 'What makes you ask that?'

'You mentioned you were transporting the hides for Accobrán. How often do you do that?'

Gobnuid stood uncertainly. 'Well, I do jobs for him when I have time. Is there something wrong with that?'

Fidelma smiled sweetly at his defensive tone. 'Not at all. It is just that transporting hides is not that rewarding for a talented craftsman.'

'I often shoe his horse and now and then sharpen his weapons,' replied Gobnuid.

'The tanist seems to do a fair and regular trade in hides. I wonder where he gets the hides from in the first place?'

'The question is best put to him. I suppose he buys them from farmers hereabout. It saves them having to do the business themselves.'

'Yet I would have thought that Lesren the tanner was best equipped to conduct the trade in hides,' Fidelma pointed out. 'Still, I suppose there is not a great deal of metal working here these days. I mean, what with the mines closed down. Do you do jobs for the abbey, for the Aksumites who stay there, for example?'

She noticed Gobnuid stiffen.

'What is it you want, lady?' he demanded, turning and glaring pugnaciously at her.

'This land used to be full of metal workings,' she went on, ignoring him. 'Did you ever work in the mines?'

The smith turned from her and bent over his furnace, stirring the charcoal into a spitting display of sparks. 'The mines closed when I was a young lad.'

'Did you know that one of the Aksumites, Brother Dangila, worked in the gold mines of his country? You know Brother Dangila?'

Gobnuid was tight-lipped. 'I have seen the man.'

Fidelma slowly stood up. She realised that Gobnuid was stubborn.

'If you know Brother Dangila, I was wondering why you supported that cousin of yours, Brocc, in his attack on the Aksumites?'

The smith glowered at her. 'Strangers are strangers, family is family. Anyway, I have already admitted that I took part in the attack on the abbey.'

'I'll bid you a good night, then, Gobnuid,' Fidelma said in resignation. 'I will see you tomorrow.'

She turned and began to walk away, feeling his curious gaze upon her. Gobnuid had an obstinate nature. It would be impossible to wring the truth from him but she felt that she had learnt enough.

The guest house of Becc lay on the far side of the great complex of buildings that made up Rath Raithlen and the way to it led through a collection of buildings from which the artisans and traders of the fortress conducted their businesses. Now the buildings were dark and deserted. Only Gobnuid had been working late this dark and chilly night.

Fidelma swung confidently down the darkened alley. It was not any great length and she could see some brand torches lighting its far end, which led into the squares constituting the stables at the back of the chieftain's hall. It was only when she was halfway along the darkened alley that some sixth sense caused her to feel a tingling of the hairs at the nape of her neck. She was sure eyes were watching her. There was no logic to the feeling. But Fidelma had an acute sense of surroundings. An awareness of environment was essential to survival. Ever since she was a child Fidelma had trained herself to notice anything out of the ordinary. She rather admired old Liag, the apothecary, for while he might overdramatise his sense of environment in the woods, the basic concepts were right. Without that sense, a person was blind.

She did not show her concern by altering her step or turning her head but the feeling grew stronger. From the corner of her eye she identified a shadow in the darkness of the buildings, just a slight movement. Something, someone, was there. She continued her steady pace, head erect, but eyes alert to the dark. She was only a few yards from the lighted area by the stables when she was aware that the shadow was on the move, moving rapidly and moving towards her.

She spun round on her heel towards the oncoming shadow, which grew into the shape of a burly man. One hand was upraised and the faint light from the burning brand torch at the end of the street glinted on something in that hand which reflected and shone for a moment.

The learned ones of Éireann, both in pre-Christian times and now that they were the repositories of the New Faith, used often to journey far and wide. Travellers were frequently the object of attacks by thieves and bandits. But those learned ones believed it was wrong to carry weapons even to protect themselves from attack. Violence was abhorrent to them and against their teachings. They were therefore forced to develop a technique which they called *troid-sciathagid* – battle through defence. Fidelma, like other members of the religious who journeyed abroad, was taught the method of defending herself without the use of weapons.

In a split second, she saw the danger. She stood, waiting for the man's assault as he bore down on her. As he reached her, her two hands shot out to take the raised arm and she grasped the wrist, swaying backwards and allowing the momentum of the man's assault to carry him stumbling forward. He went crashing to the ground, unable to stop that forward movement, while Fidelma heaved on the wrist holding the knife.

The man was strong and he managed to retain hold of the knife. When it became apparent that she could not break his grip, Fidelma let go of his wrist for fear that she would be dragged down with him. She skipped backwards and shouted: 'Guards! Guards! Help!'

The figure on the floor scrambled up and had turned and was facing her once more, wielding the knife. He was moving forward again.

But two warriors had suddenly appeared at the end of the alley and one gave a shout as they bore down on Fidelma, swords in hand.

The attacker was disconcerted for a moment, glancing behind him.

Fidelma moved forward, turning slightly sideways, and aimed a swift kick, using the flat of her foot in a jabbing motion, at the attacker's genitalia. There came a scream and the figure dropped to its knees. In another second the two guards had reached them and one rested his sword point lightly on the figure's neck.

'Move and you are a dead man,' he said curtly.

The second guard, whose eyes seemed well used to the dark, had obviously recognised Fidelma. 'Are you harmed, lady?'

'I am not. But let us see who it is that would wish me harm.'

The first guard had disarmed the man and he and his companion took an arm each and dragged the still moaning figure out of the darkness into the light of the brand torch.

Fidelma was aware of a babble of voices as people, disturbed by the commotion, now came forward. She saw Eadulf, his face pale, pushing through them.

'Fidelma! Are you all right?'

She nodded briefly.

Accobrán had also come forward.

'Is it the moon killer?' he demanded.

The two warriors pulled their captive forward so that the light fell on his face.

'Brocc!'

There was a gasp from the crowd.

The tanist stared at the burly man, who glowered with hatred at them.

'So you were the moon killer? Even when you tried to stir up the people against the strangers it was you all the time!'

Brocc scowled. Fidelma moved forward and returned Brocc's glare with a slight smile.

'It is true that you tried to kill me in that dark alley, Brocc, but I doubt whether you are the moon killer.'

'You know I am not!' snapped Brocc.

'Why did you attempt to kill me?'

'Because you are protecting the real murderers.'

'How do you make that out?' she said with a frown.

'I knew it when you first came to Rath Raithlen. You religious are all the same, protecting one another. It was obvious that the strangers killed Escrach, killed Beccnat and Ballgel. Yet I have seen you meeting them and being friendly with them. You are protecting them and therefore you must accept the guilt with them.'

Fidelma looked at the man with an expression of astonishment, which dissolved into sadness. Then she shook her head.

'How anyone can become as confused as you are is beyond me, Brocc. And it saddens me. I do not know how to answer you. But you must know that what you have done is a serious crime. You have attempted to murder a *dálaigh*—'

'Worse still,' interrupted Becc, who had joined her, the crowd having parted respectfully to allow the chieftain to come forward, 'worse still, you have attempted to kill the sister of the king.'

Fidelma grimaced, dismissing the fact. 'It is more important to consider the law above all things and what this man has done is not an affront to me but to the law that I represent. That is the more serious of his crimes. There is a fixed penalty for homicide and attempted homicide, which is seven *cumals* irrespective of rank. But this matter goes deeper—'

'It does go deeper,' interrupted Brocc, his temper not yet controlled. 'It goes deeper in that you are the guilty one in preventing the truth coming out and blame being laid where it should be. At least I struck a blow for the truth!'

Fidelma sighed and shook her head sadly. 'You struck a blow for your own prejudice, which is eating your very soul, Brocc, so that it blinds you to the truth. The most serious offence one can commit against another person is to deprive them of their life. In some lands it is called justice to balance the taking of a life by taking another. Even those of the New Faith are beginning to say that we should adopt the way which demands "life for life, eye for eye, tooth for tooth". But we are an old and wise people and we allow a killer to atone for his crime by compensation and entry into a process of rehabilitation. We have an ancient system of law that says that evidence must be gathered against a person first, then the person is allowed to answer in public and counter that evidence. Only when it is judged that the evidence is overwhelming is the person convicted.

'I have been sent to gather the evidence and, until tonight, I have still been gathering that evidence. That you think you can stand above the law and its process, and even assassinate the appointed representative of the law system, is something I have never encountered before. All I can say is that you must be suffering from a loss of sanity – whether permanent or temporary needs to be judged at a later time.'

Brocc continued to scowl in defiance. 'Your words are designed to disguise the truth, lawyer. All lawyers have lying tongues.'

Fidelma was sarcastic. 'I thought it was the fact that I am a member of the religious that caused you to think I was hiding the truth?'

'Lawyers! Religious! Black dog and white dog, both are dogs,' snapped Brocc.

Becc looked towards Fidelma in a troubled fashion. 'What shall we do with him, cousin?'

'There is little to do but to confine him until tomorrow. Then we can bring a resolution to the case of the moon killings.'

The chieftain of the Cinél na Áeda sighed unhappily and motioned for Brocc to be led away. As the crowd began to disperse he said quietly: 'We are approaching the feast of Samhain, Fidelma. It lacks only a few days. Are you sure all will be resolved tomorrow? It would certainly be best if we could see a resolution before Samhain. I would hate bad luck to be visited on our people.'

Fidelma turned towards the entrance of the chieftain's hall. Becc and Eadulf followed her inside and Fidelma took a seat before the fire.

Becc was regarding her anxiously.

'Are you recovered from the attack?' he asked nervously. 'Are you sure that you were not hurt?'

She made a negative gesture with her hand.

'I have survived worse things,' she said. 'Brocc's attack was very clumsy. However, he is a very stupid man and his stupidity makes him dangerous.'

'What is the concern about this feast of Samhain?' Eadulf demanded.

Becc regarded him for a moment or two and then decided to explain. 'The significance of the feast of Samhain is that it is the one time of the year when the Otherworld becomes visible to this world. From sunset until sunrise those who have departed to the Otherworld in the preceding year can return to this one and wreak their vengeance on those who have wronged them.'

'But that is an old pagan belief,' said Eadulf dismissively.

'So it might be,' intervened Fidelma, 'but a change in religion does not necessarily mean that people have ceased to believe in the ways of their fathers. In Rome, fifty or so years ago, Pope Boniface decreed that the old pre-Christian Roman feast of the dead, Lemuria, held in May, should be sanctified as a festival to commemorate all the martyred saints. So even Rome clings to its pagan past.'

'It is true that the people of the Cinél na Áeda continue to celebrate the feast of Samhain with full rigour,' added Becc. 'They believe that the wraiths of Beccnat, Escrach and Ballgel will return and seek revenge on all the people here until justice is given to them.'

Eadulf shook his head in bewilderment. 'Surely if such ghosts existed they would come back seeking only their killer.'

'The belief is that the whole clan is responsible if the killer is not caught and punished. The clan is the kin and the entire kin is responsible for what one of its members does. So unless the killer is caught and punishment announced, then, on Samhain, any one or all of us might be visited by the vengeful wraiths.'

'Well, have no fear, Becc.' Fidelma smiled.

The chieftain looked at her expectantly.

'When we meet at noon tomorrow in this hall, then I shall reveal the guilty to you.'

Eadulf and Fidelma had retired to their room and were preparing for bed. Eadulf was very quiet. From time to time, Fidelma glanced across at him with a worried expression.

'You appear pensive tonight, Eadulf,' she finally remarked. 'Is it about tomorrow?'

He responded with a troubled sigh.

'I have been through many such hearings, Fidelma. I have little doubt that you will be successful in this matter as you have been in the past.'

'I fear you take too much for granted,' she replied seriously. 'Don't we have a saying – the end of the day is a good prophet? You are usually interested to know how I plan to approach a hearing,' she continued when he did not respond. 'Yet tonight you have scarcely asked me any questions about who is the guilty party and how I will set about demonstrating it.'

Eadulf turned to her with a quick movement, his gaze fixed on her face as if examining her expression closely.

'Have you thought any more about our discussion involving little Alchú?' he asked brutally.

Fidelma's face altered slightly, becoming an impassive mask.

'Of course I have thought about it,' she replied, terseness in her tone.

'And?' Eadulf delivered the word like a blow.

'I would have thought that we had other matters to consider as of this moment,' she responded. 'Once we have finished, then we can . . .'

Eadulf rose from where he had been sitting with a shake of his head. He strode across the room and back again, his movements demonstrating his agitation. When he spoke again his voice was tense.

'Each time I have raised the matter, you have tried to put it off. What has happened since you had our child, Fidelma? You have become almost a different person.'

Fidelma was about to launch into a scathing attack on his insensitivity at this particular time when she suddenly realised that such an outburst would be no more than camouflage on her part. She was prevaricating. She was putting off the time when she had to deal with the matter.

'You are right, Eadulf. I do feel a different person,' she replied quietly.

Eadulf stood still for a moment, her words suddenly deflating him, and then he reseated himself. She sounded so vulnerable.

'Is it something I have done?' he asked.

Fidelma shook her head, frowning. 'I don't think so. I don't know. Since we returned to Cashel and I gave birth to Alchú, it seems that things have changed.'

'In what way? All that has happened is that we now have a son. I know that you are not concerned by the likes of those who are trying to make the religious celibate. You have always denounced those ascetic religious before.'

'I am not at all concerned with them,' Fidelma assured him firmly. 'There is plenty of room in the Faith for those who pursue the ascetic path as well as we who pursue a religion based firmly on society as it is and not as it is envisioned by those who would suppress all emotion and human instinct. Let the celibates live in their caves or island hermitages. We are here to minister to society as part of society.'

'Then if that is not the concern, can it be that you feel ashamed of Alchú because his father is a Saxon?'

'Ashamed?' Fidelma almost spat the word. Her eyes flashed as she spun round on him. For a moment, Eadulf thought she would strike him. 'How dare you think that I am ashamed of . . . of . . .' Her voice faltered and she ended with a sob.

Eadulf shrugged helplessly. 'I do not mean to upset you, but I am simply at a loss to understand. You are troubled. You are behaving differently. What am I to make of it? What has gone wrong?'

Fidelma sat, head bowed, for a few moments. Then she sniffed and tried to draw herself up.

'Can I make a bargain with you, Eadulf?' Her voice was controlled and very quiet.

Eadulf regarded her with suspicion.

'What sort of bargain?' he demanded.

'A bargain that you allow me to concentrate on this matter which will be resolved one way or another tomorrow. After that, we shall immediately return to Cashel. There I promise that we will discuss these problems and sort matters out.'

Eadulf compressed his lips and thought for a moment or two. 'It would be better if I had even an idea of what it is that needs to be sorted out.'

Fidelma looked at him sorrowfully. 'If I could give you that information now, Eadulf, there would be no problem to sort out. Can we make that bargain?'

Eadulf remained silent. Then he said: 'I have been aware of some changes in you since the birth of Alchú. I have had to live with these changes during the last few months. I don't suppose that one more day will make a great difference, will it? Very well. I agree. We will leave this matter between us in abeyance until the present case has been sorted and finalised.'

Fidelma reached forward and laid a hand on Eadulf's arm.

'Thank you,' she said simply. 'You are always there for me when I need a staff to rely on, Eadulf. Although you may not appreciate it, I value that support.' There was an uncomfortable silence for a few moments and then she forced a smile. 'Now, before we retire for the night, I want to go over what I shall say tomorrow and you may see, as you always do, if there are flaws in my logic.'

Eadulf gave in with reluctance.

'Where will you begin?' he asked, trying to put enthusiasm in his voice.

Fidelma relaxed and sat back.

'I'll begin with the gold mine,' she said thoughtfully.

'The gold mine? Who is your main suspect for the murders of the girls?'

When she told him, Eadulf swallowed in amazement.

'I hope you can demonstrate that,' he whispered doubtfully. 'If not, things could go very badly for us tomorrow.'

Fidelma slowly began to explain her case.

Chapter Eighteen

The Great Hall of Becc, chieftain of the Cinél na Áeda, was packed so that there was little room for anyone except officials of the clan to find seats. So many people had sought entrance to hear the findings of the famous *dálaigh* from Cashel that some of Becc's warrior guards had to hold people back at the doors. Becc was seated in his chair of office which, as usual on such occasions, was placed on a wooden dais at the far end of the hall. Fidelma was seated to his right and on the same level. Behind her chair stood Eadulf while Accobrán, the tanist, was standing behind his chieftain's left shoulder. Immediately to the left sat Abbot Brogán, as senior cleric of the clan, attended by his steward, Brother Solam.

In the first row facing them was a small group of petty chieftains and religious representing the abbey. At Fidelma's request, the three Aksumite brothers were among them. Behind them, attended by two of his warriors, was the tall, dark-faced warlord of the Uí Fidgente, Conrí the Wolf King. They had ridden into the fortress that morning under their banner of truce, protected by Fidelma's guarantee that no harm would be visited on them. She had ordered Adag to ensure that Accobrán and his warriors were kept as far away from them as possible. Even so, everyone treated the Uí Fidgente with deep suspicion and scowls and they appeared to form a vulnerable and isolated group.

As Fidelma examined the waiting crowd she could see all those she had especially requested to attend in the hall itself. Even Liag had been persuaded to come after Menma had put some pressure on the old recluse. Menma and Suanach sat near him. Gobnuid was scowling in the crowd, seated near Seachlann the miller. Seachlann's brother Brocc had been brought from his cell and stood to one side, against a wall, between two watchful warriors. Goll and his family were there. Tómma and Creoda, the assistant tanners, with Sirin the cook, were pressed into a corner. In fact, all Rath Raithlen was represented.

Adag the steward moved forward and, unnecessary as it was, called for attention and silence. He glanced at Becc who, in turn, inclined his head towards Fidelma. She rose and gazed thoughtfully at the crowded hall for a moment before speaking. She spoke slowly and deliberately.

'I came to this land of the Cinél na Áeda and found evil. What is evil?' She paused as if expecting an answer. 'Philosophers for many ages have argued over its precise nature. Evil is doing or intending to do harm, causing discomfort or pain in either a physical or a mental sense and creating trouble and anguish. It is the antithesis of good. Yet Brehon Morann, my mentor, once said that if we tried to abolish evil from the world, then we could know very little of the nature of our being. For often those who perform evil deeds are persuaded that what they do is honourable and necessary. Indeed, unless we all share the same moral codes of behaviour, we cannot propound a definition of evil and we must accept it as a natural part of the world in which we live.'

The people stirred, shuffling their feet, most of them not understanding her words.

'If we wanted a sermon, Sister, we would have gone to the church,' cried Brocc, still aggressive in spite of his bonds and not cowed by the warriors standing guard next to him. One of them pushed him roughly to make him quiet.

Fidelma smiled sadly. 'Even the church does not possess a monopoly on goodness. Evil is to be found there just as it is found among those who do not follow the Faith.'

Abbot Brogán looked as if he were about to respond but snapped his mouth shut, while Liag was actually smiling with cynicism.

'I have come here and found malevolence,' continued Fidelma with emphasis.

'We know that!' cried Seachlann. 'Have we not lost our daughters? Stop your sermon and tell us who is responsible.'

'I shall come to it,' promised Fidelma in a patient tone. 'I shall come to it in the proper time. Our culture and our laws are our indication of evil and we must use that as our definition. We seek those responsible for evil, for Seneca once wrote that the most important evil is the evil of cringing to evil and surrendering to it. We must always defy evil and face any suffering before we give in to it.'

Becc leant forward and nodded approvingly. 'This is true, Fidelma, but show us where this evil lies.'

Fidelma's expression remained grim. 'Three crimes have taken place here. The crime of murder, the crime of deception and theft, and the crime of abusing the laws of hospitality. From these three evils, several other small infractions of our law code have flown.'

There was a sudden sense of expectancy among the people in the Great Hall. Fidelma gazed on their upturned faces. A variety of emotions showed in their features: excitement, like dogs waiting to be unleashed in the hunt; consternation and apprehension and, here and there, fear.

'Let me begin with the crime of the abuse of the laws of hospitality. That is the least serious of the offences that have been committed against the Cinél na Áeda. But we deem it a grave misdemeanour nevertheless.'

She turned and looked down at Brother Dangila and his companions, then glanced towards Brother Solam. 'Since I have to speak in our own language so that the majority of people may understand, I charge you, Brother Solam, with translating my words into Greek for the convenience of the three brothers of Aksum.'

The steward of the abbey inclined his head, left his place and walked to where the Aksumites were sitting and swiftly interpreted what Fidelma had said. The solemn-faced Brother Dangila bowed slightly in a gesture of acceptance towards her.

'The three brothers from the far-off land of Aksum have abused the hospitality of the abbey—'

'I was right!' interrupted Brocc raucously. 'They are the killers. I said so all along and I demand—'

Fidelma swung fiercely round on him. 'You will demand nothing. If you do not remain silent I shall have you removed back to your cell.'

Brocc blinked before her fury and fell sullenly silent.

'The three brothers from Aksum, being strangers, may themselves have been misled and might use that argument to defend their actions,' Fidelma said.

Brother Dangila spoke directly to Fidelma, with Brother Solam translating for the rest of the people. 'We have no understanding of this alleged abuse, Sister. Please explain.'

'You came here, so you have told us, to study the works that are in the abbey of Finnbarr. Correct?'

'Correct.'

'Abbot Brogán gave you hospitality at the abbey on the grounds of that study and for no other purpose. But you had another reason for coming here, didn't you?'

Brother Dangila's eyes narrowed slightly and he made no reply.

'Before you entered the brotherhood of the Faith, Dangila, you told me that you worked in the gold mines of your country, the mines of Adulis which produce gold that is exported all over the world. And was not your father a worker in those same mines?'

Brother Dangila nodded slowly. 'I do not deny it. I did work in the mines in the shadow of Ras Dashen before I joined the brotherhood of the Faith.'

'Your words to me were that you learnt more than just how to spot a rich vein of gold or copper,' Fidelma continued. 'In fact, you were a craftsman in your field. You knew all about mining techniques.'

The Aksumite shrugged indifferently but made no response.

'We know how you were saved from a ship that foundered off the shores and take to the house of Molaga. You were there some time. Do you remember telling me how you decided to come here and stay in the community of the abbey of Finnbarr?'

'My memory is not so short,' replied Brother Dangila. 'And yet I cannot see—'

'Be patient. You told me that you came here to study the writings of Aibhistín about the moon and its effects . . .'

There was an uneasy murmur from those assembled.

'That was not entirely true, was it?' snapped Fidelma.

Brother Dangila said nothing. His two companions, Brother Nakfa and Brother Gambela, exchanged glances. Their expressions were not lost on Fidelma.

'Perhaps you did not even tell your companions the truth of why you really brought them to the land of the Cinél na Áeda,' she went on confidently, hoping she was interpreting the movement correctly.

Again, Brother Dangila was silent.

'It was Accobrán who suggested that you came to this abbey, wasn't it?' Fidelma prompted.

The young tanist, who had been lounging with a cynical smile on his face, suddenly tensed.

'What are you implying?' he demanded, moving forward, but Becc reached out a hand and held him back.

Fidelma ignored him.

'What did Accobrán offer you in return for coming here to use your talent in spotting gold veins in the old mines here?' she said.

'Outrageous!' cried Accobrán, taking another involuntary step forward but this time finding his path blocked by the stocky frame of Eadulf. 'How dare you . . . ?'

Sister Fidelma smiled softly at him. 'I dare because I am a *dálaigh*. As Brother Dangila seems reticent, perhaps you will tell me what you offered him to come and be your mine surveyor?'

Becc leant forward, frowning at his nephew. 'A tanist has a duty to clear such a matter not only with myself but with the council of the Cinél na Áeda. He could not act arbitrarily.'

Fidelma continued to look questioningly at Accobrán but replied to the chieftain. 'Your tanist was not intending to share any wealth that he discovered with you or the Cinél na Áeda. This leads me to the

second of the crimes that I have said have been committed here – a
betrayal of trust by your tanist, the man whom you appointed your
heir-apparent.'

Accobrán had grabbed his sword hilt to unsheathe the weapon but
Eadulf seized a short sword from a nearby warrior and placed its point
lightly against the tanist's midriff. He smiled apologetically.

'*Aequo animo*,' he said softly, advising the man to be calm. '*Aequam
servare mentem.*'

'This affront cannot be tolerated,' growled Accobrán, but he made
no other movement.

Becc was looking on in confusion. 'We must hear more than
accusations, Fidelma.'

'Oh, so you shall. I am not sure how long Accobrán, Gobnuid
and Brother Dangila have been working an old mine on the Thicket
of Pigs.'

Gobnuid, still seated, groaned and placed his head in his hands.

'Can you prove this?' demanded Becc.

'I have witnesses to all I say. And when I went to explore the mine,
I found a missing piece of an Aksumite crucifix that Brother Dangila
had dropped there. When I had previously taxed him with its loss, he
told me he had left it in the dormitory of the abbey. But I found it in
the mine. Brother Solam will bear testimony that he has seen Accobrán
and Dangila going by wagon to the mine. Menma and Brother Eadulf
have seen Dangila outside the mine and also Gobnuid. Earlier, I had
also witnessed them together with Eadulf.'

She turned back to Brother Dangila with raised eyebrows in silent
interrogation. The tall Aksumite seemed to have slumped a little in his
seat. But Becc interrupted again.

'You are accusing Accobrán and this stranger, who hardly speaks
our language, of collusion? In what language could they have conducted
such subterfuge?'

Fidelma smiled easily. 'Did you not know that Accobrán spoke
Greek, Becc? He was some years studying for the Faith in the house
of Molaga and learnt a basic Greek. I learnt that the second day I was
here when your tanist started to recite some Greek poetry. Anyway,
Brother Dangila, what do you have to say to the charge?'

The tall man raised his eyes to her. 'During the course of conversation
at the house of Molaga, Accobrán found out that I had once been a
surveyor in the gold mines of my own land. He told me that he thought
he had discovered some gold in his own territory, a place where there
had been rich mines until not so long ago. He said he knew a little of
how to recognise gold . . .'

'That I can confirm,' nodded Fidelma. 'When we were in Bébháil's *bothán* I chanced to pick up a gold rock and remark on it. Accobrán was knowledgeable enough to glance at it and assure me that it was fool's gold. He seemed relieved by the fact.'

'But he did not know enough to follow a seam and mine it from a rock face,' continued Brother Dangila. 'He asked me if I would survey it and find out whether the seam would yield riches or simply wither after a short while. For this I was offered a quarter of everything that could be extracted. I believed that this mine belonged to him.'

Fidelma raised her hands, palms outwards, to still the crowd, which had begun to mutter in astonishment.

'Do not leave us, Gobnuid,' she called, espying the smith, who had risen and was heading towards the doors. 'You probably received another quarter, didn't you?'

Rough hands pushed Gobnuid forward to the front of the crowd.

'I've done nothing,' he said in surly fashion.

'On the contrary. I feel that you have done much,' retorted Fidelma. 'There is no need to tell you how rich the lands of the Cinél na Áeda were in mines and how a generation or more ago those mines were worked out. Along came a ruthless young warrior. An intelligent warrior, who had once studied in the Faith. He found a cave on the Thicket of Pigs in which he saw gold. He saw a plan to get personally rich and powerful instead of sharing his find with his people. He found a smith who would mine and transport the gold to traders on the river and he found a mine surveyor so that he and the smith knew what seams to follow.'

She paused for a moment.

'I saw Gobnuid not so long ago driving a wagon which he said was loaded with hides sent by Accobrán for traders on the lower river. Hides? The wheels of the wagon were rutted so deeply in the track that the weight must have been considerable. From such a wagon a gold nugget fell on the track near the Ring of Pigs which was picked up by a boy called Síoda. Innocently, the boy took it to Gobnuid who sought to persuade him that it was only fool's gold. But it was not, was it, Gobnuid?'

Gobnuid hung his head, flushing, confirming the truth of her words.

'The trouble was that Accobrán gave the game away when he went to the sea port looking for a pliant captain to help transport the gold out of this territory. He made a mistake in sending some samples of his prospective cargo with the captain of a trading ship. That man was in the country of the Uí Fidgente when fate overtook him. He was dying and confessed the source of the nuggets he had to a warrior named

Dea. But all he managed to tell Dea was that the rich source was on the Thicket of Pigs. He did not know where the mine was but he knew that a hunter lived at that place, a hunter called Menma. He suggested to Dea that the hunter must know. Menma did not. However, Dea had joined a host commanded by his brother Conrí who were going to the lands of the Corco Loígde for the annual games.

'Dea and his band of warriors, without the knowledge or permission of Conrí, raided Menma's cabin in search of him. You already know what transpired. They took Suanach as a hostage to force Menma to follow them.

'They did not realise that they would be pursued by Cinél na Áeda warriors led by the very man who was the source of the gold. Accobrán realised that the merchant had betrayed his gold find to the Uí Fidgente. He did not know details, of course. When he chased them, he had one thing on his mind. He resolved that no one among the raiders should live to breathe a word of their purpose. That is why he killed them all.'

There was a gasp from those assembled.

'Menma and Suanach will testify that the Uí Fidgente were not given a chance to surrender.'

Becc was sitting back with a combination of sadness and anger on his features. 'A tanist takes oath to pursue the commonwealth of his people. I have become increasingly aware that Accobrán's actions are questionable. I have made the excuse that he is young and untutored in the code of chieftainship. But this . . . ? This is against law and morality. This is an evil betrayal of the trust of the Cinél na Áeda.'

'There is more,' went on Fidelma. 'I happened to question Gobnuid the smith about the gold nugget that Síoda had found. He panicked and thought I was on to the secret of the mine in the cave. He tried to arrange an accident without consulting Accobrán. The next morning, Eadulf and I had climbed onto the watchtower at the gates of the rath. Gobnuid joined us, saying that he had a message from Accobrán. He had loosened a rung of the ladder. When we started to go down it was sheer luck that Eadulf, who went first, did not fall to his death when the rung gave way.

'Subsequently, Accobrán must have assured Gobnuid that we were too concerned with the deaths of the three girls to bother about the gold mine. It was a stupid mistake, for Gobnuid had now alerted me to the connection.'

The tanist was standing silently, still covered by Eadulf's sword. Fidelma had already motioned a warrior to take charge of Gobnuid.

'Cousin Becc, your tanist has betrayed you and the office of trust that he held among you. Avarice! When all the sins are old, avarice will remain young. It is the oldest and the strongest of motives for evildoers.'

Becc leaned forward with an angry frown. 'Are we to take it that Accobrán and his conspirators were responsible for the killings of the three young girls? Had they discovered his secret and were their deaths a means to still their tongues?'

Fidelma answered in the negative. 'In that matter, Lesren was actually correct in his charge.'

The youth, Gabrán, leapt from his seat and struggled to reach the door through the crowd. It took a moment for the people to recover from their shock. Two men caught and held him while Fínmed, the boy's mother, started to scream and wail in hysterical desperation.

'How can that be?' gasped Becc. 'He was cleared by my Brehon Aolú, and even you said . . .'

'You were all wrong about Gabrán,' replied Fidelma firmly.

Fínmed fell to silently sobbing, while Goll had risen and moved forward to the dais. His face was filled with shock and growing anger.

'You are wrong, Sister Fidelma. You are wrong. We protest against this prejudice . . . you . . .'

'If you are silent awhile, Goll, I will explain.'

Her voice was quiet but commanding. When the murmuring of the crowd in the hall died away, Fidelma began.

'It is true that Gabrán and Beccnat were going to get married. But it is also true, exactly as Lesren claimed, that Beccnat had changed her mind.' Fidelma turned to where Lesren's widow Bébháil was sitting next to Tómma, her head hung low. 'Now that Lesren is no longer a threat to you, Bébháil, perhaps you will tell us the truth of what happened?'

The woman raised her head slowly. 'You already know what sort of character Lesren was and why he did not want our daughter to associate with Gabrán. That much is certainly true.' She paused and licked her lips. 'It is also true that Gabrán wooed our daughter and they did, indeed, plan to get married. They used to meet regularly and they went to Liag's place for his instruction, more from the opportunity to use it as a meeting place than a real interest in star lore.'

Liag, the apothecary snorted in disgust but Bébháil went on.

'Lesren also spoke the truth when he said that Beccnat had decided not to marry Gabrán . . .'

'Lies!' shouted the boy, struggling between the two men who held him. 'Becc, you have dealt with this before and dismissed the case against me. It is lies.'

'It is the truth as Beccnat told me,' insisted Bébháil quietly.

'What caused her decision?' asked Fidelma.

'She heard that Gabrán had been seeing Escrach in secret. He had told Escrach that he was only pursuing Beccnat because he wanted to avenge himself on Lesren for what Lesren had done to his mother.'

'Who told Beccnat this?'

'It was Escrach herself, who was horrified at the idea, and as Beccnat was a friend had decided to warn her quietly. But Escrach was, at the same time, in love with Gabrán and could not denounce him openly nor desert him. She merely thought to warn Beccnat about him. Beccnat decided to break with the boy and, in truth, she was already finding consolation with the tanist there.'

Eyes once more turned on Accobrán, still held covered by Eadulf's short sword.

'We have already heard from a witness that Accobrán and Beccnat were meeting and behaving as lovers. Gabrán also displayed a hate of the tanist because he suspected him of having some affair with Beccnat,' said Fidelma.

Goll stared at her in anguish. 'But this does not mean to say that Gabrán killed Beccnat. The Brehon Aolú showed that he could not.'

Fidelma smiled quickly.

'I will come to that. So now,' she said, turning to the people in the hall who remained as if mesmerised by her, 'we have the seeds of a first motive. The terrible feud between Lesren and Fínmed, which grew into the hatred of Fínmed's son for Lesren and his desire for vengeance. If not directly on Lesren then on his daughter, Beccnat. From then on, there came cause and effect.'

She turned and sought the tanner's assistant. 'Creoda, stand forth for a moment.'

The youth came reluctantly to his feet.

'You were attending sessions with Liag when he taught you about star lore.'

'I have told you so,' the young man said nervously.

'Now tell me again, who were in these sessions with you?'

'Beccnat and Gabrán, Escrach and Ballgel, and sometimes Accobrán came along.'

'These sessions, did they usually take place at night?'

'Of course. When else can you see the stars?'

'Just so. Cast your mind back to the night of the full moon two months ago.'

'You mean the time when Beccnat's body was found?'

'I mean just that. Did you have a session then?'

'We did.'

'Who was there?'

'Only Escrach, Ballgel and myself.'

'Were there any nightly sessions after that?'

'A few.'

'And can you confirm that at these sessions, after Beccnat's death, you saw Escrach and Gabrán quite friendly towards each other and so confirm what Bébháil has reported to us?' When the youth confirmed it, Fidelma went on: 'Indeed, I think we can accept that there was close friendship between Escrach and Gabrán. Until Gabrán found out that he – according to his warped reasoning – had been betrayed to Beccnat by Escrach. Whether it took him some time to find out or whether Beccnat had told him before he killed her, we will have to leave it to him to tell us or not. I think he deliberately chose the night of the next full moon to arrange to meet Escrach at the Ring of Pigs, near where he had killed Beccnat, and there he slaughtered her in the same way.'

She glanced at the angry and pale-faced youth. If looks could kill, she would have long been dead.

'Gabrán had nursed his hate for some time and I think by this time his reasoning had deserted him. He became filled with Liag's stories of the power of the moon and the knowledge that is power. Maybe the terrible thing he had done to Beccnat had unbalanced his mind and that was what made him wait until the full of the moon for his second killing.'

'And the third killing?' questioned Becc, rousing himself like some somnambulant. 'Why would he kill Ballgel? You are not saying that he also had some affair with Ballgel?'

'That is not so!' shouted Sirin the cook in protest from the side of the hall. 'I would have known it.'

'The death of poor Ballgel. Even that killing, at the next full of the moon, had a motive. Ballgel was the third of the three girls, three friends, who had been close to one another and studied star lore. Maybe Gabrán suspected that what Escrach had told Beccnat she might also have mentioned to Ballgel. Perhaps Beccnat herself might have said something to her. He knew that the three of them, as young girls do, shared secrets. Creoda told us that the girls were, in his words, "thick as thieves and no secret safe with any of them but was shared between them". Gabrán had to be sure that no secret knowledge remained outside his own. He decided to kill her as well.'

A deep, collective sigh seem to resonate throughout the hall.

'If you asked my opinion, I would be hard pressed to judge such a person as Gabrán in terms of his responsibility in law,' Fidelma added. 'Is he truly a *dásachtach*, a person of unsound mind, who is unable to plead in law? Do not forget our law is concerned not only to protect society from the insane but also to protect the insane from society. I suspect I would consider that he started out as a *fer lethchuinn*, a person who under our law is only half sane.'

'You have been very clever, Sister Fidelma,' sneered Goll. 'You have almost made the people here believe your story.'

'Everything I have said is based on the evidence as it has been told me,' Fidelma assured him. 'Surely you wanted the truth? You yourself were not sure about your son. That's why you were following him when you encountered Brother Dangila and Gabrán on the Thicket of Pigs the other day.'

The shot went home. Pale-faced, Goll sat back. Then Fínmed rose, having calmed herself. She spoke steadily.

'Yet there is one thing that you have forgotten in spite of your cleverness, Sister Fidelma. That is the very thing that has shown my son to be innocent of Beccnat's murder, and so every other accusation that you have made against him falls. It is the very point by which the Brehon Aolú judged Gabrán innocent, and under that judgement he cannot be tried again.'

'Before you go further,' Fidelma replied gently, 'Aolú did not find Gabrán innocent. He looked at the evidence and said that there was none to charge Gabrán with the crime. Under law, he has not been tried. So my arguments may still stand in court.'

'Clever, *dálaigh!*' the woman replied triumphantly. 'But too clever. You have forgotten the crucial point of the evidence. Gabrán was not in this territory on the night of the full moon. He was at the house of Molaga. We have the evidence of Accobrán the tanist who was at the same place and I am sure you have already checked with Brother Túan, steward of Molaga, when he was visiting our abbey. This evidence proves my son was not in the territory when Beccnat died.'

Fínmed sat down, staring at Fidelma with a look of victory. There was a momentary quiet in the hall. Then Accobrán slapped his thigh with a laugh.

'You are checkmated there, *dálaigh*! Too clever by half! I can vouch for what Fínmed has said in spite of my dislike for Gabrán. He was in Molaga on the night of that full moon.'

Eyes turned expectantly on Fidelma, but she did not seem to be perturbed.

'Along with everyone else, I am guilty of overlooking a crucial point here,' Fidelma confessed quietly. 'It is good that it falls to Fínmed, Gabrán's mother, to bring it forward.'

Accobrán was still chuckling and even Goll was smiling in relief and turning to his son as if to congratulate him.

'The crucial point is that Beccnat was not murdered on the night of the full moon.' Fidelma's sharp voice caused everyone to be still. 'That fact has made me reason that Gabrán was not initially a moon maniac when he started these killings, even if he developed the tendency afterwards.' She turned to Liag the apothecary. 'You examined the bodies, Liag. Do you remember our very first conversation when I asked you about that?'

The old apothecary stood up and nodded suspiciously. 'I do.'

'You told me that Beccnat's body had been found on the morning after that night of the full moon.'

'I did.'

'So?' interrupted Accobrán. 'That would mean she was killed during that night – the night of the full moon.'

'I asked you why it was that you had guided people away from the initial idea that the savage onslaught on her had been made by some wild animal,' went on Fidelma, ignoring him. 'What did you tell me? Can you remember your words?'

Liag thought for a moment. 'I said that once I examined the body, it was clear that a jagged knife had been used. It had been difficult to examine the wounds at first.'

'Exactly, and why?'

'I told you that it was difficult to see beyond the dried blood, and there was some decomposing for the body must have lain out in the woods for two or three days.' His eyes widened as he realised what he was saying.

Fidelma turned to the hall. 'Two or three days! That is what everyone was overlooking. The body had been found on the morning after the full moon but Beccnat had been killed two or three days beforehand.' She swung round to Bébháil. 'Lesren told me, and you confirmed it, that Beccnat had gone out one night to tell Gabrán that she was ending the betrothal and that was the last you saw of her until her body was found *three days later*.'

Bébháil looked shocked. 'It is true. I had not thought . . .'

'So where did you think that she had been for that time?'

'She often went to stay with friends after rows with her father. We thought she might have gone somewhere with one of her girl friends. I don't know. Everyone said she was killed on the night of the full moon and we did not question it. The question of where she had been before that did not occur to us once she was dead.'

Fidelma had turned back to Fínmed with a sad expression. Then she looked directly at Goll.

'When I first spoke to you and your son, I asked Gabrán in your hearing when he had last seen Beccnat and he gave one of his few honest answers – he said it was about two days before the full of the moon.'

Goll was standing with his shoulders hunched, tired and defeated as the truth dawned on him. Fínmed was sobbing silently again.

'Just confirm for me one other thing that you told me, Goll,' Fidelma said gently. 'Was it your idea or Gabrán's that he go to the house of Molaga a day before the full moon following the feast of Lughnasa?'

Goll raised haggard features to face her. 'You know the answer well enough, Sister. It was he who suggested that he take the goods that day.'

Fidelma turned back to where Gabrán was still being held under restraint.

'A killer influenced by the moon?' she mused sadly. 'Not in the case of Beccnat. The murder was coldly and cunningly planned. Having killed Beccnat, he made for Molaga to establish an alibi. He even started the story of the moon killer, for Adag told us that he had pointed out this fact to Aolú, the Brehon, when being questioned following Lesren's accusation. It was only later, with the second murder, that Liag pointed out it had been committed on the night of the next full moon.'

The youth regarded her calmly. He even smiled.

'I am avenged and have come to power. Knowledge is power and I have the knowledge.' He intoned the words like a priest giving a blessing before beginning to giggle hysterically. At a gesture from Becc, he was led away.

Epilogue

A small flock of choughs, flying with their wild excited call – 'keeaar . . . keeaar . . . keeaar!' – rose in the air above the mountain crags. Masters of the air, they soared high before, as if in unison, they rolled and dived towards the ground, performing aerobatics that entranced Fidelma and Eadulf as they crossed the shoulder of Cnoc Mhaoldhomhnigh and began their descent towards the plain below.

'They are a little far inland,' Fidelma observed, indicating the birds that were easily identified by their glossy purple-black plumage and long, red curved bills and red legs.

Eadulf knew that the chough – the *cosdhearg*, or red shanks as the Irish called it – was usually a coastal bird, nesting on sea cliffs, but sometimes they were found in mountains not far from the sea. However, he was not concerned with the birds. His gaze was focusing across the long, lower slopes of the mountains through which they had passed. From there, the plains below spread to where he could, in the bright late October sunlight, see the broad glinting strip of the River Siúr, the 'Sister River' as it was named. He could see where it joined the Tar to curve eastwards on its journey to the sea. It was not far to Cashel now.

'Do you think that Gabrán is truly sane?' he asked.

'Thankfully, that is not my task to ascertain,' Fidelma replied. 'He is being sent to the house of Molaga where there are trained men of medicine who will see whether he can be adjudged fit to answer for his crimes.'

Eadulf was silent for a few moments.

'Well, at least you have averted another conflict with the Uí Fidgente. And Accobrán will be a long time working to repay compensation to all he has wronged.'

'At least he will never hold any other position of trust again,' agreed Fidelma. 'I feel sorry for the three Aksumites, though. Brother Dangila and his companions probably did not know about the law of hospitality and the extent to which they transgressed it.'

'At least they have their freedom and have been sent to the seaports to look for a ship back to their own country. I hope they make it. What happened to Gobnuid, the smith? I am not clear.'

261

'He was forced to sell his forge and implements to pay his compensation and has already entered the abbey of Finnbarr. They needed a good smith.'

Eadulf laughed. 'I cannot see him as one of the brethren devoted to a holy life.'

Fidelma's mouth thinned in answer.

'There are many I cannot see as suitable to follow that calling either,' she said.

They had descended the hill and entered along a stretch of open road through tilled fields. Eadulf glanced at Fidelma and grinned happily.

'We will soon be in Finan's Height. We can cross the Siúr there and seek hospitality at the abbey of Finan the Leper for midday refreshment. By this evening we should be in Cashel.'

Fidelma smiled at his enthusiasm but there was sadness in her smile.

She had given little thought to her feelings about the prospect of being cooped up in her brother's fortress again during these last few days. She had been too busy enjoying the freedom of the chase, the inexorable coming together of the threads which would join into a solution of the puzzle. The burst of adrenalin as she revealed that solution. Above all, the wonderful feeling of freedom which she experienced in her quest for the answers; in her quest for the truth. And now – now she was faced with the return to Cashel from which she had had her few days' escape. Now, as she had promised Eadulf, there would be no avoiding the problem that faced her. She would have to come face to face with her self and her own problems.

Behind her smiling mask Fidelma felt a terrible sense of guilt at the thoughts passing through her mind. She felt that she was betraying Eadulf. Not for the first time in recent months was she questioning her thoughts and strange feelings that she had been experiencing with the birth of Alchú. She felt in a constant state of depression, even questioning her relationship with her Saxon companion. It had taken her a long time to agree to become his *ben charrthach* less than a year ago. The term was not used for a legally bound wife in Brehon Law but one whose status and rights were recognised under the law of the *Cáin Lánamnus*: a trial marriage lasting a year and a day, after which, if unsuccessful, both sides were able to go their separate ways without incurring penalties or blame.

The trial marriage had been Fidelma's decision. She had been concerned that, under the law, her marriage with Eadulf would have been a marriage between unequal persons. Fidelma was of royal rank and Eadulf would not have had equal property rights with his wife.

Knowing Eadulf's character, she had believed that such a marriage might not be a good prescription for happiness if Eadulf felt less than her equal.

She cared for Eadulf to the extent that rather than rush into easy decisions she wanted everything to be right. Logically, she knew she loved Eadulf and could not contemplate an existence without his support, his tolerance of her sharp temper, which she knew was her biggest fault. But in the months since their baby was born she had begun having all manner of depressive thoughts. She had even begun to wonder if she was ready for marriage? She turned her head aside and pulled a face, expressing her inability to form logical conclusions from the emotional turmoil into which her thoughts had descended.

Did she resent the birth of Alchú? Was that what this was all about? Often she thought how much more freedom she would have without the child. It troubled her yet she could not dispel such thoughts.

She tried to turn her mind back again to her original thought. Why was she unhappy? She loved Eadulf. She had had one unhappy affair before with the warrior Cian and thought she would never experience the agony of falling in love again. Then Eadulf came along and there had been a strange attraction. She remembered the time when they had parted, when she had left him in Rome to return to Cashel. She had felt a curious isolation then. She had not wanted to admit that she missed the company of the Saxon monk. However, she kept comparing Eadulf to the men she had met such as poor Cass, the warrior who had been killed helping her. She remembered her excitement and joy when she and Eadulf had met up again.

It was love. Surely? She enjoyed Eadulf's company, his friendship, and his love. But she wanted to be sure that she was doing the right thing. Last year, she had decided that he should return to his homeland while she went off on the pilgrimage to the Tomb of St James and when she received the message that he was in danger of death, she came rushing back to his assistance. Surely love?

What was wrong with her? Why did these thoughts afflict her? She was surely not physically ill. The previous night, Eadulf had tried to make her drink some noxious brew made from *brachlais* – what was it? St John's Wort, he called it in his own tongue. She was not stupid. She knew the apothecaries of Éireann applied it to women who became dispirited and despondent after giving birth. She was not suffering such melancholia – surely? Even as she asked herself the question, she began to realise the answer.

Her mind was so engrossed in these thoughts that she found that they had arrived at the ford before the monastery of Finan the Leper already. The place had been built fairly recently, and around the collection of buildings which constituted the monastery and chapel a small village had sprung up. It was a good location set in pleasant scenery. An excellent base for traders coming up river and transferring their goods to wagons before continuing on to the more inaccessible reaches of the kingdom.

They navigated the ford, which was still deep, the currents fairly strong. The monastery provided a 'watcher at the ford' to ensure that no accident went unobserved. A bell stood ready to be rung if help was needed. But Eadulf, not the most brilliant of horsemen, was able to pass across the river first and wait while Fidelma came easily across. They turned towards the monastery, where they knew hospitality awaited them.

'Lady! My lady!'

The harsh cry came from the doorway of a tavern they were passing. A tall, swarthy warrior emerged from the shadow of the doorway. He wore the colours of the warriors of Cashel, and at his neck, the gold torc of Cashel's warrior élite. Fidelma turned with a frown. She recognised the warrior by sight but not by name. The man came quickly forward to stand at her stirrup.

'Thank God that I have found you, lady.' He glanced to Eadulf and gave a swift salute, raising a hand to his forehead, adding: 'And you, Brother Eadulf.'

'What is God to be thanked for?' muttered Eadulf curiously.

'I was just setting out for Rath Raithlen in the lands of the Cinél na Áeda.'

Fidelma was solemn. 'Then we are pleased that we have saved you such a long journey. Why do you seek us? I presume that you have some news from Cashel?'

The man shifted his weight uncomfortably from one foot to another. He looked sombre. 'That I have, lady.'

Fidelma saw his downcast features and a fear began to clutch at her heart. 'Is it my brother? Is it Colgú? Is there bad news?'

'Your brother, the King, is in good health but not in good spirits. The news is bad, lady—'

'Then speak it quickly or not at all!' interrupted Eadulf, irritated by the man's prevarication.

'It is your nurse, Sárait. She has been killed.'

Fidelma regarded him in bewilderment. 'Sárait killed? By whom? How? Why?'

'Lady.' The warrior drew a deep breath and his words came out with a sudden rush. 'Sárait has been murdered and your son, Alchú, has been kidnapped.'

THE INTERNATIONAL SISTER FIDELMA SOCIETY

Come visit the Society's Web site at www.sisterfidelma.com for further details, news, merchandise, and updates.

Annual subscription for members is $29.95
(U.S. funds drawn on a U.S. bank).
Checks to be made out to:

David Robert Wooten, director & editor
The International Sister Fidelma Society
PO Box 1899
Little Rock, Arkansas 72203-1899
U.S.A.
david@sisterfidelma.com